EROS
EMPIRE

EROS EMPIRE

by JORDAN OWEN

BearManor Media

2011

Eros Empire
© 2011 Jordan Owen

For information, address:

BearManor Fiction
P. O. Box 71426
Albany, GA 31708

bearmanorfiction.com

Published in the USA by BearManor Fiction

ISBN—1-59393-376-2
978-1-59393-376-0

For Lex and Skye,
Twin furies to the upsetting
of my throne

Chapter 1

THE JUNGLE SPRAWL gave way to a sandy clearing, its dense network of impassible wildlife arranged by some primitive force into a circle outlined by flat stones. It was into this rounded expanse that three intrepid explorers stepped, each one wearing a beige archeologist's uniform, each with the top knotted just under their ample breasts to expose their midriffs, and each brandishing a machete. Leading the trek through the web of flora was Flora, her peroxide blonde hair tied up in a bun.

"I think this is it, you guys!" she said, annunciating each word as though it were the beginning of its own sentence. The other two explorers followed, one a brunette and the other redheaded.

"Is this the place where the ancient rectal ritual took place?" asked the brunette.

"There's only one way to find out," said the redhead "We have to perform the Summoning Ritual of the Double Tongues."

"Do you really think we'll summon Slamdingo?"

"We can only hope," said Flora. "Our research grant from the University depends on it." This time she said each syllable of the word 'university' as though it were the start of a sentence. "Minnie, you read the sacred text and Felicity and I will act it out."

Minnie, the frizzy redhead, took her backpack off and rummaged around in it, eventually removing a large leather bound book, which she opened to a marked page. "Begin the ritual by removing your clothes and getting on your knees." Both Flora and the brunette, Felicity Hatchback, began untying their tops, rubbing each other's nipples as they became exposed then stripped off their tiny shorts, exposing their shorn crotches. "Now assume the most sacred 69 position." They complied, and began licking each other's genitals with

1

ravenous abandon. Similar directions followed, the girls eagerly taking on each new act with the same decadent charisma.

After some twenty minutes of Sapphic performance, there was a rustling in the nearby trees. All three women ceased their participation in the ritual and watched with exaggerated suspense as a humanoid figure stepped through the bushes. Standing almost seven feet tall, the figure's Nubian skin glistened in the tropical sun, his bulging muscles all seeming to carry one's eyes on a rippling journey down to the massive penis that hung in a proud arc over his softball sized scrotum. The figure wore a rectangular, wooden mask that was outlined with parrot feathers and painted in wildly intersecting streaks.

"Who dares interrupt the slumber of the almighty Slamdingo?" boomed the voice behind the mask.

"We do," said Flora, looking up from the shorn pussy before her. "It's for our grant at the u-ni-vers-i-ty."

"Are you fair skinned maidens prepared to complete the rectal ritual?" boomed the voice.

"Yes," said Felicity Hatchback.

"Then choose you a sacrifice!"

"I shall be the sacrifice," cried Minnie, throwing the book down in the sand and ripping at her clothes. Naked except for her Doc Martins, Minnie placed her hands on Felicity's back, using her interlocked companions for support, as Slamdingo stepped behind her, his intimidating tool stiff and ready for action. With cool precision he guided his prick to Minnie's little pink tail hole, pressing the head slowly into the orifice that opened begrudgingly.

As his tool entered his victim completely, Slamdingo began to thrust in and out, both he and his partner grunting passionately as their pace intensified. Soon they built up a rhythm, the act seeming to build towards an inevitable climax until the feral god noticed that a light brown liquid was beginning to course from Minnie's anus. Withdrawing his prick, the ancient god Slamdingo realized that it was covered in thick chunks of feces.

"What the fuck?" shouted Luther 'Slamdingo' Stevens, pulling off the costume mask.

"Goddamnit—CUT!" barked an unseen voice. The voice belonged to Dominic Daniels who sat just out of the camera shot in a black director's chair. "What the hell is this?" he spat, stepping between two tripod mounted video cameras in the large warehouse where the island set had been constructed for *Jungle Bunnies 2: The Shaft of Slamdingo*. The warehouse had been cleaned out and converted into a soundstage a couple of years ago by Dominic's employer, Alston Image.

"Slam, I'm sorry," said Dominic, motioning for one of the crew members to come over with a hose and wash the actor down.

"Damn right you sorry," said Slam, a hint of his street background creeping into his irritated voice. "You better get me a stunt cunt for the penetration shots."

"We'll get you cleaned up and do this right next take," replied Dominic, patting Slam on the back as he headed away from the set and across the open, echoing stone and steel chamber to a side room, where Minnie Asstrix had locked herself in a bathroom stall. "What the hell is wrong with you?" growled Dominic as he entered the restroom.

"Fuck off," said Minnie, sobbing from inside the stall.

"You're supposed to be *the* anal queen—don't you know how to prepare for an anal scene?"

"I said fuck off!"

Dominic cursed under his breath and stormed out of the restroom, his steps echoing around the soundstage as he extracted a cellular phone from his pocket and dialed the front desk at Alston Image.

"Alston Image," replied the perky voice on the other end.

"It's Dominic. Put me through to Isaac."

"Yes sir, Mr. Daniels."

There was a single ring and then a man's voice answered. "Dominic— talk to me." The voice belonged to Isaac Alston, the CEO and founder of Alston Image. The voice carried the same smooth, elevating sensation as being in an airplane during liftoff.

"Isaac—I'm on the set of *Jungle Bunnies 2* and Minnie had an ass malfunction. Now Slam will only do the rest of his scenes with her if we use a stunt cunt for the penetration shots."

"Go ahead with it. I'll have Casting send somebody out."

"Even with Minnie's new ass toy launching next month? I thought this was supposed to be the official tie in product for the first run."

"Just shoot the footage and I'll see if I want to use it. And Dominic-"

"Yes?"

"Tell the cast and crew to go ahead and break for lunch, then come back to the office. I have something I want to bounce off of you."

"You got it Isaac, over and out."

Dominic flicked the cover down on the cell phone and returned it to his pocket. "All right cast and crew," he boomed, bringing his megaphone to his mouth. "Alston says you get an early lunch break. Report back in one hour."

Dominic heard the rustle of crew members setting down various pieces of equipment and became aware of the echoes of feet as they plodded towards cars, lunchboxes and the catering table. The sun hit his eyes in a blunt force wave and he pulled on a pair of sunglasses as he unlocked the driver's side door of his Audi TT. Climbing in, he set the megaphone on the passenger's seat next to a stack of manila folders.

It pleased Dominic to find that the streets were relatively empty, lunch hour still being thirty minutes away for most. Strategically arranged clusters of palm trees zipped past Dominic's car as he navigated the pleasant roads of the San Fernando Valley. In that moment, Dominic allowed himself to fall into the thought process that he had perfected over the years to help make life wonderful. He reflected that this was a beautiful late summer morning in a vibrant city and that as he drove his favorite car from the set to his office, his greatest worry in life was covering for this minor glitch in the film he was making about beautiful naked women. Life was good.

But even so, the word "something," spoken by Isaac Alston, lingered in his mind. It hung in his thoughts like a child that insolently stuck out its tongue and refused to leave. With this word, Isaac had seized control of the pleasant frame of mind that Dominic fought so hard to attain.

The word hovered in his mind as he reached the Alston Image main office, a ten story tower of black glass that shot upwards like an extraterrestrial spire from the lush ground below. The building bore a single indication of its interior nature: the company name printed on the upper right hand of the building in large, white cubic letters. Bold and plain in their brazenness, the letters stood as a solemn challenge to the reader. They were a raised chin in the face of those that would decry Isaac Alston as a smut peddler or his company as a maggot festooned corpse in the graveyard of capitalism. Where one expected to see a lurid outline of a naked woman or a cartoon pair of breasts made to jiggle by alternating neon tubes, they saw only those letters, bound in the bulwark of professionalism.

Above the letters, in the penthouse office, was Isaac Alston. If one brought binoculars, stood about five feet into the alley across the street, and looked at the perfect angle it would be possible to see Alston high above, always working diligently, as though there were a flow of life blood being generated by his quiet, constant labor that ran through the veins of the building, giving the entire construct the imposing dignity it demanded.

There were often protestors on the sidewalk outside the pitch black marble walls that surrounded the property. They usually came in specific groups with specific causes and specific fashions. Today there were hippies next to the wall, brandishing signs that declared *Alston Hates Women* and *Down With Female Exploitation*. As Dominic handed his badge out the window to the security guard in the booth by the front gates he heard one of the protestors shout "eat this male oppressor!" Dominic hit the automatic window controls in the driver's side door and the glass panel slid up just in time to block a rotten egg that splattered across the window in a comical gush.

Dominic opened the car door, stepped out, and took the night stick offered by the security guard. His once pleasant mood hitting rock bottom, Dominic stormed across the concrete sidewalk to the small mob and cracked the egg thrower across the jaw, the satisfying snap of bone reverberating up the night stick and into Dominic's arm, settling in his chest as a modestly elevated heartbeat. The punk kid lay on the ground sobbing as he struggled to move his jaw which hung limp and shattered from the skull to which it had once been attached. The blue and purple patch on his face was framed by teeth and blood on the sidewalk.

Dominic took out his phone and called 911. "Yeah—hey it's Dominic Daniels. Yeah, I beat up another protestor. Better get an ambulance out here." He pocketed his phone and turned back to his car.

"Hey man—you can't do that!" said a hippie girl with braided dreadlocks as she stepped into Dominic's path.

"Be glad I don't hit women," replied Dominic with disinterest. "Not many male oppressors can say that." He stepped around the stammering girl and returned the guard's nightstick.

The gate opened as Dominic climbed back into his car and drove through into the parking lot, his good mood returning.

There was an implied violence in the young man's green eyes. Not the sort of brimming mania found in the perpetually intoxicated vision of a blood thirsty sociopath, but the steady assurance that the capacity for that level of brutality existed but was mediated by the stern focus of a cold, regimented mind. Framing those sharp, disarming emerald eyes was a wild mane of crimson hair, punctuated by blond streaks. Anyone who looked at that face, its harsh juxtaposition of uniformity and anarchy underscored by a strong jaw line and high cheek bones, would want to speak to the man behind it; to learn about the personality that brought these opposites together.

His form was toned and muscular, his naturally pale skin tinged a healthy light brown by the California sun. His arms, reaching symmetrically out of his black tank top, gave an amphitheater countenance to his bulging chest. His black and white camouflage pants terminated at a pair of polished jack boots, their shine catching the sun light that poured in from the glassed-in canopy.

"Mr. Steel," said a woman's voice from the onyx reception counter. The young man, Hank Steel, turned from the neon colored abstract painting that adorned the eastern wall of the Alston Image lobby to face the receptionist. The room was laden with white marble tiles that caught the light from the arched half-dome of glass that covered the entrance and bounced it all around the room, making up for the natural light that was muted by purple walls and matching sitting areas on either side of the room. The vaulted ceiling and walls, which created the impression of a Frank Lloyd Wright inspired cathedral, culminated in the stucco stone wall behind the receptionist's desk which featured a large crest with the Alston Image logo. To either side of the front desk were elevators whose stark, placid reflective metal stood in sharp utilitarian contrast to the flamboyant artistry of the surrounding architecture.

"Yes?" Hank replied, his disarming eyes mellowing slightly when he raised his eyebrows gently.

"Mr. Alston will see you now. Take the executive elevator to the top floor."

Hank turned and walked towards the elevator, which had a card slot in lieu of a call button. "You'll need this," said the receptionist, leaning around the corner of her desk and extending a digital keycard.

"Thanks," said Hank, glancing down at the card, which read *Guest Pass: Useful for Six Hours After Activation*.

Hank returned to the elevator but just as he placed the card in the slot the doors parted to reveal a creature of supreme, sacred beauty. He saw her eyes first and then saw *into* her eyes. They were deep azure pools that seemed to brim with a haunting amusement, as if they probed every visage for a source of jocular passion and demanded that every moment of life be filled with this intangible merriment. After a prolonged instant Hank became aware that the mouth beneath the eyes was gently contorting into a confused smile and that his own was hanging open stupidly. This angelic woman, her long brown hair falling to her breasts, was familiar in some way and Hank's stunned brain groped for a realization that would manifest his wonderment.

"You—you're Billie Solar," he said finally, the words coming after a hard swallow.

"I certainly am," she chuckled; her smile still confused but somewhat more inviting. "So are you a new model or did you just get past security?"

"Ah, both I guess. Hank Steel." Hank extended his hand and Billie took it, her graceful poise guiding her hand to his in the lilting, downward facing posture of an antebellum lady or mediaeval maiden. "I'm sorry, Billie, I don't normally get star struck. I'm a fan of your work. It got me through some hard times."

"I'm sure it did," she replied, a wiseass coquettishness replacing her face's previous reservation as she stepped past him. "Now if you'll excuse me, I need to jet." As she left, Hank stepped backwards into the elevator, watching Billie walk away. Her mid-drift t-shirt drew attention down her lower back to her jeans, where her apple shaped butt danced invitingly as she walked towards the front door.

As Billie walked out, another figure entered: a tall, slim, man with curly, graying hair who wore a beige photographer's vest. He bumped fists in passing with Billie and Hank heard him say "movie night tonight?" to which she replied "You know it."

"Good morning, Mr. Daniels," said the receptionist.

"Hey Carol," said the man in passing. "Hold that door," he barked to Hank, who put out an arm to catch the closing elevator door. Mr. Daniels slid past Hank, who was still watching Billie walk out into the morning sun that welcomed and enveloped her like warm molasses being poured over cherries.

"You wanna finish puberty some other time kid? I've got work to do." Hank snapped out of his trance at the older man's words, and pushed the top button. He glanced at the other passenger and nodded questioningly at the button panel. "That floor's fine—I'm going to meet with the boss."

"Me too," replied Hank, extending his hand. "I'm Hank."

"Dominic," the other replied, shaking the offered hand as the door slid shut.

"Are you Dominic Daniels?"

"That's me."

"I saw your movie *One Blew Into the Hoo-Hoo's Nest*. That got an AVN award, right?"

"Yeah. Best gangbang."

"It was good."

"Thanks—I agree."

"You're more honest than humble, I take it," observed Hank as the express elevator shot up to the top floor.

"Most successful people are," replied Dominic.

There was silence at that point and Hank retreated into himself, thinking about meeting Billie Solar, the way she had seemed to look so deeply into his heart and soul for that instant. It was uncharacteristic of him to be rendered so vulnerable by a woman but as he thought on it further he realized the experience was not entirely unpleasant. Much to the contrary—he found himself wanting to be in her line of fire again as soon as possible.

The elevator opened, revealing that the entire top floor of the building was Isaac's office. Plates of black oak lined the walls, each sporting a framed poster of a different Alston Image landmark film—everything from a poster for the company's first film, a bisexual threesome reel called *Hi Honey I'm Boned,* to their more significant successes in feature length productions. The wall opposite the elevator was a mural of windows, in front of which was Isaac Alston's desk, its glass surface adorned with a wafer-thin computer screen and Hank noticed that it was transparent and he could see the reverse of the on-screen image through the back of it. The keyboard was a hologram that hovered just above the table.

In contrast to the sleek efficiency of the computer, the rest of Alston's desk was covered in stacks of papers, each sectioned off into colored folders, but within those folders were reams of paper that shot out at wild angles with color coded tabs at various intervals. Hank was impressed that the flamboyance of the papers flourished under the rigidity of Isaac's organization.

Alston sat behind the desk, wrapped in his work. Hank took him in with quiet revere. Alston's black Durango harness boots rose into his neatly pressed blue jeans and white button down shirt. The shirt had a wild floral design coming up the back and over one shoulder, orchids blossoming along the left breast. Hank felt as though he were in the presence of a religious ritual that required the utmost calm as he watched Alston work.

"Hey Isaac," said Dominic after a moment. "It looks like I got here a little early."

Alston looked up, as if seeing them both for the first time. His face was hard and sharp, cutting tight angles that suggested maturity without the sagging wrinkles inherit to age. At forty three, a spiky shuck of grey hair was the only indication of his years. "It would seem that you did," replied Alston. He glanced to Hank. "Are you the new prospect?"

"Yes sir."

"Dominic, could you hang out for a moment while I do this young man's interview?"

"Sure thing Isaac." Dominic crossed the room and sat down among an arrangement of leather sofas, returning to the contents of the file folder he carried.

Alston took a folder from the top of the stack and looked inside. "Hank Steel?" he asked.

"That's me."

"Have a seat, please." Hank sat as Alston removed the contents of the folder, which contained Hank's head shot, his resume, and medical records. "You have an impressive, if somewhat short resume, Mr. Steel."

"Thank you, sir."

"You don't list any product licenses."

"No sir, my previous employer said I wasn't ready."

"No wonder—it says here you worked for Intersect Productions."

"Yes sir."

"Artie wouldn't know a good product if it bit him on the ass. Your endowment is eleven inches?"

"Yes sir."

"Prove it." Alston handed a ruler to Hank, who rose and unzipped his pants, removing his tool. Even flaccid it was obviously the full eleven inches, but Hank held the ruler against it, showing the tip to stop just short of the end of the wooden strip. "Outstanding," said Alston, taking back his ruler. Hank zipped his pants and sat back down. "There should be at least three dildos based on that dick on the market right now. I'll hire you for that alone. Do you do boys and girls?"

"Absolutely."

"Did you have another name for gay shoots?"

"Yes."

"Scrap it—if I'm going to put out toys based on your anatomy they will be easier to sell with just one name associated with them. How much was Artie paying you for gay shoots?"

"Artie doesn't do gay shoots. Actually, that's why he fired me. I was contracted to him for straight scenes only, so I started doing gay scenes on the side since Artie hasn't put me in a movie in god knows how long. When he heard about it, he freaked and kicked me out."

"How much did he pay you for straight scenes?"

"He paid me five hundred a scene, but he only filmed a handful of them and fewer ever saw the light of day."

"I see. How much were you making for gay shoots?"

"Eight hundred."

"I'll pay you eight hundred for straight scenes, a thousand for gay scenes and twelve hundred for transsexual scenes. We'll roll out the straight scenes first along with heavy solo content for your website. We can broach the gay market quickly that way. How does that sound?"

"It sounds great, sir."

"Outstanding. How many come shots can you do in a day?"

"I average three, but my best was seven."

"Sounds good, but I'll put you with the company trainer—she'll give you an exercise routine to help improve that."

"Cool."

"I want to get you started on something as soon as possible. Hey Dominic—do you have any spots for this guy coming up?"

Dominic looked up from his papers. "I still need somebody for that BDSM shoot I'm doing with Billie Solar next week." The name made Hank's heart jump a pinch.

"I thought you had a guy for that or I wouldn't have green lighted it."

"Kid broke his arm skateboarding—I had Casting looking for a replacement."

"You free to start this coming Wednesday?" asked Alston, returning to Hank.

"Absolutely."

"Ever do BDSM scenes before?"

"No, I haven't."

"Can you tie knots?"

"Absolutely. I grew up in Scouts. Learned to give head there too."

"So tell me more about yourself—why did you decide to get into the porn industry?"

"Well, I enlisted in the military when I turned eighteen—it's a legacy thing for the men in my family—and was stationed in Afghanistan when a road side bomb hit my ATV. I was in traction and honorably discharged after recovering and when I got back home to Nevada, I started teaching martial arts and doing MMA tournaments but the whole time I kept hearing politicians—mainly the conservatives—talking about 'the troops' and how they were 'fighting for our freedom.' But it was always in the context of admonishing someone with a dissenting opinion. Some fat cat politician sees someone in his district opening a porn shop or protesting pollution or the government, etc, and he says 'just think of the troops that are out there fighting for your right to do that!' It was the weirdest thing—like it was supposed to make the person receiving the statement feel real guilty about what they were doing. It's like, the soldiers were fighting for our freedom, but god forbid you should actually use it! So I started thinking about that—about what it really means to 'love the American way of life' and decided that I was going to find a way to take full advantage of everything I had 'fought for' that these scumbags were being such dildos about. And when I got my knee fucked up at a Muay Thai tournament and had to stop fighting professionally, I decided that the only bone I hadn't broken was my dick, so I started looking into porn since that was something those politicians were always reminding us we'd fought for. Got hooked up with Artie and you know the rest."

"Sounds good. Thank you for your service."

"Thank you for yours."

"Go see Becky in HR—she'll run your paper work and get the contract printed up. Feel free to take it to any attorney you might have in mind, but have it back to us no later than Monday so we can process it before that BDSM shoot or find someone else if you decide to back out."

"Okay."

"I'm thinking what we'll do is a few photo shoots and some solo videos to start building a website around, and then we'll shoot some gay and straight cock worship scenes to sell it. After that gets rolling we'll announce the release of your dildos, but I want to go ahead and get them molded as soon as possible."

"Sure thing."

Isaac Alston stood up and extended his hand. Hank stood and took the outstretched palm, giving him a firm handshake and twinkling smile.

"Rest up," said Isaac, returning the starry eye look with one of warm confidence. "You come to work for me next week."

Barely able to see over the heads of the scantily clad women and flamboyantly dressed men that surrounded her in the Los Angeles Convention center, the rotund, miniature shape of Andrea Danvers navigated the aisles of booths that made up the Adult Business and Media Convention. The vast, utilitarian chamber had been remade into a smorgasbord of erotic diversity with the slick, polished veneer of modern business colliding smoothly with the carnival ambience of the lovingly garish lights and decorations of the various corporate booths. Danvers took notice of the projection screens and hi-def televisions in various booths that showcased company product and played engaging music. *Sickening displays of horrific, body punishing cruelty are projected onto all four walls of the convention center to remind women that they exist as plastic, disposable objects for the pleasure of men,* wrote Danvers in the notebook that she held at the ready as though it were a holy scroll on which the names of the damned were logged.

As she moved through the facility, Danvers was struck at just how available the various models were. Stopping at one booth, she observed a platinum blonde with a large fake bust posing for a picture with what was presumably a fan. The blonde wore a single piece silver dress made of some sort of vinyl material that seemed ready to burst. As the camera clicked she placed one leg against the crotch of the bemused college age boy that had requested the picture, put one arm around his shoulder and the opposite hand open against his chest, giving the appearance of desiring him sexually. The camera flashed and the boy thanked the model then took his camera back from the fellow convention patron that had taken the shot. The next man that approached the booth asked for an autograph on a DVD case and a lipstick impression next to the signature. She consented coquettishly and gave the cover a smooch, leaving a glittery residue below which she swirled off the rapid application of her autograph. A third man approached and asked to take a picture of the model's posterior, which she was apparently famous for. She smiled and turned away, pulling up her minimal dress to reveal the legendary buttocks which hung between a transparent thong. *Models are routinely forced to perform degrading acts of misogynistic humiliation for the enjoyment of pornified men who cast them aside as disposable fuck objects,* she scrawled furiously.

There was a froth building between her teeth as she elbowed her way over to a cluster of three businessmen who appeared to be discussing industry matters with each other. "Excuse me, are any of you available for an interview?" she squeaked, standing on her toes and trying to catch their attention.

None of them noticed her and the sound of the convention's thumping, bass heavy dance music drowned out her shrill voice.

"Thing is," said one of the men, "there's only so much you can do with gonzo as a medium before it starts to get dull and repetitive. I mean, you interview the girl, pan slowly up and down her body, and then you fuck her. And we know the sequence—blow job, bend over the couch, cowgirl, reverse cowgirl, anal, then jerk off and come on her face. You have to start contextualizing the event and pretty soon… you've got a feature on your hands!"

"I agree," said another of the three. "I think the fetish providers have it easy in that sense. For them it's more about the context than it is about the sex!"

Interviews with industry heads revealed that they are out of ideas and looking to sexual torture as the next big thrill for their sex saturated male audience.

Danvers moved on through the crowd, finding herself at the more expansive and elaborate booths that showcased the larger companies and their more high-budget, feature length products. All of the major players were there but one stood out above the rest, seeming to preside over the entire chamber with the regal countenance of a grand emperor: Alston Image. In contrast to the surrounding booths, the Alston Image venue occupied most of the wall against which it stood proudly, with three large projection screens showcasing clips from recent films with a shimmering outline of the Alston Image logo superimposed on them. A long line of buxom young starlets from the Alston Image contract stable and their muscular male counterparts sat signing autographs and conversing with the endless lines of fans that filed past, their polite smiles and open demeanor not waving in the least. As her eyes probed up and down the long row of performers, looking for one that was not surrounded by convention goers. None were available and a security guard stopped her when she tried to push her way through the crowd.

Irritated, Danvers looked around for a more vulnerable quarry and saw a booth nearby for Darcy's Mainframe. DMF had been started a decade ago by a former Alston Image contract girl, Darcy Collins. After leaving the company on good terms she'd entered semi-retirement from performance and applied what she'd learned about the business to launching her own company. Although it was marginal in the face of the success of Alston Image (as most other companies were) it was highly profitable, turning in an annual profit of eight million dollars based largely on lesbian and solo female content.

The titular founder of Darcy's Mainframe sat at table in front of her booth, which was festooned with posters from her recent releases, all of them featuring the kind of floral artistry commonly associated with female folk rock singers and upscale 90's alternative hippie ambiance. *Female culture is frequently exploited for the piggish enjoyment of patriarchal tyrants* scrawled Danvers as she approached the booth. There was a noticeable but not distasteful scent of a watery lilac perfume in the air around Darcy Collins as she signed copies of DVDs and various posters for the steady line of fans. Danvers took a moment to observe Darcy's clothing: she wore what at first glance appeared to be the top half of a pants suit, but terminated in a wisp of fabric that barely passed as a miniskirt, letting the woman's long, slender legs drift lusciously down to cute feet that seemed to beg for the tender grace of an expert masseuse. The top half of the pant suit was unbuttoned and revealed Darcy's ample—and legendary—natural breasts to the world. Unavoidable to the eyes the richly maternal glands filled their black leather bra to the fullest and Danvers sensed that the top had been purposely chosen as a size too small.

Danvers looked at Darcy's voluminous golden locks and thought of the dull sprigs of hair that formed her scalp and burned a little inside. She clenched her teeth at the sight of Darcy's slender neckline and sculpted, chiseled jaw line and fumed at her own bulbous set of chins. The fluidic blue of Darcy's animate eyes made Danvers clench her teeth in disgust. And the breasts—no breasts should be that big. Why can't she have a mastectomy out of respect for the less endowed? Didn't she realize that her beauty was an affront to real women?

"Why are you dressed like that?" asked Danvers sharply.

"Like what?" replied Darcy, her attention still focused on the line of patrons.

"Like a female chauvinist pig," replied Danvers.

"Female chauvinist pig?" Darcy chuckled distantly. "That's a new one. I thought you were going to tell me that I look like a brazen hussy."

"No, that term is sexist and outdated. We've liberated your sexuality for you."

"And what does that mean?" Darcy was still focused more on the fans than the annoying hag to her right.

"It means that you're free to express your sexuality the way you want, not the way men want."

"Then I choose to wear this outfit."

"No—if you wear that outfit you're reinforcing the patriarchy."

"We don't live in a patriarchy. If we did it would mean that women had no rights whatsoever. There may be inequality in this country, but that doesn't mean that we live in an oppressive dictatorship. It just means we have room to grow as a nation."

"It's not about the society we live in. It's about the society men *think* we live in. If you wear that outfit you're telling men that your body is open for all comers and you're encouraging men to rape you. You have to keep your body covered and out of sight at all times so that men won't be tempted to rape you."

"That sounds like the kind of thing they would say in heavily Islamic countries," said Darcy, now turning to face the pestering woman. "When you characterize the nature of rape as being something the rapist can't control then you take the blame off of the perpetrator and put it onto the victim. I get that you think you're being progressive here, but really all you're doing is repackaging the same old arguments that people have used against female sexuality for thousands of years: that women are temptresses that will get raped by men if they aren't careful and therefore must keep as much of their bodies covered as possible."

"Well, you've obviously been brainwashed by the patriarchy."

"Fuck off."

"There's no need to get so testy," said husky, eternally condescending voice. Danvers turned to see a tall, rail thin blonde that wore a black cocktail dress. Her towering face swept inward to form a half moon from which her nose shot out like a twisted beak. Her complete lack of femininity was underscored by her incredulous attempt to appear woman-like and for a moment Darcy thought the creature was a transsexual, but couldn't imagine a company that would hire such a poor specimen.

After a moment, it dawned on Darcy who this was. "You're Alice Grausam, aren't you?"

"You mean the right-wing pundit from the news shows?" hissed Danvers. "I should have known you'd be here."

"Why do you say that?" asked Grausam, her condescending tone only slightly modified for the sake of pleasantry.

"Well, you're a conservative—don't you love capitalist industries like porn?"

"Actually no. I'm here to review the convention for my column. We conservatives are completely opposed to porn. The real ones, anyway."

"Well, it is ruining our children."

"I couldn't agree more. And it's turning our men into pigs."

"Oh absolutely. And it's a civil rights violation."

"Totally. You want to go for coffee?"

"Certainly! Well, we're going to take off," said Danvers over her shoulder, suddenly chipper.

"Umm… yeah whatever," said Darcy, having already returned her focus to the autograph seekers.

"Oh," said Danvers, "Would you be willing to come to a lecture I'm giving in a few weeks? I'll make sure my school pays your appearance fee."

"Have my people call your people," said Darcy, wishing the two clowns would depart.

Darcy apologized to the fans that had been eyeing the pair with morbid amusement after Danvers and Grausam disappeared into the tightly packed crowd. Darcy spent another two hours at her booth and went back to her hotel suite where she enjoyed a pleasant dip in the Jacuzzi before meeting some friends for dinner. She gave no further thought to Andrea Danvers and Alice Grausam who spent the afternoon agreeing on many things.

Chapter 2

WHEN ISAAC ALSTON had been twelve years old he had lived in Boston, Massachusetts and had worked part time at a newsstand. It was here that he discovered the caustic nature of adult entertainment. The stand had been on Boylston Street, near the library, which left it in close radius of a large, sprawling monstrosity of a Catholic church. Although the stand was closed on Sundays, there were the usual weekday congregants: those going and coming from weeknight masses, the elderly who wanted to be in the right place when god came knocking, the teenagers who had just discovered religion as a form of rebellion against secular parents, homeless people looking for a heated doorway, and the never dwindling flow of patrons for the confessional. Isaac's newsstand was a regular stop for those en route to the church, especially those coming from the subway train. As such, it was common practice for those going to the church to purchase tissue packets, breath mints, and lip balm while people leaving the church usually bought cigarettes, newspapers, chocolate and whatever magazines caught their interests.

In the steady flow of patrons to and from the church, there were always those who pulled up their coats tightly against the frigid New England winter, leaving only their squinting eyes exposed to the cold. Perhaps it was the harsh cold or the flurries of snow that obscured vision, but something about those cold Boston winters—and on the opposite end of the spectrum, the sweltering Boston summers—that drove the passersby to a harsh, abrasive temperament that was only exacerbated by the withering, guilt laden sermons they heard inside.

It was in one of the winter cycles that a nun stopped in front of the newsstand. Whatever she was about to purchase became irrelevant when she saw that Isaac, who was unloading a box of newly delivered magazines, had just placed an issue of Playboy on the lowest, most visible tier of the magazine rack.

"Remove that magazine at once!" burst the nun, her eyes becoming wide and bloated at the sight.

Isaac had stopped, stood up, and looked at the magazine in question. "Oh—right. That one goes on the top shelf. Thanks," he replied.

"No—remove it from the stand altogether! And the others like it!"

Isaac had paused for a moment, confused by what he was hearing. "It's not my call what we carry, ma'am."

"Remove that vile, revolting, despicable filth at once!" She shrieked.

Alston looked at the cover image, which was of a nude woman sitting in a large martini glass, and back at the nun. "What's wrong with it?" He asked, genuinely confused and curious.

"It glorifies sin and filth and perversion and paganism!" She howled, barely able to contain the rage that surged through her. Alston remained puzzled. "And I want it out of this newsstand!"

Alston's twelve-year-old vocabulary could not articulate a phrase like *I'm very sorry, ma'am but you don't have the legal authority or moral right to tell me and my employer what we can and can't stock in our establishment* so he put it in a way that most could understand by dryly responding with "frankly, sister, I just don't give a damn."

"This magazine *will* be removed!" The nun bellowed.

Isaac pointed to the woman on the cover of the magazine. "I think you're just mad cause she's hot and you look like a St. Bernard in a penguin costume."

The nun gasped and stormed off. Puzzled at her explosive display, Isaac had taken the magazine, put it in his backpack, and put enough money in the till to cover it. That night at home, under the sheets of his bed and with a flashlight, he'd gone through the magazine page by page, trying to find the source of the nun's outburst. He studied the pictorials as one examines a crime scene or a medical text book, taking in every line and every curve and constantly wondering what the fuss was about. For the life of him, he couldn't tell what they women were doing wrong. They were naked, not shooting guns into crowds of people. They were naked, not mugging people in dark alleys. They were naked, not driving drunk. They were naked, not ripping people off with cards on a folding table. There was nothing wrong with what they were doing. Was being naked itself a sin? And on what grounds?

Isaac began putting aside some of his pay to purchase more magazines, and continued to examine the pictures quizzically. In Penthouse and Hustler he discovered men and women fucking. They were fucking, not molesting children. They were fucking, not raping. They were fucking, not robbing banks. They were fucking, not cheating the elderly out of their social security. They were just… fucking.

Determined to understand the origin of the nun's bizarre behavior Isaac got a copy of the King James Bible from the library and began to read it. He realized quickly that nakedness was one of the first sins after the first one and that it was the first thing that was found to be shameful when man and woman gained knowledge of good and evil. The next thing he realized was that the text was unbelievably, brain crushingly boring—especially the genealogical records. Having not been brought up in a religious house hold, the young Isaac had never known the smiling, cartoony picture book interpretations of the bible that many children grew up with. Where most children saw colorful images of Noah loading animals onto an ark, Isaac saw a maniacal god that treated his creation like an ant farm belonging to a spoiled rich kid.

Through the sickening tales of rape, murder, incest, genocide, suicide, and flying zombies, Isaac learned that the Judeo-Christian ethos contained a great deal of hatred for nudity and sexuality, but could never offer a rational reason as to *why*. In fact, asking "why" seemed to be forbidden in most cases.

The nun returned a few days later and found Isaac reading the Bible. "Nice to see you've changed your ways," she said with grim, bitter satisfaction. Isaac looked up, irritated but masking it well. Without a word he reached under the counter, took out a bag of marijuana, and ripped a page from the holy text. In a series of fluid motions, he used the paper to roll a joint, and smoked it. The nun gasped and stormed off, her rosary swinging back and forth with extra piety.

Isaac didn't see the nun again for weeks and in that time assumed that she'd given up. Instead, the opposite was true: while Isaac worked his shifts the nun was conversing with the clergy. While Isaac did his homework, Bible study groups became planning sessions for the revolution that would take place.

The revolution eventually took place when a group of nuns and churchgoers with protest signs stood blocking the front of the newsstand. Isaac phoned the police, who arrested several of the protestors that refused to move. The owner of the newsstand took the matter to court, where the judge ruled that the crowd had a right to protest, but that they could not block the newsstand. From then on, a small crowd of protestors would gather around the kiosk, verbally harassing anyone who purchased pornography. Again the judge ruled, this time stating that the protestors had to maintain a distance of at least twenty feet from the kiosk. The crowd intensified, and all-day sit-ins were organized. Few of the people involved were sure whether they were protesting the pornography or the fact that a nun had been insulted repeatedly, but they sat there nonetheless.

The protest lasted six weeks. In that time, sales of pornography at Isaac's newsstand skyrocketed.

Thirty-one years later, Isaac Alston stood at the wall of windows in his penthouse office and looked out on the busy San Fernando street where a small gaggle of protestors had gathered. They all wore yellow t-shirts and held signs like "God hates porn" and "Jesus loves you Isaac Alston!"

"You know," said Dominic, now sitting where Hank had sat a few minutes ago. "Right now they think we're in here sacrificing babies to Satan and having blood orgies."

Alston shook his head absently. "No, Dominic. They may say that, but what they think we're doing is making movies about people enjoying sex—which is true. And if you take away their gods, their devils, and their sniveling pseudo academic pomposity, that's really what's pissing them off."

"You're absolutely right."

"There's another dark age coming on." Alston began to pace back and forth in front of the window, looking down.

"You mean another moral panic?"

"Absolutely."

"With a democrat in the oval office?"

"The only time the religious right gets more worked up than when they're in power is when they're not. But they aren't the only ones. Did you see those hippies that were out there today?"

"Yeah—one of them threw an egg at my car and shouted 'male oppressor.' Apparently filming men and women with their clothes off makes me comparable to the Muslims that dismember women for not wearing burqas."

"That's the problem with a free society—let the people pursue happiness and they'll start inventing inane things to get upset about. In that sense, Fascism has a noble quality—it gives the proletariat something real and legitimate to react to: those wish to oppose abusive authority have an actual abusive power to battle and those that live to be abused by authority have an actual physical entity to submit to rather than a collection of statuesque iconographies. It's a sad reality—every time this country has real problems to deal with its populace turns into a nation of bored housewives that obsess endlessly over sexual scandals and rigid, Sunday school decorum."

"Then we need to find a nation of muscular repairmen to come over while our husbands are out." Dominic saw Alston laugh a little for the first time in a long time. "So aside from advancing third rail politics, what's on your mind, Isaac?"

Alston returned to his seat and pulled the rolling chair up close to his desk. He laid his elbows down on the surface and rested his chin on his clasped fingers. This placed his line of sight directly into that of the person sitting opposite him.

"I'm going to find that script," Alston said after a moment. Dominic raised an eyebrow quizzically. "I'm going to find the script for *The Lotus Wave.*"

Dominic now raised both eyebrows in alarm and not voluntarily. This was, however, as far as he would go to respond wildly to any of Alston's blunt force ideas. In their years of working together, Dominic had learned that trying to rest Alston's wild ambitions was at best futile. It was a true skill of Alston's, however, to be able to concretize those wild ambitions into the disciplined process of corporate strategy. Where one might expect to see some wild eyed, devil may care attitude in the face someone making such a wild pronouncement, Alston bore the balanced focus of a businessman who was planning a potentially risky venture and sought to instill a firm sense of confidence in those who worked under him.

"So how do you plan to do that?" asked Dominic, taking the role of advisor to the sultan, "you know there's only one copy of that script and that it's banned in most of the countries it surfaces in. What's your lead on this?"

"I don't have one—I don't even know if the script still exists, but I'm going to find that out if nothing else."

"Why do you want to find that script, Isaac? And spare me the obvious—yes, it will seal your place in history. Yes, it will make Alston Image even more of a household name than it already is. Yes, it will make you wealthier than a Saudi oil prince. Yes, it will make your company the standard by which the rest of the porn industry is measured, but what's the deep down personal reason? Cause if a project like that failed…"

"I want it," said Alston, cutting Dominic off with his eyes more than his words "because there's a good chance that it may rub out those picketing dimwits once and for all."

"How so?"

"Our country is coming to a head, Dominic. This whole 'culture war' thing that the social conservatives rail about cannot go on forever. If they push any harder then they'll either alienate the rest of humanity and be reduced to a few websites and occasional get togethers at the local Holiday Inn, like the Neo-Nazis, or they'll take us over entirely and we'll be trading women for livestock both in the marketplace and the bedroom. What they need—what we all need—is a good controversy to force the stalemate one way or the other."

"I knew you were ambitious, Isaac, but Jesus Christ."

"Dominic, if this is successful, those pious fools just might see fit to stop waiting for the second coming."

"Mr. Alston?" said the intercom.

"Yes, Carol?"

"Your son's school just called—they want you to come have an emergency meeting with your son's teacher."

"What's it in regards to?"

"They just said that it was an urgent issue involving his behavior."

Alston turned back to Dominic. "We'll pick this up later," he said. "Go ahead and tell Slam I'm going to put an extra hundred on his paycheck for what happened today."

"Sure thing," replied Dominic. The two men rose and boarded the elevator.

The elementary school which Timothy Alston attended was a bland, utilitarian set of four white boxes, punctuated only by the Spanish villa style shingling so popular in Los Angeles. Alston parked his Bugatti Veyron in the visitor's parking and entered through the pale yellow double doors in the front of the building, finding the sea green tiling on the floor of the main hallway to be similarly bland and uninviting.

A small reception office sat just off to the side of the main entrance and Alston entered to find a young woman sitting at an orange desk, her dyed-copper hair only a trace darker than the table before her. "You must be Mr. Alston," she said as he entered.

"That's correct," replied Alston, recognizing the beaming, vaguely worshipful glint in her eyes that told him she was either an admirer of his work or someone who got wet at the sight of financial abundance. He took the guest ID tag she gave him, signed the check-in list and headed down the main hall, watching the numbers for his son's classroom.

Mrs. Simmons' classroom was walled in a flowery pattern that seemed like it would have been more appropriate in a bathroom than a teaching facility. Harsh on the eyes in their blunt contrast to the puckering wallpaper were reflective, multicolored tin foil letters that spelled out "Learning is FUNdamental!" along with various cut outs of cartoon animals reading books and writing on chalkboards. Mrs. Simmons, a rippling sphere of a woman, sat beneath the cut and paste menagerie taking a quiet, if somewhat sadistic pleasure in striking red X marks across papers from a large stack of homework. Tim sat in one of two chairs on the other side of the teacher's desk.

"Mr. Alston," said Mrs. Simmons with a vaguely derisive perkiness. "Please have a seat."

Alston complied, though he was taken aback that there was no obligatory "thank you for coming out in the middle of the day like this" sort of greeting. Indeed, he felt as though he were in trouble as well. His son sat staring at his feet, clearly ashamed of something. Mrs. Simmons continued to mark Xs on her papers as though she were dolling out lashes on a slave barge. Alston's eyebrows arched with annoyance—this woman was trying to make him wait.

"I'll be with you in a moment," she snapped softly when Alston opened his mouth, never looking up from her papers.

"I'm a busy man," said Alston calmly.

"I'm busy as well, Mr. Alston," replied Mrs. Simmons, her gaze still fixed on the papers she graded. "I will be with you in a moment, but if you insist on interrupting me you'll only have to wait longer."

"Mrs. Simmons, it is totally inappropriate for you to pull me out of a meeting under the pretense of an 'emergency' only to bring me here and play disciplinary parlor tricks with me. Now either you will tell me what the issue here is or I will return to my office."

"Mr. Alston," began Mrs. Simmons carefully, capping the red pen and looking up at him with excessive formality in her rigid posture and haughty face. "Your son brought a pornographic magazine to school today."

"Oh really?" Alston asked with a voice that was cold and analytical. "Why?"

Mrs. Simmons kept the surprise from showing on her face with a lower chin motion akin to a toad taking in air. This was most unusual: parents were supposed to turn to the child at this point and demand an explanation. All parents understood the separation between child and parent that occurred when a child entered the public school system. "Mr. Alston," she replied, still careful and in a sing song voice that she had perfected over years and years of PTA meetings, "Here at Crabapple Elementary, we strive to foster a strong relationship between parent and teacher and as such we need you to take on a disciplinary role with your son so that he is not alienated from his teacher. Perhaps you should be asking him why he brought the magazine."

"You're the one accusing him of wrong doing; you present the charges."

Mrs. Simmons felt a further frustration growing inside her like a black fog that mixed with still darker waves of guttural smoke. This was not supposed to happen. The child was supposed to be handed over to the state education system after a certain age. It was in all the handbooks. But Alston remained staunchly fixated on the teacher. Finally, she spoke: "Mr. Alston, the magazine was one published by your company."

"What difference does that make?"

Mrs. Simmons was deeply distraught, though she concealed it as best she could. The calm, unwavering focus of the man sitting opposite her was going beyond frustrating. The teacher's handbook didn't say anything about this. By now the parent was supposed to start yelling at the child. The experts all said it was critical for the child to realize that parent and teacher were a united front and that the child would receive no sympathy from either until they confessed to their wrongdoing. "Mr. Alston," she began in carefully measured tones, "I think it would be most constructive if you interacted with your son on this matter."

"Let me see the magazine in question," Alston replied. The teacher reached into her desk and took out last month's issue of Alston Image's popular gothic fetish publication *Angel Bodies & Demon Hearts*. She laid it on her desk as though it were forensic evidence in a plastic bag. Isaac glanced down at it and back to the teacher. "I have a press check in one hour on this very magazine. Now you will either explain to me the nature of the offense or I will give your phone number to my press operators, my advertising execs, my delivery boys, my share holders, and everyone else who has had their *very* busy schedules thrown off so that you can explain the delay of the pressing, shipment, stocking, and sale of this magazine." The words were calm and soft spoken, but the steely-eyed certainty of the delivery made them echo around the room as if they were booming and monstrous.

"Mr. Alston, I had asked the children in your son's class to write an essay on what their fathers did for a living and bring in an example. Little Jimmy Jefferson's father works at Kirspy Kreme, so he brought doughnuts for the class. Maggie Saunders' father is an airline pilot, so she brought a model of the type of airplane he flies. But your son, with no advance warning, walked to the front of the room and read this essay…" and she reached into her desk, produced a single sheet of notebook paper that had been marked with a red F and read aloud: "My dad is a multimedia entrepreneur. He sells magazines like this one. His company is also involved in internet and digital media. He makes films that are available on his websites and in some hotels and stores. His movies are called 'pornography' and they show adults having sexual intercourse. I think that what my dad does is important because it makes people happy and has beautiful pictures of beautiful people. Thank you." She laid the paper down on the desk and held up the magazine. "*Then*, Mr. Alston, he tried to hand the magazine to little Debbie Richards in the front row. The whole class was laughing at that point and little Debbie started to cry. Within an hour the children had given her the name 'Porn Rag Debbie.' She threw up at lunch and had to be taken home."

"Why did my son try to give her the magazine?"

"It was part of the presentation to pass around the item that each student brought in so that the class could look at it."

"Is that the entirety of what my son did wrong?"

"Yes, Mr. Alston. Your son may be called before the school board."

"Why?"

"For bringing pornography to class!" Mrs. Simmons shrieked unexpectedly. Alston's demeanor was unchanged by the outburst and the teacher realized that she had given him the upper hand.

"Let me see if I understand this," began Alston, a note of irritation showing in his voice but played with masterful precision. Unlike the teacher, this note was controlled, melodious, and penetrating. It pierced into the teacher like a soprano that smashes glass with her voice. Alston's elegant composure was not lost, only augmented. "You told my son to write an essay on what I do for a living," he continued, "then you told him to present an example of the product of my labor. Then you told him to pass the item around to the class."

"That was when I gave the assignment, Mr. Alston. I had no idea you did..." she stammered for a moment then pointed to the magazine "that."

"So you're punishing my son for doing the assignment correctly?"

"Mr. Alston, one of the students in the class has a father who is in prison. He came to me and told me that he didn't want to tell the class about it so I told him to pick a career and write about that as though his father did it. Your son had every opportunity to approach me about the matter and I would have given him the same option. He did not, and that made his offense even worse."

"So now you're saying that I'm comparable to a criminal?"

"Well, you cater to the same element..."

"Mrs. Simmons, I don't know you terribly well but I am certain that if I went into my subscriber database, I could find many people that you know on a first name basis. My customers cover a full range of genders, ethnicities, social strata, nationalities, religions, cultures, sexual preferences, and income levels. There are so many demographics in my database that we create specialty publications like this one to cater to each of them," he said, picking up the magazine and handing it to his son, who sat it on top of his book bag.

"Mr. Alston, your son presented this magazine as if there were nothing wrong with it."

"In case you missed the subtext of what I just said, that was the point."

"Mr. Alston, you obviously haven't educated your son on the dangers of viewing pornography."

"There aren't any."

"Mr. Alston-"

"Mrs. Simmons, you will either explain to me the nature of my son's transgression or he and I will be leaving. I have taught my children that there is nothing morally, spiritually, or philosophically wrong with what I do because there isn't. My son followed the instructions he was given perfectly and you failed him in spite of this."

"Mr. Alston-"

"If you think that calling me by my formal title will lend you credibility in my eyes, I assure you it will not."

"Debbie's parents have put her in therapy."

"Debbie is none of my concern."

"Every child in a community is the responsibility of every adult in that community."

"We do not live in a tribal society in the middle of the jungle. You and your ilk may have gotten it in your heads that we're all one big happy family but I have no interest in delegating my parental responsibilities to people who think that I am some sort of criminal."

"You are you sick pervert!" Mrs. Simmons realized that she had shouted again, and that now she was completely exposed. The truth of her intentions had been revealed. She hadn't wanted to discipline Tim or see him disciplined by his father. There was absolutely nothing wrong with what the boy had done—she had just wanted to use it as an opportunity to rake a smut peddler over the coals. But what coals? As she stared into Alston's unflinching, unthreatened eyes she realized she'd never seen one of *them* up close before. She looked at the man across from her and tried to force herself to see some wisp of that construct she'd built up in her mind. She tried to find the slobbering, leisure suit clad sleaze bag of her nightmares but couldn't see it in the handsome, refined, polite and clear spoken man on the other side of her desk.

Mrs. Simmons also became aware that without any difficulty, Alston had seized control of her every action. He somehow knew the full range of potential responses that she could give and was prepared to counteract them as one knows all the potential moves in a chess game. She realized that she was in far over her head and that realization terrified her.

For the first time in the course of the meeting, Alston renounced his passive posture and sat forward, resting his elbows on his knees, though his firm gaze never changed. "Mrs. Simmons, your opinion of me and what I do is completely irrelevant. My son has done nothing wrong and you should be ashamed for pulling me away from my work to deal with this thoroughly idiotic matter. Since you seem to want some sort of acknowledgement of change on my part in this matter then let it be this: starting Monday I will hire a private tutor for my children and they will homeschooled. I will not have their minds and their young lives manipulated by the brainless agenda of a fool like you." He rose to his feet and looked down at his son "come on, Tim. It's time to go home."

They stood and turned to leave, Tim pulling on his backpack slowly, still frowning but no longer out of shame. As father and son walked out the classroom door, Mrs. Simmons whispered "I should call child services."

In a howling instant Alston spun around and slammed both of his hands down on her desk. "You will NOT threaten me!" he thundered, the eyes once placid and thoughtful now filled with a horrifying rage. The statement was not a challenge, but a command. It was merely an amplification of the sort of order one gives a guard dog during its training. Alston held her gaze for a prolonged moment, then turned and walked out the door with his son, slamming it shut behind him.

Mrs. Simmons sat alone for a few minutes, looking out at the room for awhile before realizing that the sharp, pungent odor of ammonia was reaching her nose. When she finally did stand, she found that she had wet herself.

Isaac and Tim walked to the front door of the school, stopping only at the front desk to sign Tim out for the day. They left and got in Isaac's car.

"Are you really taking me out of school, dad?" Tim asked.

"That's correct. When this school's teachers are sufficiently open-minded you can return if you want but until then you and your sister will receive home schooling." Alston started the car and pulled out of his parking space.

"Why do people hate what you do?" his son asked as they pulled back onto the main road.

"Well, hatred starts with being scared of something," replied his father. "And a lot of people are taught that anything related to sexuality is shameful and wrong. So when someone like me comes along and makes magazines and movies depicting it, they think that we're trying to spread evil and that scares them."

"But why would people be taught that sex is evil?"

"Well, you've never been brought up in a religious household, but religions are institutions for people who never quite grow out of believing in ghosts and as such they believe that there are ghosts controlling their lives."

"What does that have to do with sex?"

"Long ago there was a time when they didn't understand things like sexual reproduction, the spread of disease, bacterial infection, etcetera, and they believed that ghosts and spirits took over your body and controlled you in these cases. They made up intricate stories and mythologies to help them understand these things. The problem is that even in our modern age there are people who prefer this primitive fantasy world to real life and they have a deeply ingrained fear of sexuality. Did you notice the cross your teacher wears around her neck?"

"Yes."

"Do you know what that comes from?"

"Christianity, right?"

"That's right. Do you know what it means?"

"Not really. Jesus or something."

"Right. Christianity teaches that a god created the Earth and at first he created only two human beings—a man and a woman—and they lived in a little utopia called the Garden of Eden. What he planned to do with the rest of the Earth is never really explained. They were told to obey god at all times and never question him but god decided that the man and the woman shouldn't know the difference between good and evil. Instead, he made a tree whose fruit would make them magically have the knowledge of good and evil."

"So they ate the fruit."

"No, god told them not to eat the fruit of the garden but they did it anyway. Then, because they disobeyed god, they found out that they had committed the first evil, which was called the original sin."

"How could they have known that was wrong or that obeying god was good if they had no knowledge of good and evil?"

"They couldn't, but Christians believe this crap is the inerrant word of god and doesn't have any contradictions. So after they ate the fruit god was furious and threw them out of the garden and they lived in sin and suffered for thousands of years until god finally decided to 'save' the human race."

"Save them from what?"

"The rules he'd created with zero oversight."

"If they're his rules, why doesn't he just forgive them?"

"Well, Christians think that god is perfect and that being perfect he can't change his rules. The problem with that is that if god is omnipotent and omniscient—meaning he can do anything and knows everything—so anything he does would be perfect which means if he changed the rules that would also be perfect."

"That's confusing."

"It certainly is. But anyway, a few thousand years later he decided that he would forgive everyone by sending his 'son,' which was actually just a manifestation of himself, to earth so that this earthly form could be sacrificed for the sins of all humanity. So he died by being nailed to a cross, which is the symbol your teacher wears on her neck. So basically, god 'saved' everyone from being punished for breaking the rules he created by sacrificing himself to himself."

"And after that everyone was forgiven?"

"No, there was a condition. To be forgiven, people had to believe that it happened."

"What?"

"Right—the worst sin you can possibly commit, apparently, was to think that god wasn't real or that none of this happened."

"So you believe and you're saved?"

"No, if you believed then you were expected to devote most of your time to bizarre rituals and abstain from everything that made life enjoyable."

"That's crazy."

"It certainly is. But that's only one group of people that dislike what I do. There are many others, but ultimately they all fall under the label 'authoritarian.' An authoritarian is someone who can't be happy unless they're making other people miserable."

"So why do the rest of them hate what you do?"

Isaac Alston laughed. "I could write a book on that."

They reached Alston's office and crossed the security barrier. "Good afternoon, Mr. Alston," said Floyd, the security guard in the booth between the entrance and exit gates.

"Good afternoon, Floyd."

The gate opened and they drove in, rolling over the row of inverted spikes designed to regulate the entrance and exit ramps, and pulled into Alston's reserved space. Alston opened the front door of his car and got out while Tim took a book from his back pack and began to read. "You can come in this time," said Alston, leaning back into the car. "It's time you saw where I work."

Tim got out of the car and joined his father as he entered the Alston Image headquarters. They entered the lobby and Isaac introduced Tim to Carol the receptionist, who gave him a laminated visitor's pass. They took the regular elevator to the fifth floor of the building, where the presses were.

The printing press room was a large warehouse chamber that echoed with every step they took and the presses themselves looked like long steel caterpillars that chewed into the reams of high-gloss paper with metered voracity. Tim looked up and around the room as they entered, finding it to be not unlike an aircraft hangar. The boy watched the presses as they sucked the paper through their serpentine pathways, systematically inking page after page. It was fascinating, though not as sexually explicit as he had hoped.

There was a small table with a drafting board set up next to the press nearest the door, and Alston stopped here to examine the pages that had been laid out for the new issue of *Angel Bodies & Demon Hearts*. He picked up a magnifying glass and began to cover each two-page spread in detail.

"Check the margins on this page," he told one of the employees that stood over his shoulder, "It's a little off. Also this ad should be half page, horizontally. Run the editor's DVD picks in the back if you have to."

"Yes sir," replied the employee. Alston continued for about half an hour, making small observations until his cell phone rang.

"Hello?" he answered. "Yeah—I'm at press check right now. No—it's no problem. Just let me finish here and I'll be right up. Can you keep her calm while I finish this? Tell her I'll be up in a minute. Okay—see you soon." Alston pocketed the phone and looked to the man next to him. "I need to go put out a fire up on floor seven. I want to see a corrected version ready for my stamp in thirty minutes. Doable?"

"You got chief," the other man replied.

"Come on, Tim," said Alston as he walked out the two double doors that led back to that floor's elevator rotunda. "I have to go over the details of a new contract with one of my models—she's throwing a fit about something. I hope this isn't too boring"

"Nah—it's cool," mumbled Tim as they boarded an elevator.

Arriving at the second floor they stepped out into a wide open room with reflective steel walls and a stone floor. Dominic Daniels was waiting there next to a pretty slender blond with bulbous tits. She wore jeans and a dark brown turtleneck, much to Tim's disappointment.

"Dominic, have you met my son Tim?" asked Alston as he stepped off the elevator.

"Don't think so—how's it going there?" asked Dominic, turning to Tim and shaking his hand.

"And this is Janet," said Isaac, indicating the woman next to Dominic. "She's one of our models." Janet managed a tight smile and a nod, though she was clearly more interested in the contract she held in her hand. "The three of us are going to go discuss some things and I want you to wait here for me, okay? I'll be back soon."

The adults departed for a small conference room, leaving Tim alone. There were black benches on each of the walls and Tim sat down on one, glancing around at the movie posters that were framed on the walls. Tim knew that somewhere in this building, at this very moment, there was a naked woman. There had to be. After a few minutes he got up and began pacing the room. He went and looked in the window of the conference room and saw his father with Dominic and Janet, pointing out various things on the contract and explaining them to Janet, who would nod and look at Alston when he spoke then shift her eyes back to the contract.

Tim resumed his pacing then heard two people coming down a side corridor, talking happily. One was masculine, the other feminine. After a moment, Tim saw that the voices belonged to a slightly overweight bald man in a pink t-shirt and greenish cargo shorts talking to a gorgeous brunette in a silver robe that came down just far enough to cover her backside. They were laughing about some amusing anecdote and then parted ways when they reached the main room.

"Hey," said the bald man to Tim in passing has he boarded the elevator.

The woman went into a room just off the main chamber and Tim heard the door close. He snuck around the corner and noticed that there was an air vent next to the upper right portion of the door. Finding that he was unable to reach the vent standing on his toes, Tim pulled a trash can with a flat top over to the spot and climbed up on it. He could see into the room and found it to be a dressing room lit only by the light of a series of bulbs that ran the length of the mirror on the opposite end of the chamber. The girl sat in front of it in a folding chair, removing make up.

Tim watched her for a few long moments, suddenly aware of his heartbeat, which pounded at his chest like a ball peen hammer. His hands and feet felt unnaturally cold as he watched her, hoping that she would take the robe off… But then she wasn't looking at herself in the mirror anymore, she was looking at the upper right corner of the mirror. At him.

Tim dropped down from the trashcan and padded off down the corridor, hoping to get out of her eye shot as soon as possible.

"Hey," he heard the woman's voice whisper sharply and he stopped cold and then turned slowly. The girl in the silver robe was leaning out the door of the dressing room, an irritated scowl on her face. "What do you think you're doing?" She hissed. Tim couldn't answer. Her eyes moved down to the guest badge he wore on his lapel.

"You're someone's son?" she asked. Tim nodded. "Whose?"

"Isaac Alston."

"Really? I work for him."

"I kind of guessed," he mumbled.

"I'm Billie, what's your name?"

"Tim."

"Pleased to meet you, Tim. Why don't you come in here for a second?"

Tim found himself moving towards her as if possessed. He wanted to remain rooted where he was or better yet turn and run, but he was propelled forward by some alien force that extended from her hard gaze and ensnared him.

"Come on in," she said and Tim entered the dressing room. Billie closed the door behind him and led him over to the fold out chair, which she turned sideways to the mirror. "Sit."

Tim complied and looked up at Billie who, standing, seemed to tower overhead. She crossed her arms and looked down at him, a stern look on her face. "You do realize that I was in here because I wanted privacy, right?" Tim nodded, feeling like a smaller, littler boy than he actually was. "And do you realize that when you spied on me you were stealing from me?"

"What?" Tim asked, suddenly confused.

"This body is mine. I sell it to Alston Image in exchange for money and to my closest friends and lovers in exchange for their love and friendship. When you looked in on me you were stealing from me. I don't give this body away for free."

"I-I'm sorry." Tim realized he was blinking back tears.

"You should be. I'm guessing you've never seen a woman naked before."

"Not in person."

A generously forgiving and eternally warm smile spread on Billie's lips. "Let's take care of that."

Tim watched as Billie's long, articulate fingers undid the knot in her sparkling silver robe and parted the fabric. The robe fell to the floor with a graceful, fluid descent and Tim found himself sitting inches from Billie's stomach. She had a silver ring through the top of her belly button, and it suspended a tiny diamond bead over her naval crevice that caught the light from the mirror bulbs and refracted into an interlocking, holographic rainbow web that cast dim light on the inner crevices of the small cavern. His eyes traced down to the soft patch of brown hair between her legs and he became aware of the wonderful scent that came from the area. Her breasts hung like sloping rice bowls in sacred symmetry. Tim found himself reaching slowly for them. She placed a gentle hand on his.

"Just look," she whispered.

Tim returned his hands to his knees and looked more closely at her nipples, taking in every subtle nuance of those perfect, concentric circles. He examined the little wrinkles at the top of each tip, marveled at the changing skin tones between the nipples and the rest of the breast, and traced up to her face, finding her to have a warm, inviting, compassionate smile; the sort of smile that wrapped him in blankets of comfort and serenity.

"Are they real?" he asked.

"Yeah."

"How big are they?"

"34C. They just seem smaller because I'm tall."

"How tall?"

"Five eight."

"You're so beautiful..."

She said "thanks," but it was with a kind of warmth that said *I know how much this means to you.*

Tim felt her image coating his brain, encoding it with the truth that this moment was one from which all future points in his life would spring. That this would be the mark of wonder and beauty by which all other experiences would be measured. And it was an innocent moment—a moment that was less sexual than it was loving, heartwarming, and carefree. The glow from the bulbs was like a halo that surrounded her and elevated her, as though light itself knelt to accommodate the angel in its presence. Tim became aware of just how *complete* she seemed. It was as though he suddenly realized that clothing on women was a hindrance to the psychological equilibrium attained in seeing them in their most natural state. It occurred to him that this state of nakedness was the truest state of a person's physical being yet it was the state most alien to the rest of the world.

"You should take a look at this too," she said, turning around so that he could see her butt. There was a tattoo of a winged human creature flying past a moon and trailing stardust just above the crack in her ass. She shook her hips, which made her cheeks jiggle, and they both laughed.

"One more thing," she said, and sat down on the table in front of the mirror, spreading her legs. Tim looked in and saw something that looked like the inside of a flower made of interwoven layers of engorged flesh. His mind raced over all the pet names he'd heard for this thing, and his mind settled on one.

"Pussy's my favorite word for it."

Billie smiled. "Mine too."

"What does sex feel like?"

"It's like being slowly filled with warmth until all of a sudden it explodes into sunlight."

"Wow."

"Yeah." Billie stood up and tussled his hair. Tim watched her butt move as she walked over to a pair of jeans and a t-shirt hanging from a rack. Putting them on she said "Now let's go find Isaac—he's probably worried."

"Will this get you in trouble with him?"

"I don't think so. I've known your dad long enough to kind of know how he feels about these things." She tied her hair back in a pony tail and then said "besides—if he was worried about you seeing naked ladies, he wouldn't have brought you to this floor."

They left together, and found Alston and Dominic standing in the main room talking. Alston turned when Billie approached and smiled when he saw that Tim was with her. "There you are," he said. "I was wondering where you got off to."

"I was giving him the tour," said Billie with a photogenic smile.

"I'm sure you were," said Alston. "Now say good bye, Tim."

"Bye Billie."

Later that evening, Tim lay in his bed, reading a book. The lights were out except for a small desk lamp on his nightstand that was turned so that he could see the text. He was startled for a moment when he heard a knock at the open door, and saw the outline of his father.

"Whatcha reading there, champ?"

"Huck Finn. We were supposed to read it for school, but I wanted to go ahead and finish reading it anyway. It's the school's copy. They'll want it back."

"I'll have my assistant run it over there when you finish," replied his father, who moved into the room to sit on the edge of the bed, becoming illuminated by the small desk lamp. "But what I wanted to talk to you about was what happened with Billie today."

"We didn't do anything, dad. She didn't touch me or…" his father raised a hand to stop him.

"I'm aware of that. I trust Billie. What I was more interested in was something else. You saw her naked, correct?"

"Yes sir."

"I'm glad it was her. She's a very kind, caring, good person. How did you feel about seeing her like that?"

"It was amazing."

"I thought you'd say that. What I want to make sure of is that you know that she's a person, a woman, and thinking human being, not just a thing."

"Well, yeah."

"Good. I want you to think about that, though, when you look back on what you saw today. There are guys who never learn that. They spend their entire lives treating women like free toys and never learn to appreciate the person behind the body. It's important that you appreciate women for all of who they are, not *just* the looks."

"Okay."

"I also want to touch on something else. I was a little out of line in the car today. Everything I said about Christianity and my feelings about it is true, but it would be irresponsible of me not to say that there are many, many people in the Christian faith and other faiths that are very decent, wonderful people. They may believe in some whacky things that I don't, but they are good, decent people and don't deserve to be lumped in with nut jobs like Mrs. Simmons. See, there are people in any group who will serve as bad examples of that group, and that's why I wanted to make sure you had a healthy perspective on seeing a woman naked because there are people out there who think the men in my business only treat women badly, lie to them, abuse them, hurt them, and treat them like they aren't even human. I'm not like that, my company isn't like that, and I don't want my son to be like that, okay?"

"Okay."

"Good. Now you know you can come talk to me about anything that might be on your mind, right champ?"

"Yes sir."

"Good," said Isaac rising. "You can read for as long as you want, but go to sleep after, understood?"

"Yes sir."

Isaac left his son's room and smiled quietly to himself, realizing he envied his son for have such a wonderful introduction to the majesty of the female form.

Chapter 3

A **PLEASANT SMILE** crossed Dominic's lips when the vocals started on the Manhattan Transfer record he'd just thrown on the stereo. The new media tower had been a gift to himself when he'd gotten a huge bonus for his exceptional directing on Alston Image's gay Holocaust epic *The Boy in the Stripped Pajamas*. Dominic mouthed along quietly as the Transfer sang their rendition of *Let's Hang On* by the Four Seasons. The music cast wide ripples around the room from a set of twin speaker towers on either side of a large plasma screen television in his living room. The speakers, shaped like upside down coffins, were covered in a black silk mesh that complemented the equally dark border of the television and the matching marble coffee table. A wrap around leather couch enclosed the three sides of the large rectangular coffee table, leaving the television side open.

The living room, into which the front door opened, was a dark grey in the walls and carpet, but not in a depressing manner. Quite the opposite: this was the grey of slick computer surfaces and glossy postmodern office buildings. Several abstract paintings and the hardwood finish of the kitchen, a room that opened onto the living room like a concert stage, broke the trend of cool professionalism that dominated the main room of Dominic's condo. In truth, Dominic could afford much more, but he was content in his little nook, polished as it was with all the amenities of a successful show business career.

In stark contrast to the spotless constructs around him, Dominic was dressed in his usual thrown-together fashion with the haphazardly assembled corduroy pants, grey t-shirt and blue flannel work shirt completing his simple attire. It was only on special occasions that Dominic put any significant thought into his wardrobe, when emitting a certain aura was relevant to the utilitarian function of wardrobe. Where Isaac saw every thread of his clothing as forming a piece of the larger concept that was Isaac Alston,

Dominic preferred to think of clothing as a vehicle for accommodating a desired state of being. Where no such accommodation was required, no fashion sense need be observed. Dominic had often considered that were it not for his reclusive nature, Isaac would have been great as a military parade leader. He understood the science of presentation and precision. It reflected in his clothing as sharply as it did in his running of the company.

In the nearly twenty-five years that Dominic had worked for Isaac he had noticed the imperial nature of the man's aesthetics and found that his own sensibilities contrasted those of his employer in a somewhat Yin-Yang fashion. Because Isaac's background was in business he had handed the creative reigns over to Dominic almost immediately at the start of their long standing collaboration, instead applying the artistic flare in his nature to facilitating Dominic's creativity. Isaac's poise had always been that of a great, majestic vulture who, far from the predatory creature of the wild, was instead vigilant to swoop down and pluck up the best possible talent, arranging them together in combinations that were dynamic and beautiful, like a pioneering composer who found new harmonies with new instruments. He saw the socio-synaptic connections that made for great porn. His art was the ability to find these relationships and hand them over to a filmmaker who could only enhance them. Where Isaac saw beauty in film as the way in which an environment was affected by its populace Dominic saw beauty in the way the populace reacted to its environment and it was for this reason that was he was the director and Isaac the producer.

Dominic placed a skillet on one of the stove's burners, its coil already bright with heat, and took a bottle of Night Train Express out of the refrigerator, popped the cork with his thumb and took a loving swig of the sweet red wine. Shaking his head and blinking in response to the wonderfully sharp taste Dominic poured a heavy dollop of the fluid into the skillet, its thick aroma filling the kitchen as it sizzled and snapped.

Dominic took a pack of noodles out of the overhead cabinet and a roast from the fridge and a canned sauce. He enjoyed cooking, even if his skills were only rudimentary. Seeing the specified ingredients come together to form a greater whole contributed to his love of creativity in general. The kitchen was well lit and spotless—a garden of stainless steel surfaces and hardwood finishes.

The intercom on the wall of the kitchen buzzed to life. "I'm at the gate." It was a woman's voice. Dominic pushed the button next to the talk-back button, opening the gate on the front of his condo complex. Moments later Billie's Jag pulled up in the parking lot outside his building.

Dominic pushed the talk button on the intercom as he heard the car door slam. "Come on in, I'm in the kitchen," he said.

The front door opened and Billie Solar stuck her head in. "Are you decent?" she asked, her signature smile filled with the mirth of an inside joke.

"Never," replied Dominic, glancing amusedly over his shoulder.

"What's for dinner?" asked Billie as she entered, tossing her purse and a tote bag on the couch.

"Stroganoff cooked in cheap wine."

"You know me so well," replied Billie, pecking Dominic on the cheek as she entered the kitchen and took a Coors from the fridge. "So how was shooting?" she asked as she hopped up to sit on the cooking island and watched Dominic stir the food.

"Minnie took a dump on Slam during filming. Fucked up the whole shoot for the day."

"Were you able to pull it back around?"

"Yeah, but we had to use a stunt cunt for the rest of the close ups. Isaac told me to go ahead and do it, but he may not use the footage. The toy division is releasing a silicone mold of Minnie's ass next month and Jungle Bunnies 2 is supposed to be the big anal feature to promote it."

"Isaac's big on authenticity."

"He certainly is. So what's the movie tonight?"

"Mmmm!" Billie murmured, taking the beer from her lips and setting it down on the counter top. She dismounted from the island and skipped into the living room, shuffled through the tote bag until she pulled out a Blu-Ray disc, then returned the kitchen and placed the plastic case down next to Dominic's skillet. Dominic looked over at the cover:

"Fellini's *8 ½* on Blu-Ray? You fucking rock!" They high fived and Billie returned to her perch on the counter and Dominic to the dinner's preparations.

"It was that or *Salò*."

"Ugh—no thanks."

"Really? I thought you included it in your senior thesis."

"I did—but Pasolini is one of those directors that you feel like you *ought* to admire, whether you do or not. Funny you should mention that though—NYU wants me to come speak to one of their classes."

"No shit—really?"

"Yep."

"You going?"

"Of course. Why wouldn't I?"

"I thought NYU wanted to pretend you never went there."

"They did. But now it's edgy and hip to have a porn director as an alum, so they're milking the hell out of it. Makes a lot of sense from a marketing standpoint."

"I guess so. What are you gonna speak about?"

"Oh there'll be some professor of some sort there, guiding the discussion. He'll ask me questions, trying to make my work sound as if it has artistic merit."

"You don't think your work has artistic merit?"

Dominic finished with the cooking and separated the stroganoff onto dinner plates. "Oh I do," he said. "I absolutely do. That's why I grit my teeth at the thought of some stuffy suit at my old school trying to force an interest in what I do."

"But I thought they were supposed to be all liberal and hip."

"They think they are, and that's part of the problem. They've convinced themselves that they're superior to the narrow-minded conservatives but all they've done is take a different route to the same destination. They claim to reject the hysterical Puritanism that keeps the religious right from enjoying sexuality, but rather than embrace sexuality and its documentation as an art form, they convince themselves that they are practicing a 'higher' art by avoiding nudity. They declare that nudity is frivolous, that sexuality detracts from the story, and come out on the other end with a creation that wants so desperately to be art but can't transcend the prudishness of its creators. They create worlds where characters prattle on at length about enjoying sexuality, but when it comes time to show an actual sex act, the camera pans away, focusing instead on sentimental music and a bedroom curtain blowing in the wind. On the rare occasion that they actually do show some sex act the actors usually simulate the intercourse. And when you look at the rare handful of mainstream films that have actual sex acts, they're often called bold and daring but they only hint at what I film all day long."

"I wouldn't expect real actors to actually fuck on camera."

"My point exactly," continued Dominic, handing a plate and fork to Billie as the returned to the living room. "You don't consider yourself a real actor, do you?"

"Well, I have to make the audience think I'm into the guys and girls I fuck, but usually I am so is that really acting?"

"You fail to understand the point of acting, Billie." They sat on the couch and Dominic turned down the music with a remote control. "The purpose of acting is not to convince the audience that you have successfully faked the nature of your character, but to bring life and realism to the character you are playing so that they may experience the story as though the character is actually present in reality. Thus, you serve only as the vessel to help manifest its reality. In that respect, who cares how you arrive at the state of performance? Method actors would tell you that you have to immerse yourself completely in the thoughts and feelings of your character while other schools would tell you that your feelings are irrelevant, so long as you gesticulate properly. But you, on the other hand, are tasked with portraying yourself in a state of orgasmic bliss. If you convey this to the audience, are you not acting simply because it's not fake? Sada Abe, the Japanese sex icon that cut off her boyfriends cock and balls went on to play herself in a stage production about her life. Was she acting? Absolutely. Did she struggle with character development? No way."

"I never thought of it that way."

"Oh you've always thought of it that way—you've just never stopped to articulate it." They ate for a moment then Dominic looked up from his plate and looked over at Billie. "You know Isaac wants to make *The Lotus Wave* now, right?"

Billie stopped and turned her head to meet Dominic's gaze. "How? I thought the script vanished years ago."

"Isaac's after it. It's like his holy grail now."

"Well he is like our King Arthur. Isn't that script illegal in a bunch of countries?"

"It was when it was written, but now U.S. law might be lenient enough to allow it."

"What's so controversial about it?"

"Nobody really knows for sure, except that even the most hardcore of grind house studios wouldn't touch it, for whatever reason." Dominic ate some more then continued: "This is what Isaac does. He's not content to just run a business—he wants to rule an empire. This would pretty much cement it for him. Forget Hefner, Flint, Guccione, this would finalize Isaac as the ruler of the Eros Empire."

"Why aren't those other guys going after it like Isaac is?"

"Well, a lot of people have passed on the script over the years, and none of them will ever say exactly why, except that they aren't allowed to discuss the content of the script itself. See, you have to understand the history of the script. It was first presented to film studios in Japan in the late 1970's by the original author, Hotei Shibasaki, and it was rejected by every single one. Eventually one of the studios reported its content to the police who seized it immediately. Later on, the script was smuggled out of the country by a boy that worked in the impound office of the Tokyo police. The kid, who was in about his early twenties, apparently shopped the stolen work around to all the major American and European porn-chic directors: Tinto Brass, Joss Franco, Radley Metzger, Kenneth Anger, Jim Clark, even Andy Warhol. Nobody would touch it.

"After all the litigation that Deep Throat had undergone and the outbreak of AIDS in the 1980s the person or persons shopping the script disappeared entirely until the late 1980's, when a script believed to be the typewritten original was auctioned off at a private event. It went to an anonymous bidder who paid five million dollars *cash* for it. He disappeared and that's been that."

"And Isaac thinks he'll be able to find it."

"You've worked for Isaac for how long?"

"Three years."

"Exactly. I've known him for more than twenty. When Isaac wants to accomplish something then that something simply becomes an understood part of reality. When you're working with him on such a thing, you anticipate the end result to be realized the same way you expect the seasons to change and the planets to follow their orbits; it simply becomes the natural order of things."

"It sounds like you have a lot of respect for Isaac."

"I do."

"It also sounds like he's got a pretty deep personal philosophy, whatever it is."

"Oh absolutely. He's never sat down and explained it to me—or anybody really—but I know that he has one." There was a pause for eating, and then Dominic continued: "And I know that we're all a part of it."

"Do you think that Isaac will go ahead with making the script once he finds out what it was that made all the other guys pass on it?"

"Well, Isaac has never backed away from challenges or controversy."

They finished the meal, washing down the stroganoff with the last of the Night Train Express and, sufficiently smashed, watched 8 ½, then played video games for a couple of hours with the latter punctuated by raucous laughter and loud demands from both players for a "rematch" at various intervals. By about two in the morning the soporific effects of their chosen beverage were kicking in and Dominic stood up shakily, chuckling absently at his own lack of motor control. "You wanna crash on the couch?" he slurred to Billie, who nodded, laughing hazily as well.

Turning off the TV, Dominic stumbled into the bathroom and watched his reflection drift back and forth in the mirror for a moment, then clumsily began brushing his teeth. While he worked the brush around his mouth he returned to the living room to check on Billie. She had removed her clothes and gone to sleep, her head rested on her right arm. Through his inebriated haze, Dominic drank in Billie's form: the soft slope of her breasts, the tender rise and fall of her hips, the light patch of brown hair between her legs, and allowed himself a moment's indulgence. Billie's beauty was majestic beyond compare. In any room she entered the whole chamber and its occupants seemed to angle themselves in her direction as if she were the sole source of light and nourishment in a botanical garden. Billie's beauty was filled with an organic magnetism—no part of her was fake and she was the sort of beauty that looked better *without* make up. Her form was the sort that seemed to drift in and out of the natural flow of grass and trees caught in a gentle wind or found in the Rorschach examination of sunset drenched clouds. But in Billie Solar, that abstract perception was made concrete and solid. "Breathtaking" was a shallow understatement.

Rallying what little coordination he had left, Dominic pulled himself from the perfect, if blurry vision, and returned to the bathroom, finishing his evening routine. From there he undressed as he staggered down the hall to his bedroom and fell onto his bed, pulling a trashcan next to where he lay, so he would be prepared for tomorrow's hangover.

As he sank away into unconsciousness Dominic let go of the awestruck worship he'd fallen into just now when he'd looked at Billie's naked body. Theirs was not a relationship that was open to sex and there was no way he could take her while she was passed out—her friendship meant too much to him.

Dominic's final thoughts of the night were of Isaac's newfound desire to locate that script. In retrospect, it had to happen. This would be the star at the top of the Christmas tree that Isaac had been building since he'd launched Alston Image over two decades ago. This would make his level of success untouchable and everybody else would be vying for second place.

Billie Solar felt the leather of Dominic's couch against her left cheek as she woke, laying for some time with her eyes shut, not wanting to let in the light outside that tried to seep in, coloring the inside of her eyelids an ebbing orange with a purple roadmap of veins. She lay wrapped in this womb for some time, part of her wanting to crawl back into unconsciousness, another part wanting to wake and confront the splitting headache that most certainly waited on the other side of her eyelids.

When she finally opened her eyelids, Billie felt the queasy waves of dehydration wash over her suddenly cold body. As her wavering focus solidified slightly, Billie became aware of a dark brown object on the table in front of her. Her vision came together enough to realize it was a brick. Next to the brick was a crumpled piece of white paper, which Billie reached for as she raised up on one elbow.

"That came through the window for you, today," said Dominic, who was sitting on the left side of the couch in a white bathrobe, drinking from a coffee mug and reading the morning newspaper. Billie took the note and forced herself to focus on it:

Listen you worthless whore: we will not stand for your harlotry any longer you vile slut. God will make you pay and we will hasten your meeting him. Renounce your ways, invite God into your heart, and apologize to your country and all of the poor twelve year old girls who are watching your videos and thinking they have to look and act like you or we will KILL YOU BITCH.

Billie balled up the paper and tossed it back down on the table.

"They rubbed dog shit onto the door handles of your car too," added Dominic. "And wrote all over the windows."

"Yeah, that's their M.O." said Billie, sitting up and contemplating the mud and dirt caked onto the brick.

"They who?"

"Whoever. I used to call the police when I got these things, but they're never any help. Besides, there's like five or six groups that send things like this to me and going after them is kind of like playing whack-a-mole."

"You should be careful, nonetheless. Once a group of people starts hating pleasure, murderous desires are sure to follow."

Billie worked through the sickening haze of her hangover, ate waffles and drank coffee for breakfast, then dressed in clothes she'd brought in the tote bag. With morning rituals completed, she and Dominic went outside and set to work washing her car. "I've been dealing with this garbage since I started," continued Billie as they opened Dominic's garage door. "When I was eighteen I started nude modeling and suddenly people started slashing my tires, spitting in my food at restaurants, and spray painting my house."

"Where were you living at the time?" asked Dominic as he lifted a garden hose from a wooden shelf and Billie filled a large white bucket with sponges and a bottle of car soap. As they returned with their supplies to the Jag, Billie replied:

"I was in south Georgia. Near Columbus. I was just out of high school and I would drive up to Atlanta to pose as a life model for art classes, then I started doing pictorials. I would come home and find the word "whore" written on my house or my door kicked in and my living room trashed." They began the washing, Billie squeezing the liquid soap into the bucket as Dominic filled it with water. "When I started college that fall it got a little easier," she continued. "My parents were Pentecostal and actually had to start going to another church when word got out about my modeling. I moved to Atlanta to go to Georgia State and things got a little less rough in the city. I was stripping through school, and eventually some guys I went to high school with came to the club I was working at. I saw them when I came out onstage, and they weren't surprised to see me. They didn't even seem to be interested in the show. They just kind of sat there stone faced the whole time I was dancing and I kept making eye contact with them even though it was screwing me up and making me appear more cautious than sensuous. After I finished for the night I asked the bouncer to walk me to my car, and sure enough they were standing there in the parking lot, just watching me go by. Two days later I found out that my parents' house had been burned to the ground."

"Sounds like some Bible thumpers," Dominic replied as he scrubbed at the obscenities on the hood and Billie worked on the door handles.

"Not really," she continued. "That was the weird thing. I mean, they were the sort that went to church every Sunday but it wasn't because they were into the whole thing—they did it more because that's what good, fine, upstanding all American good 'ol boys do on Sunday. What was weird was they were the ones who had stacks of Playboys and bragged out loud about what girl they'd gotten to do what."

"That's the thing with those types, Billie. They don't make the connection that the women who do porn are women who grew up in some community somewhere, and have real ties to real people in their actual lives. To them, the difference between the girls all around them and the girls in those magazines or up on those stages is like the difference between the local sheriff and Superman. They're both in the same category—law enforcement—but one is real and material and the other is some abstract concept that floats off in the distant reaches of the imagination. It's really breathtaking when you think about it, but some of those meatheads don't seem to grasp that the women in those pictorials or up on those stripper poles are actual women. They think that they come from some other dimension and have no connection whatsoever to the women they live around in their community. Then when someone like you actually gets into this field of employment, they freak out because it forces them to realize that the saintly little princesses that they honor for being oh so pure are just as prone to sexual displays as the ones in the magazines. It shatters their illusions. Without the illusions, they can't feel like the big stud who got little Susie-Q-Virgin to abandon her principles and suck their dicks. Without the illusions they have to accept that the women want to do those things and enjoy doing them. Their engrained misogyny won't allow that so they act like they're upholding some great honor code when they harass you. Chivalry is not rooted in a respect for women, but in the need for society to give brutishness an admirable presentation. "

"And the girls just hate me because I steal all the attention from their hubbies," added Billie.

"Well, that and you're worthy of attention that they couldn't even begin to aspire to."

Billie looked up from her washing and smiled. It was the soft, unaffected expression of one who receives a tiny moment of pure friendship. "Thanks, Dominic."

Dominic returned a kind glance to Billie. "No problem, kiddo." And with that he returned to scrubbing obscenities off the windshield.

Across the San Fernando Valley, in a quiet suburb that was humble in the face of the slick excesses of show business all around it, Mrs. Simmons was cleaning her house. Her husband, a frail man with skin so pale it was nearly transparent, was mowing the front yard while she tossed dirty clothes into a laundry basket. With grim anticipation she approached her son Matthew's room. Matthew had gone to the mall with his friends, ignoring both his mother and father when they told him to help with the chores. This, Mrs. Simmons reflected, was precisely why her classroom authority ought to extend, by law, to her own household.

She entered her son's room and scowled wrenchingly at the sock that hung from a lamp on his dresser. Dropping the basket to the floor, she knelt beside it and began searching through a large pile of dirty clothes for more socks and white clothes for the load in question.

A single sock stuck out from under the bed, and Mrs. Simmons reached down to grab it. In so doing her hand brushed a cardboard shoebox. Curious that Matthew might have finally gotten a new pair of shoes, Mrs. Simmons opened it to find a bag of marijuana, two glass pipes, and three DVDs. Mrs. Simmons fell backwards, gasping, as though she had just discovered dismembered remains. Pulling herself onto her knees, she reached carefully into the box and removed the stack of DVDs. The first one was called *Bare Ass Beach Bonanza* and the cover featured ten nude women forming a cheerleader pyramid and smiling for the camera on some tropical vista. On the back of the box was the rear view of the front image, which showed their buttocks and genitals to the world.

Mrs. Simmons was horrified that her son—raised with such good moral fiber—would fall victim to this sort of wretched evil. Her mind raced over the scout masters, soccer coaches, priests, and youth group leaders that she had trusted with Matthew's moral development and wondered which one had failed her son so horribly. With trembling horror she reached for the other two DVDs, *Surf, Sand, and Suction Pumps* and *Busty Trannies 12 Starring Sandra Bullcock.* As her watering eyes traced over the box covers, she found that each of them had the same company logo in the bottom right hand corner. It was a silver shield with two stretches of video film in place of swords, forming a crest. Across the shield were two words written in bold capital letters:

ALSTON IMAGE

Chapter 4

Isaac Alston's house was a vast network of post-modern architecture, its cavernous chambers smoothed into the luxurious comfort of wealth and prosperity by means of avant-garde layouts and hauntingly pleasant lighting. During the day specially angled windows, most shaped like warped triangles, refracted the light at odd angles, catching it and bouncing it down the hallways in a rainbow glow.

The house's curvature gave the impression of a burst of paint frozen in mid-explosion and sculpted from a series of wild arcs into a network of tunnels and chambers. In one of these chambers, a low, domed room just off the master bedroom, Isaac Alston was sitting in the bathtub reading the script for Dominic's latest film while Miles Davis' Birth of the Cool piped in over stereo speakers in the walls above him and Jacuzzi jets massaged deep into his back. A sun window overhead illuminated the room and the script so perfectly that he didn't need to turn on any overhead lights.

Dominic's latest script was another stunning example of his haunting, lyrical style. The story, tentatively titled *Awake to the Skin*, told of a battered wife who was rushed to the hospital after being beaten unconscious by an abusive husband and left in a coma in the Intensive Care Unit. The woman's older sister was then brought in to keep her sister company and speak to her in hopes of drawing her out of the unconscious state. Recalling the lesbian relationship that the two women shared as teenagers, the older woman attempted to connect with her sister by telling her erotic stories meant to stimulate her back to consciousness. The injured sister, hearing the stories only on the subliminal level, entered into a series of dream states, each scenario casting the older and younger and sister as a modern Virgil and Dante, respectively, as they toured through six surreal, sexual tales of romance and psychological symbolism. With each orgasm, which one sister experienced in dreams and the other masturbated to in reality, a white light filled the former's dreamscape, intensifying each time until she was awakened only to find that the older sister

47

had become deeply unconscious. The script left the ending ambiguous, allowing the viewer to wonder whether the older sister had merely passed out or actually "traded places" with her stricken sibling.

The script was a masterwork of erotic virtuosity. The stunning images dripped from the page as though Alston were not reading a script but remembering a movie he'd already seen. More profound than this was the knowledge that Dominic would somehow manage to deliver an end result that was almost exactly what Alston was imagining as he read.

Dominic demonstrated a skill that was at once academic in its understanding of sexual art and unapologetically pretentious in the most easily digestible way. While Dominic never missed an opportunity for nudity and sex, he never seemed to go out of his way to create those opportunities. Where less creative writers would have treated the initial dialogue of each scene as meaningless drivel meant to build up to an inevitable fuck by means of blatant double-entendres, Dominic treated the sex like a part of the scene's natural flow, with each successive encounter making the subtle transition from the incidental to the purposeful and from the naturalistic to the romantic.

The script began with a bloody and brutal rape—not sexually attractive in the least but critical to establishing the scenes set in present day reality as dark and somber—then, with opening credits still rolling, showing the high-speed panic of the emergency room as the woman's blood soaked body was jabbed and prodded by medical technicians then wheeled into the ICU stuck full of hoses and tubes.

As the sister was introduced the focus shifted to flashbacks of the two of them running around naked in the private gardens of a mansion in the summer, the nudity there serving as a celebration of the innocent joy that both girls felt at the beauty of their existence. Subsequent flashbacks would show the sisters swimming nude together, kissing for the first time while holding each other in the lake, then experimenting with sex in a nearby shack. Other scenes would show the older sister giving a boy a blow job while the younger watched from a closet, and so on.

The set of flashbacks, themselves one of the erotic vignettes in the story cycle, set the mounting tone of the film. There was no filler, no pointless dialogue, nothing to fast-forward through. Each moment of the script propelled the story as an outgrowth of the erotic structure of the overall piece; the whole script, even in the rare moments without explicit eroticism, was one long sex scene and it was this epic capacity that won Dominic awards year after year and made vast sums of money for the studio.

Finishing the script, Alston reattached the paper clip that had bound it and placed the document on top of a dry towel next to the tub. Putting his hands behind his head, he contemplated the script for a long moment as the mellow restraint of Miles' ensemble cooked in the background.

The bathroom door swung open, and Alston's wife Patricia stormed in, still clad in her silk kimono bathrobe. At thirty-eight she was seeping into middle age with the sort of bitter elegance common to poorly aging beauty and now her skin was tanned year round and her makeup was thickly and tastelessly applied and retouched frequently. She seemed less like a human being than a Barbie doll, and Alston wondered at times if she truly thought he found this attractive.

"Would you like to tell me why our children think that they don't have to go to school anymore?" she demanded. Alston clapped his hands and the stereo shut off.

"I really have no idea," replied Alston. "I made it clear I'd be getting them a private tutor."

"Did you take Tim out of school?"

"I did."

"Why?"

"His teacher doesn't approve of my lifestyle."

"I don't approve of your lifestyle!"

"Really? Do you approve of *your* lifestyle?"

Patricia turned and thundered out. "Make sure you get a good one," she muttered, leaving the argument behind. In twelve years of marriage they had gone from a time of love and passion to the present state of placid tolerance. Patricia had been one of Alston Image's contract girls when they'd met, but now the demands of motherhood had somehow altered her opinion of the porn industry. She would be overheard frequently telling friends and family that she did everything she could to make sure her children never ended up in "this life" and that they wouldn't make the same "mistakes" she'd made. There had been a time when Alston would hear these things and remind her that "this life" had resulted in the kids living in the lap of luxury and that his work would allow the kids to go to any college and study whatever they wanted. In recent years, Alston had dropped this course of argument, no longer interested in leading horses to water.

Alston hit the button to release the drain and climbed out of the tub, his feet tracking soapy prints across the floor as he toweled off and entered the bedroom. His sleeping chambers were black, with white outlines around the various pieces of furniture to help make them visible. The only color in the room came from the burgundy colored night stands and matching lamps that Patricia had insisted on. These were enough to cast an enigmatic, nocturnal glow around the blackened chamber but not enough to foil Alston's intention with the room's decor: he wanted to sleep in as much darkness as possible and even the shallow illumination of the moon on white walls feeling too severe.

Drying his face off with the towel, Alston sat down on the bed and fished a television remote out from between the sheets. Turning on the television across from the bed, Alston watched the news broadcast on one of the twenty-four hour news stations as he laid out his attire for the day. The news was the usual tripe that had been pouring out of Washington lately: rabid right wing groups protesting the president, malcontents on the left that were upset about the president's pushing for bipartisanship, and the blithering idiots in small town diners who weren't bright enough to read the place mat menus, much less offer a constructive opinion, who were interviewed for a slice of life perspective from the "real America."

After a few commercials, an editorial news program called Shouting Match with Bob Match began. Alston, disgusted by the well known conservative commentator, reached for the remote but stopped and turned to watch when he heard the opening statements from Mr. Match:

Bob Match: Welcome to Shouting Match with Bob Match. I'm your host Bob Match. You know, it seems like it gets harder and harder to police our children's behavior, especially when the porn industry is waging a culture war. At the center of that war is Mrs. Ilene Simmons, an elementary school teacher from the San Fernando Valley and a devout Christian patriot. After making a shocking discovery, she's joined the group Families for Families, which is leading a glorious crusade against the porn industry. She joins us today from the headquarters of the group's Los Angeles branch. Are you there ma'am?

Bob Match's image condensed to fill only half the screen, with a shot of Tim's former teacher smiling vacantly on the other half.

Mrs. Simmons: I'm here, Bob. Thank you for having me.

Match: Thank you for taking a brave stand in the culture war that threatens to uproot our nation. Now what got you involved in this fight?

Simmons: Well, Bob, I've been a member ever since the son of a porn producer, Isaac Alston, became a student of mine.

Match: There you have it America—proof that the porn industry is planting agents in our nation's schools with the intention of hooking children at the grade school level. Now you contacted your local FFF chapter this morning with an urgent request to speak to the media. Why was that?

Simmons: Well, this morning I was cleaning house and found a box under my son's bed, which contained marijuana and several DVDs produced by Mr. Alston's company.

Match: Did your son have any prior history of using drugs and pornography?

Simmons: None whatsoever. He's such a good boy.

Match: I'm sure he is.

Simmons: When I found this box, I was convinced that it was Mr. Alston's filth that led him to try marijuana.

Match: Another promising life in ruins. How have you dealt with your son on the matter?

Simmons: He's been sent to talk to a special pastor who deals with children affected by pornography.

Match: We have that pastor live via—satellite. He's joining us now.

An image of an emaciated man in his middle thirties with jet black, wavy hair appeared beneath Mrs. Simmons, pushing her image up to occupy the upper-right third of the screen.

Match: Mr. Melvin Crankshadow—are you there sir?

Crankshadow: I'm here Bob.

Match: Thank you for joining us. Now please, tell us a little bit about your organization and what a recent inductee like Mrs. Simmons' son Matthew can expect.

Crankshadow: Certainly, Bob. Right now Matthew is in the Room of Acceptance here at the Institute for Pornographic Addiction, which is where he comes to grips with the reality of his condition. What we do here is use positive reinforcement by telling Matthew about all of the wonderful things that will come into his life when he accepts the reality his situation.

Match: I see, and what are some of those wonderful things?

Crankshadow: Well, first that he'll start receiving food again, then that he'll be allowed to sleep in a bed, and then that he'll be allowed to spend thirty minutes a day outside in the yard.

Match: Beautiful. It's all about the simple things.

Crankshadow: Exactly—and once he's accepted that he has a problem, he'll be taken to a youth pastor like myself who will listen as he recounts all of the details of the porn films he's watched, then pray with him. Over time Matthew will be allowed to become a part of our community, having limited, observed contact with other children his age when he begins his social rehabilitation therapy.

Match: And how does that work?

Crankshadow: Well, the children are placed in groups with one another and one of our camp counselors leads them in role-playing exercises where they learn how to speak and interact with other human beings without giving off any hint of sexual leanings whatsoever.

Match: That's very impressive.

Crankshadow: Thank you. After that we educate them on the dangers of pornography and conduct special prayer sessions to help them purge any dirty thoughts from their minds. Once they have done this they become clean in the eyes of God and are given the title of "Sterile."

Match: What do you teach them about sexuality in general—do you teach abstinence before marriage?

Crankshadow: We certainly do, but in the case of the poor souls that pass through our gates, what you have to remember is that the people in our care are addicts and just like alcoholics, these children will have to do without sex for the rest of their lives if they want to have any hope of beating off this horrible affliction.

Match: It is truly beautiful what you are doing, Mr. Crankshadow. Mrs. Simmons, am I correct that the FFF is providing counseling for parents of porn addicted youths?

Simmons: That's right Bob—the FFF provides a full range of resources for parents and children affected by pornography. Presently I'm enrolled in a course called "The Demons of Self Pleasure: Coming to grips with your son's grip on himself."

Match: Mr. Crankshadow, is there anything else you'd like to add?

Crankshadow: Yes, Bob. I want all patriotic Christians out there to realize that these porn people will stop at nothing. Satan is working in their hearts and minds and they will do anything it takes to sucker people and bully them into their way of thinking so that they can manipulate the public for power and personal gain. Make no mistake—the porn industry is a dangerous cult run by fanatics that play on fear and ignorance to manipulate gullible rubes into giving them financial support.

Match: Thank you, Mr. Crankshadow and Mrs. Simmons.

Crankshadow: Thank you for having me.

Simmons: Thank you, Bob.

Match: Alright—coming up on shouting Match, we talk about the Liberal idiots who think that Jesus Christ would have been in favor of universal healthcare. But now a word from out sponsors.

Alston turned off the television and sat staring at the blank screen for a moment. He felt annoyed, insulted, and frustrated, but not surprised in the least.

"You have to understand, son," said Artie Barrel, getting to the meat of what, until now, had only been rambling, "that men are basically slimy, shitty little creatures. They go to work every day, come home, have dinner, maybe fuck their wives, but when you get right down to it, every single one of them has some deep, hidden flaw in their character that makes them worthless little shits. And what they do is stick that embarrassing little flaw into the one place where nobody will think to look—their sexuality. What they don't count on is that there are those of us out there who know where to hit and where to hit hard. We get them hooked on a drug they were already addicted to. That's what porn is good for, and that's why we make it."

Ralphie Barrel, the son and only offspring of Artie Barrel, listened somewhat attentively as they rolled down a bland stretch of suburban Las Vegas. Since naming his son as the Vice President of Intersect Productions, Artie had delighted in delivering these monologues to his now twenty eight year old son.

Ralphie, outwardly patient with regards to his father, was pleased beyond compare when he had been given the title of Vice President. He had learned over time that nothing in life was quite as important as a title. A title was like a shield that blocked you from attacks by all the assholes out there in life. He was no longer Ralphie the scrawny kid who got picked last for kick ball. Now he was the Vice President of Intersect Productions.

The title was already starting to pay off. The girls that worked for Intersect—even the ones that weren't porn stars—were sucking his dick on request. The guys who worked for Intersect were smiling when they saw him, even giving him some high-fives. Before, neither gender had so much as acknowledged him even though he was Artie's son. In fact, before his naming a VP, most people didn't even know Artie had a son.

"Is this the house?" asked Artie as they pulled up to a small blue bungalow with asbestos siding.

"Ah—yeah," said Ralphie, glancing down at the clipboard in his lap. They pulled into the driveway and Artie took out a handheld video camera, which he turned on his son. The red recording light came on.

"What's up my man?" said Artie as Ralphie bounced his eyebrows for the camera. Ralphie had a habit of nodding slightly as if he were grooving to music only he could hear and moved his jaw as though he were chewing gum even when he wasn't.

"Well, I am making my porn debut today," replied Ralphie, smirking vacantly. "And I am filming this scene for the new Intersect Productions site Breakinfantasies.com!"

"Alright boy—who's waiting for us in that house?"

Ralphie looked down at the clipboard "Today's victim bitch is Katie. It's always a blast to wake these bitches up with a dick up their butts. So without further adieu, let's get the action started!"

They climbed out of the truck, Ralphie pulling a leg of pantyhose over his head as he tip-toed up to the front door. Artie watched through the fold out viewer of the camera as his son opened the screen door then tried the door knob. "Bitch left the door locked!" whispered Ralphie to the camera. "Oh well," and with that he kicked the door in, one of the hinges breaking off as the deadbolt shattered the frame.

The house was sparse and tastefully decorated—a surprise to Ralphie, who had heard this bitch kept dildos all over the place and had posters from her movies on the walls. Nevertheless he glanced around and found a bedroom, through the open door of which was a woman lying asleep in bed, an empty bottle of Jägermiester lying on the floor next to her. Stalking into the bedroom, father and son poked and proded the body of the pretty brunette, finding it unresponsive.

"Bitch is out cold!" Said Ralphie, pulling the sheets down to expose her naked body. "I like it when they lie still like this."

Artie zoomed in on the naked woman while his son stood off to one side and stripped naked. Once his hunched, emaciated frame was fully exposed, Ralphie snuck over to the bed and rolled his silent partner over on her back, spreading her legs. Artie zoomed in on her exposed cunt and Ralphie leaned into the camera shot to flick his tongue rapidly over her large clit.

"Eat it like its turkey dinner, boy!" Howled Artie, who walked around the bed to get a wide shot of his son's naked ass. From there Ralphie turned and shoved his semi-erect penis into the woman's mouth, fucking each cheek before going all the way in, her teeth brushing against his wiry pubes. Finishing penetrating her throat, Ralphie withdrew and made a few joking thrusts of his tip into one of her nostrils.

"Time for the main event!" chuckled Ralphie, who slithered down the body and thrust his stiffened pecker into her slit, humping clumsily in and out, all the while lifting her right leg and licking up and down her calves. This proceeded for some twenty minutes, when Ralphie started to grunt harder and deeper. "I'm gonna come," he gasped.

"Spray them titties, boy" barked Artie. "Make your mother proud!" Ralphie obeyed and withdrew in time to shoot a few bursts of malodorous jissom onto the woman's bare breasts. Artie zoomed in on the come as it rolled down her chest, then clicked the record button off. "Got what we need." he said as Ralphie dismounted and put his clothes back on.

As they left the house, Artie put a hand on his son's shoulder, beaming. "My boy's a man today."

The sunlight hit their eyes hard as they left the house and both squinted as their eyes readjusted. As Ralphie blinked away the morning sun, he saw a woman standing on the front porch of the house across the street and wearing a pink silk bathrobe with her hair in curlers. After a moment, Ralphie recognized Vicky, the shoot's makeup girl, putting touches on the model's face. "Hey" called the model from across the street. "What are you guys doing over there? Are we gonna shoot this or what?"

Chapter 5

WHEN ISAAC ALSTON was sixteen, he got his girlfriend Mandy pregnant. When she told him of the news Isaac asked what she planned to do about it and she broke down crying, saying that her parents would disown her if they found out she'd been sleeping with someone and so an abortion would be necessary. Isaac dipped into his savings to pay for the procedure and on a crisp spring morning he drove her to a clinic, which was located in an unassuming beige building. Mandy was silent for the entire journey but her eyes were red and puffy and tears rolled soundlessly down her cheeks.

They reached the building and parked out in front and when Isaac climbed out of the car to put coins in the meter, he noticed the line of protestors across the street, each of them wearing duct tape over mouth and eyes. In their hands was a large banner reading "because they have no voice." At least they're quiet, thought Alston.

Escorting Mandy from the car, Isaac made his way up the stone steps with his girlfriend in his arms. Looking down at her he felt as if he were watching the mother of a condemned man on her way to watch the execution. While she wept silently, Isaac struggled to identify the victim.

Sitting in the waiting room while Mandy received the procedure, Alston glanced out at the silent imbeciles on the opposite sidewalk and wished they'd thought to put tape over their noses as well. On this Saturday morning these people could have been out in the public gardens, drinking in the morning radiance of the dew-soaked grass as it refracted the new dawn through beads of tiny, fluidic, prisms. Instead they were standing out in front of an abortion clinic with tape on their faces.

Isaac contemplated the protestors, wondering where their connection to these aborted cells came from. These "babies" that they fought so hard to protect were only small collections of cells. They had the long-term potential to become human beings, but presently they were only microscopic groups of matter. They hadn't loved and lost or been to rock concerts or been given social security numbers. There was no doubt they were living but were they human? No. Not in the romantic sense that led people to protest on the street. These people weren't protecting the rights of a human being, but the projected rights of a projected human being. They were protesting the destruction of their vacant idealism.

What would that baby become if it was born? Another damned soul bound for eternal hellfire. These people, who were claiming to be "pro-life," were the same people who treated existence like a crushing burden to be endured in flamboyant agony. Why were they so eager to commit people to such a fate?

After the procedure was complete, Isaac took Mandy home and didn't hear from her for several days. When word of the abortion spread around the local community, Isaac was shouted at. He was shouted at by parents, by teachers, by his fellow students, by homeless vagrants and clergymen alike. The shouting became screaming, its volume and pitch entering the shrill, ravaging timbre of distorted lunacy. Over time the screaming began to blend, each voice melding into the next until all that remained was a single, unbroken stream of enraged static.

It no longer mattered what verbosity fueled the anger, it was all a part of the wall of noise. And the wall became a dome, one that surrounded Isaac and contained him inside its dimly lit interior. This was not, however, detrimental to Isaac Alston. In this newfound den of din, he was free.

Wrapped in the cool darkness of his bedroom, Isaac Alston contemplated what he had seen on the television. He considered the newly revealed truth— Mrs. Simmons had been aware all along that he was a pornographer. She had known that Tim would present such a project and allowed it to go forward.

Alston picked up his cell phone from his bedside table and dialed his assistant. "Hey—get Abe Lattimore and Duke Cunningham to my house— pronto. I don't care what they're doing. I want them over here now." With that he dressed in comfortable weekend attire and went downstairs for breakfast.

Patricia was a decent enough cook, though Alston preferred their chef. Nevertheless, the smell of waffles and bacon that drifted up the stairs was a bright, heartwarming smell that, coupled with the sound of cartoons on the living room television, lifted him into a wisp of nostalgia and, for an instant, away from the crazy lady on the TV. When he entered the kitchen, its wide dome shimmering with the cool steel of modern appliances, he could see the kids from in the living room. Tim was playing a handheld video game and Jesse, Alston's four year old daughter, was watching a cartoon on the flat screen television.

Alston ignored his wife as he passed and poured himself a glass of milk before going out on the patio to read the paper. Patricia had already tossed it on the chase lounge, and he as the headline caught his eyes as he sat:

WHITE HOUSE CAVES TO INSURANCE LOBBY
By Blair Dithers
WASHINGTON D.C. —In an unexpected move, the new ad-
ministration has announced that it will reach across the aisle
in an unexpected show of bipartisanship. "I think we can all
agree that partisan agendas are second to the ability to form
alliances with one's adversaries," said the President, his infec-
tious grin reflecting the morning sun from the White House
rose garden. "And so it pleases me to announce that my ad-
ministration will advise congress and the senate to fully em-
brace the healthcare plan proposed by the Republicans." When
asked why the administration was going to fully-support a bill
that was in complete contradiction to the promises made on
the President's campaign trail, he responded by saying "Now
don't think for a minute that our partisan ideology will sway
the glorious ship of American unity that has sailed all these
years on freedom's compromising waves. We Democrats had
to spend the last administration as the minority party and as
I recall we didn't like it. What sort of Americans would we be
if we stomped on the downtrodden party with our filibuster
proof majority in both houses?"

Alston couldn't stand to read anymore and cast the paper aside as Patricia brought him breakfast and called for the kids to come join them. They ate amidst the pleasant formalities of a family breakfast, complete with the light hearted chatter of mindless conversation. There were times when Alston would have done anything to avoid this sort of open-ended chit chat, but in anticipation of the meeting he was about to have with Abe, his Vice President, and Duke, his attorney, Alston relished the private moment, free as it was of the blithering insanity of the outside world. Alston found himself laughing warmly along with his wife as Jesse attempted to retell a joke she'd heard on television, her missing baby teeth causing her to slur and squish certain words comically. The children had been the one light in the dull grey of domesticity that Alston cherished. When they finished eating Alston kissed Jesse on the forehead and tussled her hair before collecting the dishes and taking them into the kitchen. Once there he washed them off and loaded the dishwasher, the utilitarian nature of the action again allowing him a moment's escapism.

Abe Lattimore and Duke Cunningham arrived together shortly thereafter, having taken the same car. Abe was a somewhat tall man with sloping white hair and a slight beer gut. He wore large belt buckles and cowboy boots, both a throwback to his Texas heritage. Despite his eccentric image, Abe was a trustworthy and insightful right hand, having brought to the table a wealth of experience managing fortune 500 companies when Isaac was just launching Alston Image. Abe had come out to California to get into something more exciting than the soporific boardroom seminars of his Dallas ventures. He'd been skeptical about going into porn at first, but when he'd seen the commanding presence and glittering ambition of a young Isaac Alston, he'd been quickly convinced of the potential and taken the office of Vice President and Alston Image.

Duke Cunningham had been a high school friend of Alston's who had gone to Harvard law school. The experience had left him a bit hardened and cynical, with the drive towards academic excellence slowly withering his capacity for social enjoyment. In the years since then, however, he had sculpted that vaguely bitter nature and augmented it with some of the industry's inherent charisma to produce a persona that was at once formidable and reassuring. He had been Alston's personal attorney and primary legal advisor since the inception of Alston Image.

"If this is about *The Lotus Wave,* I still haven't got any leads," began Abe as he and Duke entered Alston's vaulted foyer.

"It's not," replied Alston, shaking their hands quickly and formally. Both men exchanged worried glances as Alston led them into his formal dining room, giving them both the feeling of entering the War Room. Alston pulled out the chairs closest to the far end of the polished mahogany expanse and sat between them, with Abe facing him on his left and Duke on his right. With a calm but hurried tone, Alston told them about the *Shouting Match* interview and the preceding encounter with Tim's teacher. "As you know," he finished, "I don't care when these whack jobs go after me, but I can't put my kids in the line of fire. I want to know what this Simmons woman could do to us and what I can do to her."

"She really doesn't have fuck all on you as far as calling child services goes," replied Duke Cunningham. "The best she could do is say that your line of work exposes your kids to sexually explicit materials and situations, but that's a rather flimsy argument. It would depend on how puritanical the Child Services worker she spoke to was."

"I took Tim with me to work the other day—how risky was that?"

"It depends—what did he see?" asked Duke. A distant look of realization came to Alston for a moment. "Never mind—don't answer that. It's unlikely that she would have any significant traction going after you like that—not after appearing on the news and admitting she joined an anti-porn group when she found out your son was in her class. It would tell any judge that she had an agenda and was trying to fuck with you. Anyone else I would tell them they were overreacting, but with you I'll just say not to stir this pot before you have to."

"What Duke is saying," continued Abe, "is that right now you have the upper hand. If you lash out violently—or lash out at all for that matter—you forfeit that superior position by admitting their baseless arguments have merit. And since they know that their arguments are baseless, they'll only perceive weakness if you respond. You've never given interviews so don't start now. I'll handle the press if it gets to that point."

Alston nodded slowly, his eyes cast softly on the tiny waves in the brown hues of the table. "I still want everything you can give me on Families for Families. Who they are, what they do, what they *really* do. All of that. I didn't like the look in that pastor's eyes. There was too much Jim Jones mixed in with the Jerry Fallwell."

"I'll see what we can find," Abe replied. "But I will say this, though I know it won't slow you down: if there is anything to this FFF bunch and they do come after your family then now would not be the time to take on a project like *The Lotus Wave*."

"You're absolutely right," said Alston. "That wouldn't slow me down in the least." They watched him for a time, his once mild gaze now wavering on the verge of combustion. Still, his features were calm and collected. Only the unspoken fire of his defiant eyes stood out from the placid mask of his outer self. Both Abe and Duke had known Alston long enough to be familiar with this state, though neither had seen it burn this brightly before. Usually Alston sank into this deep contemplation when he sought to shake off the impudent fools who questioned his ambitions but now Duke and Abe could see him sinking deeper—the darkness inside him welling up not as a destructor but as an ally. His eyes clicked up again, the darkness suddenly restrained. "Gentlemen, thank you for coming out today," he said, standing abruptly and shaking their hands. "Tell Dominic I'm green lighting *Awake to the Skin*. With that title—I think it's a good one."

"I'll do that," said Abe. "I'm sure he'll be glad to hear it."

Abe and Duke left, Alston escorting both of them to the door and bidding them a polite farewell with a tight but sincere smile. As they departed, both of them were secure in the knowledge that their meeting today had carried more weight than the words that had been exchanged. It had been a dark, visceral performance, with Alston securing a fundamental truth in the minds of his seconds in command: that a lion, no matter how majestic and beautiful, was still a lion. That the delicate poise and graceful speed of its interwoven frame were still fueled by a primal adrenalized killing mechanism. By extension, a leader such as

Isaac Alston, no matter how diplomatic and peaceful in his lavish grandeur, was still an emperor and still commanded a wellspring of vigilant brutality, ready to be tapped at all times, in the hearts and souls of his power structure.

With much to contemplate, Abe and Duke returned to the Alston Image building, the heart of Isaac Alston's Eros Empire.

Andrea Danvers lived in a notably lavish home in a trendy suburb of Weston, Massachusetts. Her tenured position at Whitland College afforded her a home that occupied the perfect center of a wide, well manicured lawn surrounded by a high wrought iron fence that was gated at the driveway. The gate was operated by a keypad on a post that was at the level of a car window. Cars were not parked by their drivers but stopped under a stone awning at the side of the house where the family's private valet would then relieve the driver and navigate the car the remaining fifteen feet to dock in the garage if it belonged to the family and the parking lot just off the backyard pool house if it belonged to a visitor. The front of the mansion was outlined with a gold border that stood in harsh contrast to the green marble columns and white stucco exterior. A line of palm trees bordered the sidewalk up to the front door.

In the mansion's expansive dining room, Andrea and her husband, Mercer Thompson, sat on either side of an ornate table made of a dark oak. Mercer Thompson stared down at his plate of bean curd and tofu with an expression that would have been contemplative if it hadn't been straining to be as blank as possible. Distantly, he heard his wife expounding on her findings at the recent porn convention as though her tone were teetering precariously between lecture hall grandeur and sewing circle gossip. "And that was when I met Alice Grausam. You know, I never thought I'd say this, but she and I had so much in common. I mean, imagine—a capitalistic right winger like her and a Marxist like me being so much alike. I had lunch with her and I told her about how I wanted to have a law passed that would re-move African-Americans from positions on professional sports teams and the entertainment industry so that they wouldn't have to suffer the humilia-tion of being entertainment for white people and wouldn't you know it, she said she wanted to get blacks off of the sports teams, TVs and radios too! I told her about my research into how pornography destroys families and she completely agreed with me. And best of all, she totally agreed with me when I said that pornography was a failing of modern liberalism."

Mercer Thompson wanted to ask his wife if she'd said anything to Grausam about how the patriarchal underpinnings of marriage made it a pro-cess of rape by contract but realized that this would sound like a challenge and decided not to pursue it. In doing so, however, he missed the rhythmic window in the conversation in which he was supposed to have interjected a polite observation and this sudden failing caught Andrea's attention. "You haven't touched your dinner," she observed. "And your bowel movements have been irregular lately—have you been sneaking fatty foods at lunch again?"

"No ma'am," he muttered as Andrea lit a cigarette.

"Well something's obviously on your mind, so out with it."

"I—I—well, I got that research grant today."

"Oh. Well that's good," she replied with excessively sharp formality.

"I'll be able to do that study for my new book project."

"You do realize," began Andrea with calculated irritability "that you getting your research grant before I get mine will reinforce the patriarchal values of our enemies, don't you?"

"Yes, darling. I just thought that-"

"You just thought that you'd flex your testosterone drenched sense of entitlement, is that it?"

"Well, no. No not at all."

"Well why then?"

"I just thought that we could… celebrate."

"You want to *celebrate?*"

"Yes, dear, I do."

But they both knew that Mercer did not want to celebrate—he wanted to numb the pain of satisfaction. Getting the grant money for the book was supposed to make him happy and happiness was a thing that he watched from behind rain soaked glass. From this vantage he'd been able to learn that happiness was the ultimate expression of elitism—it meant putting oneself into a state of willful ignorance to the sadness of the rest of the world. As a child, Mercer had been left out of the sports and outdoor games that the other children played due to a bronchial condition that caused him to cough up large chunks of phlegm if he got to running too hard. When he became a teenager his father feared that the apparent lack of an onset of puberty was a sign of Mercer's latent homosexuality and began to feed his son a steady diet of the kinds of powders and health supplements used by professional body builders. This left Mercer with a gastric condition that required he wear diapers through his high school years and beyond. Forever relegated to the role of wall flower (specifically the wall with a restroom,) Mercer had watched in silent frustration as the girls around him had blossomed and with their blossoming came an awareness of his own sexual desires. As he grew (chronologically, if not literally,) Mercer began to recognize the types of boys that the girls around him favored. They wanted boys with muscled bodies, smooth skin, full lips, and inviting smiles. While most of the girls around him were too polite to say anything that was outright cruel, few of them had any time or interest in the kid that the jocks referred to as "diaper boy."

In his early years one of the first lessons of courtesy and consideration for others that Mercer had learned was that it was inappropriate to brag openly about your material possessions to children who came from less financially affluent backgrounds. It made sense to Mercer and he often wondered why the other kids were so outwardly pronounced in wearing stylish, ornate clothes that demonstrated their worldly opulence. The lesson sank deeper into the moistened driftwood of his shame drenched being and began to gradually shape Mercer's worldview until he began to wonder why nobody was being considerate of him at all. The actual bullies weren't the worst part—it was the utter indifference to his suffering that made him angry. All around him were cheerleaders with breasts that bobbed up and down and long smooth legs that kicked up in the air to flash the single piece of fabric that covered their young crotches and members of the girls basketball team that ran around in little mesh shorts and bent way over to touch their toes during practice and there was a place called a locker room where they all changed in and out of various garments, the transitional period of nakedness being the topic foremost on the lips of the boys in the opposite locker room. These discussions irritated Mercer to the point of profound depression: how could they be so ignorant of his presence that they would talk about things that were eternally beyond his grasp but not theirs? It was as if each of the other boys thought that they had a right to have sex with the girls by virtue of their existence. But their existence was wrong because they had something that another person did not have.

In the dark recesses of this adolescent despair, Mercer began to look for a tunnel of deliverance into a rationale—any rationale—that could put all of this into perspective. It was by chance that he stumbled on to some radical feminist literature and suddenly it all made sense: the other boys thought they had a right to have sex because they had grown up in a society that had conditioned them to expect rape as an entitlement. His eyes had been opened: he no longer felt contempt for the poor boys around him because he knew that he could help them. Contrary to popular belief, these radical feminist writers didn't hate and despise men but wanted to help them, much like Christians claimed to love the sinner and hate the sin.

Mercer's early attempts to evangelize his newfound truths were unfruitful—lacking any of the outwardly pleasant social graces that would have allowed him to communicate with most people, he was generally ignored by those around him and those who did respond usually said "aren't you the diaper kid?"

College revealed itself to be a more workable environment: nobody was aware of his diapers, his congestion, or any of the preceding twelve years and though generally isolated as he had been before, his migration to the halls of Whitland College placed him in the ranks of a small number of serious students whose minds were devoted entirely to academics. Here, he'd been able to study the kind of feminism that had been a beacon of radiant hope throughout his teenage years. There were classes on Women's Studies that expounded exactly what he wanted to hear and he took to it with an odd commitment: his study was thorough and academically well received but it was devoid of the kind of energy that would have otherwise indicated an enthusiastic pupil. Instead his professors noted that he seemed to be fixated on some blurry internal logic, as though the classes were not a process of education, but an intentional attempt to reshape his view of reality—as if he hoped that flexing only one part of his cognition would cause the rest to atrophy.

The self crippling was complete when Mercer handed in his doctoral thesis titled "The Illusion of 'Sex Positive' Feminism: how advocating for women's right to enjoy their sexuality contributes to rape culture." The paper was well received and caught the attention of one of Mercer's classmates, Andrea Danvers. A year younger than Mercer she'd just begun work on her doctoral thesis titled "Pornogrphy: rape as a consumer product" and had wanted to meet the man behind a thesis as remarkable as his. For once, he connected with someone and realized that she was the ideal woman: where most women shaved their legs and crotches, Andrea's lower body was consumed with a thick web of black, curly hair that also filled her armpits. Where many women were slender and lithe, Andrea was spherical and bulbous and where most women sought to walk with an erotic swaying of their hips Andrea would cast her bloated legs outwards and pull the rest of her body along in their wake. She was the ideal woman: one devoid of femininity. And she made him feel like the ideal man: one devoid of masculinity.

Together they graduated, married, and eventually returned to teach at Whitland College. Mercer was paid a handsome salary to teach a course that advocated Marxist economics as a means to freedom from gender inequality and Andrea found considerable fame and fortune on the book tour circuit giving lectures on how the porn industry turned a profit and was therefore immoral. Mercer had wanted to write a book as well but his wife kept reminding him that his success would make it appear as though he were trying to exert a patriarchal hold on her career and he relented. He liked that she kept him feeling safe and secure—not letting the perversion of happiness creep into his otherwise reverently bleak life. With her guidance, it made sense that they should live in such luxury because they were incapable of enjoying it and being numb to one's own prosperity was the height of moral completeness.

But the college had wanted him to write the book and he had accepted the research grant. Now, he needed to celebrate. In their long and involved history as advocates for radical feminism, Mercer and Andrea had frequently been accused of being anti-sex. In public Andrea was quick to reply that they were not "anti-sex" but rather "committed to a proactive analysis of the rape oriented nature of the biological reality of sexual indulgence in a contemporary capitalistic environment whose intrusive consumerism reflected the invasive horror of penetration and the self indulgent insanity of orgasmic release." In private, however, they used sex for what it was meant to be: a means to nullify potentially elitist feelings of happiness with quivering disgust. They took mutual satisfaction in their ability to perform that act without pleasure and without passion as was required of a relationship based on equality. To ignore sexuality would have been to acknowledge that their weakness towards it. To have sex without enjoyment was to demonstrate ownership of their sexuality.

Mercer could tell that his wife's eyes were asking if by "celebrate" he meant sex and his delicate nod while looking down at the table indicated that he did. The research grant was something that a perverted elitist would take pride in. It was time for Andrea to subdue that feeling. She rang the little bell that made one of their house servants come running.

"Clear the table," said Andrea when the girl arrived. The young woman—who could have been shapely were she not concealed in a thick black cloak—picked up Mercer's plate of bean curd and tofu then came around to take Andrea's bucket of fried chicken and extra large soda when her employer sniffed loudly. "What is that I smell?" boomed Andrea to the suddenly panic stricken young girl. "Are you wearing *perfume*?"

"Y-y-yes. Yes Ma'am," whispered the girl in response.

"Oh so you're supporting the cosmetics industry now are you? Haven't I taught you not to indulge in the deceit of corporate enterprise?" she demanded as she lit a cigarette.

"I'm sorry," said the house keeper, tears streaming down her reddened face. "My boyfriend is picking me up after I leave tonight and-"

"A boyfriend? A boyfriend? I bet you shaved your cunt for him too didn't you? Bend over and raise your dress."

"Ma'am?"

"Let me see your cunt! Now!"

The petrified girl bent over shamefully and raised her dress. Andrea jerked the servant's panties down and leaned in close. "Shaved to the bone. So you're dating a pedophile."

"What?"

"That's why you shaved your pubic hair. You may not realize it, but as someone who understands media theory, I can tell you that you've shaven your crotch because you've been brainwashed by the very same corporate giants that have turned your boyfriend into a pedophile. Are you seeing this?" she turned the girl's buttocks towards Mercer and spread her legs further apart. Mercer could see that the vagina had indeed been shaven but did not allow himself to linger too long on the sight. "Apologize."

"For what?"

"For buying into the pro-pedophilia agenda of the corporate rulers of America."

"I don't know what that means!"

"I do. And that means you need to apologize!" shrieked Andrea, slapping their girls buttocks with both hands.

"I'm sorry!" cried the humiliated girl. "I'm sorry!" she cried again and again as Andrea continued the spanking.

When at last the spanking subsided, Andrea rose to her feet. "You are on leave from your job as my house keeper until such time as you have hair on your crotch. You will not style it or trim it. And you will inform that boyfriend of yours that if he does not undergo treatment for his latent pedophilia, I will report him to law enforcement."

The girl reached down and pulled her panties up as she hurried from the room, the dishes she'd removed from the table now scattered all over the floor. Andrea stood in stern silence as she watched the girl leave out the servant's entrance in the kitchen. After the door slammed Mercer began cleaning the food and dishes up off the floor.

"You know what the worst thing of that convention I went to was?" asked Andrea returning to the hybrid tone of vacant rambling and academic credibility that she wielded so well.

"What's that, dear?"

"It was how indifferent all those girls were to the degradation that they were enduring. Almost as if they didn't consider it a bad thing at all. They even seemed to be enjoying it. But if there's one thing that kept me going through that thing its knowing that one day those girls will learn how degraded they were and how mistreated they've been. They'll be educated—they'll know what a horrible thing it is that they do to their fellow women and they'll change their ways. I just wish they were more self aware."

Mercer nodded as he washed the dishes and put them away. When he finished, he and his wife went upstairs to "celebrate" and, much to Mercer's morbid satisfaction, he forgot about that pretty servant girl and her sweet smelling vagina when he took off his clothes and moved trembling towards the swampy expanse that was a fully nude Andrea Danvers.

Chapter 6

THE CHAMBER WAS WIDE and black, with the room's only visible contours coming from the slight changes in the shade of the darkness that ebbed and flowed in and out the distorted architecture only to be pulled taught at hard, unexpected angles. The chamber was massive—it stretched off into the distance like a vast aircraft hanger—but the ceiling was too low and the only lighting came from bare light bulbs that hung like smoldering sunflowers from long wire stems, each flaring out with hypnotic intensity. Hank steel pushed one of the low hanging bulbs aside as he walked toward the camera.

The room had been modified by zigzag corridors that distorted the vastness of the chamber into intersecting voids, each darkness penetrating the next. The camera was mounted on a track that rolled slowly backwards as Hank Steel approached it, a thick black bull whip wrapped around his left hand and held tight in his right. Dominic Daniels sat perched on a stool that extended sideways from the thick metal post that supported the camera. He watched Hank advance menacingly on the lens and held a blank focus that suggested subtle analysis of his performer's every move.

Hank mirrored the focus that Dominic cast up at him, using Dominic's eye level, which was just above the camera lens, as an organic target for the ominous stare that he cast down on the mechanical eye. He moved down the network of the off kilter hallways that went nowhere except the center of the disjointed room, all the while staring into the camera as if it were the eyes of someone who, fallen to the floor, was now crawling backwards slowly like Daedalus before the Minotaur in that ancient labyrinth.

They came to the mouth of the corridor, which opened onto the center of the room. "Cut," whispered Dominic, and Hank stopped in place, watching the red record light go off. In the center of the room was a large cage bathed in stage lights that gave it the effect of being surrounded by a thundering ritual bonfire—as though it were the scene of a jungle sacrifice in the middle of the night.

Dominic dismounted the track camera and motioned for Hank to follow him into the center of the room, where the giant cage stood. *This must be what method acting feels like,* thought Hank as he stepped through the intricate network of cables that ran beneath his feet. *To never leave character, not even when the camera stops rolling. But what character am I? What am I tapping into here? This primal beast creature is me, but not the me I want to be.*

Dominic gave Hank a hand held video camera. "Now we're going to shoot some viewpoint shots," he explained. "Just hold this camera up to your eye level so that it seems like the audience is seeing what you're seeing. Billie is going to come out in a moment and get in the cage, and when she does you're going to walk around the outside of the cell, videotaping her as you circle. Understand?" Hank nodded.

Hank's heart leapt when Billie walked onto the set. Her bare feet pressed against the cold stone floor as though each step were notes in an ocular melody. As she approached she cast her robe aside and entered the cage naked, winking and flashing a smile and Hank as she passed. He watched her move into the cell, watched the way her ass swayed, the cheeks moving in and out of one another and felt his heart swoon.

As Billie got into position, Hank noticed how the mood on the set remained as it had during filming. Before Dominic the directors that Hank had worked with had made no attempt to maintain an atmosphere on the set. Pointing the camera in the direction of two people fucking seemed to be the extent of the effort expended by many directors, but Dominic brought a delicate precision to the scene, almost as if he, the director, had created a special character for himself to play on set so that he could move as a ghost through the shoot without breaking the focus.

With Billie in position Hank went to his mark and began to circle the cage when Dominic whispered "and… action." As Hank came around to the side of the cage where the door stood open, its metal bars catching one of the overhead lights, Hank began the dialogue he'd memorized the previous Monday:

"Hey there Billie Solar," he began, pointing the camera straight into her face but careful not to get the film crew into the shot.

"Hey," she replied with faux meekness, her hands clasped behind her back and one foot toeing the ground innocently.

"What did you come here for, baby?"

"I need to learn to be a good girl." He panned the camera up and down her body, returning to her shimmering eyes, which emoted in such a way that she seemed to have learned to flex them like muscles.

"And why is that?"

"Well, my hubby wants to fuck me in the ass, but I'm too tight back there."

"So did you try wearing a plug?"

"Yeah... but I'm not a good girl—I kept forgetting to put it in. So my man sent me here to be disciplined."

"Well I think we can handle that. We'll get that ass stretched out with some of our favorite toys, but first you need to be paddled for disobedience, don't you?"

"Yeah..."

"You say 'yes master' to me, is that understood?"

"Yes master."

"Cut," said Dominic. Hank pushed pause on the camera and handed it through the bars to Dominic, who watched the footage for a moment before nodding and saying "looks good. Let's set up for the first activity."

Two of the roller-mounted cameras were moved into place, and a third unit, this one shoulder mounted, was carried into the cage by one of the camera men.

"Okay, explained Dominic," we're going to shoot thirty lashes on the ass, fifteen on each cheek alternating left to right and back. I want thirty from each angle we just mounted for, so that's going to be ninety total."

"Can you handle that?" whispered Hank.

"Yeah—I'm an ass queen," said Billie as Dominic passed a cat-o-nine whip through the bars to Hank. "Can't get enough." Her voice had a warm sweetness to it even when she was all business.

"Hank," said Dominic, returning to his director's chair. "What we want is to see are her cheeks bouncing when you whip them, so come down from above, not from the side. Think of each stroke as starting in your shoulder and ending in your wrist."

"Got it," said Hank, whipping the air experimentally.

"Lower the cuffs, please," said Dominic and a pair of leather wrist restraints lowered from the ceiling on a chain. Hank attached them to Billie's slender wrists and pulled them just a little too tight. He watched Billie close her eyes and breathe in deep and as the chain was raised again until she stood on the tips of her toes, taking a private pleasure from the act.

Dominic commenced the scene and Hank brought the lash down on Billie's bottom, her bottom bouncing as it welled up red. A wave of desire filling him, Hank struck her right buttock, which yielded the same result. He increased the force of the strikes and Billie yelped playfully, her kinky self coming out in the performance. Her passion for the action gave Hank something to feed off of and he found himself embracing his sadistic character whole-heartedly. As the administrations increased his heart melted tenderly at the way her jaw trembled, the way her lips seemed to grope for words to articulate the guttural groans that she produced, and the way her long dark hair swayed gently back and forth as her body responded to each strike.

The cameraman operating the shoulder mounted unit finished taping his thirty and ducked quickly out of the way of the first mounted camera, allowing it to pick up without a pause in the action. Dominic nodded quietly to himself, impressed with how well these two were working together. Their heat was combustible. When Hank finally finished all ninety repetitions Dominic called "cut" and the cameras were moved again as another set of cuffs, this one for Billie's feet was lowered from the ceiling.

Hank watched silently as Billie drank in the pain with a soft smile on her face. The skin on her bottom was bright red, though unbroken, and Hank reached and stroked Billie's buttocks with the knuckles of his hand, and she looked back at him with a welcoming smile.

"Am I doing okay?" he whispered.

"Outstanding," she whispered.

"Okay—next scene," said Dominic, his voice careful not to violate the chapel of the set. "You guys cool on the dialogue?"

"Yeah," said Billie. Hank nodded.

"Good. Okay—cameras in place? Awesome, take it away guys."

The red record lights ignited and Hank fell back into his role as though he were slipping on a warm glove.

"It's time for your suspension, Billie," said Hank with feigned disinterest. "Are you prepared for this?"

"Yes," she replied. Hank pulled her hair, forcing her to crane her neck backwards. Her eyes were big and round as they looked into his. Just over her shoulder blades he could see her stiff nipples, the hard tips appearing to strain against her heaving breasts.

"Yes, what?" he asked darkly.

"Yes master..." she groaned, and he released her hair. As he took hold of the foot cuffs and knelt to put them on her ankles, he felt as though he were not playing the part of a torturer but of an acolyte kneeling at a sort of mass he had never believed could exist: it was a rite that celebrated the naked, the sensual, and the ravenous. In the past he had felt as though each act he performed in, while not shameful to him on an intellectual level, had carried a strong emotional repugnance, as though he were doing something that, in the name of decency, should fill him with disgust. But that smog of guilt was not found here with Billie and Dominic. Instead, the part of him that would breathe it in and cough it out was left to cast about wildly, looking for something to grab onto only to find Billie's naked ankles, where he lovingly attached the cuffs.

Though Hank's harsh performance demeanor was unaffected, he watched Billie's ascension with an innocent fascination. She closed her eyes and gave herself over to the levitation as though she were being lifted off the ground not by a series of chains and pulleys but by some form of eastern meditation. One of the track cameras came around to capture Billie from below as she ascended, the set lights bathing her in an angelic glow.

The rest of the set progressed through a series of kinky acts, each lasting about two to three minutes. Billie was tied, suspended upside down, her nipples clamped, and pleasured with several vibrators before she was lowered again and stripped of her restraints so that Hank could bend her over his knee and spank her with an open hand for some time, transitioning to the anal segment by teasing her tail hole with his right middle finger, feeling the tender outer ring loosen gradually. He realized then that she was crying—that she had been since the suspension. The tears ran down her face as she breathed in deep for air, her heavy breathing accentuated by thick sobs. Sensing that he had noticed her tears for the first time, Billie turned her head slightly, looking back at Hank as he worked his finger into her anus up to the knuckle, followed by his index finger as the orifice loosened. He looked into her eyes and found that his breathing had begun to match hers in tempo and depth. Her eyes willed him on with a look of hunger that said that her tears were the sort cried by a patient of psychoanalysis who just had a breakthrough. It was a look that told him to go on, that her love of pain was her strength and he could not hurt her.

After loosening her anus sufficiently, Hank was given a bowl of ice cubes and told to insert them into her. This he did, finding he was able to force twelve into her ass before it was stretched to capacity. The lines from the script came back to him from another dimension:

"Time to fuck you," he whispered, as he unzipped his boiler room jumpsuit, letting it fall to his boots as Billie crawled across the stone floor, placing her mouth on his dick. Hank pushed Billie's hair to one side as a camera came around to zoom in on the act. Billie arched her butt into the air like a cat, the melted ice cubes running down her legs in a glistening stream. Her mouth worked up and down his shaft, her lips, jaw, and tongue moving like three parts of a bio-mechanical machine that knew hidden secret spots in his gland only reached by such a virtuoso performance as hers.

Dominic called for vaginal penetration and they repositioned, with Billie laying on her back and Hank spreading himself over her with bestial countenance to begin with missionary sex. Hank pressed the underside of his cock against her pussy lips, rubbing his dick up and down the length of her slit before entering her hard and deep. They kissed and their tongues intertwined, tasting each other's saliva with hedonistic abandon. Their positions changed and the rhythm increased, but whether Billie was pressed up against the bars of the cell or sitting on top of Hank, their focus remained constant and metronomic, never losing its momentum.

When Hank finally felt that he could hold off no longer, he motioned for the shoulder cam operator, who rushed in to get a close up on the money shot. Dominic raced over as well and handed Hank a hand-held camera through the bars. Billie fell to her knees as Hank held the camera with one hand and jerked his prick with the other, roaring and red in the face when his load finally sprayed her tongue with wave after wave a his thick, milky seed.

There was a moment's pause as the camera focused on Billie's face, and then Dominic called "Cut." Handing towels to Hank and Billie through the bars he said "that was serious business you two. That'll be the box shot for sure."

Hank lowered a hand to help Billie to her feet. "Thanks," she said, with a curtsy. Hank let his eyes hang on Billie's for an instant too long before he left the cage and headed into the shower room that was located off to one side of the studio set. The little room had three nozzles, each with one knob. Hank flipped one of them on and let the warm jets cast over him, purifying him of the sweat that stuck to his body. "Mind if I join you?" He turned, to see Billie in the doorway, her makeup smeared and hair askew from the shoot.

"Not at all, Ma'am," Hank replied. Billie entered and flipped on the spigot next to Hank.

"Thanks—I'd give you some privacy but I hate to let come dry in my hair."

"No problem. You were really something out there."

"You too," she said with a wink.

"I've never done bondage before. You're famous for it, right?"

"Yep—got my start in the fetish community before I went mainstream."

"I'm kind of, well, curious about that..."

"Oh?"

"Well, during the shoot you started crying..."

Billie turned around and leaned her head back, letting the water soak backwards down her head. "Yeah, that's something I've always done on set. It's like another kind of orgasm, so I don't try to stop it."

"It's not... from some sort of abuse?"

Billie snorted sarcastically. "That's what everybody thinks. They assume that women who do bondage must have been molested and men who do bondage must have been beaten by their stepmothers. Why do my kinks have to be negative? I like getting laid in dark, creepy settings the same way other people like to watch scary movies. I like getting chained up and whipped the same way boys like getting in a boxing ring and beating the hell out of each other. And I cry because sex is the performance of beauty and when it's performed on a virtuosic level, it moves me to tears the same way a symphony does."

"Wow. I never thought of it like that." Hank washed his chest for a moment and then asked "what got you into this business?"

"I like having sex and I like being watched. I didn't get forced into it because I was supporting a drug habit or any of the other stereotypical stories you hear about. I was a college grad, I was working a good gig, but I kept fantasizing about cameras on me while I fucked."

"Did you start out with Alston?"

"Yeah. He had me shoot some test shots and hired me on the spot."

"He's got an eye for talent."

"That's the truth. Did he sign you already?"

"Yeah—sounds like he's got big plans for me."

"Big plans for big glands," chuckled Billie as she smacked Hank's ass and switched off the water. Then she leaned in close, put her hands on his stomach, and whispered in his ear "you were great today. I'm sure we'll work together again sometime." A kiss on his neck and she left. Hank stood under the warm jet of water, eyes closed, breathing in and out each memory of her body, her voice, and her eyes. He thought about the back of her neck and they way it drifted up to meet her jaw line in a delicate swoop. He thought about the way her hips curved around her tummy. And he thought of the way her eyes seemed to use her smile to breathe.

"That was money what you did out there today." Hank turned to see Dominic leaning against the shower room doorway.

"Thanks," said Hank.

"Most guys in hetero shoots assume they're just background players, and their performance suffers as a result. Thing is, the guy is just as responsible for making the scene hot as the girl is. You seem to understand that."

"I figure if a guy watches the flick, he's living vicariously through me, so I ought to give him something to live for."

Dominic smiled. "I like you kid. Isaac just gave me the go ahead on my new feature film, and I'm sure I'll have a part in there for you."

"Outta sight," said Hank, beaming.

Word of the *Shouting Match* interview with Tim's teacher spread like the California brushfire and public outrage scorched up and down the arid streets of the San Fernando Valley, pulling in protestors with a magnetic voracity. Where Alston Image had previously been protested by bored housewives, now it was being protested by their husbands as well. Where it had drawn throngs of directionless hippies, now it was also being protested by their misguided professors. And where it had been protested by small groups of religious fundamentalists, now hundreds of members of Families for Families stood with crucifixes and megaphones, proclaiming the horrors that went on inside the walls of Alston Image.

They lined the sidewalks each day, their chants and cries shifting from one target to the next when an Alston Image employee would pull up to the gate. Police in riot gear were a regular sight and they bordered the gates to the office building with cold precision.

Inside the office, the day to day activities remained largely unchanged and for this the employees were silently grateful. The Alston Image office became an oasis in the midst of the public hysteria on the outside, and Isaac Alston poured himself into the solemn passion of his work, his calm stoicism keeping his employees satiated and upbeat. He played solo piano recordings through the PA system; Beethoven, Thelonious Monk, Scott Joplin. It seemed to help keep the mood mellow.

Hank signed a three year contract with Alston Image and was amazed to watch the corporate machine moving in his favor. Where the Intersect Productions office had always seemed lethargic—as though the very suggestion that he ought to be treated like an employee was highly presumptuous and the implication that they should operate like a business even more so—Alston Image was a well oiled machine that flowed with compulsive efficiency. Several photo shoots were conducted with Hank stripping off a cowboy costume, biker gear, a navy sailor suit, a toga, and several other costumes that left him two or three machismo professions away from a disco vocal group.

Dominic directed three gay videos and two more straight videos for Hank's website, which launched shortly thereafter. The five videos lacked the same intimate heat that had come out with Billie, but each showcased a highly technical performance from Hank, which was reflected in each of his partners. With each shoot, Dominic was impressed with the manner in which Hank took control of scene, drawing the focus with a harsh demand on the camera. Even when the camera was locked onto the penis that thrust into Hank's asshole he still glared into his partner with a feral challenge in his eyes that made it impossible not to return to his stone cut face.

Hank's scene with Billie was released on a compilation of bondage scenes directed by Dominic Daniels and every person within the company who watched the video said that Hank and Billie's scene should provide the DVD's cover shot. The release was met with high critical acclaim, with both newsstand porn magazines and industry trades commending the particular scene with exclusion to all others. The notoriety was enough to generate a million hits and three hundred subscribers in the first month of Hank's website.

Three weeks later, Hank received the script for *Awake to the Skin* and was told to memorize it. Hank sat up nights in the extended stay motel room that he had rented and read the script over and over, finding it to be a thing of beauty that he had never encountered before. This was what it meant to be naked, thought Hank as he poured over the text. Not just bereft of clothing, which was nudity, but to use nudity as a means to expose someone to the very heart of their being—that the slopes and curves of a human body carried a poetry that was beyond words, music, paints, or any of the other frail mediums that human beings had used to recreate the natural beauty of their species' own form. As Hank reread the script, he understood what Dominic had understood for so long: that rather than try to use artistic mediums to replicate human beauty, they were best used to accentuate it. Dominic didn't create films; he created environments that allowed that pure nakedness to run free in a certain direction.

After the fourth reread of the script, Hank thought of his time with Artie's people, how he'd felt like little more than a meat puppet in a trailer in the desert that sat around and waited for Artie to call with some work. Sitting in that scorching little hovel, he'd felt like one of those dogs that was kept locked up in a little pen until it was needed to chew up another animal in the back of a warehouse while white trash and day laborers placed bets.

But here—in Isaac Alston's world—Hank felt like he mattered. But it wasn't like with Artie—Artie made you feel like you mattered for the expanse of time that he was shooting you, then you felt worthless again. Artie was like heroin. Alston projected a different attitude: that you were always important and he was honored to work with you. Still, that honor didn't seem to come at the price of Alston's own self-esteem.

As the days since their performance passed, Hank found himself looking for reasons to speak to Billie again. Once or twice a week they would pass in the halls and Billie would always smile and wink or make some light conversation but never with the time or convenience to resume their previous interaction. When their scene was finally released on DVD, Hank received a complimentary copy and set about hunting down Billie. He found her in the lobby, stepping off the elevator as she walked in the front door.

"Hey," he said, and she turned to him, realizing that there was a tone beckoning her beyond the usual familiarities. "Look what I got," said Hank, holding up the DVD case. Billie smiled.

"And where did you get that?" she asked.

"Hot off the press—they've got one for you up there too."

"I'll be sure to get that," she replied. There was an ambient moment in which Hank wasn't sure whether he ought to attempt further dialogue or let her go on her way, but when he looked into her shimmering blue eyes, his mouth spoke ahead of his brain:

"Want to hang out and watch it tonight?" he asked.

"Sure," she said playfully. "But it'll have to be your place. Someone put a dead skunk in my ventilation system and I still haven't gotten the smell out."

"Oh—okay. But it's nothing fancy."

"No sweat, babe. Need a ride home?"

"Sure."

"I've got to shoot a scene with Rod Wielding right now—you want to hang out and we'll hook up after?"

"Okay."

They rode the elevator up to the seventh floor, where Billie led Hank down the main corridor to a soundstage where Dominic and his crew were already in position to shoot Billie's scene. Judging by the nature of the set, Hank decided that the content of this scene would deal with a gynecological exam gone haywire. Billie found a chair for Hank then went into hair and makeup.

"Oh shit—I've got the master watching today," said a hardy voice over Hank's shoulder. Hank turned his head to see Rod Wielding in a bikini brief holding canned drinks. "Pepsi?" He asked, offering Hank one of the two he carried.

"Sure," replied Hank, taking the can and cracking it open. While they waited for Billie to prepare, Hank and Rod chatted pleasantly, and Hank indulged one of his greatest joys: learning about where people came from. Rod, born Rodney Zombrowski some thirty eight years ago, had grown up in Portland, Oregon learning the logging trade and got into the business to pay for college. After studying aimlessly for two years without declaring he'd returned to porn full time, putting his money away and making some wise investments. Despite having to take a year and a half off about five years ago to kick a cocaine habit, Rod had always been a welcome presence on the Alston Image talent roster for his rugged looks and easy going drawl. They chuckled over anecdotes of the small town life they'd both grown up with and debated briefly over the merits of various Depeche Mode albums.

Billie returned and got into position on the set, disrobing, as always, as if it were an afterthought. Hank watched Rod work, impressed with his performance. It was wise of him, Hank thought, to get me comfortable with him before I watched him fuck Billie. It was another example of the difference in working for Isaac Alston, he decided. After an hour of various positions, Billie swallowed Rod's money shot and blew a kiss to the camera before Dominic called "cut" and the technicians began to deconstruct the set.

After a shower and a last kiss goodbye, Billie and Rod returned to where Hank sat. "How did we do?" asked Billie.

"Outstanding as always," replied Hank.

"Let me get dressed and I'll be ready to go."

"Okay," said Hank, smiling after her as she left for her dressing room.

"She's into you, bro," said Rod after she left. "I saw the footage you guys shot. Don't think I've ever seen that kind of heat at on camera."

"Cool," said Hank absently, thinking how the hallway Billie had just walked down had been endowed with a certain inebriated wistfulness in the course of her passage. She called down the hall, saying she was ready, and Hank gave Rod a fist bump before nearly skipping down the hallway to meet her.

They took the elevator down and headed out into the parking lot. The security guards were clubbing a protestor who had jumped the outer wall.

"It's never been this bad before," said Billie as they crossed the lot to her car.

"Have you seen that interview with his son's teacher?"

"Yeah. Pissed me off."

They climbed into her car, the interior leather hot from the California sun. When Billie turned the keys her radio came on, and it blocked the sound of the crowd noise with cool jazz. The mellow lamentations of George Benson filled the car's interior as they pulled up to the front gates. On their approach, the two riot police on either side turned their shields on the crowd and laid into the seething mass, blocking the street lice that screamed and beat on the hood of Billie's car.

As the gate closed behind them and Billie turned out into the open street, Hank watched the angry throngs that yelled hoarsely at their passing. He'd been taking a bus to the headquarters most days, and this was much nicer than the cold rush of stepping off the bus onto the sidewalk with these maniacs. He watched them under furrowed brow as they flowed in and out of each other as one, multifaceted glob of public outrage. They looked as though they didn't have faces but were instead wearing a mask modeled after Much's *The Scream* but had left them on too long in the sun, which had caused the masks to be welded permanently and form fittingly to each of their faces.

"Why are they so angry?"

"Apparently someone is forcing them to look at our movies," muttered Billie dryly, her warm and patient persona showing signs of strain. Hank chuckled humorlessly. The mob went on for several blocks before trickling out, and then Hank and Billie were left to drive in pre-rush hour traffic towards Hank's temporary lodging. "So you don't drive?"

"When Mr. Alston agreed to see me, I sold my car and my trailer to get the money to come out here." Hank chuckled again, this time in self awareness. "I don't know what I was going to do if he turned me down. I guess with so many studios in town I'd be able to find work somewhere."

"Where did you work before?"

"Out in Nevada. For Intersect."

"Those scum peddlers?"

"Rub it in."

"Sorry—I wasn't judging you. I mean, you just seem like you're a cut above the kind of men Artie Barrel normally works with. I don't feel like your desire to have sex with women is motivated by a deep seated hatred of vaginas."

"Well, I was young and naïve when I got involved, but I never did really gel with Artie's stable. Or with Artie for that matter. The guy oozes public restroom floor muck."

"That's what I've heard. How do you like the valley so far?"

"I love it. It's bright and sunny but without that Wild West vibe that makes Nevada so difficult to enjoy. I'm just kind of surprised at all of these protestors. Again, I don't get it."

"I don't think they do either. They just think that there's something about the human form that's automatically wrong. They can't put any concrete definition on what that is, they just know it's there and they need to react strongly."

"Do you think anyone knows why?"

"I think Isaac does."

"But he doesn't talk to the public."

"I think that's why."

They arrived at Hank's hotel and headed upstairs to his suite, heads turning in recognition of the presence of Billie Solar. She brought a sacred elegance to the utilitarian surroundings, and the tenants noticed, some of them appreciatively and others with the same inexplicable contempt that Hank had seen in the raving throngs outside the Alston Image building.

Hank's room was a simple chamber: an all purpose kitchen/bedroom/sitting area with an adjoining bath. Hank's harsh, violent looks cut a stark contrast to the middle America décor of plaid bed sheets and nautical artwork.

Billie tossed her purse on the bed and sat down next to it, smiling flirtatiously at Hank as he crossed the room and put on the DVD. Their scene came on the TV Hank sat down next to his partner. Brooding music played during the expository shot of Hank staring down the camera as he stalked down the makeshift hallway with an ominous, bestial stride. "That was what it felt like when you stepped into the cage," said Billie, her hand stroking Hank's arm as he smiled slyly. The show continued and Hank and Billie teased one another as they enjoyed it.

"That was awesome," said Billie as their scene climaxed. "I was really impressed with the way you handled it. A lot of first time guys would have folded under the pressure."

"Pressure?"

"Famous starlet, famous director, famous company, famous video series."

"Oh. I guess I never looked at it that way."

"That's just it—you just went in and did it."

"I guess I did."

"You sure did. Now order a pizza."

Hank leaned in and surprised Billie with kiss, lingering in her eyes for just a moment and allowing her to smile beneath suddenly rosy cheeks before turning to take out his cellular phone. After ordering, he collapsed backwards onto the bed.

"It's on the way. Large, double pepperoni."

Billie lay down next to him, propped up on one elbow.

"Are you sure Dominic won't mind that you're here?" Hank asked.

"Why would he?"

"When I held the elevator for him, I heard him ask if you were still on for-"

"Oh! You mean movie night. That's just our thing. He's just a friend."

"Really?"

"Yeah—I'm about the only one of the girls in the company that appreciates fine cinema, so Dominic and I always get smashed on Fridays and watch a classic of some sort."

"And then?..."

"I pass out on his couch."

"Oh."

"His wife passed away a few years ago, right before I joined the company. He was really distant then, so I made it a point to get to know him and help pull him back around."

"So... Alston put you up to that?"

"No. I just wanted to help."

"Wow."

"Hmm?"

"Where I'm from, people don't usually help each other."

"That's a shame."

"I guess. Most of the time when people want help it seems like what they really want is control."

"That's because the people you help have to earn it."

"That sounds cold hearted."

"No, it just means your senses are accurate. When a person needs help—and you're the one to give it to them—you can feel this hollow place inside them and when you give the help, it fills that hollow place, and when the hollow is filled, the overflow comes back to you and that overflow is called gratitude. There are people who don't want help, they just want you. When you sense one of those people, you'll find that hollow space but you won't be able to fill it. You'll look into that hollow place and feel like you're standing on a cliff overlooking a black void. And when you give to those sorts of people, it feels like everything you're giving them just disappears into that void. And it's like once you start throwing things into that void… they have you. And the more you give them, the tighter their grip."

"That's it exactly. You nailed it."

"I always do."

The pizza came, and they ate it in bed as the last rays of sunlight succumbed to darkness. There was a black and white B movie science fiction film on one of the classic movies stations, and they laughed at the time-worn campiness of it. By the time it was over, Billie lay on top of Hank, her left hand stroking his jaw line.

"Do you always do this with your co-stars?" Hank asked, regretting the words that he could not hold back any longer.

"No. You'd be the first."

"Really?"

"Most male porn stars aren't the commitment type, even to one date."

"Makes sense." And they kissed again, this time each of them savoring the act with a lingering contemplation. Hank began to caress up and down Billie's back, his hands pulling her shirt out of her jeans, probing up towards her bra and sliding under it, the soft flesh beneath feeling all the more tender with the elastic tension from the undergarment against his knuckles. Her clothes slid off with languid precision, her body writhing against his in a way that seemed to render them naked of its own accord.

He wrapped one arm around her waist and laid the other around her shoulders, pulling her close as he entered her. She led the thrusting, sliding her body up and down on his. Hank wasn't used to going this slow and as their sweat intermingled in the cool, darkened hotel room, he let go of chasing that single, white-hot burst of orgasm and focused on the process, thinking of it as an extension of the playful intimacy of just making out with a girl. In this giving of himself to Billie's rhythm, he was able to let her orgasm bring his and sustain it in long waves as he throbbed inside her.

Afterwards they went to the shower, made love again, and returned to the bed to sleep. Laying there in each other's arms, contemplating the ceiling, they drifted again into quiet conversation:

"So are you going to be in *Awake to the Skin*?" asked Hank.

"Yeah. Dominic wants me to play the older sister. You?"

" I'm going to be one of the male leads in the big finale."

"Have you read the script?"

"Have I? I can't put it down. It's beautiful."

"You're going to like working on one of Dominic's feature-length films. He really shines on those."

"Isaac seems to have a lot of respect for Dominic's work."

"He sure does. Have you heard he wants to make *The Lotus Wave*?"

"You mean that famous banned script? How—does he have a copy?"

"No, he's just looking for it."

"Damn—if he makes that…"

"That's what Dominic was saying."

The conversation faded away, their eyelids growing heavy. As Hank fell asleep he found himself immersed in a sense of cautious satisfaction. Doors were opening all around him and while most of them were doors for his career to pass through, there were also the deeper, dustier doors that Billie seemed intent on prying open. Those were doors that led into rooms padded with a soft, listless feeling of ethereal bliss. As a kid he'd gone through those doors all too often, having let too many girls pry them open.

Billie nestled into him as she drifted off and his defenses fell.

Chapter 7

HANK GRABBED the executive pass off the receptionist's counter. It had been waiting for him since twenty minutes ago, when he'd gotten a text message:

MY OFFICE. NOW.
– ALSTON

He'd shown the text to Billie as he pulled his clothes on and her eyes had widened from groggy haze into vivid concern. "I'll drive you," she'd said. The protesters outside the building seemed like mosquitoes as Hank and Billie rolled into the parking lot. A quick kiss and Hank was on his way into the building.

When the elevator doors opened onto Alston's floor, Hank was startled to not see Alston absorbed in work, but staring straight ahead as though expecting the arrival of a firing squad that he intended to dishearten with his gaze alone. Abe Lattimore and Duke Cunningham stood on either side of his chair, their normally pleasant expressions washed in the same sober, serious tone that wrapped their CEO's features.

"You wanted to see me, Mr. Alston?" asked Hank with measured cordiality as he entered.

"Have a seat, Hank," replied Alston, who turned his computer monitor around to face across the table as Hank sat in the chair indicated. "Why do I have this email?" asked Alston and Hank leaned in to read:

ISAAC:
HEY GOOD BUDDY! HEARD YOU'RE PLANNING TO MAKE THE LOTUS WAVE AND I HAVE A LITTLE PIECE OF INFORMATION THAT MIGHT PROVE USE-

FUL TO YOU. WHY DON'T YOU GET OVER TO VEGAS
AND LET'S CHAT ABOUT IT?
-ARTIE

"I don't know, Mr. Alston," said Hank, sitting back from the monitor. "I really don't."

"Well that's the problem, Hank," replied Alston. "In light of this email, your history with Artie raises more than a few eyebrows. I haven't seen Artie in years and his pleasantries aside, we've never been friends. I've told a few people inside my organization that I was interested in making *The Lotus Wave* but I never told you. Who told you about it?"

"I'd rather not say, sir," said Hank carefully.

"So you did know about it?"

"Yes sir."

Alston sat forward in his chair, placing his elbows on the desk and crossed his wrists on the glass top. The epic glare that Hank had seen when he walked into the office narrowed as though it were now targeting a single crosshair, trained on Hank. "Listen to me very carefully, Hank. I'm not accusing you of anything. Yet. But I will tell you this—I have chosen to do a great deal for you because I think that you are talented and naturally endowed in a way that is beneficial for my company. Now, I am not like Artie. I'm not a vindictive little shit and I won't make some outlandish threat like 'you'll never work in this town again,' but I will tell you this: if I find out that you're just spying for Artie, I'll have you out on the curb so fast your head will spin."

There was a pause, and Hank realized that Alston was studying his face, like a champion poker player looking for a tell. *He's just trying to see what my reaction will be*, thought Hank as Alston's eyes probed over him with laser beam precision. "Sir," began Hank slowly, "the time that I've been here has been amazing. Working for you is like… well… it's a dream come true. Working for Artie was a nightmare. I felt like a walking cliché around him and any attempt to be something more would just get laughed at. Have you ever heard him laugh? Like he's being amused by something deep down in your soul, like he's found the most precious private memories in your brain and taken a piss on them? When I worked for him, I was living in a trailer and selling weed to make ends meet. I felt like a used up, dried up wash rag. I don't think there's enough money in the world to make me want to do something nice for that man. There's a Judas in your midst, sir, but it's not me."

Alston noticed a hair thin quiver in Hank's jaw line and knew that the last sentence had been pushed out with a touch more emotion than Hank wanted to show. Alston's cold, contemplative demeanor remained but now it was softened and milder. He stood up and said "come on then—you're going with me to Vegas."

"Don't I need to pack, Mr. Alston?"

"I have a private plane, Hank. We'll be back in time for dinner."

"Oh. Right."

Hank rose and followed his Boss to the elevator. Abe and Duke were close behind them. As they exited the elevator, Hank saw Billie chatting casually with the receptionist. "Carol," said Alston, leaning politely into the conversation, "Call the airstrip and tell them to have my plane ready with a pilot. I want to leave for Vegas as soon as I get to the runway."

"Yes sir, Mr. Alston," replied the receptionist, picking up the phone. Hank touched Billie's arm, assured her that he'd see her later, and then fell back in step with the boss. Abe and Duke broke rank and headed for elevators that that went to floors other than the penthouse.

Alston's car was parked in the spot closest to the door, and Hank was, for a moment, in awe of the vehicle. As they sat down and closed the doors, Alston took a pair of sunglasses out of his jacket pocket and put them on. "Oh by the way," he said as he pulled out of the space and headed for the front gates. "Don't speak ill of Judas. He's the noblest character in that whole story."

Hank wanted to ask for an explanation, but Alston seemed to have absorbed the car in that aura of contemplative silence that he exuded in unguarded moments. As they passed through the gates and turned out into the main road, Hank was struck by the way in which Alston ignored the protestors. It wasn't like Billie, whose aggravation at the angry throngs had been readily apparent but it wasn't like he was suppressing strong feelings either. It was simply as if the crowd wasn't there. Hank almost commented on the odd neutrality he saw in Alston, but felt as if doing so would rupture the quiet membrane that blocked and silenced the cretins outside.

As they approached the air field, Hank realized that he was seeing Isaac Alston as the man truly was: that the anger and suspicion he'd seen earlier were not deep seated passion, but rather a performance that had been what the interaction called for. A convincing, if mechanical portrayal. This contemplative, monk-like demeanor seemed more appropriate for Alston but it was not without implications of its own. It told Hank that Alston's was not the sort of emotional palette that flared wildly without control but was instead a trained and precise beast that was made all the more threatening for its gentle placidity. For an instant Hank felt almost sorry for that elementary teacher that had tried to take on Alston directly.

When they arrived at the airstrip they were met by one of Alston's bodyguards, a large, dark skinned man named Terry who did little more than nod and fall into step with his boss when they approached. Rocking left and right as he walked, he seemed to have been specially designed for the sole purpose of taking up a formidable amount of space.

Alston's Boeing BBJ was waiting on the runway, and when he climbed the mobile stairs and stepped into the cabin, Hank's eyes widened. The jet's interior looked like a posh living room that had been rolled up and stuck in a tube. The carpet and leather chairs were a deep burgundy, accentuated by darker but shiny wooden borders and fixtures. Alston dropped into one of the reclining chairs and put his feet up on the wall-mounted couch across from it as though this extravagant surrounding were nothing new for him. It wasn't.

"Where... should I sit?" asked Hank curiously. Alston smiled gently, his amusement a brief relief to Hank.

"Wherever you like, Hank," replied Alston. "It's all first class." Hank looked around again—Terry had taken a spot near the door and gone to sleep. Finding a circular couch that surrounded a small table, Hank sat and waited for takeoff. After the plane was in the air he looked out the window, watching the San Fernando Valley diminish beneath him. This is Isaac Alston's life, he thought. This world is something I'm just lucky enough to visit on the VIP list. This way of life is an extension of who and what he is.

The flight was fairly short, taking a little less than an hour, and when they neared their destination Alston checked the wrinkles in his clothes in the bathroom mirror and put on a new suit coat.

When they stepped off the plane and down the stairs to the runway, there was a limousine waiting for them and standing against it, smug incredulity evident in his smirking features was Ralphie Barrel. Those features expanded when he saw Hank, as though the sight amused him immensely.

"Hey there guys," said Ralphie, his head continually bobbing up and down on his scrawny neck as he chewed on gum. "Pops told me who was coming over, and I said 'I gots to pick these fuckers up.'" He shot a hand out to Alston, the skinny fingers rattling as if suspended by rubber. Alston shook it with a utilitarian sense of formality and climbed in to the open limo. "Suck any good dicks lately?" whispered Ralphie as Hank passed. Hank boarded the vehicle, ignoring the bipedal rodent that Artie called an offspring.

Inside the limousine were two voluptuous women in tiny single-piece garments that were held together by a single silver ring in the back. Ralphie sat between the two of them and put an arm around each one, his head continually nodding and one half of his face smirking as though it had gotten halfway through a sly wink and stalled.

Terry took up most of the space on the opposite side, leaving Alston pressed against the left-hand door and Hank wedged in the middle. As the vehicle departed for Artie's place, Ralphie examined the three people sitting across from them, remembering that his role was to try to demoralize Alston before they arrived at his dad's house.

"So…" began Ralphie. Isaac looked at him with undisguised disinterest and Hank pretended to look out the window. "You guys have a good flight?" he asked after a moment, irritated that he couldn't think of a devastating put down.

"It was without incident," replied Alston. "How is your father? I haven't seen him in quite some time."

"Pop's okay. Had cataract surgery a few months back."

"Has he still got that horse ranch?"

"Ah—no. That went belly up awhile ago."

"I'm sorry to hear that."

Ralphie's aggressively cocky demeanor became slightly darker and strained, his perpetual chewing motion slowing and the whites of his eyes showing a little wider. A single strand of his slicked hair fell down in his face. You one, me nothing, he thought irritably.

"Dad said you had some big project in the works."

"I always have a big project in the works. You?"

"We…" Ralphie stuttered. "We've been doing a lot of gonzo shit lately."

"I've never cared for gonzo personally but when my company does it we bring as much artistry as possible. Most companies don't."

"No, but its…" Ralphie trialed, realizing what he'd opened himself to.

"Cheap to produce?" asked Alston casually.

"Yeah," said Ralphie. "It's cheap to produce." Not only was he loosing the game, but this was making Ralphie look bad in front of his bracelet bitches.

Hank was aware of the impressive skill with which Alston navigated every nuance of the conversation, not only shifting it in his favor, but forcing Ralphie to be the one to concede defeat in each exchange. It was like watching a master chess player who forces an opponent to take foolish, sacrificial moves.

Despite getting to watch Alston's impressive technique, Vegas was unearthing too many bad memories for Hank. Even though he'd only been gone for about a month and a half, the city seemed to have bent and twisted itself, transmogrifying into the looming monstrosity of his nightmares. This was a town that pimped the pale nectar of human frailty. He thought about what Billie had said about the void. This was a town that didn't give, it only took. From time to time it paid out, but it was with the cackling glee of certainty that the payout was really an investment in the pathetic truth of human nature. There were whispers in the buildings—each a snickering beckoning to sink back into the cold comfort of lies and intimidation that had been working for Artie Barrel.

Why would I have a secret inclination to return to this? He asked himself. Did I not leave here to escape this craziness? And why is Alston bringing me back here? Surely he wants to see how I'll behave. He's looking for any hint that I'm sympathetic to these cretins. He's holding my feet to the fire—that much is for sure. But is it possible that I'm supposed to learn from this? Perhaps he's showing me the difference between him and the Barrels so that if I were in cahoots with them, I'd change my mind and come over to his side…

The limousine pulled up in front of Artie's house, a squat bungalow in a neighborhood of similar structures. There were palm trees, though unlike those in the Valley the leaves of these were brown and black, with only a slight burst of green close to the trunk. Las Vegas, reflected Hank, is not a city to see during the day, when the neon lights stand naked in their transparent casings.

They walked up to the house, Ralphie leading with his ladies, and entered. The living room was strewn with beer cans, and a TV dinner lay half eaten on the coffee table.

"Isaac Alston," said a husky, inebriated voice. Isaac turned to see Artie Barrel descending a short flight of stairs, his beer gut leading the way. One of his eyes was milky from the cataract surgery; the other was glassy from a state of perpetual intoxication. Grey stubble covered his sagging chin, creating a contrast with his dyed blond hair. He mirrored the cocky swagger of his son, though it was refracted by a certain world weariness that made the swagger tragic in its belligerence.

"How did you find out?" said Alston evenly but impatiently.

"Oh, word travels fast around these parts," chuckled Artie. "Now come on—let's you and me talk in private."

Alston glanced at Terry and back to Artie. "How private?"

"Step into my study." Alston looked into the room from which Artie had just emerged. It had beige carpet that was stained with vomit and piss. There was a couch at the far end, in similar disrepair.

"I can break that door if I need too," said Terry. Alston nodded and followed Artie into the rank chamber.

"Cut to the chase, Artie. What is this about?"

"Well, I heard you're going to make the *Lotus Wave*. How's that coming," asked Artie as he closed the door and took a bottle of scotch off a shelf on the wall.

"That's none of your business. What did you want to tell me?"

"Well, I was hoping we could have a little talk about that. Wanted to make sure you'd thought that through. See, you're a big cheese in this business. What you do affects all of us. Are you aware of that?"

"In fact, not spirit."

"That's the problem, Isaac. See, we porn people have to operate under the radar, you know?"

"No."

"We're the seamy side of things, Isaac. What we do has to be done quietly so that those upper class folks don't take notice. After that little stunt you pulled with that school teacher, those upper class folks are all up in the air about you. You can't just do whatever the hell you want. You have to take the rest of us into consideration."

"Why?"

"Because we're all in this together, that's why."

Alston glanced around the room. "What part do I have in any of this?"

"That's another discussion altogether, son. Look, if you make that movie, those special interest clowns are gonna clamp down on all of us. We've got to do what we can to keep them happy. It's the only hope we have to keep the business alive."

"They'll never be happy."

"Right—the best thing we can do is stay off their radar. They think that we're scum so we need to act like it. We need to play their game. What pisses them off is when we do like you're doing—start parading around like we're high class. Like what we do is okay."

"It is okay."

"See—right there. You're actually believing your own bullshit. That's why we need them high society types. They keep us in line."

"You might need them, I don't."

"Look, Isaac, you pretend you're high society all you want, but I'm not letting you make that movie." Artie took a swig from the bottle and offered a hit to Alston.

"I don't drink what you drink," replied Alston.

When Alston left the room with Artie, Ralphie turned to Hank and stared into his eyes with a great, stoic display of smug satisfaction, all the while trying to ignore the part of his mind that kept asking: *satisfaction for what exactly?* But it seemed that this was important—that each interaction with another person could only be considered a win for Ralphie if the other person were reminded of Ralphie's superiority. Ralphie struggled for a moment to find some psychological armor that would make him exude the same regal magnificence that Hank projected simply by entering the room. Then it occurred to him: his title.

"I thought you should know," said Ralphie, his smile returning for the purpose of teasing, which, as far as Ralphie was concerned, was what smiles were for. "That since you were fired, I have been promoted to vice president of Intersect Productions."

Hank spread his lips and arched his eyebrows in a manner that said *Oh really?* Then he said "does your father know about that?"

The verbal wound spread across Ralphie's face in a red burst on either cheek. He rebounded quickly, and returned to his smirking ready stance. Still, the bored, disinterested tone with which Hank's eyes gazed into his own was a penetrating, aggravating drill that bore down to his nerves. Hank could accomplish with indifference what Ralphie struggled to attain with all his being and it was this that infuriated Ralphie. It was also a component of that hidden part of his mind that he fought so hard to ignore.

He realized, in that same dark tiny world of inner honesty, that he stared into Hank's eyes not for the sake of staring Hank down, but for the sake of showing Hank that he could maintain the focus. This quivering truth, which Hank understood all too well, infuriated Ralphie: that even as he sought to stare down his adversary he did so, albeit secretly, with the intention of impressing that adversary. Even flanked by one of Isaac's bodyguards, Hank still seemed like the greater threat. The bodyguard would only intervene in a professional manner to stop the violence of the situation but any physical pain Ralphie suffered at Hank's hands directly would invariably come coated in the blunt force of the truth.

Ralphie leaned deep into Hank's aura. "At least I don't suck dick for money."

Hank looked over at Ralphie, as if his personal space wasn't violated in the least. "At least I don't suck it for free," he replied. Ralphie stepped back, gritted his teeth, and stormed out into the back yard to sit by the pool and roll a joint.

A few minutes later, the door opened and Alston emerged, visibly annoyed. "Think about that, alright," said Artie, his voice devoid of a questioning lilt. Alston ignored him and nodded to Hank and Terry to follow him out. Ralphie didn't join them for the ride back to the airport and neither did the bracelet bitches. Once they were on the plane all three resumed their previous posts and Hank nodded off. After the plane was in the air, Terry leaned over and tapped Alston on the shoulder. Alston turned his head and Terry whispered:

"I don't want to get involved in things that aren't my concern, boss, but I watched Hank and that Barrel boy after you left. There was no love between those two. Felt like one would have killed the other if they was alone. If he's a mole in your company then he's damn good actor too."

Alston nodded and returned to his quiet contemplations.

Chapter 8

FOLLOWING THE TRIP to Las Vegas, Alston and Hank returned to their normal patterns within the company. Hank and Billie worked together again in a scene for the southern gothic feature *A Hose for Emilie* and Alston reviewed project proposals and magazine layouts as well as interviewing potential starlets. He moved the line of dongs based on Hank's penis into production and made a limited edition release for the upcoming holiday season to coincide with the upcoming DVD release of *Hank Steel: God of Penetration*.

Two weeks later Hank's first paycheck came in and it allowed him to move into a decent apartment and purchase his own computer. When the day came to move into his new pad, Billie came over to help him pack, although there wasn't much—just a couple of suitcases. As she reached into one of them to spread open an interior compartment, she felt something that didn't belong. "What's this?" she asked, withdrawing it and handing it to Hank.

Half an hour later Hank burst into Alston's office. "I didn't call for you," said Alston, but he was cut short when Hank slammed Billie's discovery down on his desk. Alston leaned in to see a tiny microphone unit attached to a little radio transmitter.

"Looks like I was your mole after all," said Hank. Alston picked up the device and leaned back in his chair, examining it with utter perplexity. "Billie found it in my suitcase today while she was helping me pack."

"Leaving so soon, Hank?"

"Just moving into a new apartment."

Alston nodded, setting the device back down on the desktop. "Have a seat, Hank," he said thoughtfully. Hank complied, lowering himself into the chair across from Alston, only to watch as Alston dropped the transmitter on the floor and rose to take a large, hardcover book from a nearby shelf. Returning to his desk, he dropped the book to the floor, letting it land on the transmitter before stepping down on the book with the heel of his shoe.

There were crunching sounds as he did this. "I never really suspected you," said Alston, returning to his seat. "Anybody who's anybody knows what Artie Barrel is like. I had to be sure, but I know how Artie uses people. The minute I looked at your resume I knew I'd be talking to him soon. So tell me something, Hank, how much do you know about the *Lotus Wave*?"

Hank's demeanor softened, as though he were attempting to match Alston's contemplative disposition. "I know what everyone knows. Hotei Shibasaki, legendary Japanese loaner, script gets passed around, etc, etc."

"You don't know anything about why it's so taboo?"

"Does anybody?"

"Apparently not. I've been at this for two months now, and the trail is stone cold."

"Well, I've always had one theory…"

"Oh?"

"Well… think about the legend. What happened to the script?"

"It was sold at an auction in Paris."

"To whom?"

"Nobody knew."

"You mean to tell me that some son of a bitch walks right into an exclusive auction, drops all that money on a script, then disappears and *nobody* knows who it is? There's no press? Nobody cares?"

"You have a good point."

"I know I do. And you know what I think? I think that buyer was Hotei Shibasaki."

"Where would he get that kind of money?"

"Who says he bought it? I think the whole thing was a setup."

Alston became increasingly interested. "Go on."

"Shibasaki was already in trouble with the Japanese police, right? What if the auction was all a big performance to sneak the script back into his hands without anybody noticing?"

"How would he have gotten the script past customs going back into Japan?"

"That I don't know. But that auction is your first lead."

Hank saw Isaac Alston smile widely for the first time, his teeth brimming against the triumphant V of his lips. He stood up at once and reached across the table, extending his hand to Hank. They shook as Hank rose to his feet. "Nice to see you're more than just another pretty face," said Alston, genuinely pleased.

"It's the least I could do, sir."

"Then I can't wait to see you at your best. What're you and Billie doing after you move today?"

"I don't know—go out I guess."

"Take her to the Black Chapel. It's a swinger's dinner club. I'll phone ahead and tell them to put you at my table."

"Thank you sir, but I couldn't possibly afford..." Alston raised a hand to stop him. Hank nodded, understanding. "Thank you, sir."

"It's the least I could do."

Hank left the office and phoned Billie who told him that she had loaded his meager belongings into her car and driven them over to his new apartment. Meeting her at the complex, he helped her carry them up the stairs to the unfurnished set of rooms. The apartment began with a short hallway with bathroom on the left and the bedroom on the right. Beyond that was a living area and kitchen. Overall the apartment was crisp and modern, the bright hardwood floors and marble counter tops catching the flood of sunlight that poured in from the mural of windows across the room.

Dropping the bags in the center of the living room, Hank collapsed to the floor and lay down with his hands behind his head, a secretive smile beaming up at Billie as she straddled him. "You can stay at my place until your furniture is delivered," she whispered, kissing Hank. She recoiled coquettishly after a moment, staring down into his beaming, violent eyes. "What are you not saying?" she asked, amused.

"When I showed Alston the bug, he set you and me up on the guest list at the Black Chapel."

"You're shitting me!"

"No I'm not." They kissed again and returned to their feet. Hank opened one of the suitcases and extracted a set of formal clothes then followed Billie out to the car. They took a long shopping trip for the afternoon and spent it strolling through the Westfield Topanga mall, walking a dreamy hand-in-hand to the mellower side of the Top 40. As he sat in a dressing room and watched Billie try on dress after dress, a small part of Hank worried about those songs—they were starting to mean something. That was never a good sign. Whenever those songs, with their endless waves of syrupy sentimentalism, began to go from daffy headed background euphoria to deeply resonant musings on the nature of love, Hank knew that he was falling for somebody. That was a feeling he tried to keep submerged. Steve Perry's 1984 solo hit "Oh Sheri" came on and rather than sound like a hollow echo of the anthematic majesty that was Perry's voice when it was backed by Journey, he found the tune to be a searing, honey sweet accompaniment to Billie's voice, one that seemed to reach out with auditory fingers and bend the afternoon sun that poured into the mall towards Billie's slender form.

They wandered through the neon dome of commercial paradise, eating lunch in the food court and chatting happily as though the other patrons of the mall were only mobile props and this entire structure had been erected solely for Hank and Billie. Through waves of ever deepening conversation they had filled each other in on their pasts. At each land mark in the other's timeline they would find a commonality: from their small town upbringings to the sense of awe they'd felt entering the Alston Image fold.

Even so, Hank noticed a contradictory thread: where each landmark sexual event in his life had been celebrated, Billie's had been decried. When Hank had played doctor with a little girl in the neighborhood at age five and seen her genitalia, his father had poured a glass of apple juice for Hank and a beer for himself, toasting the occasion. But when Billie had played naked in the sprinkler in the backyard at age ten, while the neighborhood boys of various ages had watched through the slats of the wooden privacy fence, her parents had slapped her around and taken her to their church's Pentecostal preacher to be prayed over. When Hank had lost his virginity at age fifteen it had been met with high fives by the other guys on the JV football team. When Billie had lost her cherry, the other girls at her school had stopped speaking to her and started speaking about her. When Hank had screwed a four-star General's wife late one night in the mess hall, the other soldiers had treated him to a round at the bar during the next R&R. When Billie had dated a professor who was twenty years her senior, she'd been threatened with expulsion.

Hank tried to drift over these hypocrisies in conversation, but found that with Billie his eyes could imply a certain awareness of the contradiction in their stories and that she would accept it patiently. Despite all of this, they shared a mutual love for the shimmering Eden of rebirth that had been the valley. The world outside their paradise—beyond the greater Los Angeles area—seemed to exist in some sort of distant realm where large populations could be launched back and forth into one another by vast, impartial buffers that tossed them about like a game of sociological pinball.

As the hours melted away it came time to go to dinner. They returned to Billie's house and showered together, nuzzling noses under the warm spray. Billie dressed in a jet black dress with matching pumps and purse, the sheer dress only a suggestion of clothing that drew attention to the soft strength of her form through its delicate roughness. As Hank buttoned his shirt he beamed at her, savoring the reality of her dressing so beautifully for an evening with him. It was an honor, one he had earned.

As he took her hand and escorted her to the car, Hank thought about Ralphie's bracelet bitches. Where Hank found reward and satisfaction in Billie's presence, Ralphie erected a shallow smoke screen of respectability. When Billie was on Hank's arm, he felt elevated to her level. When those girls hung from Ralphie's arm, they were lowered to his level under the pretense of raising him up. Only a fool wouldn't see such a hollow, vacant façade, but that was what the Barrels dealt with: fools.

The Black Chapel had been an actual Catholic church at one time, but interest in Catholicism in the San Fernando Valley had quickly waned and the building had been converted into a nightclub. As the Valley became a porn industry Mecca, the owners had capitalized on the scene and turned the facility into a gourmet swinger's club. The name had come from the wood used on the building's exterior, which was a pitch-black cut of ebony. An imposing presence, it functioned better as a swinger's club than it did as a church. During its days as an actual chapel, the circular window that adorned the second story of the building's front had been filled with a stained glass depiction of the Virgin Mary, her head cast down, as if in shame. When the building had been born again, the stained glass image was changed to a set of red tones that appeared to open like a vertical flower. All night long, strobe lights would play around the image, shooting the red hues out into space with a feral glare.

When Hank and Billie walked up to the door, the bouncer recognized them at once and moved the velvet rope that blocked fifty feet of potential patrons from entering. They ascended the stone steps that lead up to the main entrance and the interweaving muscles in Billie's legs and the way her ass shook in the little black dress drew wolf whistles from the crowd.

Nestled deep into the throng of wannabes—but craning his neck to watch Hank and Billie enter—was a man who had been following the couple all day, since he'd watched Hank enter Alston Image and leave shortly thereafter. He'd watched them at a distance as they'd shopped all afternoon and when he'd overheard them talking about the Black Chapel during lunch, he'd gotten into this line early so that he could stay on top of their business at the club. He was a man who wore a smirk mask and bobbed his head to music only he seemed to hear. He was a man who chewed even when there was nothing in his mouth. He was a man who regretted leaving his bracelet bitches in Las Vegas.

"Beat it, shrimp," said the bouncer when Ralphie finally arrived at the front of the line. "This aint the place for Leisure Suit Larry."

Ralphie managed the feat of grimacing without losing his smirk and replied "Do you know who I am? I am the vice president of Intersect Productions!" The bouncer was unmoved. Ralphie shook his head and took five one-hundred dollar bills from his wallet and pressed them into the bouncer's lapel pocket. The bouncer rolled his eyes and moved the velvet rope, admitting the once more cocky and unrestrained Ralphie Barrel into the club.

The main hall of the chapel had been converted into a wide, raised platform where general admission tables were arranged amidst exotic plants. The platform—which lined three walls of the main room—opened by sets of circular stairways onto a dance floor that stood before a massive stage. Tonight

the entertainment consisted of a smooth jazz ensemble that had been enjoying a month long residency at the Black Chapel. In that time the individual
players had melded together and become a tight, funky unit of interlocking
majesty. As their melodic lines intertwined, the crowd at their tables nodded
in warm affirmation to the sweet sadism of the slapping bass and weaving
alto sax that transpired beneath beaming stage lights.

Hank and Billie were met by a hostess who escorted them up a flight of
stairs just inside the door. "Mr. Alston's private box is right this way," she said,
leading them down a corridor with red walls, ceiling, and floor. They passed
several doors before arriving at one with a plaque bearing the words *Reserved
for Mr. Alston*. The hostess opened the door with a passkey and both Hank
and Billie marveled at the chamber, which was just larger than the hotel room
Hank had moved out of. There was a bar with a drink station on the wall
alongside the door, and on the left wall a leather mattress with two recently
fluffed pillows. In the middle of the room was a quartet of matching couches
that surrounded a small coffee table. At the end of the room, just before the
balcony railing was a table set for two. "The menu is on the touch panel attached to the railing. Just enter your order and it will be brought up to you. In
addition to our gourmet dining selection you may also use the screen to send
a sex invitation to any of the other tables or boxes in the club and if they accept they'll be brought to you. If that's the case you're welcome to make love
here in your box or you can visit any of our three specially themed play areas.
You can also use your menu to purchase adult novelty items, DVDs, and private dances from members of our staff, myself included. Mr. Alston will pay
your tab this evening up to five thousand dollars. Enjoy your stay!"

With that she left Hank and Billie to wander the room for a moment.
Hank examined the various bottles at the drink station, finding the most exotic of imports he'd ever seen. They convened at the table, Hank with his back
to the stage. Billie was all that mattered. Bathed in the lustrous light from the
concert, her eyes shimmered with a haunting, radiant splendor.

Hank collapsed backwards into his seat, floored by Alston's generosity. "I
can't believe he's doing this for us. He must be more grateful than I imagined."

Billie shook her head dismissively as she tapped the menu to life. "This
is his life, Hank." She said. "This is nothing for him. Like the drive thru at
McDonalds."

Hank ordered a full rack of ribs and Billie had the spaghetti. The food
was exquisite, each bite granting the transcendent elevation of a spiritual revelation injected into delicious food. They made no attempt to speak as they
ate the magnificent food but conversed with their eyes all the while.

When the meal was finished they savored the afterglow of the exquisite
food and the sensual sax melodies. Hank opened his mouth to speak, but

there was a knock at the door which broke his train of thought. Answering the door, Hank found a cheerfully nude Rod Wielding on the other side, flanked by five women that stood proud in their nakedness. Hank recognized them as Alston Image contract players.

"Didn't want to interrupt your meal, mate," said Rod with a beaming smile. "But it's your first time here, and you two have to go through a little initiation.

"Oh yeah? How does that work?"

"Well, these five women stay here with you and get freaky, while me and my four mates take care of Billie, if she's so inclined."

"Is that right. Hey sweetie—what do you think about-" but Billie was already waving across the amphitheater chapel to a luxury box where four of Alston's male models, Slamdingo among them, waved back with one hand and jerked their cocks with the other. "I think she's sold," said Hank, unbuttoning his shirt.

"Hey love—see if there's rubbers under the bar," said Billie as she stood and pulled her dress over her head. There was applause from the four spectators across the room and she shook her ass while twisting her nipples in response. Hank found a fishbowl full of condoms under the bar and set it on top, taking out a large handful and turning them over to Billie as she approached. "Thanks babe," she said, kissing him as she left with Rod.

The girls filed in and surrounded Hank, following him to the bed. Among the Alston Image luminaries that pulled his clothes off were Janet Drillride, Melanie Moaning, and the company's recent Russian acquisition Ivana Sukitov. The other two girls were lesser known models, but their tenacious removal of his garments made introductions impractical.

They fell to the bed and began a passionate, if somewhat frenzied ritual. Hank tasted each of the ten nipples that hung before him, shaking the breast that it hung from with his mouth as he did. His mouth sensitive after the meal, he savored all of the tastes that these women had to offer, drinking deep in the fine variations in texture from their nipples to their breasts to their tongues and lips. Soon he felt one set of lips on the shaft of his dick as another of the women straddled his face.

Their sex was majestic, and after making each woman come, Hank was exhausted and gasping for breath when the girls finally allowed him to climax.

Across the room, in the opposite box, Billie lay on the bed grinning as the boys each kissed her goodbye and left her to go rendezvous with their ladies. Billie drank in the warm waves of pleasure that rose and fell through her thoroughly drained body.

Her eyes closed for an instant and when they opened an unknown figure stood before her, naked. His body, however, lacked the muscular majesty of the men she'd just enjoyed. By contrast, it was a scrawny, wiry frame with a single line of thick, black chest hair between two oversized nipples. A penis hung quivering below the abdomen in roughly the same way that a ring finger extends when the rest of the hand is making a fist.

"Saw this little get together, thought 'I need to get me some of that!'"

"Who are you?"

"Baby, I am the vice president of Intersect Productions."

Hank heard the screams as they cut through the music and he was on his feet in an instant, catching only a glimpse of Ralphie pouncing on Billie before tearing off down the hallway, following the curve bend around the inside perimeter of the building, knocking over a waitress with a tray of martinis as he went. "Get security!" he shouted as he turned the next corner and ran headlong towards the open door. He ran as fast as he could but despite every muscle in his body pumping with locomotive efficiency he still felt as though he were moving in extreme slow motion. Forcing his whole body against his stunted perception of time, Hank flew into the box, his hands under Ralphie's arms before either was aware Hank had crossed the room. Ralphie fell to the floor and started to scramble away before Hank dove on him and struck him in the kidneys with an open palm. Ralphie screeched hoarsely under a dry heave, but found his footing and made for the door, running headlong into the door frame in panic. Hank was on him again and spun him around, slamming his fist into Ralphie's stomach. The vice president of Intersect Productions had only a moment to stagger backwards into the hallway before Hank's fist flew into Ralphie's nose, the cartilage flattening audibly as Ralphie feel backwards onto the carpet, this time looking down at his left hand as it filled with one heartbeat dollop of blood after another from his nose and mouth instead of attempting to get away.

Hank regarded Ralphie, who lay with gelatinous decomposition in a puddle of himself on the crimson carpet. The punch had felt as though it had burst through the back of his skull and was still flying down the hallway. He knew that Hank's fist was throbbing and felt the pulsating pain by proxy, as if the blow had created an immaterial leash between the two of them; a leash that had always existed though Hank had never wanted to wield it.

"The hell do you think you're doing?" Hank said in harsh but controlled tones.

"I was gonna fuck Billie."

"No, Ralphie, you were going to rape Billie."

"I just saw her fuck five guys in a row."

"That doesn't mean she has to fuck you!" Hank bellowed, though even his rage seemed cool and mediated.

"I don't see why not."

"I know you don't," whispered Hank, and kicked Ralphie in the nose as hard as he could. Ralphie squealed like a stuck pig, knowing the true pain of physical combat for the first time. All of his life he'd amplified the childhood scuffles in which he'd emerged the victor as being some great testament to his alpha male prowess but now the truth of that tile was standing before him. Ralphie's eyes traced up the naked form of the muscle ripped Centurion. This was why the early Olympic Games were run in the nude: to allow the spectator to fully appreciate the majesty of these men. This was why Hercules was thought to stand halfway between man and the gods.

In every one of those misguided acts of rebellion—against teachers that had sought to educate him, law enforcers that had sought to block him from anti-social behavior, against school administrators that had tried to reform him, in all those instances when an authority had stared him down, there had been that same undercurrent, one that said *you might not like me, but you* will *respect me.* That was not an undercurrent for Hank: it bathed him like the sweat on his body.

Ralphie wanted to sink away into the floor, to get away from the blunt wall of humanity that stared him down. "I know you aren't real good at understanding things, Ralphie," whispered Hank "so I'm going to say this as nicely and as simply as I can: if you ever lay a hand on Billie again I will fucking kill you. And being vice president of Intersect Productions will not mean a god damn mother fucking thing."

The snarling anger in Hank's face ebbed as he stepped back and it was replaced by the same look of disinterested disgust Ralphie had always seen when Hank looked at him. Ralphie sat up slowly as Hank went into the box where Billie sat sobbing on the edge of the bed. Leaning into the doorway, Ralphie could see Hank take Billie into his arms and hold her close, whispering reassuring things to her. He waited for one of them to turn and look at him with glaring anger, like it always happened in the movies, but neither of them did. A wavering anger made Ralphie's jaw quiver. Even though he sat in a pool of his own urine, blood pouring down from his blackened nose, he was angry at Hank and Billie. How dare they have this moment? By what right was Hank so arrogant that he could pretend to care about Billie? Why was he carrying on like this? He was already getting to fuck her—why did he keep acting like he gave a shit about her? But even more, how dare he and Billie have this moment that excluded him? How dare they be happy together when their embrace was making him so miserable?

Ralphie watched as Hank and Billie walked past him, their arms around each other's shoulders, heading towards Alston's box. They didn't look at him, they didn't speak to him, and they acted as if he wasn't even there. He wanted to beg them: *please yell at me again. Please kick me and punch me again.*

Please make me feel like garbage instead of nothing... but all he could do was weep quietly on the floor as the sound of one of LA's hottest smooth jazz combos reverberated up through the floor.

Thirty seconds later the bouncer came for Ralphie, dragged him down the stairs and threw him out the front door. Ralphie landed on the sidewalk, still naked and shaking, only to be scoffed and jeered at by those who still waited in line. "Don't you fucking laugh at me," spat Ralphie, staggering to his feet. "I am the vice president of Intersect Productions!"

Hank drove home with Billie, who sat silent and shaken in the passenger's seat. The noise of the club truncated by wavering silence, they made no attempt to speak as they drove back to her house. When they finally arrived at the house, Hank helped Billie undress and get into the bath tub, where he bathed her quietly for nearly an hour. The ritual was not for hygienic purposes but for Hank to return Billie's body to an awareness of a tender, empathetic touch. When she finally stood up he showered the soap off her body and dried with an honest, sexless deliberation. They went to bed, Billie still silent but her arms wrapped tightly around Hank's neck as she placed her head on his left breast.

As Billie drifted off in his arms, Hank stared up at the whirling blades of the ceiling fan and contemplated the woman that laid against him. He wanted to pull the sheets over them both, wrap up as tightly as possible and close his eyes, eliminating everything except Billie and the darkness. In that infinite womb of blackened space, he felt as though he saw the truth of love: that human beings were just concepts, thoughts, suggestions of existence that whirled endlessly through this dark void that was life. In this swirling void they cast out groping hands to catch hold of one another for a short time before being pulled off in opposite directions, the quivering strains of love drifting away once more. His heart pounded inside a cold chest as he felt the sands of love draining through his fingers.

More so than this, he thought about the mindset that had propelled Ralphie to attempt rape this evening. Clearly Ralphie didn't comprehend the violation of a woman, couldn't understand why she had a right not to be forced into sex and why Hank stood apart from his fellow men in this regard.

It had always been there—the withering sense of male camaraderie that had seemed, for so many men, to be the point of sex. They celebrated sexual conquest the same way they celebrated hunting trophies or successful sporting events. It was as if sexuality existed as something that was not a part of their own identity but something that had been relegated entirely to women. It was as if the men who overstepped the boundary of consent and attempted an act of rape did so not because they were over sexed or under sexed but because they resented sex the same way racists resented the xenophobia of the unfamiliar. Perhaps, in that same vein, Ralphie hated Hank for being in touch with his own sexual identity in a way Ralphie never could be.

Hank, being unschooled in the field of intellectual debate, was unable to put these ideas into words and experienced them only as feelings and impressions. He held Billie close in the darkness, feeling her body rise and fall with her breathing.

Chapter 9

ARTIE BARREL was reclining by the pool, reading a copy of Guns & Ammo magazine when he heard knock at his front door. "Come in!" he shouted, only glancing up from his magazine. The knock repeated and though Artie started to raise his voice louder he thought better of it and forced himself to his feet, picking up the bottle of scotch next to his chaise lounge and dropping the magazine in its place.

As he forced aside the liquid haze, Artie tried to get some bearing on what the nature of this visitor might be. He vaguely remembered having some kind of appointment today, but was unable to remember beyond that. As he got closer to the front door he could see a young woman's face framed in the front door's ornamental window. She was cute—a naturally tanned face with a smooth little nose. Her hair was dyed blonde but black roots showed underneath. When Artie opened the door he saw two huge tits that were straining against a pink tank top.

"Those things real?" he grunted.

"Ah, yes sir," she replied cautiously.

Artie looked up into her eyes for the first time. "You sellin' something, doll?"

She looked confused. "Are you Mr. Barrel? I was told to come here to audition for Intersect Productions."

The light behind Artie's eyes flickered on and off. "Oh—yeah. Right," he replied after a moment. "What's your name?"

"Christina Holcombe."

"Naw—I mean your porn star name."

"Oh. Right—I was thinking Bambi Bangs. Do you like it?"

"Ah—sure, whatever. Come on in."

She followed him through the living room, wincing at the disrepair. They stepped out onto the back porch and Artie flopped back down where he'd been. "Alright," he said, "Get them clothes off."

"Just like that?"

"Well yeah, sister. You wanna be a porn star, right?"

"Yeah, I guess."

"You guess? You guess? What the fuck are you doing here if you just guess? I'm in the business of makin' fuck tapes and I don't need gals that're gonna go pussy shit on me if I tell 'em to take their clothes off. Now either get naked or stop wasting my time." Artie returned to his magazine, ignoring Christine/Bambi for a few seconds. Nervously, she reached up and began to remove her top, feeling surprisingly cold for a warm Nevada afternoon. Artie glanced up from his magazine when she began to move. "That's it, honey, make your daddy proud." Then he returned to his reading.

When Christine/Bambi was finally naked, Artie tossed the magazine aside and sat up again, motioning for her to come closer. Nervously, she stepped within arm's reach of him. "Gonna evaluate you like a piece of meat," he grunted, grabbing her tits and squeezing down on them and moving them around to see different angles. Finished with his inspection he turned her around and pushed on her lower back, making her bend over. He spread her ass cheeks and stuck his index fingers into her anus, spreading it apart before moving down to her pussy, giving it the same treatment. "You know how to suck a dick?" Artie mumbled aggressively.

"Yeah…" she whispered.

"Well make it snap," he replied, pulling his dick out and returning to his magazine. Christine/Bambi knelt by the lounger and carefully placed her glossy lips onto the head of Artie's half flaccid prick. As she winced and began to sink her mouth on the pecker, Artie's cell phone rang. He took it out, not interrupting the blowjob. "Yeah?" he growled.

"Ith me, Dadth," said Ralphie on the other end.

"Yeah—you in the Valley?"

"Yeth."

"You following Alston and his people around like I told you too?"

"Yeth."

"So why do you sound all stopped up?"

"Becauth Hank Thteele beat me up."

"Why the fuck did that happen?"

"I thwied to fuck Biwie Tholar."

"And he beat you up for trying to fuck some Alston Image bitch?"

"Yeth."

Artie clenched his teeth for a moment as he shot his load into Christina/Bambi's mouth. "Well fine then—that is just fine. It sounds like ol' Isaac Alston needs a little publicity to keep him in line. You stay in the Valley awhile and I'll give you the go ahead on your next move, alright?"

"Ukay Dad."

Artie hung up his phone and returned to his magazine. Christine/Bambi was wiping come from her face. "So how did I do?" she asked, choking back tears and sinus drainage.

"I'll be in touch. Beat it."

Alston sat back in his chair, reading over the company website for Le Trésor Perdu Auction House in Paris. The facility had been established in the late 1800's and had played host to countless works of fine art and rare artifacts, including Greco-Roman sculpture and hard-to-find first editions of major works of literature. He had told his assistant to contact curator to schedule a phone interview, and now he waited for the next shoe to drop.

His cell phone rang—it was Dominic. "Hey Dominic—How's New York treating you?"

"Fine so far. Turn on *Shouting Match*. They're about to talk about you again."

"Is that right?"

"Yeah. Turn it on—you don't want to miss this."

Dominic hung up, and Alston crossed his office to an arrangement of leather furniture pointed at a large television screen and turned on the broadcast. There were some commercials and then the show's logo flew onto the screen.

Bob Match: Welcome back to Shouting Match with Bob Match. I'm your host, Bob Match. Nation, we ran a story a few weeks ago about a heroic mother whose son was driven to madness by the horrific filth of porn kingpin Isaac Alston. We received a tremendous amount of viewer mail from that story. Bessy-Mae T. From Starkville, Mississippi writes 'Bob—love the show and god bless you for bringing the truth to all of us conservative patriots. Wanted to know if there were any developments in that story.' Well Bessy-Mae, I can report that Mrs. Simmons' son is doing well but I can't say the same for our country's moral fiber. It seems that Mr. Alston is planning a full-fledged assault on our country's family values. Now, nation, I know that most of you are too moral and upstanding to admit to being aware of this, so I'll take the plunge for you. You might remember that there was an era known as 'Porn-Chic,' with movies like Deep Throat, Behind the Green Door, and the Devil in Ms. Jones threatening to turn the pornographic film industry into a mainstream genre of cinema. Now the great moral crusaders of the time were able to put a stop to such corrosion, but through it all there was a script from that era that has become the stuff of legends. That script, The Lotus Wave, has been banned in several countries and was never produced. Well, Mr. Alston has decided to change all that. Yesterday we received a tip from Artie Barrel, who is himself a pornographer, that Isaac Alston is producing The Lotus Wave, *a film so sickening in its perversity that it was denounced by the Vatican. Now the actual contents of the script are something of a mystery, but we've heard that it involves children sodomizing puppies at gunpoint.*

Nation, this is undeniable proof that Isaac Alston is a tool of the liberal media. He will stop at nothing to achieve their agenda of destroying the American way of life. Why? I'll tell you why—he resents the fact that Jesus Christ died on the cross for the sins of humanity. Nation, your rights are only as secure as the number of guns in your house and if a vile film like this gets made it'll only fill your mind with the kind of hippie-dippy garbage that will vote your second amendment rights out the window. This is what the dark prince wants, America. He knows that Jesus was a capitalist who would have never approved of socialized medicine and now he's using pawns like Isaac Alston to turn this into a Communist state in time for the rapture.

When I think about this great nation, tears come to my eyes. I think of little Billy McGunderson in Spokane, Washington who writes "Mr. Match, why does Isaac Alston hate the American people? My granddad fell off the wagon because he was watching Alston Image smut. And after that he started drinking again." Well, Billy, I couldn't agree more. Isaac Alston wants to destroy the good, honest, conservative Christian values that our country was founded on. We're going to keep you posted on this story, America. The time is 12:45.

Alston turned off the television when the commercials began, placed the remote control on the glass coffee table before him, then stood quietly and crossed to the window, looking down on the seething multitudes below. In a few hours (or moments, if any of them had cell phones with web access) they would receive their latest slab of raw meat, courtesy of Bob Match.

"The Tisch program at NYU has been home to many outstanding alumni. From Woody Allen to Martin Scorsese to Oliver Stone, some of the greatest directors of all time have passed through our halls. We have always sought to celebrate the masterful work that such distinguished alums have bestowed on the cinematic world. As part of our ongoing interview series with these outstanding persons, we are pleased to present Mr. Dominic Daniels.

"Controversy followed the announcement of Mr. Daniels' appearance here, as it has followed him through most of his career. When Mr. Daniels graduated from this fine institution some twenty five years ago, he entered the field of adult film after meeting Isaac Alston, who was himself a student at Harvard University. Together they launched Alston Image with such landmark titles as the masturbation epic *The Cheese Stands A Bone,* The Greco-

Roman period piece *The Penis de Milo,* and the cautionary tale of female felching set in the wild abandon of hippie drug culture, *Blow Ass, Alice.* While these parody titles were well received within their, ah, target demographic, it was with his high-brow erotic films that Dominic Daniels and Alston Image achieved international recognition and even mainstream critical acclaim. The first of these, *Ice in the Heart,* was as mature in its intellectual themes as it was explicit in its love scenes. Daniels followed *Ice in the Heart* with his Prison Society trilogy, three films which each dealt with a different form of love considered taboo in the time period and locale in which it is presented. The first of the three, *A Mind's Broken Eye,* was a study of interracial love set in the American south of the 1950's while the second film, *She Waits Beyond The Bonfire,* was a transgendered coming of age story and the final piece of the three, *Autumn's Favorite Son,* told a complex story of incest with intense, often violent surrealist imagery. Since the critical and commercial success of the trilogy, Daniels has gone on to direct consistently successful art films for Alston Image in addition to the vast majority of their parody, gonzo, and fetish output and his most recent project, *Awake to the Skin,* is set to go into production next month. Ladies and gentlemen, please join me in welcoming Mr. Dominic Daniels."

The speaker at the podium turned and applauded with the audience as Dominic Daniels walked out from the wings and into the bright stage lights. There was polite applause as he shook hands with the professor who had introduced him and sat at one of the two chairs on the stage. The professor took the other seat, and microphones came on next to each of them.

"Well, Mr. Daniels," began the professor.

"Call me Dominic." It always amused Dominic how academic professionals would take on a sort of cowering pomposity in his presence, as though his affiliation with pornography made him a delicate creature, privy to some mystical knowledge from a far off fairyland.

"Certainly. You've had a very prolific career in your field. Why is that? Does it have anything to do with the cheap productions?"

"Isaac doesn't do cheap productions, first of all," replied Dominic. "In fact, Alston Image was founded on the premise that audiences would respond to pornography as a legitimate entertainment medium if it was presented with the same kind of cinematography and quality production that goes into well made films and television. Generally speaking, though, we're able to be more prolific because we don't have to deal with the theatrical release cycle that most Hollywood studios pander to. We know that our work is going straight to DVD or straight out to the internet or magazines, and because we don't do mainstream advertising, we have the budget to move a lot faster than the more accepted industries. That allows me to film gonzo compilations—that is to say collections of sex scenes with no plot and little dialogue—and release them on a very short production cycle and the sale of those DVDs affords me the time and industry support I need to create my feature length films."

"That's what's curious to me and I'm sure many students here, Dominic. Critics have said that you'd make an outstanding mainstream director. That your writing would put you on the level of Woody Allen or Robert Altman and that you have the production scope of James Cameron, the surrealist bent of David Lynch and the striking intensity of Roman Polanski. So, with that level of high praise, why would you sell yourself short by directing porn?"

"Well it's the simple fact that my interest is human sexuality and when it comes to the depiction of such things, Hollywood is a giant pretense. They can't show actual fucking. I'm sure there are even people in this room who felt a slight twinge of disgust that I would even use the word fucking. But in the porn world, that pretension is off. I can show the most explicit of sexuality and the viewer won't be distracted from an overall appreciation for the film."

"But isn't faking a love scene convincingly part of the skill required of a good actor?"

"It can be. But why is it necessary? Should an actor be more interested in his ability to convey their ability to convincingly fake a performance, or their ability to render a performance? Jackie Chan performs his own stunts in their entirety. Is he *less* of an actor because he does his own stunts, or is he more of an actor? How is his performance less enthralling than that of a martial arts movie star that throws a couple of punches then needs a stunt double and trick photography to make the rest of his performance convincing? Countless films have featured actors jumping off buildings and every one of them has been filmed with special effects but Jackie actually jumped off a building and caught a rope ladder from a helicopter in *Police Story 3*. Sure it was probably arranged so that he wouldn't actually hurt himself—but the intensity was real. That's what porn allows me to capture."

"Wouldn't you rather be using real actors, though?"

"What do you mean 'real' actors? You mean people who can deliver dialogue correctly? People who know how to develop a character? Porn stars, believe it or not, are people too and many of them have skills, interests, hobbies, and ambitions that have nothing to do with porn. A person who is willing to learn the craft of acting can learn it. All I require is a performer with an open mind and a strong will to succeed. There are intelligent people in the industry that can really understand dialogue and plot and character development. Sure, there are also no talent imbeciles, but Hollywood has plenty of those in its blockbusters as well."

There were appreciative chuckles at this sentiment and then the interview was interrupted by the garbled feedback of someone approaching one of the microphones that had been set up in the aisles for the upcoming Q&A. Both Dominic and the professor turned to see a portly student in thick glasses and a black turtleneck standing at the microphone. He seemed to be perturbed by something but even more he seemed to be looking down his nose at Dominic, which was an odd angle considering that Dominic was above him. "Excuse me," he said with an heir of practiced elitism "but what are we even listening to this guy for? When my friends and I sit up nights talking about directors, his name certainly hasn't ever come up. Is this school really so desperate for guest speakers that we have to pretend that there's something of artistic merit in the dark, bottom feeding filth he produces?"

Dominic's gaze narrowed as he took in the boy who had interrupted him. With a gentle version of the deliberate pace with which he had approached the protester that egged his car, Dominic stood, took the microphone next to his chair, and walked to the front of the stage, standing about five feet away from the boy and three feet above him. In the stage light Dominic's frizzy hair was bathed in an angelic halo.

"You know," began Dominic, his disdain hardly masked "I knew if I came back I'd run into one of you little shits and you know what it really is that sickens me about that? It's knowing that in all of the education you've gotten here, nobody has bothered to kick you in the balls, slap your face and tell you to grow the hell up. You kids think that you're so goddamn special because you're film students at NYU? Well guess what—that is pretty damn special and that's why it makes me sick. You've got a fantastic opportunity here and you squander it looking down your noses at people whose boots you aren't even fit to kiss.

"You think you're the only smug film school brat that sat up till four in the morning talking David Lynch movies over Starbucks coffee with his fellow Andy Warhol impersonating post-grunge slackers? You think those late-night bull sessions make you some kind of apprentice to the gods? When you graduate from this school and move back in with your parents you'll have a whole new perspective. Come talk to me again when you've directed a few toothpaste commercials and wedding videos. After that directing porn won't seem like such a step back for you. The very idea that you'll have even the creative freedom to tell people what position to fuck in will seem like a shimmering beacon of hope. You'll hear the clapperboard drop and feel like you've really and truly made it.

"And when that day comes, you'll have to ask yourself a question: 'Am I doing this because I love directing, or because I wanted to be a snooty little artsy-fartsy bitch at a bunch of Hollywood coke parties?' And if you answer the former—that it's your love of directing that draws you to it—you'll find that your creative opportunities will open up exponentially because the big wigs—those entertainment execs that you claim to disdain—don't hire creative people for the sake of nursing their bloated egos. They hire them for their ability to direct and produce.

"And if there's one thing you don't know yet, it's that creative people can't produce under compulsion, no matter how financially lucrative the project. If you don't love the act of creating then you won't create. You'll coast along on trends and word of mouth for awhile, then bottom out and be completely forgotten. If I were directing Marlon Brando in a five hundred million dollar Hollywood epic, I would not enjoy it any more or less than I enjoy directing two peroxide blondes in a sixty-nine because I do this for the love of what I create, not for the love I need.

"Substance comes when you stop looking for it and start creating it. When you open up your soul and embrace the joy of filmmaking it will stop mattering what the nature of the project is and when that happens everything you put out will be Citizen Kane. And that's not to say you shouldn't strive to direct those big budget Hollywood reels if that's what you're after. Go for it—chase after it. But you shouldn't go for the goal if you don't love the race.

"If the commercial goals of the product can be captured simply by filming people fucking, then there's no limit to the artistry that I can bring into it. When I bring artistic flair to a project, I bring something that is pure and undiluted by the demands of shallow Hollywood trends. It's a bare tapestry laid before me and I can work exactly to my liking and Isaac Alston will approve of it under one condition: that I produce something that is a perfect mirror of my creative desires. You see, porn is a genre that works when it grabs the viewer on a primal, sensory level and as such if the director is not as naked in his artistic fulfillment as the performers are in reality, then the audience will know it in a heartbeat and the whole thing will fall flat. If I'm not one hundred percent open to my deepest desires in every single shoot that I do, then I am not doing my job correctly. Now you go out and find one snooty little art house studio that not only requires but *demands* that level of personal truth.

"Do you call me a bottom feeder because I create films that are dark and disturbing? Films that make you question the true extent of what human beings will find pleasurable? I create those films because I am not only willing but capable of falling face first into the depths that mainstream studios only hint at.

"Have you ever stopped to wonder why people scoffed and pissed at Paul Verhoeven's *Showgirls* and gave it such crummy reviews? The acting, the cinematography, the soundtrack, the choreography, the plot, all were equal to or superior to that of top Hollywood blockbusters. Naysayers will tell you that the acting was abysmal, that Elizabeth Berkeley gave a terrible performance, but they never can explain *why*. How was her performance any worse than that of Jennifer Grey in *Dirty Dancing*? It's rather simple: *Showgirls* contains nudity and lots of it. It's devoted to nothing nobler than the promotion and performance of sexuality and I promise you that if you could get the people who really hated that film to be honest with themselves they would tell you that they just aren't comfortable with taking sexuality seriously. They can't bring themselves to admit that there is true artistry in sexual performance and their bashful prejudice cost several actors their careers.

"Turn that around and look at a movie like *Boogie Nights*. Makes the career of several rising actors and gives several more a comeback. Why? Because it portrays professional sex culture in a profoundly negative light. It's chock full of nudity and sex and explicit behavior, but it kept the viewers securely assured that what they were seeing was bad and filthy—that they, by virtue of not being in this industry—were automatically superior to those who were, then had the audacity to still allow you to look into our world and enjoy it!

"The San Francisco Chronicle said that *Showgirls* was about a woman who wanted to accomplish something that was 'not admirable, just ridiculous.' How was aspiring to be a showgirl ridiculous? Lighting a bag of shit on fire is ridiculous. Drinking and driving is ridiculous. French kissing a pencil sharpener is ridiculous. What's ridiculous about wanting to dance naked? Nothing. It is courageous and commendable and the men and women who do it are kind enough to share their beauty with the world.

"I bring this up because if that same movie had been made as a porn flick, the acting, the cinematography, the soundtrack, the choreography, and everything else would have been commended and held up as evidence that a porn film can stand on par with Hollywood mainstream excellence. Separate but equal, if you will. But instead they tried to make that film a mainstream Hollywood project and the impotence of Hollywood is that it can't give you actual sex! When I watch Hollywood movies with their simulated sex it cracks me up because no matter what lengths they go to, they're just tiptoeing around what we show on a daily basis. And you think that mainstream cinema is higher brow because of its puritanical limitations?

"Do you think I sit up nights sobbing because I'm directing porn instead of being a 'real' director? Fuck no! I do what I do because it satisfies me and allows me to create my art with the kind of freedom that 'respectable' genres can only hint at. I'm only as real a director as the professionalism I bring to my projects and I bring quite a lot; not because I'm hoping to prove to you 'real' directors that I'm 'good enough' to earn your respect but because this is an avenue where I can respect myself!"

There was silence in the lecture hall as Dominic returned to his seat and the questioner sat down, sinking low in his chair.

Ninety minutes later, Dominic emerged from the theater into the adjoining hallway, nodding distantly at the dean of students, who had been apologizing furiously for the student's outburst. The remainder of the interview had not gone well. The professor leading the discussion had asked overly softball questions, abandoning the penetrating manner of his initial inquiry. Dominic had been sober and utilitarian in his answers and when the floor had been opened for Q&A, one of the ushers had announced that there wasn't enough time for questions.

With a tight smile and slight nod, Dominic dismissed the dean and began a slow, mellow stroll down the corridors of his alma-mater. The dark greens of the passages had a homey feeling, but this nostalgia was intercut with brash splashes of the new: posters, flyers, and campus announcements that he didn't recognize. As he walked on he found his pace quickening as he sought escape from his corroded memories.

"Mr. Daniels," said a husky, out of breath voice. Dominic turned just as he was about to descend a flight of stairs and saw the young miscreant that had started the evening's downward turn. It occurred to Dominic that he must have been moving faster than he'd thought since the lad seemed to be flushed as if from a chase. He skidded to a halt before Dominic and sputtered: "You—you were right."

"I know I was."

"But I mean it—I'm sorry. Really. I shouldn't have done that. The whole rest of the time I sat there and felt really stupid and I just wanted to tell you that I was sorry before you left. I just felt so dumb I—I mean I…"

Dominic put out his hand "Hi, I'm Dominic."

The boy was caught off guard and his mouth trembled for an instant before he took the offered hand and shook. "Peter. Peter Wingrove."

"Nice to meet you, Peter. Who's your favorite director?"

"Akira Kurosawa."

"Good choice. *Redbeard* was always my favorite of his. That and *Dreams*."

"I saw *Dreams* when I was a kid—it made me want to get into directing."

"Is that right?"

"Yeah—I was living in Japan at the time with my dad. He was studying filmmaking from a porn director over there."

"With such a background you should have more respect for the craft."

"I guess there was a certain amount of rebellion involved. It sort of embarrassed me growing up. Dad never broke it down for me like you did."

"Who did your dad study under?"

"Hotei Shibasaki."

Dominic raised an eyebrow. "Want to go for coffee?"

They made tracks for a nearby coffee shop, one that had been installed into what must have been a small bank at one time. Dominic had made polite conversation as he and Peter traversed the few blocks to the shop but the young man knew all the while that the name Hotei Shibasaki had suddenly made him someone of great interest in the eyes of Dominic Daniels.

The coffee shop was the sort of smooth, modern design where the edges seemed to slope into one another, the deliberately diverging shades of wood providing a wisp of log cabin ambience amidst the otherwise ultra-chic veneer. In contrast to the changes in the college that mutilated his memories from two decades ago, Dominic found the ambient design of the modern chamber delightful and inviting, the new space warming his heart as the stereo played Coltrane's "My Favorite Things."

Dominic ordered an espresso for the kid and a mint tea for himself. Peter had barely taken a sip from his mug when Dominic began a line of inquiry:

"I want you to tell me everything you know about Hotei Shibasaki."

"May I ask why?"

"You haven't heard?"

"I guess not."

"Well, it got leaked to the media earlier today, so I guess I can tell you. Alston image is looking to buy the script for *The Lotus Wave*."

"It can't be done."

"Why?"

"Because Hotei Shibasaki isn't about to let that film be made."

"He doesn't want it to be made?"

"No—he wants it to be made more than anything in the world. The problem is that there's nobody willing to make it on his terms."

"And those terms are?"

"It must be made exactly as he wishes to see it made."

"That's not uncommon—a lot of directors are like that."

"But that's just it—there's parts of that script that, well, most people would want to have filmed with special effects. Shibasaki wants them filmed for real."

"So you know what's in the script?"

"My dad did. He passed away a couple of years ago and he never explained it to me. He would get violent with me if I brought it up too much. It wasn't long after he read the script that my dad stopped working for Hotei Shibasaki. Something about the script just disturbed him too much."

"You still haven't answered my first question—what was your experience with Hotei Shibasaki?"

"My dad was big into the porn-chic era films. He wanted to break into the industry as a director, but the market in America was difficult to penetrate, so he started working in Europe, where he met Hotei Shibasaki at a party thrown by Radley Metzger. They hit it off and Shibasaki liked my dad and invited him to come to Japan and work on his crew for a film he had coming up. He and my mom moved to Tokyo and my dad became a part of the Shibasaki Pictures production team. A few years later I was born. I was about four or five when dad left Japan and Hotei Shibasaki for good."

"What was his motivation for that?"

"He read the *Lotus Wave*. Also, he called the police after he read it."

"And that's why it was seized?"

"Yeah."

"Peter, I don't think you took your stance against me in the hall today because you were rebelling. I think you were trying to uphold your father's legacy."

Peter nodded. "I could see that."

Chapter 10

RALPHIE BARREL sat in a wooden cube of a chair next to the mural window of his hotel room. There was a police officer standing in the doorway talking while Ralphie stewed in the corner. "From now on you are to retain a minimum distance of five hundred feet from Billie Solar, Hank Steel, the offices of Alston Image, and the Black Chapel night club," said the cop with dry conviction.

"Yes sir, officer," muttered Ralphie sarcastically, scowling out the window all the while. "Won't let it happen again."

"Sure you will," grunted the cop, turning to leave. "The only people who get restraining orders are the ones who don't honor them."

After the officer left, Ralphie stroked the metal brace on his nose gingerly. He felt like he needed to touch it every few minutes to get a residual hit of the pain that Hank steel had inflicted on him, as though the pain were a fuzzy tape recording of a lesson Hank had taught to a captivated audience of one. He wanted to review that lesson not because there was a test coming up but because in some quiet, secret way, he enjoyed stewing in his own personal incredulity.

Some time passed and Ralphie became restless. He wasn't sure what he wanted to do or who he wanted to do it too, but the plain beige walls of the hotel room were wearing on him with their sullen reminder of the blandness of his current state. He pushed himself up out of the chair and walked into the bathroom, flipping on the light and looking at himself in the mirror. The nose brace looked like a piece of crude costume jewelry for some sort of robot outfit. The brace was complemented by his two black eyes.

Ralphie began combing and gelling his hair instinctively, not in an attempt to mask the awkward protrusion of his swollen, splinted nose but out of a spiteful reflex as though gnashing at his scalp with the comb would prove something to the pathetic figure in the mirror.

When at last he was dressed completely, Ralphie left the hotel and meandered through the streets of Van Nuys, not certain what it was he was looking for. After an hour or so of this he became hungry and stepped into the grocery store section of a nearby gas station. As he took various items from the different shelves and bins, he noticed the magazine rack and instantly focused on the three black shelves that held the pornography, deciding to see what they carried. There was one shelf devoted entirely to magazines from Alston Image. Ralphie flicked through the different publications, snarling at the way they seemed to make all the bitches look like something greater than bitches. Like angels or some shit. Then he stopped on one of the Alston Image fag rags. Hank Steel was on the cover, stark naked as he had been at the club, staring into the camera with a militaristic solemnity as though he were proud and honored to be on the cover of a fag rag.

Ralphie picked up the Alston Image magazine, *Men's Flesh,* and thumbed through the pages until he found Hank's pictorial. Having seen the man in person, Ralphie knew that the pictures were not airbrushed but even so he found it difficult to believe that the body was real. Hank's chosen surname was certainly accurate: every piece of the form seemed to have been hammered out by a master blacksmith. Of particular magnitude was Hank's tool, which was showcased in varying degrees of erection in the pictorial in which Hank masturbated to a pulpy climax. In the final two shots his jissom was captured first in an elegant arc from his cock head and in the next in a thick, semi-transparent mess on his abdomen. An additional strand of it was suspended between his first and second finger, his tongue reaching out as if to break the liquid bridge.

"He's beautiful isn't he?"

Ralphie turned and jumped back, realizing some scrawny guy had been looking over his shoulder. "Fuck off, fag," he spat, tossing the magazine onto the rack and storming off towards the checkout counter.

When Isaac Alston was seventeen, a vandal had spray painted the word "cunt" on the wall of the boys' room at his high school in bright red letters. Isaac, having become known as a smut fiend, was assumed to be the culprit, though no evidence was brought against him. He was ordered to repaint the disfigured wall and accepted the punishment without complaint.

The following morning, school faculty found that the young Isaac Alston had not repainted the restroom but had instead painted over the poorly written "cunt" with the same word, only now presented in insular half-uncial calligraphy. The administration had reacted fiercely, demanding that Alston do the assignment properly. Alston refused and was suspended for two weeks while the janitor painted over the offending letters.

Though he would never know it, the art teacher and one of the English teachers had stood in the restroom for nearly an hour prior to the repainting, discussing the quality of Isaac's work. The art teacher commented on the excellent use of shading that captured the glow of the fluorescent lights and gave it an almost three-dimensional flare while the English teacher brought up the willowing Baroque swirls that engulfed the border of each letter and Celtic lattice work that filled the interiors.

Two hours ago, the glass bottle had been carefully emptied of its contents and refilled with gasoline. After this a dry rag was stuffed into the bottle's opening. Finally, a lighter was flicked a few times and held to the outer tip of the rag. Whoever built this simple bomb, lit the fuse, ran up the alley that opened onto the street parallel to the Alston Image offices, and flung the burning glass container over the lot's outer wall, was unimportant. The bearded wastrel, clubbed into submission by riot police moments after the flamboyant launch, could have belonged to Christians for the Abolition of Lust or the Student Committee for the Advancement of Sexual Dignity, or Moms Against MILFs or any of the other hundred or so civil action groups that surrounded the office building but that was irrelevant—the fact of the matter was simply that after the bullets ripped through his chest, all of the thousands of people surrounding the building rushed in on the police.

High above the street, in the penthouse office, Dominic Daniels and Isaac Alston stood at the window and watched as the Molotov cocktail spiraled over the outer wall and landed in Billie's Jaguar. There was an elegant flourish in the first moments of the spreading flame, like a conductor raising his arms and, by extension, the rest of the players in a symphony. The conflagration spread outwards across the upholstery of the open convertible and in raged silently for a moment before the car exploded in a seizure of incinerated clouds.

"Did you have any trouble coming back from the airport?" asked Dominic.

"No—I don't think they recognized me until I was pulling into our lot."

Alston crossed to his desk and clicked on the intercom. "Carol, please tell Ms. Solar that her car just exploded and that I'll have my lawyer handle the insurance."

"You got it, Mr. Alston."

The public hysteria since the leaking of the *Lotus Wave* project had been steadily brewing since yesterday. A conservative religious group had been alternately singing protest songs to the tune of *Onward Christian Soldiers* and *Up, Up, and Away, Junior Birdmen* for most of yesterday morning when the news had begun to spread among their ranks and gradually the songs had dribbled away into a moment of silence before the choirs were reborn in a bloodthirsty roar of overdriven hysteria.

By early afternoon various senators and congressmen were decrying Alston Image, demanding that the president have Alston arrested. In response, the president had delivered a speech on the importance of family to the American way of life which conservative commentators began to analyze in search of a hidden socialist agenda.

And as Dominic and Alston watched Billie's car explode, Artie Barrel was awoken from a hangover by the sound of his telephone. Through the crushing throb of dehydration he fumbled for the receiver and pulled it under the covers with him.

"Hello?"

"Mr. Barrel. This is Melvin Crankshadow from the Institute for Pornographic Addiction."

"Uh… okay."

"We here at the IPA were greatly impressed by your noble decision to expose Isaac Alston's horrid intentions in filming *The Lotus Wave*."

"Uh… Thanks." Though the late morning haze wore too heavily on Artie's brain for him to make much of an analysis, he had a vague impression that this man's voice was a delicately refined, quietly penetrating tone that, were it given tangible substance, would be in the form of tiny water bugs that could land on the surface of a pond without breaking it.

"I wanted to call you today because I'm always interested in making friends with a noble man such as yourself. Such people are severely lacking in our modern world, don't you think?"

"Yeah, I guess they are."

"You're probably wondering why I've contacted you today and I won't waste your time—I can't help but think that a noble man such as yourself would be interested in lending some merit of public integrity to your industry which is, let's face it, reprehensible."

"Sure, I guess."

"That's why I wanted to extend my hand to you, Mr. Barrel. My organization's purpose is to help people with their addiction to pornography. We get so demonized for doing this noble endeavor—helping others with the addiction we've taught them they have—and I can't help but think that with your alliance could help both our causes exponentially."

"Yeah—that's true." Artie was warming to the idea.

"We've recently received a great influx of financial support from those who, like you, are opposed to Mr. Alston's behavior. We wish to put that good fortune to good use, and we wish to do so by filming a television commercial about our cause. It seemed appropriate for us, then, to enlist your help in the matter as such a reaching across the aisle would lend credibility to our cause, not the politics surrounding it."

"Okay."

"In that regard, Mr. Barrel, would you be willing to film our commercial?"

"Ah… yeah—sure. Sounds fine."

"Wonderful, Mr. Barrel. I shall have my business people contact you for the particulars. A blessed day to your, sir."

"Thanks. You too."

Artie held the phone for a long moment after Melvin Crankshadow hung up. When he finally moved to hang up his own receiver his sore, reddened eyes caught the light spilling in around the vertical blinds that cloaked his windows. For a moment he stared into the sharp, downward angles of that light, considering dimly the glow which, while painful to look at, it had never before seemed so beautiful.

When Alston was informed that Darcy Collins wanted to see him on urgent matters, he made sure his daily calendar was clear enough to allow her a few hours of his time. Since her time as an Alston Image contract girl, Darcy had kept in touch with Alston on a professional level and he'd found himself in the role of business mentor. Certain that Darcy's interests in promoting her own product line would never offer a threat to his own business endeavors he'd given her powerful insight into marketing her products with the most important of them being "remember: the vagina sells itself. Your job is only to distinguish yours from the rest. The sale has already been made. But at the same time, never forget the eons of shame you're reaching through in the process of collecting on that sale and, as such, always appeal to the best within your customer, not the worst." While Alston had never dreamed that Darcy's business would take off as it had, he felt not the threat of a potential rival but rather pride in seeing the student rise to the level of the teacher. Their relationship had, throughout the years, retained the stiffly professional tone of all of Alston's discourse, seldom punctuated by the informal relaxation Darcy assumed he must reserve for his innermost circle.

When Darcy arrived at Alston's office he greeted her with a hug that retained the formal grandeur of his natural distance from real intimacy but still managed to convey fully and completely the comfort and camaraderie the moment called for. It was this odd ability to project genuine support in the guise of professional detachment, Darcy reflected, that had made him such an outstanding businessman.

"What's the urgency, Darcy?" asked Alston as he broke the embrace and gestured to one of the chairs on the visitors' side of his desk. "Please sit."

Darcy lowered herself into the chair, and it was in the careful hesitation of her movements, which were normally fluid and naturally sinuous, that he became aware of a much darker problem as he returned to his side of the desk.

"I'm in trouble, Isaac," she began softly. Alston was seated now, the full focus of his being directed at Darcy. "I let one of them get to me."

"One of 'them?'" asked Alston, gesturing with a turn of his head in the general direction of the crowd outside.

"One of the worst of them. I was at the Adult Business and Media Convention signing autographs and such. Then this woman came up to me and introduced herself as Andrea Danvers. Do you know of her?"

"I've heard the name. What happened?"

"She kind of butted her way into a conversation with me and tried to argue about her particular brand of feminist 'theory.' I tried to brush her off, but then she told me that she was doing a lecture on the role of women in society. She said she'd pay my full appearance fee if I'd come and debate her. I told her to have her people call mine, just to try to get her to go away, and she did.

"So a few days later my agent gets this call from a liberal arts college in New England and I tell him to ask for twice my usual appearance fee just to get them to back down. Well, they said they'd pay it. I couldn't believe it and I couldn't turn it down. They asked my company to send a few samples of our products for reference material and even paid for them. So we shipped the stuff off to this college and I took a flight out there the day before the lecture.

"I landed at Hartsfield-Jackson and there was a student there to meet me. It was strange—she addressed me with this rigid formality. No smile, no handshake, just a dry 'how do you do' after she asked my name then she turned and started walking towards a car. If I hadn't already known that she was there to pick me up I would have never thought to follow her. When we got to her car she took my bags and put them in the trunk and it was then that I got a chance to take her in. She was the kind of girl that's meant to be skinny—narrow hips, flat chest, slender neckline, but she was pudgy in this bizarre, almost purposeful way. When she bent over to pick up my bag, her T-shirt slid up and I could see these awful stretch marks. Not only that, she had pubic hair from her ass crack coming up her lower back. When she reached up to close the trunk lid, I realized that her armpits were unshaved as well. We got in the car and I realized that she had this odd smell to her. She was certainly bathed, but there was no hint of deodorant or perfume of any kind. I said 'I don't mean to be rude, but do you shave at all?' I expected her to be taken aback, but instead she responded flatly and formally, with a kind of accent that sounded like the typical idiot teenager drawl being stretched to the breaking point into some semblance of intellectual authority. She said 'no, I don't shave my body hair. Doctor Danvers says that shaving body hair is the patriarchy's way of making women look like little girls to reinforce childish gender identity and encourage latent pedophilia.' She said the words almost as if they were some kind of deadpan ritual chant. I asked her about 'Doctor Danvers' and she replied 'Doctor Danvers is the foremost authority on pornography and its damaging effects. She understands its role as a capitalist engine for the enslavement of human beings by delivering patriarchal programming to men through their penises.' I asked her what kind of research went into that conclusion and she said 'well, you have to understand that although there's no scientific data supporting her argument, Doctor Danvers is someone who studies media images and knows how they affect our society.' I said 'how does she know?' and the girl wouldn't say anything. I tried to push the issue a little more and when we came to a stop light, the girl looked over at me and said 'look, I was told not to let you engage me in conversation, okay? You'll have to wait until the lecture tonight.' In that moment, I saw something strange in the girl—when she said 'look—they told me' it seemed to carry with it a vague suggestion of someone who was crying out for help from behind a barbed wire fence. But there was also this dismal sense of grey resignation.

"We arrived at Whitland College which was in some small town in Massachusetts. I was given a room at the alumni house and told that I would have lunch and later dinner brought to my room. I asked if I could tour the campus and the kid at the front desk told me that they thought it would be best if I stayed in my room until the lecture. I asked if they thought my presence would be a disturbance or if they were concerned for my safety and he just said 'they told me it would be best to keep you in your room.' So I asked if I could borrow a copy of Andrea Danvers' book to read until then and he picked up a phone at the desk, dialed a number, and then said 'she wants to know if she can have a copy of Doctor Danvers' book to read. Ah ha. Ah ha. Okay.' And then he hung up the phone and said 'a copy will be brought up to you with lunch.'

"So I settled into the little suite—which was little more than a common hotel room in size and accommodations—and waited. They finally brought me some food—brown rice and vegetables with flat water—and a copy of Danvers' book *Smutscape*. I sat there and read the thing and it was horrible—I read the whole book in a few hours with morbid curiosity. The whole argument was that capitalism is designed to reinforce patriarchal rule by creating and exploiting gender stereotypes and that they slowly train men to see sexual violence as acceptable and then use mass media to render the violence invisible and that the long term effect of this was that men would start needing 'harder and harder' porn just like 'any other drug' until they started raping women, then raping children, then having children of their own and raping them. She talked about how rape was the result of teaching men that women wanted to be hurt and it made wonder if she even knew what rape was. She made it sound like any man could rape a woman if he was exposed to too much sexuality and she made it sound like all women were asking to be raped if they flaunted their sexuality too much. It wasn't like rape was something that only a few malicious individuals were capable of because of genuine misogyny but rather that it was something that bubbled just under the surface of all men and that they all had the same hair trigger that would send them into some sort of psychotic rape mode. The weird thing was, she said that was no peer reviewed, scientific data to support this but, just like the girl in the car had said, she kept saying that she was someone who studied media images and knew how media images affected society, as if that declaration were something that overruled any objections and required no further justification. As if her claiming to know better than the rest of us was all that her argument required. I sat there and thought *how can she be a doctor of anything?*

"When they finally came for me, I was escorted to the campus auditorium by two young women who bore the same detached yet alert expression as the girl that picked me up and the same lack of attention to personal grooming and seemingly deliberate commitment to weight gain. They brought me into the auditorium and gave me a seat in the front row. I looked around while the students and faculty filed in. There was no hubbub of dialogue like I expected. The students there were mostly women, but they were stiff and quiet in their demeanor. They did act like they were happy to see one another, they didn't show any hint of life whatsoever, and they all held their heads very upright, but it didn't seem to be out of pride or confidence but rather some kind mask of down-the-nose condescension that wasn't directed at anyone in particular but rather held fast like some sort of parade dress uniform.

"The lights dimmed and some frail emaciated man named Mercer Thompson came out and introduced Andrea Danvers. After he gave a few words about how she wasn't anti-men or anti-sex but only saw them as the tools of class distinction that they were, Andrea Danvers emerged. The applause they gave her was so dead and robotic that it almost sounded synchronized. She got up there and started speaking, and it sounded like she was quoting her book word for word. I recognized the same shallow arguments, the same hollow conclusions, and the same vacant, ill-informed interpretation of the timeline of porn history. She said that Jenna Jameson was the first ever porn star with any mainstream recognition as if Linda Lovelace and Marilyn Chambers never existed. She said that pornographic feature films try to make 'a few stabs at a simple storyline and a few stabs at a Hollywood production' as if feature films were something we only tossed off without any thought. She acted as if movies like *Caligula* were never made. She tried to portray gonzo porn as being entirely devoted to torturing women by making them vomit and cry. She kept talking about 'hardcore, body punishing sex' and how this was some kind of problem that needed to be fought against.

"But the worst thing of it all, Isaac, was that she said that even though women signed contracts to appear in porn, it was still rape. She said 'I don't care if you sign a million fucking contracts, that's rape.' Those were her exact words. I mean, if you can't sign a legally valid contract saying that you consented to have sex, how *can* you give consent? I realized then and there that for all of her token garbage about empowering and liberating women, *she* was the one that didn't respect a woman's right to choose. She didn't want women to be able to consent to sex; she wanted to be able to control their consent. It was scary, looking at all those dead, expressionless faces that stared up at her like children that had been watching television for several straight hours. It wasn't a lecture—it was the gathering of a cult. I was certain all of them had read the woman's book already and heard all of these arguments before and that they were simply meeting to hear the same sermon that had brainwashed them in the first place—like they need a recharge or something.

"That horrible woman stood on that stage and towered over them like she was some kind of puppet master. She talked about 'our bodies' and how porn was hurting 'our bodies,' as if she thought that all women's bodies were directly interconnected. She talked about 'our sexuality' as if she were not only presuming but proudly proclaiming that she had a stake in every woman's body. I felt sick and violated then—no piggish brute of a man has ever made me feel as inhuman and preyed upon as I did in that moment. I suddenly realized that I was alone in that room—that I had no allies in the faceless, vacant throng that stared up at that wretched bitch. I had gone from feeling sorry for those young women to feeling terrified for my own safety.

"But you know what the creepiest thing about it all was? The way that horrible woman said things without saying them. She talked about porn out there that show grown women dressed as little girls and then said 'what happens when the men who look at these images start having daughters?' She was obviously saying that men who look at that kind of porn would start molesting their own children, but in the Q&A segment—if you could call it that—someone asked her to further explain the psychology that would make a man who was attracted to fully grown women somehow want children because he was sexually attracted to adults in over sized children's clothes. She said 'I didn't mean that. I meant that as someone who studies media images, I can tell you that these images will sexualize child abuse in the minds of men and that will have a deleterious and potentially sexually hostile affect on the children that these men raise.' It was this dizzying, nauseating feeling that if you tried to put your finger on exactly what she meant she'd just dress it up with elaborate wording and use that to make the actual point sound more profound while still dodging responsibility for what she was really saying. I tried to follow her logic—I really did—but I felt like I was flailing in some purgatory where everything around me was transparent and the truth was something I could see but not grab onto.

"They started asking her questions and she explained that the women would all get to go first and then the men later, if they had time. She said that was because men were the ones that usually dissented and therefore they needed to be constrained. When it was finally time for the men to speak the ones that did started crying and going on and on about how sorry they were—that to see the dark secrets of their sexual perversions up on a screen like that was too much. Then—and this blew my mind, Isaac—she asked them one by one if they'd like to come up to the stage and apologize for rape. Some of them actually did. They apologized for rape as if it was something that all of them were guilty of by the fact of their gender. I looked up at that stage and it broke my heart—I thought about all the women that had crusaded for my rights—for my right to vote, to own property, to have a career, to have control of my body and here was this vile cunt taking advantage of all that for some hateful authoritarian fantasy.

"And it was right then that I realized 'Doctor' Danvers was speaking about me. She said my name and a spotlight hit me. She asked me 'Ms. Collins, your company sent us some porn DVDs, is that correct?' Then she stuck the microphone down in my face and I said 'yes.' Right then cops came up on either side of me and one of them told me I was under arrest for the sale and shipment of obscene materials across state lines. They put me in hand cuffs and led me away. Danvers didn't say anything and neither did the kids. I looked out and realized that all of them were now directing that condescension at me, as thought they'd finally found a target for it. I was put in a holding cell at the local precinct all night. I was arranged the next day on obscenity charges and, well, my trial is coming up in a few months, Isaac. I want Duke Cunningham to represent me."

"He's all yours, Darcy. I'll make sure his fees are taken care of throughout."

"Thank you, Isaac," said Darcy, realizing she'd begun to cry. "I just feel so stupid—I let the money lead me into their trap."

Alston rose sharply to his feet and came around the desk to sit in the chair next to her. He put a calm, honest, and reassuring hand on hers. "It's okay, Darcy. All you did was put a price on your services and that's a noble, decent and honest thing. They were the ones who deceived you. They were the ones who lured you there under false pretenses and they were the ones that led you into their trap. They think we're a bunch of predatory creeps because that's what they are and they can only see the world in terms of creeps that support their cause and creeps that don't. But I'll put Duke on this right away. He's helped me beat the obscenity rap countless times. Don't worry." He drew her in and embraced her again and in that moment Darcy felt a surrender of one of the layers of Alston's formal exterior. She was able to feel the passionate, raging authenticity that boiled deep within him and had warmed herself at its fire.

Chapter 11

AWAKE TO THE SKIN entered production a week later. The massive soundstage that Dominic had used for the filming of *Jungle Bunnies 2: the Shaft of Slamdingo* was transformed into the coma ward of a big city hospital. The soundstage was several miles from the main offices and indistinguishable from any of the other studio lots that filled the Hollywood sprawl, which kept the protestors at bay. The set was relaxed and the crew efficient, all thriving under the fluid guidance of Dominic Daniels.

Hank's role in the film was twofold: in the "real" world, he would appear as an orderly who took an interest in the two sisters and then in the dream world as various symbolic figures, each central to the scenario in question. Billie played the elder sister, who served as the film's narrator while another Alston contract girl, Diana Arland, portrayed the incapacitated sister. Hank was struck at how they truly seemed like siblings.

Filming of the framing story got underway and moved smoothly, wrapping in just ten days. From there it was a matter of filming the vignettes themselves, starting with the flashback to a youth of Sapphic experimentation between the two sisters. To this end a luxury villa in Sacramento was rented, and Hank was brought along because, as Billie informed him, days filled with eating pussy would leave her starving for dick in the evenings.

With a foolish grin, Hank snuck away from the Valley to join his girlfriend for a week of extraordinary splendor. The weather was warm and mild, its satiating temperature giving a sharp, Technicolor radiance to the California country side. Renting a car in the wake of the bombing, they took long winding roads through the carefully sculpted countryside that, by virtue of their own blissful arcs, turned even the most mundane of California freeways into botanical tapestries. They listened to the first seven Chicago albums on the way to the villa, and Hank found himself smiling with affectionate amusement each time Terry Kath and Peter Cetera's guttural soul and soaring harmonies made him cast sideways glances at his lady. Love songs meant something to him again and, for the first time, he was comfortable with that. The car bombing, Ralphie's wormy attempt at rape, and the maniacal protestors all seemed distant to this fantasy life he'd softly sunken into.

The villa was a post modern cubist visage with a dark wooden front door etched with exaggerated Egyptian hieroglyphs in the front surrounded by oblong columns, the latter sporting oil powered sconces. Tall cactuses rose from clay pots on either side of the entrance. The double doors opened to reveal that their wall was merely the surrounding structure that enclosed three free standing houses, each of them a house of its own, each maintaining the sharp edges of the cubic theme. The three houses stood facing inward on a vast swimming pool and were connected by a series of stone walkways that arched playfully over the water, connecting in the center at a circular island that seemed to float on the water. The island sported an open bar that cast a neon purple glow out across the pool.

The film crew stayed in one of the houses, Dominic in another, with Hank, Billie, and Diana taking the third. There were three bedrooms in each house, but Hank and Billie were unsurprised to feel Diana's slender, naked frame slide into bed next to them. She sank into the lavish, plush bed and joined the sensual feast that Hank and Billie were already preparing.

The villa opened onto a back yard that was manicured into delicate submission to resemble a lush, colorful wilderness and it was here that Billie and Diana ran naked among the trees, making love under shimmering, leafy canopies. Hank, watching from behind the scenes, was amazed to watch Dominic's crew and their cameras seemed to probe across the surface of the intimate embrace of the two women, as though the slightest harsh brush would shatter this sacred moment. The days were filled with Billie and Diana's elegant portrayals of a pair of teenage sisters discovering their sexuality in a manner so innocently free that it was as heartwarming as it was arousing. The nights were filled with the blessed relief of the throbbing erections Hank sustained watching his girlfriend perform.

There was, however, a certain amount of tradition that could not be shaken by the filming schedule. Friday night was still movie night and it was a ritual that would be observed regardless of the circumstances. These circumstances, however, were most conducive to such a viewing as the villa had small theater with three rows of white leather couches. Dominic had arranged for a showing of Kyoshi Kurasawa's *Kairo,* and while Hank wasn't familiar with the director, he knew that this time was important to Billie and her satisfaction was close to his heart.

"I got a call from Isaac earlier today," said Dominic as he and Hank stood at the wet bar over the pool, preparing drinks. "He said he took your advice and contacted the auction house in Paris where the script was sold." Hank looked up from his mixing and raised an eyebrow. "They put him in touch with the old curator from that time period, who said the buyer's name was officially unknown, but that it was obviously Hotei Shibasaki himself. You were right, Hank."

Hank smiled, picking up a tray of drinks. "You know it," he beamed. Dominic placed two more glasses on a tray of his own and together they carried their concoctions to the theater. As they crossed one of the arching bridges, Hank's demeanor darkened, the concerns of the real world coming back to him slightly. "Isaac isn't concerned about the car bombing?"

Dominic shrugged. "God knows how Isaac really feels about anything. Right now I think he's just tickled pink that I put him in touch with this kid I met whose dad knew Hotei Shibasaki."

"Has he always been like that?"

"Yeah. We met in college and he was every bit as formal and introverted as he is now. He was studying business at Harvard and I was at NYU. He had come down to New York for Spring Break and we met at a party at my school. He'd wanted to check out the porn theaters on Time's Square and I knew the landscape.

"So you hit it off?"

"Yeah, but it was weird. The whole time it was like I was being evaluated for a job I'd always wanted, but I didn't know what it was. "

The filming at the villa wrapped shortly thereafter and Hank returned with Billie to the sound stage, which had been converted into a series of exotic rooms for the filming of the dream sequences. The filming progressed at its usual efficient clip, with Alston dropping by every few days to watch dailies with Dominic. Over time, Hank found himself fascinated by the filmmaking process and the intelligent discourse between Alston and Dominic.

One night at home, Hank and Billie turned on the television and saw a commercial that used hand puppets to tell children not to look at pornography and always report it to their parents if they ever found any lying around the house. The commercial's point was lost in its waffling nature and Hank and Billie stared in confusion at the screen until the visual faded out to be replaced by the words *Paid for by Focus for Families with the help of Intersect Productions*. Later that evening, Billie found that the commercial was already generating responses on the internet. "Artie Barrel is a turncoat!" announced one pornographic news site. "Barrel is in league with the religious Right!" declared another.

One of the articles read:

Artie Barrel, aging porn also-ran, is back in the news for the first time in nearly two decades after it was revealed that he produced the Focus for Families recent anti-pornography commercial targeting young children. The ad, which premiered on four major networks during their primetime lineups, has been meet with extreme reactions on both sides, with supporters calling the piece proof that there are in fact some decent people in the porn industry and detractors saying that Barrel has foolishly gotten in bed with the enemy.

Barrel is the founder and current CEO of Intersect Productions, a company whose output has steadily dwindled in the last ten years to the point of near non-existence. Presently the company releases a bi-monthly DVD installment of its long running Rape 'em in Their Sleeping Cunts *series as well as the infrequent release of other titles. Originally considered the king of 8mm sleaze reels, Barrel and many of his contemporaries experienced a dramatic plummet in popularity with the rise of Alston Image, the company famous for the mainstreaming of modern pornography. The long standing rivalry between the two companies came into public light when it was revealed that Barrel had been the one to leak Alston Image's intention to produce* The Lotus Wave, *a controversial script by erotic auteur Hotei Shibasaki. Many have speculated that Barrel's renewed animosity against Alston Image and its eponymous founder, Isaac Alston, is due to Alston's recent acquisition of Hank Steel, formerly a background player in various Intersect Productions releases and now a major star in the Alston Image contract stable.*

Billie realized that Hank was leaning over her shoulder as she read the article. "Can you really call it a rivalry if only one side is fighting?" he asked.

Chapter 12

FILMING ON *Awake to the Skin* was soon completed and entered post production. Word of the film's imminent release generated interest among independent art house cinemas across the country and the initial plan for a direct-to-DVD release was scrapped in favor of a theatrical release. Posters were printed, emblazoned with an NC-17 rating. Mainstream critics were sent advance copies of the film and it generated overwhelmingly positive reviews. "Dominic Daniels' latest feature film for Alston Image has once again proven not only that the porno chic ethic is not dead but that artistic vision can be 20/20, even when it's looking through sex colored glasses," said the New York Times. The Los Angeles Free Press wrote "With breathtaking virtuosity, Mr. Daniels shows that as a director he is a master pianist, one whose actors are the keys on his limitless instrument."

The press was not entirely positive, however. Alice Grausam, writing for the Conservative Moviegoer blog called the film "a two hundred minute glorification of the kind of pagan values that are destroying this country" while Women Overcoming Womanhood magazine ran an article by Andrea Danvers that called the film "a sickening embodiment of the kind of subliminal rape common to modern pornography." Neither had seen the film.

In general, however, the level of buzz surrounding the film's release was such that Dominic found himself doing interviews for two days solid. Most of them were over the phone while others asked him to appear in person or on their radio broadcast. The most public of these appearances, however, was when Dominic was asked if both he and Billie Solar would appear on a nationally syndicated afternoon talk show called *Helen*. Both agreed and drove to the television studio in Dominic's car. It wasn't until they reached the green room backstage that they learned they would be on a panel with Andrea Danvers and Alice Grausam.

"This sort of thing is part of why Isaac doesn't do interviews," said Dominic as he and Billie sat in one of two green rooms.

"What's weird about it," said Billie as she touched up her makeup in one of the room's mirrors, "is that the felt it necessary to separate us from them, but not them from each other."

"Really? I hadn't noticed."

"Yeah—Danvers and Grausam are in the other green room together right now."

Dominic snorted. "I guess those two have more in common than I thought."

Half an hour later one of the show's techs came and escorted Billie and Dominic to the set, sitting them down on the left most side of the semi-circular table at the center of the show's set. Danvers and Grausam were brought out and seated in identical chairs on the other side of the center chair where "Helen," the host, would sit to moderate the panel.

The set was dark, with only the dim, neon blue work lights illuminating the chamber. Across the table, Danvers and Grausam were sheathed in voracious daggers of pale azure light and they stared back at Billie and Dominic with a cold uniformity that seemed to grow outwards from their dim illumination. Beyond the boundary of the stage lamps set the audience, the light only just reaching far enough to catch vague outlines of the mass of faces. The few faces that were visible were cold and motionless, their features further shrouded in darkness.

Finally, the lights came up and the stage was illuminated, revealing itself to be modeled to look like the living room of a modern town home and suddenly devoid of the ominous, brooding countenance it had known just a few moments ago. Neon signs about the audience bearing the word "applause" began to light up as Helen, the show's pantsuit clad middle-aged host walked out, beaming vacantly at the crowd as the clapped their hands with Pavlovian fervor.

Helen moved at the center of the show's stage and waited for the applause to die out before speaking. "Hello everyone, thank you for joining us today," she began. "Since the invention of the camera, pornography has been a hot button issue in our modern society. For some people it's just harmless fun while for others it's seen as degrading and dangerous. My panel today comes from both sides of the debate.

"On the left we have Dominic Daniels and Billie Solar. Dominic is the director of the recent erotic film *Awake to the Skin*, which premiers this Friday in select cities. His work has previously been met with critical acclaim, so much so that it is regarded as successfully crossing over into the mainstream. Next to him is Billie Solar, one of the sexy leading ladies in *Awake to the Skin* and a frequent player in Dominic's work.

"Across the table are Andrea Danvers and Alice Grausam. Ms. Danvers is the author of *Balls Without Testicles: a New Perspective on Women in the Work-*

place and is an outspoken critic of the porn industry. Her next book, *Smutscape: How the Porn Industry Has Enslaved Humanity* has just been released. Next to her is Alice Grausam, prominent conservative commentator and the author of *Red, White and Aborted: How Liberals are Destroying America one Blood-Soaked Fetus at a Time.* Give them all a hand!" The audience resumed its euphoric applause as Helen took her seat at the center of the table.

"Alrighty then," chirped Helen as the central camera zoomed in on her. "Dominic, why don't you tell us a little bit about your film *Awake to the Skin?*"

"Well," began Dominic, trying his best to remain cordial in the face of Helen's smarminess, "it's an art film which uses human sexuality as the focal point for a series of psycho-dramatic vignettes that illustrate a woman's rebirth as a sexually uninhibited being. This occurs because she is beaten into a coma by her abusive husband and while in the hospital is told erotic stories by her sister, with whom she has shared a long running sexual relationship."

"And when she wakes up, she's got a new perspective on life?"

"I don't want to give away the ending, but that's the idea."

"Mrs. Danvers, have you seen Mr. Daniels' new film and what do you think of it?"

"I haven't seen it, Helen, but I can tell you what I think about it," began Andrea, her gelatinous body rippling as she spoke. "The porn industry has realized that we feminists have seen through their little games. 'Free love' during the 1960's was just a declaration by men that women better be ready to bend over and service their male overlords whenever those slave-drivers demanded it. Then when the pornographic film industry got going full steam in the 1970's it wasn't long before we feminists realized that these were just brainwashing recruitment films for male chauvinism. Ever since then we've fought bravely to help these women realize that they're being exploited."

"They are being exploited," Dominic interjected.

"So you admit it?"

"Exploiting something means 'to utilize, especially for profit.' That is what I do, but it doesn't mean I think less of the people who I 'exploit.'"

"See—that was my next point, Helen. This man is just uses people."

"I use their abilities the same way any other employer would with any other skill set."

"But this is different."

"How?"

"Because its *sex*."

"So?"

"So sex has been used throughout history to enslave women!"

"I agree. But that's not what I'm doing."

"Yes it is—you're a man."

"And you're a bigot."

"No I am not—all men are rapists. And those that haven't raped yet benefit from rape in general."

"How?"

"Because rapists enslave women."

"What about the ones who rape other men?"

"That doesn't count."

"Why?"

"Because those are other men!"

"So rape is sometimes okay?"

"I didn't say that."

"And I didn't say that I'm a male chauvinist slave-driver but you seem damn well ready to put words in my mouth."

"You see this, Helen? See how he makes references to mouths? That's how you know where his mind is at all times. His warped, perverted brain is thinking about inserting his penis into my mouth!"

"I wasn't talking about your mouth and it was just a figure of speech."

"See, Helen—he's making fun of my figure!"

"Ummm… yeah…" began Helen, her show business veneer cracking slightly as she searched for words. "It is my understanding that Mr. Daniels' new film is meant to show the higher brow artistic side of porn, or rather erotica."

"Erotica is just repackaged pornography for a high class of consumer."

"Then you admit that there are higher classes of people who can appreciate pornography?" asked Dominic.

"No—just people who use a higher class of posturing to hide their perversions."

"How do you know this to be true?"

"Because I'm an expert on feminist theory."

"It sounds like you're just an expert on your own opinion."

"I am a feminist; therefore my opinion reflects the opinion of all women."

"What about the ones that don't agree with you?"

"Those are just women who have been brainwashed by the patriarchy. They watch pornography like yours that exploits racist and sexist stereotypes and are coerced in thinking that their sole function in life is to make men happy."

"Why do you bring up racism?"

"Well as I understand it you've got a film out called *Jungle Bunnies 2: The Shaft of Slamdingo*. How can you justify a title such as that?"

"It's just making fun of political correctness. And it's a bad pun."

"Oh that's not the purpose of it. I'll tell you what its purpose is."

"Oh yes—please, Andrea. Do tell me what *I* meant in *my* movie."

"Well, as I'm sure you know, white men are the primary viewers of interracial porn."

"They are?"

"Yes, they are. And the reason they like it is that they can see the white woman being degraded by the object of their hatred: the black man."

"That's completely inconsistent with the history of racism. Racists of all stripes have always and without exception been opposed to interracial relations and regarded the women of their cultures as being sacred and untouchable by people in other races."

"That's not true."

"Why not?"

"Because I'm a feminist."

"So your point of view is superior to hundreds of years of observed and documented history?"

"No, my opinion determines what is and is not observable history. And you're constantly using that same black man in your films."

"Slamdingo Stevens?"

"Exactly. In another one of your films he plays a high school principle that enforces discipline by having sex with unruly students."

"That was one of the first movies we used him in. It was called *Lean in Me.*"

"And you don't realize how that communicates that it's okay for men to tame and control women using their sexuality?"

"No, Andrea. I think it's meant to be seen as an intentionally bad pun to give people a laugh."

"And how does Mr. Stevens feel about it?"

"He thought it was hilarious."

"No he doesn't. He's in an oppressed minority and therefore he needs to be educated on what he really wants."

"So you're saying that you know what's best for all people in all minority groups and what they think about everything all the time but I'm the one who's bigoted because I did a play on words?"

"Yes, that's correct."

"How do you feel about all this, Alice?" asked Helen.

"How do you think I feel, Helen" clucked Alice Grausam, straightening her cocktail dress as she sat up. "I'm having to sit here listening to two liberals bitch and moan about semantics when everyone can see that they're both wrong."

"And why is that?"

"Because they're both liberals!"

"Do you consider yourself a liberal?" asked Helen, turning to Dominic.

"I'm certainly no conservative, but I'm definitely on the left side of libertarian. I support the right of all persons to live as they wish but I still want to make money and keep it."

"Exactly—you're a capitalist and therefore opposed to social progress." spat Andrea.

"Why does wanting to make my own money and keep it mean I'm opposed to social progress?"

"Because rich white men have been opposed to social progress in the past."

"That's true. I'm not."

"Yes you are."

"Why?"

"Because you have money!"

"So?"

"So if you were in favor of social progress you'd be in favor of doing away with money altogether."

"Why?"

"Because worldwide poverty is the only way to guarantee equality."

"Then to hell with equality."

"And you're the one that's joining forces with a far right wing conservative anyway," interjected Billie.

"Is that true, Andrea," asked Helen, "do you think of yourself as having allied with the far right?"

"No, Helen, we haven't allied. Rather, we've conjoined our goals around the common issue of pornography and have restructured our agendas to accommodate this partnership.

"So you've joined forces with a conservative, as if that's going to help your socially progressive goals."

"It was a conservative who freed the slaves," Alice interjected.

"No, Alice," replied Dominic in a tone that suggested he was speaking to a child, "it was a *Republican* who freed the slaves. You can be a liberal Republican just like you can be a conservative Democrat."

"No you can't."

"Yes you can."

"No you can't."

"Yes you can."

"No you can't."

"Yes you can."

"Okay, okay, okay" gasped Helen, visibly worried that she was losing control of the room. "Alice, do you see yourself as having anything in common with Andrea?"

"Well we're certainly opposed to pornography, Helen. We both agree that pornography is degrading and insulting to women. Liberals have always tried to position themselves as being the ones who are progressive and forward thinking on women's issues, but ultimately it is the conservatives who have always said that race, gender, sexual orientation, etc, are irrelevant and that people should just be judged for who, not what, they are."

"That's complete crap," said Billie. "Conservatives have always fought tooth and nail against social progress for disadvantaged groups and then when change finally does occur they pretend like they were for it all along and the other side was just making a big stink about nothing."

"You're all so politically correct that you won't even think of talking to someone on the other side of the table."

"We're doing it right now!" shouted Dominic.

"Yeah—and don't talk about political correctness," said Billie, her irritability showing. "You conservatives are the ones who demanded that 'safe sex' be rebranded as 'safer sex.' You demanded that creationism be taught alongside evolution out of respect for your religious views. That's political correctness through and through. Why is it worse for liberals to be politically correct?"

"Well, for example, you're the ones who say that we have to call black people African Americans."

"And why do you think that is?"

"Because you're trying to recast conservatives as the racists when in reality-"

"No—it's because you conservatives can't seem to call African Americans by any names that aren't disparaging."

"Oh you need to grow up and grow a pair. You think that blacks today are offended by being called niggers? They say it to each other all the time."

"Oh give me a break, cunt."

"How dare you call me that?" screamed Alice, hellfire blazing in her eyes.

"Why are you so offended? We're both women so can't we call each other cunts?"

"But I mean blacks say 'nigger' when they like each other."

"So it's okay to throw epithets at people you *like*?"

"Are we still talking about my movie?" asked Dominic.

"You better believe we are," said Andrea. "And I'll tell you something else, Dominic Daniels. It breaks my heart that a beautiful sister of mine like Billie over there—"

"I'm not your sister."

"Yes you are—you're a fellow woman."

"That fact of my existence doesn't make me your ally, you bigoted fool."

"You need to shut up and learn your place!" barked Andrea.

"My place? My place? You're the big feminist loud mouth and you're telling me to learn my place? Aren't I one of your majestic, beautiful, sisters that's just as valid and important as you?"

"Yes, but that doesn't mean you don't need my guidance. You're brainwashed into supporting this rapist."

"Dominic's never raped anybody."

"He rapes you every time he looks at you."

"Do you even know what rape is?"

"I sure do—it's when men—all men, every single last pee-pee waving one of them—succeed in objectifying all women as nothing more than come dumpsters. That's what rape is."

"I thought rape was when one person forces another to have sex with them," said Dominic, eyes rolled to the heavens.

"A male rapist like you would seek to pervert the reality of rape but the fact of the matter is that your kind raped Billie when you took away all of her job opportunities and forced her to be a whore."

"I didn't take away her job opportunities—if anything I provided one."

"That's what the patriarchy does—it takes opportunities away from women and puts them in a position where all they can do to survive is sell their bodies. If Billie here were actually a feminist-"

"ENOUGH!" shouted Billie, slamming her palms down on the table as she rose to her feet. "Don't tell me that I'm not a feminist. A thinking woman with self respect, independence and an awareness of the values inherit to adulthood is a feminist. And the only thing that is implied by such feminism is that women are equal to men. And the nature of that equality is only that gender is not a determining factor in the assessment of a person's ability and character. All else is just empty, bitter superiority.

"You assume that I was forced into this business by a society that wouldn't allow me to earn a decent income or hold a more respectable office. I would counter by saying that I am a university graduate with a degree in music and a concert pianist. Before I entered the porn industry I was a first call session player and very in demand as a soloist at private functions and I still give concerts from time to time. Whether you want to acknowledge it or not, there are women in porn who are college graduates, come from affluent families, have doctorates from legitimate schools, and consider themselves intellectuals. They might be a minority in the porn industry but guess what? They're a minority in society at large. I got into the music business because I wanted to make money doing what I loved and I got into porn because I wanted to make more money doing something I loved more. By making the assumption that I became a porn star because I was too weak, foolish, uneducated, and low class to choose something better, you make yourself the bigot. Do not attempt to say that you are not a bigot simply because you think your bigotry is justified by your platform. A platform founded on bigotry can butt heads with preexisting forms of bigotry, but it can never rise above their primitive notions of prejudice.

"The very best in the feminist movement were the ones who fought for the right to make choices with the understanding that some women would choose lifestyles that they themselves did not agree with; the ones who understood that it was the right to make a choice that was the goal, not the installation of women in token positions of power and influence. Those who shrieked that women ought to overthrow and enslave men because all men were only a hair's width away from committing rape are bigots. They are just as narrow minded and ignorant as the man-favoring prejudice they claim to oppose. Less than a century ago, people in this country actually believed that African Americans needed to be controlled because otherwise they would only descend into rape and sexual violence. We now realize how sick and distorted a perspective that is, and yours ought to join its ranks.

"I am not objectified by pornography. I am objectified by my gender. Pornography is only the observation and documentation of the natural state of my existence. All people are objects of lust in the eyes of those who are attracted to them. It is the intelligent person who can see and recognize that the ability to arouse feelings of lust does not represent the totality of a person's existence and appreciate the people they lust after for the complete person that they are. An objectification means that a person's existence is defined, in its perceived totality, as representative of a specific and limited set of concepts. In the sex-negative view on pornography, the charge of objectification means that a woman is to be viewed as a means of sexual gratification and nothing more—that she is devoid of feelings, thoughts, dreams, desires, hopes, fears, philosophies, or any other traits of a deeper human existence. This supposition is logically flawed because it neglects to consider that all persons are objectified by their professions. If you go to the grocery store you see the checkout clerk as nothing more than a checkout clerk. You see them as the person who will scan and bag your items, take your money, and return the correct change and nothing more. By your logic you have objectified this person as a functionary and are guilty of objectification. You have not taken the time to make a personal connection with this person to ensure that you are interacting with them on a human level before asking them, out of mutual respect and a relationship grounded in equality, to perform the task for which they were hired. This is true of every type of occupation—you and the employee both understand the pre-determined nature of your relationship to each other and are content to act accordingly. Indeed, it would be impossible for the checkout clerk to perform their job if they were to develop personal relationships with each person they served. Similarly, the terms of sex work carry with them the understanding that one party shall provide and the other receive sexual gratification and that the mark of respect in the exchange is money, not emotional connectivity. If you cry 'no—that's not always the case—sometimes I meet store employees who become by friends' and so on, then you shoot yourself in the foot: if you can make this connection with a person whose service you pay for, why is it impossible for the clients of sex workers or the consumers of pornography to make the same connection, especially when the act being traded on is of the most intimate possible nature?

"Don't say that pornography motivates men to violence. Throughout the ages of artistic expression there have been those who are convinced that the necessary moral ambiguity of artistic appreciation will inspire others to violence. Mark David Chapman said he was inspired to shoot John Lennon by reading *Catcher in the Rye*. Charles Manson claimed to be inspired by the White Album. John Hinckley Jr. was inspired by *Taxi Driver*. People who are prone to violence are prone to violence whether they have any external stimulation or not. There is no reason for the vast majority of persons—who are more than capable of self-control—to pay the deficit created by those who choose to lash out violently."

"Yes, women have been oppressed throughout history. But to simply exchange women for men in the position of power is missing the point. Do that and in another thousand years men will just be marching in the streets, demanding their rights and civil liberties. Progress is not made simply by exchanging the roles of slave and master. Progress is made when both sides realize the futility of the master/slave relationship.

"I grew up in a psycho-religious household and as such I found escape in the philosophies of the great feminist writers. The ones who advocated gender equality. The ones who said women should receive equal protection under the law. The ones that taught me to be proud of my sexuality and proud of the fact that I wished to experience it and call it my own. My life has been built around the teachings of such people and I live my life everyday grateful for the courage that those women showed to the phallocentric traditionalists that had oppressed them. But I also live in the real world. I understand that not everybody is a bully. I understand that there are people who are different from me but still want to be treated with kindness and respect. In other words, I'm a feminist because I celebrate my womanhood and make it into a thing of artistic beauty without becoming a narrow-minded, militant shrew. You're a feminist because you looked between your legs and found something to complain about.

"But what you don't understand about feminism," said Billy darkly, "and the most important thing of all is that-"

"My producer is telling me that we need to go to commercial," said Helen, visibly relieved. "When we come back I'll be showing my studio audience and all of you at home how to make scented candles out of chocolate chips and crayons. Do you have any parting words, Alice?"

"Just how glad I am not to be a pimp and a whore like those two over there, Helen."

The applause signs flashed on and the audience responded enthusiastically.

Chapter 13

IT WAS A SUNNY AFTERNOON in the Valley and Rod Wielding was enjoying lunch with Janet Drillride at the outdoor pavilion of a hipster-chic restaurant. Lost in the conversation, gourmet salad and fine white wine, Rod was unaware of the buzzard shaped newspaper columnist that approached his table.

"Excuse me, you two work for Alston Image, right?" he said with feigned politeness.

"Ah, yes," said Rod, reservedly irritated with the approach.

"I wonder if you two would care to answer some questions."

"Probably not, but go ahead," said Janet.

"Well, I'm doing an op-ed on the spread of STDs in porn."

"Okay," she replied.

"Well, what do you think of them?"

"I don't," said Rod.

"You don't? You don't think about syphilis and herpes and gonorrhea?"

"No, I don't."

"They're rather unpleasant," added Janet.

"But are you aware that according to Cal-OSHA regulations, it's illegal for bodily fluids to touch human skin?"

"Cal-OSHA can kiss my cunt," she spat back.

"More precisely," continued Rod, "We choose to do our jobs in full knowledge that our bodies will come in contact with other people's bodily fluids and we consent to have that happen. OSHA safety regulations should protect us from things we don't want to have happen."

"You're essentially telling us what we have to do with our bodies." Said Janet. "What about mixed martial artists? They come in contact with bodily fluids all the time in their fights. Do they have to be shut down as well?"

"Well, no, but that's different."

"How?"

"Because it's not porn."

"Oh," said Janet and Rod together.

"What about if I have unprotected sex with someone on my own time," asked Rod.

"That's fine, I guess," said the reporter, his crooked countenance recoiling slightly.

"So it's not okay for me to choose to do something for work that it's okay for me to do in my private life?"

"Look, what about the spread of AIDS? Don't you realize that there have been six cases of HIV reported in the porn industry in the last ten years?"

"So?" replied Rod. "There are parts of the world where rate is six in every ten *people.*"

"At best," added Janet.

"Doesn't that worry you?"

"Does it worry me that there are risks associated with my job?" she asked.

"Yes."

"Certainly. That's why I take steps to minimize them. That's why I get tested every month."

"But testing didn't stop those six people from getting infected," retorted the reporter.

"The point of testing isn't to prevent individuals from getting HIV," interjected Rod.

"Then what's the point?"

"The point is to stop HIV from getting loose in the industry. People will get HIV—it's an STD and whenever people have sex there's the potential for the spread of STDs. Think about safety testing in cars—the goal isn't to stop the crash from happening; the goal is to minimize the damage when a crash does happen. Our industry has an excellent track record of stopping the subsequent spread of HIV once it's identified in one of our performers. Can you name any other field of production where the entire industry would halt production because of one person's health problems? All these Marxist assholes that go around demanding regulations for everything sure don't acknowledge when and industry is regulating correctly on its own."

"But the point is that industries can't be trusted to self-regulate, so they require compulsory government regulation?"

"Even when they already are regulating themselves?"

"Well of course—it's obvious that any business that claims to be effectively self-regulating is just lying."

"Would you please go away?" asked Janet.

"Fine," sputtered the reporter, "but you're industry still operates illegally."

"Well whoopty-shit," said Rod, wiping salad dressing from his mouth. "We're operating illegally. Go down to the local police precinct and tell them that they have to stop protecting the taxpayers from murderers and rapists and robbers so that they can go shut down an industry that brings in a massive chunk of tax revenue for Van Nuys because some people are fucking for fun and profit and you don't like it. I'm sure they'll jump right on that."

The Families for Families agent who had introduced himself as a reporter stormed off and, when he was out of sight of Rod and Janet, drew the portable tape recorder from his inner jacket pocket and erased it, annoyed that he had been unable to get them to say what he'd wanted.

"You'll be in charge until I get back," said Alston. Abe Lattimore was sitting across the desk from him, turning pale as he watched his boss packing a briefcase with various documents and files followed by a laptop computer. "Just keep me posted on things, but otherwise you know what to do. All the projects that will get the green light in the next three months have already been approved."

"Isaac, with all due respect," began Abe, aware as he was that Alston's plans to fly off to Japan were inflexible, "*Awake to the Skin* just came out."

"So? It's been out for one weekend and it already made double its production costs."

"Well, yes, that's true but surely you've heard the outcry in the wake of the *Helen* disaster."

"Heard it? I've been actively ignoring it," replied Alston, nodding to the window wall behind him and the crowd below. "Dominic won't be doing interviews for the time being."

"But Isaac... those two ladies—Grausam and Danvers—are coming together in support of Families for Families. The PR department is pulling its hair out."

"I don't see why. Since when has Alston Image ever acknowledged our antagonists publically."

"We don't. But this is worse than before. There are more people picketing out there every day—hell they've shut down all the streets in a two mile radius. Surely you've noticed that?"

"Of course I have. That's why I've been taking a helicopter to work."

"And you don't plan to do anything to remedy this situation?"

"Of course I do. I'm going to make *The Lotus Wave.*"

"How will that change anything? You've already got one controversial new movie out there."

"How are our subscription numbers?"

Abe sighed. "Higher than ever."

"Exactly. You of all people should know better than to reason with me. I know you don't understand how this film will change things for the better, but I do and I think Hotei Shibasaki does as well." And with that he picked up the briefcase and headed across the room for the roof access, where his chopper waited.

Thirty minutes later, Alston was on his jet and the jet was in the air. Alston sat at the circular table in the cabin and spread the documents in his briefcase before him. The first thing he took out was a legal pad of hand written notes he'd made about the whereabouts of Hoeti Shibasaki based on his correspondence with Peter Wingrove. It read:

* *Believed to be living among the burakumin.*
* *Would have to be in his mid eighties if still alive.*
* *Was living in Shibuya, Tokyo when Peter's father knew him.*
* *Had no permanent soundstages, preferred to work abroad to evade the strict Japanese pornography laws.*
* *Family owned a slaughterhouse, which he was poised to inherit.*

The last point was underlined several times. Alston regarded the page and drummed a pen on the table top as he contemplated the current state of affairs. In the few days since the *Helen* incident the protestors, forever on the verge of riot, had swelled exponentially and Alston had chartered three armored vehicles to transport his actors and employees to the building. Across the country companies were laying-off workers in record numbers while their CEOs made record bonuses from government bailout money. When news crews interviewed the protestors outside Alston's building they inevitably spoke to blue-collar laborers that had been laid off. It seemed, Alston pondered, that they thought that their economic woes were not the result of a stoppage in the trickle-down economics so long advocated by the right, but rather because of some great moral degeneracy that had displeased the job-giving gods; that their moral outrage at pornography would forestall their disillusionment with the American Dream.

The protestors were finding new angles, however. Many pointed to the liberal in the white house and the supposed liberals at Alston Image and alleged that the government was secretly working in conjunction with the porn industry to corrupt America. They could not understand how Alston Image, out of all other porn houses, seemed to be recession proof. Spiritualists declared that there was a spell cast over the business and Alston was in league with Satan. Secular moralists cried that with no jobs, society had become so lost in its purpose that people no longer had any moral grounding to keep them away from pornography. The speculation of both camps did not, however, affect the reality that Alston Image had not needed bailout money nor asked for it. Their brash declarations that pornography spread disease did not change the fact that out of the three hundred people that worked for Alston Image, three hundred of them were negative for HIV, hepatitis, herpes, syphilis, gonorrhea, and most other STDs, with minor, curable infections being the only things infrequently exchanged. And their angered cries that pornography catered to the worst elements in society did not change the fact that most mainstream multi-media entertainment shops stocked Alston Image products. It seemed to be the inflexible state of reality—in the face of their shrill and increasingly hysterical assertions to the contrary—that seemed to be at the root of their mania.

Andrea Danvers and Alice Grausam had announced that they would put aside their differences and—in a landmark display of bipartisanship—collaborate on a new book bashing the porn industry. The spirit of unrelenting bipartisanship seemed to be sweeping through Washington as well, with Democrats caving to every single demand made by their minority counterparts. The president spoke frequently on the importance of the strong serving the needs of the weak and that in an effort to put aside petty bickering over who was right or wrong his administration would be devoted entirely to serving the needs of the down-trodden conservatives. The backlash among Democrats had been negative to say the least, but they'd taken it with the same kind of couch-slumping apathy that washed over the nation as a whole.

It was almost perverted, Alston mused, how apathy fueled the outrage. Within every lazy eyed tree stump of a human being there was a stale, fragile child that feared change. It was a cold, quivering thing in a glass box that clung to its meager shelter with wavering cowardice. It was the ultimate contradiction to survival: a thing that, when confronted with the knowledge of its own vulnerability would cling to the vulnerability rather than embrace the knowledge. The conservatives had long claimed that this contradiction was the province of the left, with its preference for the welfare state but Alston felt more and more certain that all along this had been nothing more than posturing on the right; that conservatives knew their so called "strength" was little more than a hollow façade and that the slimmest of hairline fractures to that façade would send them reeling into a panic more commonly associated with 1950's housewives and domesticated drag queens.

Next to the handwritten list was a photograph of Hotei Shibasaki in his prime. The picture showed a man whose jaw line held the chilling squareness of his countrymen that underscored a set of eyes that burned with a steady, mastered passion. Alston found the face to be a mirror and secretly felt himself molding his face from the inside out, so that Shibasaki would find the same mirror when they met one another face to face.

Though it was the middle of winter, the San Fernando Valley seemed oblivious to the season. This observation briefly crossed Melvin Crankshadow's mind as he looked out over the throng of onlookers, each of them baking in the afternoon sun. Sweat poured down the bridge of Melvin's nose as he became aware that the speaker and the podium—a local representative from Families for Families—was wrapping up his introduction. Rising when he heard the applause, Melvin shook the man's hand and smiled as he turned and waved to the crowd.

The small stage had been hastily erected across the street from the Alston Image offices when Melvin suddenly had news to reveal that even he had never thought possible. As he surveyed the cheering crowd he beamed to himself, inwardly satisfied that his faith had guided him to this moment.

"Ladies and gentlemen," he began, the microphone feeding back for a moment as he spoke. "I look out at this crowd and I see patriots." There was a boom of cheering and applause. "I see people who aren't afraid to take a stand for what's right!" Another boom. "I see people who have put aside their differences and come together in the name of freedom, justice, and the American way of life!" A third and even louder boom. "Before this great crusade you had many different names. Some of you were hippies, others were Christians, and still others were liberals, conservatives, left wing, right wing, and many other titles but the winds of this crusade have finally caught both wings of the American political spectrum, and we are united against pornography!" The crowd erupted again, this time stomping their feet and shaking their hands in the air.

"When I started Families for Families," Melvin continued, "it was with the humble initiative of helping to cure the addiction to pornography that afflicts so many people. Now that initiative has boomed in to a nation-wide campaign to combat this crippling social disease. Who spreads STDs? The porn industry! Who promotes violence against women? The porn industry! Who convinces teens that sex is okay? The porn industry! And the time has come to take a stand against this public menace."

The crowd erupted again and Melvin motioned to the side of the stage, where three women draped in large body coverings ascended a small set of stairs to take the platform next to Melvin Crankshadow. The coverings were long thick dress like garments that covered the women in their entirety, accompanied by similar pieces that covered their heads with only a mesh net to see out of. There was no indication that they were women—all skin was covered and no shape was visible. They stood to Melvin's right as he directed the crowd's applause to their arrival. One of the garments was blue, one was black, and one was grey.

"The latest step in our campaign," began Melvin when the crowd response had mellowed, "is to introduce these beautiful new fashion designs for women who no longer wish to be objectified. We've dubbed them 'dignity sheathes' and they guarantee that no woman will have to suffer the indignity of being ogled ever again. Now women are free from the horrible objectification that comes from a sinful mind and a sinful culture.

"Think of a bird in a cage. In a perfect world, that bird would be able to fly anywhere it wanted without a second thought. But that bird doesn't live in a perfect world. It lives in a vicious, dangerous world where predators will feed on it if it's not careful. So ask yourself which is better: the freedom *to* fly around wherever it wants or the freedom *from* being devoured? The dignity sheathe is an answer to that question. It says that no woman should have to be raped, no woman should inspire a man to violence, and no woman should inspire men to quarrel with one another. It says 'enough!' to being held in the jaws of our base level desires. And it says that we are ready and willing to stand up for what's right!"

There was another blast of applause from the crowd, during which time the woman draped in grey moved to the podium. "My name is Ilene Simmons," she began with a righteous tone that was slightly muted by the garment. "Last fall I found out that my son was addicted to pornography produced by that man" she pointed to the Alston Image building from beneath the dignity sheathe "and now my son is getting the help that he needs thanks to Families for Families. I am wearing this dignity sheathe because of my commitment to helping the children!"

There was cheering and then the black sheathed model took the podium. "My name is Alice Grausam and all my life I've fought back against the steady tide of slut-indoctrination that liberals have been forcing onto our society. I'm wearing this sheathe because I believe that it frees women from the curse that is shame over their sinful bodies. Now no human being can look upon me with lust and that is why I support the liberating efforts of Families for Families!"

And finally, the blue sheathed model took the podium. "My name is Andrea Danvers, and I am wearing this sheathe because one man too many told me to put a bag over my head when-"

"Ladies and gentlemen, the dedicated women of Families for Families!" said Melvin Crankshadow sliding back in front of the microphone. "But there's one more person that I want to thank…" Melvin looked around the audience to make sure that Artie Barrel was not in the audience "and that man is Artie Barrel! He is living proof that there is a bipartisan solution to this scourge that plagues our country!"

Artie Barrel watched the proceedings from his living room in Las Vegas. He sipped a beer as Crankshadow continued extolling his praises to the cheering crowd. It never occurred to him to wonder why he hadn't been asked to appear. Thin beams of sun cut through the largely overcast sky, providing the only illumination besides the television.

Ralphie entered from the kitchen with a beer and some chips. Sitting next to his father, he crossed his feet and propped them on the coffee table. When the broadcast finally hit a commercial break Ralphie picked up the remote and muted the television. He took a sip from his drink then spoke: "Daddy, I don't know if you've noticed, but this shit you're doing with the preacher aint exactly helping our image."

"Don't talk like that, boy. He's a nice man."

"Well, I'm sure he is but you know porn and the church don't mix."

"Don't say that, son. You heard the man. Bipartisan and such." Artie took a swig from his own beer as his son watched, nonplused.

"I guess I just don't get why you've stopped trying to be the king of sleaze like you used to be."

"Look where it got me, boy!" choked Artie with a hoarse cough. "I don't know if you noticed but the whole reason we live in this shit hole is cause of me being the king of sleaze!"

"Well what about Isaac Alston? He makes porn too and he doesn't-"

"Don't use that fucking name!" boomed Artie, throwing his beer across the room without rising from his slump. The bottle shattered against the wall, sending a burst of liquid and glass across the television set. "Isaac Alston is a fucking shit-stirrer. We had a balance back in the day—the high society types were all good and conservative and pure and we were their secret shame. We were like any drug—everyone was doing it and nobody admitted it. Then this little Yankee intellectual from kike-town comes on the scene and he starts putting out porn like he's doing something respectable. Like it aint something to be ashamed of. And he upsets the balance. He gets people talking. He raises the bar. Suddenly porn aint some shit you shoot in the back room of your house and sell in an alley. Suddenly there's all these feminist bitches in the business talking unionizing and worker's rights and shit. I mean, here I am trying to be a drug dealer and this Alston bitch starts acting like a… a…"

"Pharmacist?"

"Yeah! Starts carrying around with his nose in the air, like he's helping folks out. Like he's providing real entertainment or something. Like there's not something wrong with what we do just how we do it. People act like he's revolutionizing the industry when all he's doing is making it harder for us real types to function."

"What about movies like Deep Throat and such?"

"What about 'em?"

"Well they were getting played in theaters—I thought that was what made porn mainstream."

"They got close. But VHS put a stop to it. First people didn't have to go to theaters anymore. They could get their smut in the mail, get it at back alley stores, all of that, and so there was no reason to make movies that people would go to the theater to see. That was when I was flying high. My company could turn out thirty jerk-off titles a month and people ate it up. But they ate it up cause they understood it—they knew there was something wrong with them looking at all that smut and we knew there was something wrong with them too. The shame was what kept it going. That's how masochism works.

"But then Isaac Alston comes in with all these new ideas. Specialty cable channels. Porn on demand in hotel rooms. He trots out this Dominic Daniels shithead who starts giving the bitches acting lessons and wham! His movies are getting reviewed in serious film magazines! Oh they're every bit as perverted as what we put out, but instead of feeling ashamed, they have people laughing about their perversions! Suddenly people are talking about their fetishes over coffee like it's not vice anymore. And my videos slowly stop selling cause there aint hardly no shame going around no more. It's like somebody figured out how to sell heroin that don't make you sick and its putting all us vice merchants out of business."

"Is that really what this business is to you, Daddy? Vice?"

"Of course boy! Don't tell me you're getting that snooty pussy-assed Alston Image thinking in your head!"

"I dunno what I thought about it, daddy. It's always just been the family business. It's what I grew up in and what feels natural."

"I guess that's where I failed you, boy. The only thing natural about what I do is that it's wrong. I got into this shit cause I'm no good at anything else. The niggers had the dope trade all closed up so I needed something I could pedal. Get an eight millimeter camera and a couple runaways and you've got yourself rent money for a whole fucking year."

Ralphie thought about this for a moment. "So... I guess what I'm asking is... what makes you do what you do? What makes want to do this?"

Artie thought for a moment, realizing that his son was asking for something deeper—a frame to put around the respect he wanted to have for his father. "When I was a boy," Artie began, his voice barely above a muttered whisper, "Me and my folks lived in Kansas. Heart of tornado country. They would have those twisters come through all the fucking time, and every time they came through this siren would go off. It was an old air raid siren, one left over from World War II. And that thing used to get to me. It'd make me really afraid. I was about three when I heard my first one. I remember even back then pappy would smack me if I started crying so I just had to hold real still down in the basement and hope that it all went over okay. That sound—it was so loud you could hear the sound of the operator turning the crank. One day I was at school and a man—a meteorologist—came to talk to our class. I'd never paid attention much, but when he started talking about predicting tornadoes, I put up my hand and asked if he rang the siren. The other kids laughed at me but he said that was one of his jobs around the news station. This was a small town and I would see him around from time to time. I don't think he ever remembered me, but I would always look at him and think 'there goes the man that controls fear. That guy right there can make the whole town afraid whenever he wants to.' I respected him more than I respected my own daddy cause I knew he could make my daddy scared too. That's what's always moved me. I wanted to be the one who turned that crank."

"You wanted to be a weather man?"

"No, boy—pay attention! I wanted to control fear. I learned real early that if you control fear you control people. That's what porn should be—fear. Fear that the bitch is gonna get her throat cut. Fear that the subscribers are going to get their perversions mailed to their bosses. Fear. Plain and simple. When Isaac Alston came along, people stopped being afraid. He ruined me and that's all there is too it."

Ralphie realized he'd been looking at the floor as he'd listened to his father. "I want to put a stop to it daddy. I want to put things right. I'll kill Isaac Alston if I have to but I want to put things right for you."

"You don't need to kill Isaac Alston, son. Make that man a martyr and his descendants will conquer the world. What you need to do is just remove one piece—just the right piece—from his structure and the whole tower will come crashing down."

"What piece is that?"

"I think you can guess."

"Dominic Daniels?"

"Nope—too legendary."

"His VP?"

"Who would care? You need just the right balance."

"That faggot Hank Steel?"

"Close. But he's not the block you take out. He's the first piece to fall after you take that block out."

"So… somebody close to him?"

"Yeah."

"Who's closest to him?"

"I think you know the answer to that."

"I think I do too."

"Somebody that tons of people want dead."

"Yeah."

"Somebody that's been getting death threats as long as she's been in the business so nobody would know it was you."

"Yeah."

"Somebody that means something to every single person at that company."

"Yeah."

"You know who I mean?"

"Yeah."

Chapter 14

HANK STEEL watched as a single strand of maroon fluid poured from the bottle of wine, its majestic curves weaving in and out of itself as it fell in an unbroken arc down to the chalice formed by Billie's lips. When the luscious troth had been filled he sat the bottle on the nightstand and suckled her lips tenderly, the wine running down her cheeks in an identical bead on either side. He knew in that instant that this was the purist bliss possible. The manifold hesitations that had brought him only reservation in the face of what he'd hoped would be true love were now laid cold and dead in a long forgotten past.

Only a half hour ago he'd come home to the house he and Billie now shared bearing a sack of groceries. The house had been dark save for the light above Billie's piano, where she had been practicing for an upcoming concert. It was not the first time he'd heard her play, but in the hallowed stillness of the darkened house he'd been struck by the welling melody and the innocent, somberly playful articulation that her fingers brought to it. Hank had found himself leaning against the door frame into the living room, each angelic note stroking his heart with the same delicate revere that Billie stroked the keys. When she'd finished, the last notes seeming to hover in the swirling embers of the piece's beauty, he'd realized there were tears in his eyes. And in the fading glow of those final notes, the words that fell across his tongue seemed to be guiding his mouth for their own purposes:

"I love you."

At first the words had seemed like something his lips had groped for silently and he wasn't sure if she'd heard him. But as the words joined the last strands of the piano's resonance, she'd raised her head slightly, looking over her shoulder at him.

"I love you too."

He was distantly aware of the sound of Billie's good china rattling in the cabinet across the way as he'd crossed the living room and taken her in his arms. The next words came as a further surprise, but he'd said them never-theless:

"I love you and I want you to marry me."

Their kiss was unbroken as she wrapped her legs around his waist and let him carry her into the kitchen. They banged into the refrigerator as he opened it and withdrew a bottle of wine. Now, in bed and yielded to a naked-ness that went far beyond their discarding of clothes, they drank of the wine as they drank of each other. Hank knew that she was his life's true love and the thought of their marriage filled him with a happiness so deep and rich it made his body ache.

He'd known that they loved each other when the nature of their love-making had changed. Where it had first been an extension of the playfully ravenous lust they exhibited in their on-camera performances, it had grown over time to be an understood extension of the words, looks, and touches that they shared. When the joy of each other's company had brought them to a point that their words could not define, they found that just as a violent physical fight occurs when both sides give in to the wordless mania of their raw emotions, so was the tender embrace that they fell into when the bridge of dialogue ran short of materials. In recent weeks Hank had felt that bridge between them nearly finished and, with those three simple words, had placed the capstone that connected them forever.

The insides of his arms felt as though there were electric currents running through them, and he wrapped himself in her body to calm the burning.

When at last their mutual climax had come in slow, billowing waves, they'd lain together in the bed; his penis still nestled inside her. After a time she stroked his chin, realizing that he'd been staring at the ceiling for awhile.

"What's on your mind, babe?" she asked.

"I'm just thinking about the whole marriage thing," he replied.

"How do you mean?"

"Well, I want to marry you. Oh good god I do. But I keep thinking how there are all these rules and things that people attach to marriage. Like it's something more for society at large than it is for the two people involved."

"That's because it was originally a trading of property when the father passed his daughter to his son-in-law."

"True."

"And after that it was the Church's way of approving sexual interactions between two people."

"Also true."

"And if that weren't enough girls have been taught from the crib to re-gard marriage as the pinnacle of their existence. That after that happy day they have to spend the rest of their lives on a gracefully downward trajectory."

"Very true."

"But you know that's not what I want from this, Hank. And it isn't what you want either. You know as well as I do that even though time marches on in one direction, the lives of all people fire off at different angles through the vast void of existence. And when two of those shooting stars get close enough to one another they reach out and grab hold as hard as they can, never wanting to let the other go. And when they do that, their course spins off in a whole other direction neither of them had ever planned to go but they go that way anyway because that's the only path they can take together. And when they take off on that path, they have to celebrate with a lavish ceremony. A proud, joyous declaration, whether it is just among each other or in front of the entire world. That's what our marriage will be Hank. And no church or overbearing family members will change that. We're doing it for ourselves, not some hysterical deity."

"I love you."

"I love you too."

They kissed once more, and then slept, never noticing the line of protestors forming on the sidewalk outside.

Alston's private jet landed in Alaska and he switched over to a commercial airliner for the remainder of the flight. Even with a private sleeping cabin, he found it irksome to have other people on his flight, quickly tiring of the sound of feet clomping up and down the thin corridor between the sleep cabins and he found himself irritably pulling on a pair of headphones and listening to mellow lounge jazz for an hour before finally drifting off.

Mercifully, he found himself awakened by the sound of the captain announcing an imminent landing in Tokyo. The tiny cabin was still dark, the only light being that of a vague purple dawn that seeped over the horizon. Finding his brain to be too frazzled by the trip to work out the time zone difference, Alston resigned himself to several days of jet lag while he waited for the plane to land. There was a seat across from the bunk and Alston strapped himself in, nodding off again only to be awakened by the jagged rumbling of the landing gear touching down.

The celebrity passengers, among whom Alston was counted, were unloaded by a rolling staircase onto the concrete and escorted into the terminal by a series of attendants with glowing batons. In the hazy light of dawn the jeweled finery of the luxury class passengers seemed to carry a water-logged dreariness, as though the jostling fatigue of long distance travel had ebbed into their very clothes. The sight reminded Alston of being on set at countless night shoots in lavish mansions where the actors and actresses, ever stoic in their resolve, would smoke cigarettes, crack their knuckles, and make weary chit-chat between takes, all in an effort to retain the inner glimmer necessary to appear as though they were in the throes of early-evening seduction despite it being four o'clock in the morning. The thought of a production in progress filled him with an inward smile and a warmth that carried him out of the withering bleariness of dawn and into the utilitarian sterility of the airport.

The grinding ennui of the montage that ensued as Alston drifted from the terminal to his hotel went by as an ambient blur. He was vaguely aware of the grandeur that struck most gaijin when they stepped into the rapid-fire neon whirlwind that was the Japanese mass-advertising metropolis and with the same vagueness appreciated the delicate contours of the hotel lobby but was aware of nothing until he reached his suite.

The room was a simple one bedroom suite with brown shag carpet and matching bed spread. There was an Edo-era print framed above the bed and nearby was a night stand with a reading light.

Although the hotel was a five star affair, Alston had no interest in renting one of the luxury suites normally reserved for businessmen of his caliber. It was not out of humility or some fear of being distracted, but the simple nature of Isaac Alston: when it came to work, he was utilitarian in the extreme. At home, such posh surroundings were the norm and mundane, but on a trip such as this Alston gave no thought to bringing such luxuries with him. Here, in this vast, alien expanse, he was not the reigning king of a sprawling porn empire. He was young again and hungrier than ever. Finding Hotei Shibasaki—and navigating the delicate science of persuading him to agree to the project-would take him back to the primal stages of his career. Hotei Shibasaki had walked away from a prosperous career to live in utter poverty for decades. No amount of money would impress this man, no amount of fame or recognition. Nothing but the simple understanding that project had to be completed to Shibasaki's exact specifications and nothing else.

Alston crossed the room to the small desk and chair that faced the windows and sat his carry-on bag down on the desk, extracting two DVDs in slip cases and placing them on the flat surface. They were the two previous films in Hotei Shibasaki's *Waves* trilogy, beginning with *The Cherry Blossom Wave* followed by *The Orchid Wave*. Alston stared at the empty space to the right of *The Orchid Wave* and longed to see the trilogy be completed by the efforts of his labor the same way every president longs to fill in that one remaining space on Mount Rushmore.

Falling backwards onto the bed, Alston landed in a sitting position, his gaze never shifting from the two DVD cases. As the cold blue light of the Shinjuku Prefecture ebbed with amoebic countenance over the plastic covers, Alston tried to contemplate sleeping off the jet lag and realized that he could not. He was in an ambient limbo in which every ounce of his being longed for rest but moaned in the knowledge that if he attempted sleep he would simply lie in the bed until his back began to sweat then get up and pace around the room for an hour.

Realizing that he craved the rush of relaxation that could only be found in one act, Alston picked up the bedside phone, called a number he remembered from his last time in Japan, and ordered up a call girl.

Noriko Hana clicked the door locks on her car with the key fob and dropped her keys into the glittery leather purse that she wore on the job to bedazzle her john. It hung motionless from her delicate shoulders save for the slight swing when it was bumped by the sway of her hips. Her sharp red dress was strategically designed to appear as though it had once been longer but torn in a moment of ravenous passion to reveal more leg that was originally intended.

Her shiny black boots echoed through the hotel's concrete parking garage as she made her way to the guest elevator, not bothering to check in at the lobby. She knew this hotel well—it was a favorite of traveling businessmen and, as such, a favorite of escorts all over Tokyo. As she boarded the elevator, drawing long stares from two salary men as she passed, Noriko began preparing to slip into stereotype mode, knowing full well that most white travelers wanted an Asian courtesan to sound like a twelve year old bimbo with a mouth shot full of Novocain whose orgasmic moaning sounded like fingers rubbing the sides of a balloon.

Walking quickly down the corridor towards her client's room, Noriko seemed to bob like a firefly from one fluorescent light fixture to the next, her brisk pace adding a certain charge to the warm, inviting smells that emanated from her body. Each dash of perfume and every streak of animal scent had been delicately added to perfectly lull the client into the illusion of her genuine arousal. The reality was that Noriko had never come while having sex with a client and had never expected to. At best she might feel a kind of detached pity for the more nervous ones or a grimacing disgust for the more redolent ones. Either way, they didn't pay her to come or even pretend to come. They paid her to bend her personality into an attractive frame for her vagina.

The cynicism of her profession aside, Noriko did find that she enjoyed her life as a prostitute. When she was with her friends—the ones who had no idea what she actually did for a living—she felt as though she were more complete than the rest of them, as if capitalizing on her sexuality had made it more of a concrete element of her life rather than an abstract mystery as it was for her friends. At each lunch, shopping spree, or girl's night, she watched from behind a girlish façade as her friends talked about their sex lives as though they were these mystical currents that ran through their lives, endowing them with an enigmatic sense of disillusionment while she knew, though she fought hard not to show it, that hers was a sex life filled with certainty, not confusion.

Noriko put her pseudo-philosophical musings aside when she arrived at the door of her client's room and knocked. When the door opened she was prepared to cock her head to one side and pronounce the word "hello" as "hair-woe" but was caught dumbfounded when she recognized the sharp, disarming features of her client.

"Are you Isaac Alston?" she asked, abandoning the idiot inflection of her girly persona.

"Yes," he said with the formality of a business man laced with a strain of genuine kindness. "And you are?"

"Noriko," she replied after a moment, taken in by the first client she'd ever had who asked her name.

"Hi Noriko, please come in."

He stepped aside and allowed her to enter and she suddenly felt as though her every move were being evaluated not with the critical eye of a predatory creep but rather with eyes that were trained like the taste buds of a wine connoisseur to find the most subtle contours of a finely brewed concoction. She was suddenly aware of herself as a ballet dancer is aware of her every motion. She found the state to be both pleasant and slightly disconcerting.

Noriko dropped her purse into the chair at the desk and noticed the two DVDs. She remembered hearing on the news that Isaac Alston was looking for Hotei Shibasaki. She was about to break a cardinal rule of escorts and try to make genuine conversation with her client when she heard him unbuttoning his pants. "You were about to say something?" said Alston as Noriko turned to see him standing shirtless, his slacks falling to the floor. The polite consideration in his voice made her pause and take stock of his body. It was a strong form despite its age. The grey hairs among the darker patch on his chest gave the tanned muscles beneath the look of being sun-scorched, the vague wrinkles not marks of age but the harsh rigidity of skin that had been pulled taught against the muscular development beneath. Noriko found herself stroking up and down his chest absent mindedly before letting her hand drift down to his penis.

Though it faded further and further away as she stared into his eyes, Noriko's professional side began to ask Alston what he wanted her to do for him, but he seemed to read the vague change in her face and cut her off with an unexpected kiss. She felt herself go limp in his arms as one of his hands found the single ring that held her dress in place and squeezed it, causing the straps to pop loose. As Alston relaxed his grip the dress fell to the floor and Noriko was naked save for her boots. She felt him draw her in again and gave herself over to a moment of genuine enjoyment, relishing the taste of his lips as she realized that tonight's work might not be an act after all.

He released her completely and she fell backwards on the bed, unzipping each of her boots and shaking them off. As he lay down next to her she felt herself becoming not a sexual plaything but an instrument about to be played by a master virtuoso. His lips kissed down her neck, down between her breasts, then came to settle on her left nipple, taking it gently into his mouth, his tongue seeming to trace each of the miniscule grooves in the hardening teat. Noriko realized that her breasts had begun to ache and that the ache was the voice of a long dormant need—something she had long since abandoned out of a sense of duty to what she thought were the rules of her profession. As she began to massage her other breast, she realized that she'd begun to enjoy her work.

Though it was far from boring—quite the opposite—Noriko realized that Alston was spending a great deal of time on her nipples, sucking first the left one to erection then the right, then alternating his attentions back and forth. Trained to read her clients and emphasize their implicit desires, Noriko found herself unable to read her client's intentions. On the one hand the tender suckling seemed to be a longing for maternal validation while on the other hand it seemed like the poised embrasure of a seasoned saxophonist working tiny, but penetrating strains of vibrato into each note of a long solo.

As Alston's right hand found its way down to her pussy, Noriko realized that she wasn't meant to know the answer—that whatever psychology was motivating Isaac Alston in this act, hers was not the place to know but to experience. He slid his fingers inside of her while keeping his thumb pressed against her throbbing clit and began to administer a series of strokes that told Noriko she had become a mere vessel for the enjoyment that he conjured in her. When at last she came it was with the agonizing, stampeding build that she had known the first time she'd given herself an orgasm as a teenager. As she felt that sudden burst of sunlight echo in exploding waves through her nerves, Noriko felt her conscious mind drift away and she stopped wondering how this man—out of all the men she'd serviced—had been able to make her come. Had it been the skilled body that had manipulated hers or the tender, sensitive tone in the few words he'd spoken to her? She stopped caring when she realized that he was no longer next to her.

She opened her eyes to see Isaac Alston rolling a condom onto his tool. She relished the sight, breathing in the sudden smell of latex as her vagina, already moist from ejaculating, began to throb in anticipation. He was on her with a primal urgency, but still he seemed gentle. He pulled her to him and lay on his back, sitting her down on his stiff, purple erection. In all her time as a prostitute, Noriko had learned to disconnect from her body while men played with it, aware only vaguely of the foreign objects that entered her. But in this embrace she felt herself slipping again into the role of instrument to a master of music and when he finally came the feeling of his member throbbing inside her sent tiny waves of climax rippling through the afterglow from which Noriko was still yet to emerge.

Noriko panted for breath, sweat pouring down her body even in the cool, air conditioned room. She looked into the eyes of the man that had satisfied her and, in all her confusion, found herself thanking *him*. Alston smiled warmly, still inside her, and as she looked down at him, Noriko realized that he'd already caught the thread of the next thought to cross her mind, and answered it as though she'd already spoken: "Yes, you can stay if you want."

She rolled off him and the climbed under the covers together. Noriko found a new calm peace in his embrace as they both drifted off to sleep.

Chapter 15

TRAPPINGS, MISSISSIPPI could be regarded as a blue print for small town America: a few mismatched buildings with corroded antebellum flare surrounding a generic stone courthouse made up the entirety of the town square and beyond that the only other buildings of any significance were the school, which housed all grade levels (with fifth being the largest) in a single building, three Baptist churches, and a big box department store. Most of the buildings on the square were unoccupied, some with boards over the windows and some missing doors and windows all together. There was no theater in Trappings, no shopping mall, no cable television, and computers, let alone internet access, were considered a luxury. On Friday and Saturday nights the kids who were old enough to drive (few of them bothered to get licenses and the town's only law enforcement officer didn't care) would drive around the town square in a slow parade, honking their horns playfully at one another while the adults who needed something to do would sit on the benches around the town and remember when they had been so young and carefree.

Of the 1,256 adult-age residents in Trappings, 654 were unemployed and dependent on welfare, 831 lived in trailers instead of houses, 954 were high school dropouts, 1,034 were registered Republicans, and 1,205 attended Sunday services at the local churches. Of the 602 residents who were employed, 254 worked for one of the three churches, 100 were employed by the big box department store, and the rest had been forced to find jobs in neighboring towns.

Most of the city had fallen into considerable decay, but this did not matter much to the local residents because the churches were the most important buildings in town and no matter how decrepit the rest of the town became, the churches were always shimmering bastions of prosperity. Their lawns were always well groomed, their paint was always shiny and fresh smelling, and their air conditioning was the best in town. The churches were constantly expanding, with new additions contributing to the lavish sprawl.

After riding around the square on Friday and Saturday nights, the most popular form of entertainment was the sermons. The preachers at each of the churches wove captivating stories of flying corpses, brutal torture and super- natural disasters but were always careful to remind their flocks of the real –life demons that existed. These were demons which the townspeople were only vaguely aware of: demons that gathered at the borders of their great nation in places like New York and San Francisco. They were an alien force of faceless mutants that conspired secretly to *change* things. They were the communist, socialist, fascist, latte-drinking *liberals* who lived for the sick thrill of aborting fetuses and smoking pot and for this they were minions of Satan. Liberals, said the preachers, were people who didn't think you had to follow any rules. They thought that you could just do whatever the hell you wanted with no regard for what god thought about you. There had even been a liberal who said that the only law was "Do What Thou Wilt" and that this hippie had been a friend of Adolf Hitler who had created a lawless world where everybody did whatever they wanted. This, the preachers explained, was the long term result of liberal- ism: when society removed god from their lives and started doing whatever they wanted whenever they wanted, they would turn the world over to tyran- nical dictators who forced everyone to live a certain way, which was why it was the god-appointed duty of the US government to impose a standard of living that nobody deviated from. The rules were simple: if a Conservative was in the white house then blind, unthinking nationalism was the norm. If a Liberal was in the white house then the nationalism merely shifted to a pathological loyalty to whoever shouted the loudest for "traditional values."

There was one business in Trappings that thrived. It was the only busi- ness that contributed to the local economy and brought in customers from outside the town. It was housed in a single double-wide trailer located on a long, otherwise barren stretch of road that technically qualified as a part of the town of Trappings, on the edge of a county of the same name. The busi- ness was called the Whack Shack and it sold a full range of magazines, DVDs, video games, adult toys, and miscellaneous accessories that fell under the umbrella of "pornography."

The Whack Shack had been opened several years ago by a pair of enterpris- ing lads, Mack and Jack, who found immediate success in their erotic venture. Their business thrived and they were able to move product almost as fast as they put it on the shelves. Customers to the store seemed to be drawn not only to the products but to the festive atmosphere of the store itself, which embraced a lively enthusiasm not seen outside the decaying façade of the rest of Trappings.

The store was not, however, met with approval by the town at large and soon the Whack Shack was faced with a group of people across the street holding a sign which read:

IF YOU GO IN THIS ADULT STORE WE WILL TAKE
YOUR PICTURE, POST IT ON THE INTERNET, AND
SEND IT TO YOUR EMPLOYER. JESUS LOVES YOU
AND SO DO WE.

When Mack, who had been minding the store, saw this for the first time he hastened to call the police and was connected to the only sheriff in Trappings county, who promptly replied with "the feller running that protest is my fourth cousin's son-in-law's god father and as you know I don't arrest my own kin. Just wouldn't be the Christian thing to do" and hung up. Mack was left holding a silent receiver and staring out the shop's open front door at the beady eyed lard bucket that started back at him with the sign in one hand, a camera in the other, and a small entourage behind him.

When the preachers began spreading the news that Isaac Alston was going to make *The Lotus Wave*, none of the townspeople knew who that was or what was controversial about the movie, but they soon learned that this was one of those liberal elitists who was trying to destroy god's America with smut. The congregations stormed the Whack Shack and demanded that they hand over all Alston Image content. Terrified of the angry mob, Mack and Jack did just that, handing over some three hundred of their two thousand products. A bonfire was lit and the products were destroyed. This did nothing to quell the public outrage and two days later Mack and Jack were forced to flee Trappings County on foot, the rest of their products seized and destroyed by the angry mob.

By the end of the week 1,247 of the 1,256 adult-age residents in Trappings, Mississippi were registered members of Families for Families.

Two weeks after that the population of Trappings, Mississippi was 1,247.

A boutique that sold dignity sheathes was opened on the square.

Artie Barrel's business had ground to a halt. Intersect had not sold one product of any kind since Melvin Crankshadow's rally outside the Alston Image offices. The money in his bank account would dry up soon and with no other recourse he called Melvin Crankshadow. The pastor was immensely understanding and invited Artie to the upcoming Sunday service, saying he'd be willing to talk about an employment opportunity.

That Sunday Artie made the trek from Las Vegas to San Bernardino where Crankshadow's church, the First Grand Pantheon of Jesus Christ the Imperial Redeemer of American Liberty was located. The main building was an octagonal edifice, its imposing grey stone punctuated at each sharp edge by a long white column which, while decorative, appeared to be holding op the great, broad sloping roof that culminated in a single, unadorned spire. The church's property covered an entire square mile, with a large share of it going to parking space.

There were two three story buildings that branched off from the church. To the east was a facility that housed a gymnasium, cafeteria, various meeting rooms, a daycare center, and administrative offices. The east wing was labeled Institute for Pornographic Addiction. It had no windows or external doors.

When Artie arrived he was struck by the way in which the building seemed to dominate the landscape, as though the horizon line cowered in its wake. It was not a beautiful structure—indeed it seemed like a great, dark scab on the surface of the earth—but it was a structure that seemed to scowl at the viewer, as though daring them to challenge its ugliness. Artie was instructed to drive to the main entrance where a valet took his car and parked it. The building was like the sprawling, morbid shadow of the casinos that populated Artie's native city.

Artie was nervous at first when he stepped through the shimmering, freshly polished glass doors that towered above him. He was worried that he might be recognized and shunned, but he was surprised to find that upon entering he was greeted by two elderly women who were handing out pieces of paper—a program of the morning's events—to each person that entered. Their withered, mechanical smiles and their weak, raspy greeting was the same for Artie as it was for everyone else who entered. Lost among such guiltless equality, Artie found himself oddly at peace. The vaulted ceilings of the red-velvet lobby towered above him, sunlight pouring in through crucifix shaped windows.

Stepping through a further set of doors, Artie found himself in the main chapel which looked, as far as he could tell, more like a sporting venue than a church. The seating surrounded an octagonal main stage in traditional amphitheater style, with each row ascending above and behind its predecessor until they arrived at one of eight entrances, where Artie stood now. Not wanting to draw too much attention to himself, Artie sat down in one of the pews by the door and watched as the regular parishioners filed in and filled up the closer rows. From where he sat the stage seemed to be no bigger than his hand, but four large video screens were mounted to steel beams above it so that all would have a good view of whatever was to happen.

As other parishioners filed in, Artie noticed that many of the women wore dignity sheaths. Those things are really catching on, he thought to himself. He stood to allow one of them to pass. "This way, sister Patricia," said an usher who guided the woman beneath the dignity sheath. The parishioners continued to pour in until the venue, which must have held some 10,000 people, was filled. The house lights dimmed, bland Contemporary Christian music began to play, the booming PA system making the shallow music sound boastful and commanding.

Smoke began to pour in through one of the entrances to the stadium and the manifold lighting structures began to contort their multicolored beams to the silhouette that stepped up into the inverted spotlight. Crossing through the smoke and into the shimmering presence of the auditorium—timed perfectly with a dramatic build in the music—was Melvin Crankshadow. The audience response was uniformly overwhelming and as Crankshadow descended the stairs into the manic throng he was followed by a trio of lower ranking pastors, each holding up a copy of a bible in one hand and one of their leader's recent books in the other. Each of the members of the three man entourage smiled as though his dimples were in fact tumors on the brink of combustion. Armed guards, each wearing American flag print body armor, walked behind the pastors.

The music was building steadily as Crankshadow took the stage, now incorporating what one might assume were percussion instruments from a biblical time period and the kind of horns that might have announced the arrival of Centurions to a regal amphitheatre. He stepped up onto the octagonal plateau and into the primary lighting, showing himself to be a tall, thin man who, in contrast to the conservative, grey suit clad attire of his entourage was wearing acid-washed jeans and a beige, button down t-shirt. There was a youthful gleam in his authoritarian smile as he ran around the perimeter of the stage giving high fives to the front row. He bowed and then waved to the back rows as the music subsided.

"Brothers and sisters in Christ," he began in a chipper, almost effeminate voice that was undercut by the inherit masculinity of a southern inflection. "It is so wonderful to see you all here today. I cannot tell you how happy it makes me to see each and every one your shinning faces out there prepared to lay your lives on the line for the good lord Jesus Christ. Who here is ready to die for their savior?" There was a thunderous round of applause and Crankshadow continued: "Because, as you know, there is a war going on out there, people. The liberal media wants to tell you that rape is okay. They want to tell you that pedophilia is okay. They want you to think that bestiality is okay. And they're doing it by turning this into a porn culture. Porn culture is the most unnatural thing there is and that's why it's ruining this great, God-given, country of ours. The most natural thing in the world is God's one true path for all people, a path that leads you into the arms of the one person god has selected for you. But the liberal, secular, Satan-driven heathens out there resent God's truth. They want to be proud and continue doing things their own way. And thinking for yourself leads you into one thing and one thing only: the fiery pits of eternal damnation.

"That's what Satan wants and that's what porn culture gives you. Why, if you look around in your communities you'll see the effects of porn culture. You'll see women trying to look as vainly beautiful as possible and men giving in to the throws of these temptresses and being unable to stop themselves from raping them. It is not these poor women's fault that they were born tempt-resses, but surely these good, honest, hard working men can't be blamed for giving into the primitive urges that Satan has infected them with. That is why we have the dignity sheath and why so many of the women in our congrega-tion are wearing it today. Because men cannot be trusted to fight these satanic urges on their own, so the women must, out of our eternal compassion, have their horrible affliction covered by our innovative new garment.

"And what affliction is that? It's the affliction of beauty! The affliction of having visual features so precisely calculated for the purpose of serving Satan that men are bewitched into forcing themselves upon them! And the evil, deceitful porn culture is taking advantage of this. Everywhere you turn—on billboards, on television, on the internet—you'll find porn culture trying to corrupt men into vile rapists, just to turn a profit.

"But in these sad, sinful times, there is hope. There is a bill that is about to be put before congress which will allow our for faith based organizations to take direct action against all those who would dare oppose our faith. Soon the wretched laws that have kept us from making this a Christian nation will be struck down because when the Unlimited Sanctity Act is passed we will finally have the authority to declare unlawful all things which fly in the face of our faith. With its passing our government shall establish the Department of Offense Prevention and Enforcement. I know that many of you have al-ready committed your sons and your daughters to our sexual rehabilitation facilities and soon sexual deprogramming will be as mandatory as kinder-garten!"

There was thunderous applause and then Crankshadow finished: "And now, I want to yield the rest of my time for today's sermon to Andrea Dan-vers. Andrea!" There was more applause as Andrea Danvers, covered in a dignity sheath, took the stage. She extended a hand to shake Crankshadow's and wrapped in the dignity sheath it looked like the probing pseudopod of some massive amoebic monstrosity. Crankshadow shook the hand and took a seat next to his entourage in one of four chairs that sat in even rows along the far edge of the stage. Andrea took the microphone she was offered and held it flat against the face area of the dignity sheath to be heard.

"Ladies and gentlemen," she crowed with a stuffy, pompous tone. "We are a fighting a war against rape. What is rape? It means giving men a sense of entitlement to women's bodies! It's a sociological construct that benefits all men. All men benefit from keeping women in a state of fear and cowardice.

But now, thanks to new legislation, we have the power to strike back at this evil, phallocentric society. Finally, women will be free from rape!

"First, I'm pleased to report that new truth-in-advertising laws require realism in all manner of modeling. Henceforth, no model may endorse a product or appear in a magazine unless she is at least fifty pounds overweight. This is a bold and decisive strike against standards of beauty that exclude most women and create unrealistic expectations in the minds of men. Secondly, no woman appearing in any sort of advertisement may have an excited or happy look on her face as this can only be interpreted by men as being the 'come hither' look that tells them that women want to be raped. And why does rape happen? Because men think it's what women want! If it weren't for porn convincing men that women want to be raped then the thought of rape would not occur to these poor, sensitive, misguided and confused men.

"The next step is the regulation of the internet and for this purpose the FBI will increase its watch for potential sex offenders by requiring that every computer sold come equipped with a new chip that will report any user who accesses a pornographic or sexually suggestive website. Now I know the ACLU, that great bastion of male-dominated liberalism, has said that what private citizens surf for on the internet is nobody else's business but let me ask you this—what if the man who cuts your grass or delivers your paper or teaches your children were jerking off to bondage porn every night? Don't you think you have a right to know about it?

"People often tell me that pornography doesn't appeal only to men and that there are women who like to watch porn but let me tell you—just like the small number of Jews that voted for Adolf Hitler so those are just the women who have been brainwashed into thinking that they like pornography. Trust me—every single one of those women just thinks that she has to pretend to like that stuff to make the boys happy. No woman loves pornography. After all, what women would love watching the slow, humiliating genocide of her entire gender? It is a holocaust perpetuated by porn culture that we are trying to stop, people.

"I don't care how consensual porn actresses think their roles are or how many contracts they signed saying that they're willing participants—what they are doing is rape. They are being raped by men, raped by capitalism, raped by the entertainment industry, and contributing to the rape of their entire gender. Because these poor women can't understand that they're being raped on porn sets they have to have someone else decide for them. That's what sisterhood is—the older sister deciding what's best for the younger sister.

"Let me tell you, as someone who studies media images, I can tell you that right now we are in the middle of a massive sociological experiment that none of us consented to be a part of. And because none of us consented that means we're being raped! Everyone of us is being buggered bloody and raw by the Viagra stiffened penis of capitalism. Money is evil and sex for money is just sex for rape. I mean money for rape! I mean rape for money!

"People often ask me if I'm anti-sex and I say 'no!' Just like everyone here I think sex is a wonderful mystery and because it's a mysterious, sacred thing it must be protected from those who abuse it. Many in the feminist movement have argued that marriage is a form of enslaving women but I tell you in truth it is a way of controlling men. Marriage—and by this I mean marriage that occurs properly in the eyes of god—is designed to teach couples that their sexuality is a thing which can only be indulged in for their creator's purpose—to create children. As soon as men lose sight of that knowledge, and begin to enjoy sex, they become rapists. And women who begin to enjoy sexuality for something other than the pride of bearing children are willing rape victims. And that's a critical part of the brainwashing methods men use to rape women now—make them think they're giving consent. I will tell you this—if sex is done for pleasure it is an act of rape. Sex is not love and sex is not a connection between two people. It is a brutal, hateful form of biological servitude that men inflict on women. That is why we must always regard sex as a wonderful mystery—because the truth is too ugly to look at. Thank you."

The applause, while plentiful, was more cautious and reserved this time. Crankshdow took the microphone again and strode back to the center of the stage while Andrea returned to her seat in the audience. From where he sat, Artie could see Andrea trip and fall in her dignity sheathe as she stepped off the stage. A man in the audience stood to help her up but as soon as he placed a hand on her Andrea screamed "RAPE!" and the gentleman was led away by security.

"As we end our sermon today, brothers and sisters," said Melvin Crankshadow as the guards left the room, "it is my distinct pleasure to introduce a very special guest. Mr. Arthur Barrel!" The entire congregation turned to look where Crankshadow was pointing. Artie would have been happy to remain hidden in the darkness but a spotlight suddenly shone brightly on him. "Come down to the stage, brother Arthur!" boomed Crankshadow as Artie rose hesitantly and began to descend the stairs. He had feared that scorn would come with recognition from this crowd but he found that their welcome eyes and polite applause were quite the opposite. When he arrived at the stage, Crankshadow gave him a hand to help him up and then threw it over Artie's shoulder once he'd made it. "It is my distinct pleasure to welcome brother Arthur into our fold. Arthur, as you may know, ran Intersect Productions which was kind enough to reach across party lines and help us in our time of need. And for that, I want you all to look past the pornographer and into this man's soul! Because right now, this man is in need! Open up your hearts by opening up your wallets! Half of what goes into this week's collection plates will go to help this poor man!"

The crowd was enthusiastic in their response, and buckets were passed down each aisle. By the time the buckets were brought up to the stage, each one was full of change, dollar bills and checks. There were eight buckets, each full nearly to the brim. Artie stood and smiled awkwardly as Crankshadow led the congregation in a rousing hymn and thanked them all for coming. There was tremendous applause and Artie was led off the stage by the pastor's entourage. After ascending the steps behind Crankshadow he was led by the pastor to a side corridor that hid them from the exiting congregation. Artie was surprised when Crankshadow handed him a check for two hundred and fifty thousand dollars. "We make at least five hundred thousand every Sunday, so here's your share," he said politely. Artie took the check with an odd sense of caution. "I'm afraid I don't have time to talk about employment for you today like I thought I did," continued Crankshadow "but I want you to have this in the meantime. Come back next week and I promise I'll have my whole afternoon available."

Artie thanked Crankshadow with a kind of gratitude that seemed to have rusted from years of dormant neglect. The chapel was huge as was the parking lot, and by the time he got back to his car, Artie found that his mood was rather pleasant and worry-free. On the long drive back through the Nevada desert he found himself constantly focusing on the horizon, reveling in the opiate certainty that while he had not "seen the light" at this particular service, he would see it soon if he kept coming back.

Chapter 16

ON ISAAC ALSTON'S eighteenth birthday, he had discovered the works of Hotei Shibasaki. To celebrate the anniversary of his birth, Alston had snuck over to Boston's combat district and attended a screening of *The Cherry Blossom Wave* at a local adult theater. Having read a Playboy magazine interview with Shibasaki, Alston was intrigued at the prospect of seeing what was being touted as an artistic breakthrough in the realm of erotic cinema, but was wholly unprepared for what he saw that evening.

The Cherry Blossom Wave told the story of a young girl from a rural fishing village that was to be married off to a local boy to whom she felt no attraction. The film opened with the young girl—a breathtakingly delicate beauty whose gentle poise was augmented a harshly minimalistic bitterness—being whisked through the French country side towards a lavish mansion in the company of an older man, presumably her father, though the downward angle of his gaze indicated certain lasciviousness. They sat in the back of an antique town car, the driver occasionally looking into the mirror to catch glimpses of the young lady. What struck Isaac as he watched the scene was not the incestuous implications but the aura of control that the young woman had over the moment, as though she were aware of the magnetism that exuded from her very being.

The boy of noble birth that she was to marry assumed that her indifference to him was prudishness and, on the night of their wedding, was angered when he took her virginity in a passionless exchange. Determined to draw her forth from her perceived frigidity, the husband began to take his wife on a tour of the world's most exotic perversions, from soap massages in Japan to brothel orgies in Las Vegas, and in each instance seeing his wife come out of her shell with magnificent displays of unbridled sexuality that never transpired in their marriage bed. Through the course of the film the husband became more and more disillusioned with his wife as he began to realize that her disinterest was with him, not sex in general, and finally confronted her on the subject, asking if she can ever learn to love him. Her reply—the young woman's first and only lines of dialogue in the film—were seared into Isaac's soul:

"How can anyone love you? Love for you is a merit badge, a golden trophy, a framed plaque to be awarded by everyone on the planet except for me, the woman you claim to love. Is it any surprise to you that in all of our travels your observations of my sex life have become increasingly voyeuristic? You've looked in on me as though I were a lock whose combination you were unable to glean. You've trotted me from one mind-blowing orgasm to the next as though looking for the specialist to cure some sickness of mine, never realizing that the sickness was yours. In every instance of cuckoldry you've shoved me into I've delved deeper and deeper into my passions because I am thrilled by the knowledge that it makes you increasingly impotent. You desperation excites me—it thrills me to know that you heart sinks into your guts every time you see me come at the hands of another. Congratulations—the only way for you to get me off is to revolt me."

Following this the husband committed suicide in a most grisly fashion- he threw his wife an elegant dinner party for her birthday and, at the end of the evening, when she was opening her presents, presented her with a simple black box, which she opened to reveal her husband's severed penis and testicles. When she looked from the box to her husband, the look of scornful indifference hasher than ever, he dropped his trousers to the floor to reveal the gaping wound that pulsed with gushing dollops of black blood. The husband collapsed shortly thereafter, his wife wiping her face clean of dinner and leaving the room without looking at her dying spouse.

In the final scene of the film, the new widow was shown entering her husband's funeral at a lavish Catholic church wearing a black dress that, while ankle length, was open in the front, revealing a well groomed pubic bush. To the shock of the many attendees, the girl climbed onto the casket and squatted over her husband's face and proceeded to masturbate furiously, finally spraying him with clear fluid. The camera then turned out toward the audience to reveal that all of the minor characters with whom she'd shared erotic episodes throughout the film were now filing in through the main entrance of the chapel, each of them nude, and approaching the casket in a single file. Upon arriving they ran a train on the girl as she made out with her husband's corpse.

When the film was over Alston sat in the theater until the lights came up and the janitor told him to leave. In that interim darkness he found himself awash in contemplations of what he had just seen. It was a haunting feeling, knowing that the violence and cynicism of the piece had been transmuted into a thing of elegance and beauty—as though the cinematography, soundtrack, acting, and sex had all been the ingredients in an alchemical recipe that could only be brought to life through the direction of Hotei Shibasaki.

Controversy over the film mounted when it became public knowledge that the actor playing the husband had actually severed his own genitals and died for the film. The actor was a terminally ill man who had volunteered for the part. The US government ruled that the film, despite its graphic scenes, was not a snuff picture because the actor's death was not shown on camera. Thus, the film continued to air despite the requisite protests, and was even released on VHS and later DVD as the technology became available.

Lying in bed, the prostitute Noriko asleep at his side, Alston watched *The Cherry Blossom* wave on the computer that sat on his stomach. All these years later he was still amazed at how the work seemed so timeless and knew that it was indeed the authentic rage that boiled beneath its pastoral surface that contributed to its staying power. He marveled at the film but still wondered, as he was sure many had, why Shibasaki would kneecap his own career by using real body mutilation and death? There was an answer that stirred in him but he was reticent to acknowledge it not because he feared the truth but because he knew that if his suspicions were correct, he and Shibasaki would be more alike than he had ever imagined. He wanted to think that this would endear him to the man and better guarantee his consent to create the film but at the same time Alston knew that this longing to connect with another person would leave him naked and vulnerable to the potential of rejection. He'd never brought these feelings into his business pursuits before—the rejection of a business proposal by a potential associate was only the failure of that person to recognize that Alston was in the right. Perhaps it was better, he reflected, that Dominic was the one who handled the artistic end of things.

Sleep had come at last but not for long—his excitement at the thought of tracking down Hotei Shibasaki was too great for him to slumber at length. He rose from the bed and padded into the bathroom, drawing a steaming hot bath in the traditional Japanese bath, climbing into the barrel shaped tub.

"You want breakfast?" called Noriko from the other room.

"Please," replied Alston "call room service and put it on my bill. Whatever you want to get." As he settled into the bath, Alston could hear the girl calling the front desk in Japanese. After a moment she walked into the bathroom and joined him in the tub. Her fluid motions into the room and then the tub were pleasant, Alston loosing himself for a moment in their tranquility as her slender body immersed itself in the steaming water.

"So how long have you been doing this?" asked Alston, his demeanor vaguely taking on the tone of a formal interview.

"Three years," replied Noriko.

"I have to complement your English—it seems quite fluent."

"It's to my advantage to know the language—most of my clients are foreign and most of them are American."

"I see. Do you have many local clients?"

"A few. Mostly old men."

"Any that own slaughterhouses in the Shinjuku Prefecture?"

Noriko paused for a moment, bit her lip and looked down at the water. "I'm not supposed to give out client information, Mr. Alston."

"I'll give you five thousand dollars, US."

"There's one... he owns a slaughterhouse on the south end of Shinjuku."

"What's his name?"

"I honestly don't know—we don't usually get the names of our clients. I've never serviced him and a lot of the other girls wont because he's Burakumin, but some have and they say it's weird because he always has tons of money to pay for whatever he wants, but he lives in total shit. But ours job isn't to worry about where money comes from. That's really all I know."

Alston nodded, an index finger curled over his upper lip, chin resting in the adjoining palm. His contemplation was broken by the door bell ringing. "Come in," he said and heard the bellhop swiping a passkey through the reader. There was a rattling of covered dishes as the cart was wheeled in and Alston beckoned for it to be brought into the bathroom. After a tip the bellhop departed and Alston and Noriko were left to enjoy a western-style meal of pancakes, bacon and eggs.

Following breakfast, Alston bid farewell to Noriko, who slipped him the address of the slaughterhouse owner. Minutes later he was hailing a cab.

The slaughterhouse was contained in a vast warehouse that connected to a wide open expanse where the cattle were herded in wailing clumps by ranch hands. Entering through one of the two gatefold steel doors, Alston stepped into the arena of massacre en masse, into a sprawling chamber where the bleating, distorted screeches of feral death throws merged with the clanking grind of machinery and the moist severance of evisceration. The coppery stench of blood hung low in the air, underscoring the pervading odor of excrement. Assembly lines of young men stood ready at their various posts, each distorting the slices of meat in a certain way. Alston watched a pig squeal as it was impaled on an iron hook and lifted upwards on a chain. The pig became a plasmatic geyser as it sailed through the air, the chain finally descending next to a young lad with a machete who sliced it vertically from chin to crotch, a putrid mass of intestines vomiting out on the floor below. When exactly the pig's life had ended was unclear—that moment had been lost in the arterial artistry.

As though sensing Alston's fascinated stare, the young man abandoned slaughtering the pig for a moment and approached Alston. "Can... I... Help... You... Sir?" he asked in slow, practiced English. Alston labored for a couple of minutes with what little Japanese he knew to finally explain that he wished to see Hotei Shibasaki. The worker was confused for a moment, then shook his head and said "not here." After another minute of difficult translation, Alston convinced the worker to bring the owner to him. The boy nodded and ran off in the direction of a set of steel steps which led up to a catwalk running the inside perimeter of the complex. The catwalk terminated at the far end of the chamber, meeting with a metallic box which seemed to be the supervisor's office.

At length the worker returned, followed by an old man who was, himself, wearing a blood stained smock that indicated he was frequently among the slaughter himself. "Mikado-san...boss" stammered the young man to Alston.

"I'm Shinji Mikado—I'm the owner. What can I help you with, sir?"

Alston didn't need to draw out the photograph to recognize Shibasaki—the man's sharp, endlessly intense features—almost a mirror of Alston's own—were undeniable. "No," whispered Alston "you're Hotei Shibasaki." The owner looked back at the worker who had summoned him and gave a nod of his head towards the young man's station. After the lad had returned to work, the old man turned back and smiled with a subtle cynicism.

"Of course I am, Isaac Alston."

When Isaac Alston was a junior at Harvard, *The Orchid Wave* was released. Shrouded in controversy following the previous film, it was difficult to find a theater that would show the picture and as such Isaac was forced to navigate Boston's Chinatown to find a bootleg copy, which he ultimately located from a street vendor. Sneaking into a room with AV equipment one night to watch the film, Isaac couldn't believe his luck: he had procured not a bootleg of the film but an actual theatrical pressing. Thrilled with this discovery he spent the late night hours discovering a new wing had been built onto the cinematic utopia of Shibasaki's previous film.

The Orchid Wave returned to the kind of pastoral countryside that had been prominent in *The Cherry-Blossom Wave* and it was amidst these lush backgrounds that the story of a stunning woman who lived alone in a lavish, marble mansion unfolded. A buxom, fair skinned beauty with stunning red hair, she was seen lounging with breasts and pussy exposed in posh arm chairs, clad only in a skimpy, open robe and white heels. Throughout the day she would receive clients whom she would take into an enclosed garden in the back of the house and perform unusual rituals with and on them. The garden was contained in small, ivy covered walls with Incan designs. The flowers were a varied bunch, with pitcher plants and Venus fly traps sharing space with many different varieties of orchid. All of the plants seemed to lean towards an altar erected in the center of the garden, across which a yellow and orange cloth was draped. The redhead, whose name was never given, would instruct her clients—some of them male, some of them female—to remove their clothes and lay nude on the altar, during which time she would interview them regarding their deepest sexual desires. When they had described them, she would stand above them, place her hands on their foreheads, and transport them to an alternate reality where they would experience their fantasy in its entirety. There was always, however, a surprise for each of the clients—each experience would require that they confront whatever dark secret within themselves was keeping them from fully enjoying their sexuality before they could achieve the kind of mind blowing orgasm possible only to those who were at one with their sexual nature. With the redhead acting as a kind of Virgil to the client's Dante, clients who secretly wished to be nudists would relive the embarrassments of their lives that had made them introverted and, in each instance, resolve those embarrassments in a sexual manner before finally being able to walk nude on a sandy beach. Clients who fantasized about being raped—both male and female—would sexually overpower those who had victimized them before finally being handed over to the throws of mock ravishing by performed rapists. In each scenario, the clients found new liberation in their sexual kinks by overpowering the hang ups that kept them from expressing them in reality.

In the second half of the film's two and a half hour cycle, however, a man who had committed three rapes in his life without being punished for any of them, came to the woman's mansion with the hope of confronting his inner demons. Horrified by the man but intrigued by his request, the woman consented to perform the ritual and, to her surprise, guides the rapist on a disturbing and bleak journey into his own subconscious, with each "therapeutic" sexual encounter resulting in the rapist losing a body part until all that remained was his head which, still alive in the psycho-dramatic ritual, was ultimately fed into a massive, vagina shaped disposal drain. When the redhead emerged from the ritual, she found that the client lay dismembered on the altar, his body eviscerated in the exact manner that it had been during the course of the ritual. The credits rolled over a fixed image of his lifeless and brutalized flesh.

Though the film had been shot in Europe and featured mostly Caucasian actors, the Japanese influence in Shibasaki's filmmaking could not be denied. The achingly distant wide shots, the claustrophobically confined close angles, and the genre bending soundtrack all transcended the conventions of western film and quietly placed the film into the pantheon of majestic art. There was, on a more profound level, the meditative tone of the overall pacing which gave the film a dreamlike quality that was not interrupted by the sudden, savage bursts of violence.

This time, young Isaac Alston had already read about the film and knew why it was, in itself, controversial: although the dismemberment of the rapist during the fantasy sequences had been accomplished through special effects, the dismembering of his body had been real. The man was, in fact, a serial rapist who had been brought to justice in a small northern European village where the law was one of Kangaroo courts at best. Shibasaki had been able to approach the local authorities and was given an audience with the condemned man, in which he laid out the offer to appear in a film. The rapist had consented with full knowledge of the ultimate result.

"Don't think I haven't been aware of you and your work, Mr. Alston," continued Hotei Shibasaki as the pair ascended the stairs, his voice nearly muted altogether by the cacophony below. "I've kept a curious eye on Alston Image from the time you started making waves all those years ago. Shortly after my retirement, as I recall."

"You were a big inspiration to me," said Alston, an unexpected note of child-like worship skipping across the words.

Shibasaki raised a dismissive hand and smiled politely. "But I was most intrigued by the news that you intended to produce *The Lotus Wave*. When I heard that, I was certain I'd run into you at some point." Alston wanted to respond but found himself at a loss for words, content to merely watch the old man step past him and open the door into the little metal office box.

The sight within the tiny chamber was almost as alarming as the initial sight of the slaughterhouse only moments ago. The room wasn't merely an office, but a living space. A frail cot with a pillow and anemic looking blanket lined one corner and a wooden desk adorned the other. A stove and refrigerator were against the wall that ran parallel to the outer wall of the building and it was also into this side that a small closet and a bathroom were set.

"You live here?" asked Alston reflexively.

"Not quite to your level of opulence, I am sure."

"No... No I didn't mean to offend."

"Not at all, Mr. Alston. Please sit."

Alston sat down in the lawn chair that Shibasaki had indicated. "So I suppose you have lots of questions, Mr. Alston?" the old man asked as he turned to the kitchenette and began boiling water on the stove.

"Why the whole underhanded way of marketing the script? I mean, I understand smuggling it out of the country, but why did you have to do the whole auction thing?"

"After my first two films nobody would touch me. The authorities had raided my studio and I was going to be tried for obscenity with the certainty of a thirty year sentence. At the last minute I copped a plea bargain and was let off in exchange for the understanding that I would never write a script again."

"So does *The Lotus Wave* even exist?"

"Oh, it exists. I wrote the script and when word of my completing it was leaked to the Japanese authorities, my agent smuggled it out of the country. Then he started marketing it to all the big porn studios. They were all willing to look at it, but they had to sign a disclosure statement saying they wouldn't discuss its contents publicly until after it had been released. After reading the script they all passed. Every one of them. I was ruined by then. The courts had seized everything I had and I couldn't keep going on. I quit film entirely and took up the family business—this slaughterhouse. And that's been that." Before Alston could respond, Shibasaki turned and handed him a mug of tea. Alston tasted the tea and found it to be magnificent: in a room surrounded by disgust and failure, Shibasaki had produced a cup of tea that felt like a triumph.

"So why was it that the script was so controversial?"

"Find out for yourself, Mr. Alston." Shibasaki opened a drawer in the nearby desk and withdrew a red three ring binder, which he passed to Alston before sitting down in the chair opposite him. With the kind of reverence normally reserved for a first edition pressing of the Torah, Alston opened the note book. Inside were nearly two hundred laminated pages, the first bearing the words:

The Lotus Wave
By
Hotei Shibasaki

"It's in English…" whispered Alston as though speaking too loudly would dissolve the pages.

"No sense writing in the language of the country that had already banned it."

Alston began to read, aware of the aged person across from him whose sharp gaze never wavered and he began to know how it felt to be on the receiving end of the penetrating stare he'd always given the world.

The pages were old, crumpled and yellow, but the story the they contained still reeked lusciously of fresh typewriter ink. Alston gently turned the first page and began to read, feeling as though each time his eyes blinked he saw not the darkness of his inner eyelids but frames from the movie—frames that, as far as his imagination was concerned, were already seared into sixteen millimeter film. He read as though he stared into a shimmering well from which the complete film had surfaced and drank in every word like the nectar of salvation.

The Lotus Wave told the story of a young man who was coming home to the small fishing village of his youth to attend the funeral of his sister, with whom he'd shared an incestuous relationship. It followed him through a series of encounters with the various men and women in his family and, as a way of overcoming his status as black sheep, his having sex with each of them, sometimes consensually and sometimes by force, but in each case leaving each person with the impression that they were alone in their transgression. The dramatic tension mounted as the family members began subsequent interactions with one another, each uncomfortable with their secret. In the final scene, the protagonist was confronted by all of the relatives he'd seduced and as a final act of retaliation against them, had sex with the body of his sister. After this he was taken into custody and subsequently placed in a mental institution.

The story was simple but the pacing was such that the plot didn't seem like a series of raunchy sexual encounters but rather one of a hit man stalking and offing one victim after another. It was a cold, ominous pacing and one that seemed to seduce the viewer into the same footsteps as the film's predatory hero. Reading the script was like taking a philosophy course from an adrenaline junky: the desire to shock and offend was there and it was prevalent, but it was consistently metered by technical mastery, witty, darkly amusing dialogue, and a script so detailed in its directions that Alston felt as though it were guiding his mind's eye directly. He knew, in the harrowing instant of reading the script's final words, the threshold feeling that he'd first felt watching a Shibasaki picture for the first time. It was a moment when he knew he had to make a conscious decision to throw the film away in disgust or accept it on its own terms. It was a thrilling high—knowing that disgust and enlightenment rocked back and forth on the teetering scale that was his psyche. The smile that spread across his face seemed to be making the decision for him.

"It's amazing," said Alston.

"I agree," said Shibasaki. It was dark now and the workers had all gone home. The chamber was now lit entirely by an anemic light bulb that hung from the ceiling. Alston's features returned quickly to the penetrating demeanor that was a mirror of Shibasaki's own.

"What was the dreaded secret about the script that everyone talks about?"

"The girl's body."

"It's supposed to be..."

"Say it."

"Real."

"So just like in the previous two movies, but this time you're going to..."

"Fuck it."

"Why do you always have a person really die in your films?" asked Alston.

Shibasaki was impassive. "Answer your own question," he replied.

Alston thought for a long moment and then the truth dawned on him. "Because it's their body, their choice." He whispered.

"Precisely, Mr. Alston. Exactly. That's why the protestors go bat shit over my films—because they can't accept the reality that the people involved made a choice to participate. It grates against their psyche—they retaliate by demanding that it be taken off the market for the good of the people involved and society at large. But having someone die means that they can't be acting on behalf of the person's good. That person's good has long since expired. They have to accept the reality that the person who they want to prop up as a victim consented to my using their body in its dead and final state. It's a powerful statement: that a person's body remains theirs even in death. They accuse pornographers of giving the populace a sense of entitlement to the human body when in reality it is they who feel such an entitlement. They think every sex worker is a helpless victim whose sole purpose is to be held up as a come stained object of overt pity and underhanded ridicule. But a dead body is one whose owner has spoken. Their decision is final and unwavering. Most of the studios that I tried to market *The Lotus Wave* to wouldn't even speak to me. That's why all these rumors have sprung up.

"But I'm here. I want to make it. Why don't we just make the movie and let it speak for itself?"

"Why don't I just let my movie speak for itself? Mr. Alston, have you not understood that it is for this reason that the idiot masses remain unmoved by profound works of fiction? What else is a religion but an organized training guide for learning to accept as fact the ideas of a fiction? Yes, great art can speak for itself but only to those who can hear. I don't need to explain my work to you, Mr. Alston. You obviously understand it. But it is not the educated that require a teacher.

"We all have, in our nature, an element of man and an element of beast. By this I mean that as naturally evolved creatures we are still subject to the same hunter/prey survivalist instincts that motivate lesser creatures but there is also an aspect of each of us that is driven by consciousness and rationality and this element of the mind must be in control of the animal instincts in a rational human being. A society is a macrocosmic manifestation of this dichotomy. Though there are a near infinite number of degrees between the two, the fundamental classes of a society are the thinkers and the primitives. The failure of democracy is to allow the primitives to think that they are equal to the thinkers. Human rights are values which are extended to all people based on the fundamental nature of their species but the equality ends there. So long as human rights—the right to property, expression, and autonomy of mind and body—are not violated, then a free society must reinforce the understanding that the unthinking may not use their inability to think as grounds to legislate their morality on those who can. It is because of the inability of the primitives to understand this that the products you and I create are opposed so vehemently.

"From an intellectual standpoint, it is necessary for a line to be drawn in the sand. The morality of the thinkers must be declared to the primitives along with the declaration that those who fail to grasp those terms are free to be left behind. The founders of your country attempted to establish this in their constitution: the expressly separated church from state to ensure that the primitives could not use divine right to limit the thinkers. They provided freedom of speech, ensuring that the primitives cannot silence the thinkers. They passed freedom of assembly so that the primitives couldn't stop the thinkers from gathering. These simple rights contain all of the final authority required to control the primitives without taking their human rights but the difficulty in predicating a society on human rights is that those rights must be given to all people, including those who can't appreciate them. We the thinking must tolerate the infantile braying of the idiot hordes whose fearful reaction to the notion of freedom is to shrink and hide by electing a leader that will quickly and efficiently return them to the imperial days of long ago: to a time when their lives amounted to nothing more than an assembly line drivel, each chewed up and spat out as needed by the royal machine.

"Great works of art in all mediums have come and gone over the years, Mr. Alston and each time one has threatened to force the unthinking hordes out of their shells to lay naked in the pantheon of thought they've rallied to protest its existence. Look at the history of artistic achievement: it is a bloody tapestry of gut wrenching frustration. Of bold, brave, brilliant, innovative creators being stifled at every turn by rampaging throngs of blithering fools who declare with a shrill, wailing scream that this new symphony, rock album, painting, cartoon, television show, novel, stage play, film or whatever will destroy society. That it will piss off their god, corrupt their kids, and turn their cities into a cesspool of muggings and rapes. They protest and protest and protest and every time whatever it was that they thought would destroy society does *not* destroy society and the idiot hordes go on the prowl for the next new creation to get horrified by over and over again, never evolving. They whine and whine about their religions—they talk about Jesus but never realize that were they alive two thousand years ago it would have been *they* who were nailing Yeshua to the cross.

"They're finally getting their way, Mr. Alston. Your country has finally overdosed on political correctness and declared that people have the right to not be offended. Your founders foresaw such a thing Mr. Alston. Why else would people have the right to the *pursuit* of happiness? Can you imagine how long a society would last if they decided that their citizens were entitled to happiness? There would never be any true happiness because nobody would know how to pursue and gain happiness, just how to complain about not having any. All that would happen is that an impossible to maintain government department would be established to make sure that everybody got their wishes met which is totally impossible. Now look at the D.O.P.E. in your country. Nobody had the nerve to stand up and declare that such a department would be impossible. The effects of such a department are exponential: your government tells its citizens that they have the right to not be offended and nobody learns to stomach anything. Suddenly nobody has to tolerate anything they don't like. Every single time the idiot hordes have declared that they want the source of the offense to be removed they have hypocritically said that they want *just this one thing* removed. Everything else is fine, but this one thing is unacceptable. And THAT is where their near sightedness is revealed: every single thing banned from public consumption is another brick pulled from the tower of freedom and every time one brick is pulled it gets easier for the unthinking to pull the next one—and your country has decided to give them hammers!

"A film like *The Lotus Wave* will either set the thinkers free from the primitives or give the primitives the catalyst they need to destroy the world as we know it. Look at what's happened in the wake of rumors that you were going to be making the film. They don't even know what it's about and already they're ready to burn you at the stake! That film can never be made because it has never been represented by a producer that can fight for it. I can't—I'm too old and too crazy in the eyes of the world. They see me as the sum total of the most horrific scenes in my movies. What *The Lotus Wave* requires is a third party to advocate its principles and ideas. No such porn company has existed. Out of all the ones that were willing to discuss the project with me after finding out it involved a dead body, not one of them has demonstrated an ability to articulate and advocate the principles laid out in my films."

"I can be that person," said Alston quietly, his voice welling up distantly "I can be the person who presents this film to the world. I can make them see. I know I can..."

"How, Mr. Alston? You've never done a single interview. You've never spoken publicly. The people who work for you are among the few that even know what you look like."

"I just... I know I can."

"This is the error of your silence, Mr. Alston. You have never taken on the public—you have hidden, barricaded yourself. I know you're a good man and that you run a responsible company—even a great company—but that doesn't cover your cowardice. You've never confronted the protestors. You've never become the hero that your supporters have wanted you to be."

"I will. I promise I will."

Hotei Shibasaki shook his head and took a long sip from his cup. "Go back to Los Angeles, Mr. Alston. I'm just a crazy old man that's made a couple of good flicks. Whatever *The Lotus Wave* is, whatever great utopia could have been found in its creation and understanding, will never be. Go home, pack your bags, buy a nice little cabin in the mountains and stay the hell away from the rest of the human race."

Chapter 17

THE UNLIMITED SANCTITY ACT passed unopposed and, in one fell swoop of the scythe of bureaucracy, all Americans had the right to not be offended. Within days the Department of Offense Prevention and Enforcement was opened and complaints began to pour in from all over the country. Bookstores, video game and DVD retailers were forced to pull anywhere from eighty to ninety percent of their inventory from shelves, including nearly all magazines. All so called "decency violations" were handled first in the order they were received and then by the number of people that signed each attached petition with two hundred and fifty thousand being the number that would ensure immediate processing of a reported violation. The protestors outside Alston Image, now numbering some five hundred thousand, began circulating decency violation petitions among their ranks, guaranteeing that each issue on their agenda would get the magic number of a quarter million.

In the first forty-eight hours of the Unlimited Sanctity act, ten million jobs were lost and many businesses were required to close, including all porn shops. There were some public objections to the new law but they were quickly silenced when protesting was declared offensive. Within the first seventy-two hours, prayers to the Christian god had returned to schools and the teaching of evolution was abolished.

Desperate to find some way to draw a profit, the ad industry began running ads featuring severely deformed, diseased, or mentally retarded models to ensure that nobody would be offended by overt sexuality. Strangely, few people attempted to counter object to this practice as dignity sheaths had already become required in most states and a general sense of stagnation began to settle in. Indeed, the vast majority of the left began to spout shallow praise for the recent depiction of diversity in modern media.

The movement towards hideousness found a new figure head in the form of Cheryl Bunion, a late-middle aged church volunteer who had appeared on a British variety show singing various show tunes in a quivering, girlish soprano. Her barely passable performance was outshined, however, by her rather homely appearance. The grey caterpillars that served as her eyebrows cast wild, wiry strands of hair about her vast, flat forehead, giving her the countenance of a large, sleepy dog. The most compassionate and egalitarian of onlookers, when pressured to find some redeeming factor in her physical appearance, would be forced to fumble open mouthed for something pleasant in the wild sloping of her cheekbones and the twisted, off kilter stretching of her nose and lips. She boasted that she was forty-seven and had never been kissed, which came as a shock to nobody. When video of her performance went viral on the internet, she was pounced on by the American media and was soon signed to a major recording contract.

"What's worse," asked Billie when she saw the video on her computer, "to be celebrated and successful because you're marginally talented and pretty or to be celebrated and successful because you're marginally talented and hideous?" She sat on the couch in her living room, her laptop open on the coffee table. Hank was leaning against a window in the dining room, looking out at the mob of protestors that now packed the streets in front of the house. He'd tried calling the police, but to no avail—one of the people in their neighborhood was convinced to join the rally and it became a block party in the eyes of the law.

The police were slowly turning on them—the no longer made any great effort to control the protestors outside of the Alston Image offices, who had taken to burning effigies of Isaac Alston and attacking the armored vehicles that brought Alston Image employees to work.

Because of Billie's figurehead status among the models at Alston Image, the protestors had begun to focus in on her as a more concentrated source of their anger. Presently, the mob outside her house held up signs with phrases like "Die Harlot Die!" and "The Bitch Will Burn." At random intervals, the leader of a youth choir would blow a pitch pipe, signaling for his troupe to begin singing "Hark! The Harold Angels Sing" with revised lyrics:

> Though her hair is caked with come
> She will get the good Lord's gun
> We don't mean his holy prick
> Burning Hell awaits this chick
>
> When she dies of some disease
> All will know that she was sleaze

Raped and burned in pits of Hell
While above we're laughing well

When that cunt gets what she needs
We will laugh and watch her bleed
When at last she shows up dead
God will piss upon her head

"All I know is there coming out with a movie based on some book called *Pull*," replied Hank. I turned on the TV the other day and they were going on and on about how there was nothing in it to offend anybody—no beautiful women, no nudity, nothing pleasant or escapist whatsoever, just this slow, agonizing story about an unwed teenage mother growing up in the slums. They showed a clip from it and it was of an obese black woman running down the street eating a stolen bucket of fried chicken. How am I *not* supposed to find that offensive?"

Hank's cell phone rang and he pulled it out of his pocket. "Hello?" he answered. "When? Is everyone okay? Yeah—we'll be there in just a second."

"Who was that?" asked Billie, worried at the newfound strain in Hank's voice.

"That was Dominic. He wants us to meet him at Alston's house. A bomb just went off inside it."

They rushed to Billie's car and Hank took the driver's seat. The crowd roared when they saw the car backing out of the driveway and their fury multiplied when they realized that Billie wasn't wearing a dignity sheath. Hearing the protests Hank nodded to Billie who opened the glove box and withdrew the loaded .45 they'd started keeping there. As they backed out of the driveway and turned in reverse to align with the road, Hank took the gun, rolled down his window and fired a single shot into the air, its burst enough to scatter the hordes that had run in to pound on their car, though they quickly resumed their post once he'd driven away.

The streets of Van Nuys were similarly littered with protestors, most of them crazed from hunger and only barely capable of hollering incoherently as Billie and Hank approached. The protestors finally tapered off when they reached the gated community where Alston's home was located. In the long, winding drive up into the hills, Hank and Billie were tempted to drift off into the pleasant immersion of the lush mansions but were unable to shiver off the cold reality that loomed low in the air.

When they arrived they found that Dominic was already parked on the other side of the street from the house, which was now barricaded by a fire engine, SWAT team transport, and three police cars. Where once the house had been a towering testament to modern architecture it was now the frame to a gaping orifice from which unending billows of smoke poured, drifting up into the sunny blue sky as though its grey trail was a harsh malignancy on the otherwise tranquil beauty of the day. Vast amounts of rubble were strewn across the front lawn and where the bomb had vivisected the mansion there were broken pipes and support beams twisted off at odd angles as though cowering in the wake of an imperial parade.

Dominic stepped away from leaning against his car when Hank and Billie drove up. "Apparently the bomb went off in the living room, which is close to the front of the house," explained Dominic as the others turned to stare open mouthed at the damage. "I heard Patricia tell the cops that she was out back with the kids when it happened."

"So everyone's okay?" Billie asked.

"The kids are fine, just real shaken up. Patricia was knocked down by the force of the blast, but she seems to be okay."

"It's that fucking movie!" shrieked an angry voice. They turned to see Patricia Alston stepping from between two of the emergency vehicles. Clad in her bathrobe she stormed towards Dominic as the paramedics and a police officer followed close behind tried to calm her. The police officer seized her by the shoulders just as she reached Dominic. "If my goddamn husband weren't trying to make that fucking movie none of this would have ever fucking happened!" she was screaming in a hoarse voice as mascara ran down her cheeks in teary lines.

"There's not going to be any movie," said Dominic loudly, and Patricia was silenced for a moment. "That's why I brought Hank and Billie here—so I could tell all three of you at once. I just talked to Isaac on the phone. He said he's found Hotei Shibasaki and says there's no way to make the movie— Shibasaki wants a woman's dead body to be fucked on camera. There's no way we can arrange for that. The project's off."

"Is that what he said? That the movie was off?" demanded Patricia.

"That's what I have to assume." Patricia relaxed for a moment, her suddenly frail body sinking back slightly into the depths of her robe.

"So what's next? For Alston?" asked Hank.

Dominic shook his head, looking down at the ground as Patricia was led away. He sighed and cleared his throat as another cloud of ashen fog billowed overhead. "I don't know. We can't keep going like this. Alston Image sales in Europe are still going strong enough to keep most of us eating, but without any new product there will be layoffs fairly soon."

"What about a relocation?" asked Billie. "They could move the whole operation overseas."

"That's true but this Families for Families crap is already picking up all over there too. They've set up branches in the UK, Scotland, Ireland, Italy,

Spain… Word is they've even got one planned for Vatican City. It will only be a matter of time before they've gotten their claws sunk in wherever we decided to move, and we'd be back where we are."

"No surprises there," muttered Hank.

After awhile Duke Cunningham drove up, bearing the news that had already been circulated, adding "the sheer amount of paper work at the Offense Prevention office is all that's keeping us in business."

"How exactly does that thing work?" asked Hank.

Duke Cunningham placed his briefcase on the hood of the car and flicked the locks, opening it. He extracted a thin stack of papers bound by a metal clamp. "This is a print out of the form," he explained, holding it where the others could see. "First the complaint has to be explained in terms of who is offended by it and why. In order to qualify for immediate processing the complaint has to be filed on behalf of a minority, which consists of at least a quarter million people."

"What's the maximum on how many can be in a minority?" asked Dominic.

"There isn't one. So each complaint can have an attached petition in which the signatories claim to constitute a minority and demonstrate how the offensive thing in question is offensive specifically to their minority. If they don't get the necessary quarter million they still get what they want but it's just processed after all other forms that have a higher number of signatures. Once a 'thing' is identified it must then, by law, be removed from sale or expression and laws are passed to ensure that it cannot be seen, heard, or traded in public."

"They'll collapse the entire economy," said Hank, aghast.

"What's already been banned?" asked Dominic.

"Let's see… "muttered Duke, taking out another print out. "Porn, any movie not rated G, any book not written for children except the Christian bible, all magazines, meat products, alcohol, candy and all dessert items, sex outside of wedlock, sex within wedlock that doesn't produce children…"

"Okay, I've heard enough," interjected Dominic.

"Focus on Families circulates the petitions around to all of their churches. They can get a quarter million in nothing flat. They've already made blasphemy illegal."

"Well goddammit," said Hank, who turned to realize that Billie was back in the car, talking to someone on her cell phone. She finished the call and returned to the small huddle after a moment.

"What was that?" asked Hank.

"Nothing babe. I just need to go out of town for a couple of days."

"You'll be back in time for your concert, right?" asked Dominic. Billie nodded.

"By the way," Duke interjected, "We got a letter from Families for Families that was stamped by White House. Apparently you can no longer advertise your concert with reference to the fact that you're a porn star. Also, they want your set list to include at least six songs from the Families for Families hymnal."

"What about my first amendment rights?"

Duke sighed. "What about them?"

The next day, Artie received a call from Melvin Crankshadow. "Artie-"said Melvin with precise cheer. "Wanted to see how everything is going?"

"Fine," replied Artie.

"Well I wanted to follow up on our meeting the other day. How's the money treating you?"

"Umm... great actually," Artie chuckled a little.

"Wonderful to hear it Mr. Barrel. You know, I was reading in the Good Book the other day and I thought of you."

"Oh is that right?"

"Well, it occurred to me that the running theme through the narrative of the greatest story ever told is one of sacrifice. Sacrifice is such a beautiful thing, don't you agree?"

"Yeah, I guess."

"Think of the implications, Mr. Barrel: that you could gain immortality in the eyes of your tribe by their knowing that you had surrendered that which was most important to you to the needs of the whole. It's a tradition that began with Abraham and one that we should all continue to this very day. Sacrifice reminds us that nothing quite as important as helping our fellow man and that all of our petty personal attachments are really just hindrances in that pursuit, don't you agree?"

"Sure, I suppose."

"And that's what I love about you, Artie. That's why I'm so proud to call you my friend. You get what I'm talking about. You're a stand up kind of guy—the kind you want with you in a foxhole. Tell me something, Artie: what do you think of the current culture war?"

"What do you mean—this whole nobody can be offended thing?"

"Yes."

"Well I don't know—it kind of puts me out of business..."

"You were already out of business as I recall, Mr. Barrel."

"Well, that's true."

"But think about it, Artie. With the new prohibition, there's going to be a black market for smut the likes of which you've never seen."

"I guess so..." said Artie,

"Don't guess—know it for certain. It's everything you've always wanted—smut peddlers will be back underground and your business will be booming. But that's not all: Isaac Alston will be ruined. Nobody will be able to produce big budget porn features anymore. It will be hand held video cameras taping stoned teenage runaways in a ghetto apartment. The very thing you've been best at and the very thing Alston has never done."

"Well that does sound mighty fine, now that you mention it," muttered Artie with a contemplative drawl, the burgeoning light of realization slowly igniting in his eyes and smile.

"You see, Mr. Barrel," continued Crankshadow with a vaguely syrupy tone that was laced with practiced sincerity, "I told you I'd help you out in the long run. You're about to become a wealthy man. I'm going to give you a position within my church as a silent investor. We'll take the money you make off of the porn and give it back to you with interest. As far as the IRS will know, you're just a businessman who supports the church like a good American."

"But am I a good American?"

"Of course you are, Mr. Barrel, of course you are."

"Well that all sounds good, but what does that have to do with sacrifice?"

"Oh I'm glad you brought that up, Mr. Barrel. You see, I've counseled some remarkable people in my life. People who have turned their lives around in the name of Christ. And every time they do it's a beautiful thing to watch. You see, when the Devil takes hold of them they lose control and fall into all manner of drugs and alcohol and violent crime but every time they turned their life over to Jesus, it always improves. They get off the drugs, they get a new job, and they make peace with the people they've wronged. All because they accept the magnitude of that sacrifice that Jesus made for their sins."

"You mean to convert me?"

"Oh no, no, no Artie—not at all. I'm approaching you as a business man, not a Christian. But nevertheless, I must let my Christendom guide me in all things and for that reason I must reach out to you as one who asks for an act of charity, in recognition of the amazing things the lord has already done in your life."

"Umm... okay—what?"

"Well, a sacrifice, Mr. Barrel. My congregation has been calling for a sacrifice, one that will lift their spirits in these trying times."

"A sacrifice of what?"

"Not of what—of whom."

"Okay—who then?"

"So you're saying you'll do it?"

"I don't know."

"Well do think about it, Mr. Barrel. Think about the words of my flock—surely you've seen them in the news?"

"I have."

"And you've been hearing what they've been saying?"

"I have."

"Then think about it Mr. Barrel. They're telling you exactly what to do. Exactly who to sacrifice. I'll talk to you soon, Artie."

"Okay—bye," replied Artie, but Crankshadow had hung up before he could finish the phrase. Artie hung up his receiver and stood solemnly in his kitchen for a moment, feeling that the light that beamed in through the windows was peering into him and through him. Though bathed in the afternoon sun, Artie felt as though he were standing in a sort of photonegative of darkness—that the light which surrounded him was being refracted by the true darkness that emitted from within himself. He carried that inverted darkness with solemn contemplation into the living room where he sat down and turned on the television.

Bob Match: And welcome back to shouting match with Bob Match. You know, for the first time in a long time, I feel proud to be an American. We've got those bible-sodomizing, flag-burning, baby-aborting Democrats right where we want them. It's finally time to bring this country back to what the founders wanted all along—a limited government ruled by an almighty monarch. When we conservatives are finally back in control, we'll make sure that every Latino in this country has to carry papers verifying their citizenship at all times and we'll make sure abortion and condoms are illegal and we'll make sure that you're under constant 24 hour surveillance for your own safety and, more importantly, we'll make sure the government stays out of your lives by eliminating all forms of government healthcare, minimum wage and child labor laws, environmental protection, and all the other names that the government has for COMMUNISM! Here with me today is Alice Grausam, whose latest book "Vaginacide: How pornography causes cervical servitude" with Andrea Danvers would be a New York Times bestseller except that we've finally shut down that great bastion of Liberalism, the New York Times. How is the book selling, Alice?

Alice Grausam: Well, Bob, my supporters and I successfully registered as a majority minority whose rights were being oppressed by all Americans who refused to buy my book, so now my book is in nearly every home in America. And for those people who can't afford my book, prison awaits!

Bob Match: That'll show these evil Communist Liberals to unnecessarily burden the state. So you were at the Alston Image protest rally yesterday, correct?

Alice Grausam: I sure was, Bob, and we were thrilled to find out that some god fearing patriot had bombed Isaac Alston's house!

Bob Match: We can only applaud such valiant displays of patriotism. This will show our enemies how we deal with domestic terrorists like Isaac Alston. I understand the protestors have a new name for themselves?

Alice Grausam: That's right, Bob. While I was out there with those bible loving patriots, they told me about a new name for their movement. It goes back to the days when patriotic Americans would hear Stars and Stripes played by brass bands and get a tear in their eye. We've decided that this new movement will be all about finding that dusty old trombone that's in all of us, pulling it out, and blowing it for freedom once again. Bob, I am pleased to present the Rusty Trombone Party!

Bob Match: That truly does bring tears to your eyes. Camera 3, zoom in so that the good folks at home can see the tears in my eyes. Now tell me, Alice, what are the Rusty Tromboners saying about Alston Image?

Alice Grausam: They have realized that Alston Image is the great beast from revelation and that its absolute destruction is crucial for the return of our Lord and Savior Jesus Christ. Isaac Alston—more than anyone else in history— has profited off of whoredom and now it's time for him to face the wrath of the Christian community.

Bob Match: On that note, am I correct that Families for Families is on the verge of declaring Christianity the official religion of the United States?

Alice Grausam: We certainly are, Bob. We've successfully petitioned the government that the vast majority of the Christian minority is offended by not having their religion recognized as the official religion of the country and since our numbers beat out the Jews and Muslims automatically, we're just waiting for the paper work to process and soon Christianity will be the official religion of the United States.

Bob Match: Well that sounds fantastic, but what about the latte slurping pecker lickers on the left that will say that this is infringing on the first amendment?

Alice Grausam: The first amendment has long been misunderstood, Bob. Liberals like to pretend that it means some nonsense about free speech but really, if you read into it correctly, it refers to the right of the Christian community to regulate and reduce the size of the government. It's all covered in my new book. And besides, once Christianity is recognized as the official religion, it will be high-treason to practice anything else.

Bob Match: That will ensure we never end up like those radical Muslims. Now, we had one of our reporters down there earlier and there was a great deal of chanting. What was that all about?

Alice Grausam: That's the anthem of many of the Rusty Tromboners. They're calling for the head of Billie Solar.

Bob Match: The Alston Image contract girl?

Alice Grausam: That's right. She's been the most widely successful model on the Alston Image roster and as such she's a symbol of everything that wretched company stands for. These good patriots are demanding that bitch's head on a platter and I don't blame them.

Bob Match: That will save the American people from the scourge that is democracy. And you need to hear that nation: this country is not a democracy and it never was. It's a representative republic. When you pledge allegiance you don't say "and to the DEMOCRACY for which it stands," do you? NO! This is a republic pure and simple. Democracy is just mob rule. It says that the majority can do whatever the hell they want with no oversight whatsoever. Look at the democratic leaders throughout history—Hitler, Mussolini, Mao, Pol Pot, Idi Amin, Vlad the Impaler, Jim Jones, all of them Democractic Liberal Commie Satanic Athesists! We have a caller—caller, you're on the air.

Caller: Umm... yes, Bob. I can't help but point out that Jim Jones wasn't an Atheist. He was a Christian minister...

Bob Match: Shut up! Shut up you godless heathen idiot. Cut his line! Cut his line! Did you get his caller ID information? Good—send it to Department of Homeland Security. You hear that you godless traitor—we're going to have you hanging upside down by your nut sack before the day is done! Nobody will ever question me like that! I will not be challenged on the truth. The first amendment protects me from being questioned! Anyone who challenges my point of view is disrespecting my right to free speech and since my point of view is the point of view of all true Americans anyone who questions it will be locked away so help me almighty God Christ in Conservative Heaven! Okay... Okay... I'm calming down now...

Alice Grausam: It was pretty obvious that caller was a man who is addicted to pornography.

Bob Match: Absolutely. I could tell by the communist tone of his voice that he was a big fan of... of... what was that bitch's name?

Alice Grausam: Billie Solar?

Bob Match: That's the bitch. That one right there. God that bitch needs a bullet in her brain. Just think how much better off we'd all be if we didn't have bitches like that?

Artie Barrel muted the television and sat in the silence of his own thoughts for a moment. Not used to such contemplations, his focus was broken by the sound of bed springs bouncing in his son's room.

"Hey boy!" shouted Artie. After a moment the bouncing stopped and Ralphie stuck his head around the door.

"Yeah daddy?"

"What're you doing in there?"

"Fuckin' me a bracelet bitch."

"Don't you know that shit's illegal now?"

"Aw hell daddy aint nobody gonna touch me. I'm the vice president of Intersect Productions."

"Well, whatever. Send her home and get some clothes on. I have a job for you."

"What kind of job? I'm already vice-president of Intersect Productions."

"That aint what I mean boy. But do this for me and I'll make you president, how about that?"

"Sure as shit daddy. What do you have in mind?"

Artie attempted the gentle charisma of Melvin Crankshadow. "Son," he began, "the greatest thing a man can do is make a sacrifice, wouldn't you agree?"

Chapter 18

RAPE WAS ON THE RISE, especially in areas where the dignity sheath was popular. After Christianity was declared the country's official religion the only thing that Catholics and Protestants could agree on was that the natural role of women as the temptress was one that needed to be removed from the rest of society. As such, centers were created to house incurably perverted women. The centers, known as Slattern Salvation Houses, were privately owned by Melvin Crankshadow Industries and became a leader in the growing field of for profit juvenile and adult detention centers. As new prisons were opened to house the adult female offenders, Andrea Danvers declared that the raped women were getting their just deserts and deserved to be locked away for giving in to the vile patriarchy while Alice Grausam proclaimed the incarcerations as a much needed return to a biblical code of ethics.

When Alston returned home he first visited the wreckage of his house, finding a letter from Patricia stating that she'd gone with the kids to her parent's house in Colorado. The news struck Alston as cold breath in the fog that had been his icy resolve since meeting Shibasaki. The recent memory of meeting his idol hung thick and congested in the air above him, hovering with the demand for an analysis of the events that his weary consciousness was reluctant to provide.

Over the course of his first day back, Alston packed several suitcases full of his clothes and moved into the small overnight suite in his penthouse office. As his helicopter circled in to land on the rooftop helipad he watched the angry, screaming masses that had shut down the streets for five square miles. They were a famished, shit scented multitude that waved their signs and screamed as though they expected some act of divine intervention to decimate the Alston Image offices. Similar groups had massed around the Flynt Publications building and the Playboy offices. With men in smelly rags and women shrouded in dignity sheathes, Alston felt as though he were staring down at the throngs of Mecca, though their purpose around the large onyx cube of his offices was far from worshipful.

The dome that Alston had erected around himself was beginning to crack. No longer could the stoic attention to his work override the growing voracity of the screaming multitudes. Shibasaki had penetrated Alston's defenses with the diamond dagger of reality and while the darkly focused posture was still unmoved from his face, it was apparent in the minute implications of his eyes that he was ready to face his attackers and his mind had become more retaliatory in its planning. He had been to the mountain top and studied at the feet of the master. Now the ethereal spirit of his consciousness was at war with the throbbing muscle of his brain, forcing it with vicious resolve to accept the truth of Shibasaki's words. Deep in Alston's nerves he felt sparks coming alive—sparks that were generated by hearing the sounds he had shut out for so long and seeing the sights that self-imposed blindness had shielded from him. If the love of one man could bring enlightenment to the whole world could the hatred of the whole world bring enlightenment to one man? He placed this question on the forefront of his mind as he opened the door of the helicopter and stepped out into the sudden rush of hoarse braying that spewed up from the maggot infested streets below.

As he placed both of his feet on the ground, Alston felt the natural impulse to turn and hurry down the thin row of white stairs that led to his office but instead he strode forward to the edge of the building, set down his baggage, and stepped up on the low barrier wall that ran the perimeter. Feeling the dizzying rush of gravity, he scowled down at the seething multitudes whose screaming reached a fever pitch when they realized who they were seeing. With nothing protecting him from death, whether it came from an assassin's bullet or the unflinching pavement below, Alston placed both his feet together, held his arms apart and straight out to form a cross, and raised his chin up to the sky. He stayed in this position for some time—perhaps five minutes, perhaps ten—all the while feeling the roaring hatred ricochet off the surrounding buildings and come back to him amplified a thousand fold.

Duke Cunningham and Abe Lattimore were seated in front of Alston's desk when he arrived and rose to greet him when he entered the room. For several uncomfortable minutes they'd watched Alston stand on the ledge overlooking the riotous mob below, terrified that he would jump but wise enough not to get in his way if that were course he decided. When he'd stepped down from the ledge, Duke and Abe had hurried quickly back down the stairs to the office to leave the impression that they hadn't been watching Alston in that most naked of moments.

Alston's demeanor was that of an enlightened despot. Alston still held the reigns of his company with the iron clad grip that his sharp tone had always commanded but now the constant contemplation in his eyes was not one of potential action. It was a combustible fixation on the moment at hand that wafted in the breeze of a compassion that had always been apparent but was now acknowledged by Alston himself. When he crossed the room to his advisors the meter of his stride seemed to imply the dry, imperial tone of a battle march. When he shook their hands, both Duke and Abe found a profound reassurance of the strength that had been suspended when Alston went away.

"Alright," said Alston, sitting down at his desk. "What do I need to know?"

Duke Cunningham spoke first: "It's like this whole Department of Offense Prevention Enforcement is a Pandora's Box. Families for Families is getting things banned by the hour at this point. Have you gotten a chance to look at the news?"

"I read every paper I could get my hands on during the flight home. I know the basics about the D.O.P.E. but that's it. I guess we're off the market then?"

"Us and every other porn company. The D.O.P.E regulations have made obscenity laws redundant so for the time being there won't be any obscenity charges pressed against us. For the time being. Darcy's trial will be going forward in the next few days."

"Make sure she the full support of my legal representation."

"Indeed we will. But how long do you think we can hold out?"

"For as long as it takes to get this whole mess resolved."

"You think there's an end in sight for all of this?"

"Maybe not in sight, but it is there. Those seething hordes out there aren't bound by an ideology. They're bound by a media personality. All we have to do is take away the figurehead that's holding them together and they'll disperse."

"And what figurehead would that be?"

"Melvin Crankshadow."

"What about Andrea Danvers, Alice Grausam, Bob Match, all of those?"

Alston shook his head "those aren't of any consequence. They just serve to pump up the crowds, but what they think is their driving philosophy is really just a repackaging of what they're getting from Crankshadow. Without the momentum from Crankshadow, there's a chance that the government will step in and uphold the right's of its people for a change."

"You need to be careful going after Crankshadow, Isaac," Abe interjected.

"I don't need to go after him. He'll keep coming after me and before too awfully long he'll step out of his comfort zone."

"You sound prophetic, Isaac."

"I just know how people work. Crankshadow has the strength of his convictions behind him and because his convictions are founded on the wrong premise, they'll inevitably bring him down."

"He would say the same thing about you."

"But he's the aggressor here, not me. The validity of his convictions is what will allow him to succeed or fail on my battlefield. My convictions are founded on rationality, his are founded on faith. His require the blind unthinking masses to create the semblance of validity, mine do not. Duke—tell me something."

"Yes?" Duke replied.

"What keeps you working for me through all of this? Besides the paycheck."

"Besides the paycheck... Because I like the materials we put out. I like seeing naked people having a good time."

"Precisely. That alone is enough to invalidate the shallow whining of Crankshadow's supporters. Your support for me is predicated on something concrete. His supporters rely on him to feed them their daily dose of Heaven. No matter how convinced they are of their support for him it is a false, hollow hallucination because it has no concrete manifestation. That is the failure of all theocratic societies—that the populace will ultimately have nothing to show for their patriotism save for the promise of rewards after death."

"But not all of those people are following Crankshadow for theocratic reasons."

"Now come on, Duke—hasn't history taught you anything? His secular followers simply replace him and his cult of personality as their god. They will be the first to dissent when they come to realize that the utopia he promises by removing all pleasure can never be obtained."

"There's the reason I keep working with you, Isaac," interjected Abe. "You make porn with a purpose."

"Then I rest my case."

"So on more immediate matters, tell us about Shibasaki. Apparently he won't let you make the film?"

"Wont and can't. He doesn't trust me to represent the film properly, but he also wants-"

"A dead body," whispered Duke.

"Right. But I haven't given up."

"Why not?"

"Why not? Look at those mildewed cretins out there in the street! How do you think I could go on in the face of that without something to live for? I don't know how I'll make that film, but come hell or high water I'll either make it or die trying!" There was a concentrated mania in Alston's eyes when he said this, one that was echoed in the timid reverence of his associates.

"Whatever course you take," said Abe carefully, cautious in the face of such an unorthodox display from Alston, "you'll have to find some way to get around the mob."

"No," said Aslton, gently shaking his head. "The mob will have to get around *me*."

Melvin Crankshadow had been right—the black market was doing wonders for Artie Barrel's business. Things were back like they were in the good old days: find a run away with a decent figure and you could get her to fuck on film for the price of a drive through dinner. If they cried and begged him to stop, he could spit "what are you going to do about it, bitch? This shit will put your ass in jail if the cops find out." The videos were selling well—they had to be sold through hucksters in back allies but they were selling.

Never one to take stock of his sales demographics in previous eras of his company's success, Artie was suddenly aware of the sheer volume of conservatives and evangelical fundamentalists that were buying his products. In one of their increasingly frequent, always hushed conversations, Artie had asked Crankshadow if he'd been telling the congregation to purchase Intersect smut. The minister had given a jolly, almost condescending laugh when he'd heard this and replied "no, Artie. Sin is bound in the heart of mankind. Without you to corrupt souls they wouldn't come to me for salvation. Keeping my flock in a constant state of guilt and quiet turmoil is the best thing for them and I don't need to help them with that."

These words echoed in Artie's mind as he sat in a chair on the circular main stage of Crankshadow's megachurch. After his glorious introduction to and reception by the many thousands of people that attended the sermons, Artie had become a staple of each Sunday's performance, always sitting somewhere on the stage and standing and waving when he was expected to, but never speaking.

"I have a very special young man to speak to you today," said Crankshadow, his voice shaped by his eternally beaming smile. "Matthew Simmons was one of the first youths admitted to our porn addiction rehabilitation program and today he has completed the program. Come on up Matthew." Crankshadow turned and led his congregation in applause as Matthew Simmons, now a conservatively dressed teenager in a polo player t-shirt and khaki slacks, climbed the stairs to the stage. "Matthew is a prime example of the kind of change that needs to happen in this country. I'm pleased to report that we have a bill pending right now that will allow us to seize children from abusive homes and place them in our care. No longer will we have to wait on the United States government to do the lord's work for us! This bill, called the Universal Custody Reclamation Act, will allow us to rehabilitate the nation's children as we see fit and we will finally be able to take back the next generation in the name of Jesus Christ almighty! Matthew's life is a testament to why such a bill is so vitally needed. Matthew!"

Applause.

"Thank you," said Matthew after he was handed a microphone. "Thank you," he repeated as the applause petered out. "I wanted to talk to you today so that I could share my testimony and my truth. A year ago I was addicted to pornography. It was corrupting my mind and destroying my relationship with the living God. Now, that same God has healed me and taught me to control the impulse to sin that runs through my body.

"Let me tell you, people, that the Devil does not fool around with this addiction. He makes it feel so natural. For years I'd been an addict and felt like it was the most natural thing in the world to want to have sex with the girls around me. I would look at the girls that I went to school with and my thoughts would automatically turn sexual. I felt that this was natural and I actually enjoyed thinking these shameful things. It was like anytime I looked at a girl, the first thing I would ask myself was whether or not I wanted to have sex with her. If I did then sex with her would be the only thing I could think about and if I didn't want to have sex with her then I wouldn't think about her at all. I actually believed that this was normal and that I didn't need help.

"If that weren't enough, I began to have sexual thoughts about the women in my community. When I learned to masturbate, which the Devil left me vulnerable to by hardening my penis like he'd hardened my heart, I would touch myself and think of my teachers, my mom's friends, and various older women I would encounter and start to wonder if they knew things about sex that I didn't and could teach me. Again, I thought all of this was perfectly normal.

"I began buying pornographic DVDs because I needed to feed my unholy addiction which, at the time, I didn't even know I had. I had to fake my ID, put on fake beard stubble, and sneak into an 'Adults Only' novelty shop and looking back I now realize how hard the pornographers were trying to push their products onto children. The internet was much worse—it was as if there were no restrictions—nobody telling me I couldn't look at this stuff and with nobody telling me not to, I had no reason to think it was a bad idea. I would go on 'Adults Only' websites, ignore the content warnings, and just start looking at porn.

"When my mom finally caught me, she turned me over to Families for Families and they rehabilitated me. They taught me that wanting to have sex with girls as young as thirteen was perverted and helped me accept responsibility for my problem by registering as a sex offender. My sixteenth birthday is just around the corner and my probation officer says I might be allowed to make a supervised trip to Disneyland to celebrate! Because of my addiction—and having to register as a sex offender—I won't be able to live where I want or get jobs, but that's okay because Mr. Crankshadow has taken me under his wing and given me a place to live here at the church's Lifetime of Addiction shelter.

"From Mr. Crankshadow I have learned that looking at women sexually is evil and sinful but I've also learned from Ms. Danvers that it's also degrading and dehumanizing. We can't allow this to keep on, people—the whole world has fallen into sin and if we don't save them from sex, think of what could happen. I mean, if you tell people that sex is okay you're basically telling them that rape, pedophilia and bestiality are okay. Sex is evil and wrong and you know that it's evil and wrong because it makes you feel good and the devil always makes things feel good when they're bad for you. If you aren't in pain every minute of your life then you're prone to evil. It's that simple. So we have to keep this going people—we have to get out there and keep witnessing and keep getting our petitions through the D.O.P.E doors and get over this whole 'I'm okay you're okay' thing because that's not what Christianity is about!"

Thunderous applause. Artie smiled and nodded at the young man as he passed then jerked his head back to attention when he noticed Crankshadow glare at him sharply.

With production at a standstill there was little to do at the Alston Image offices. Alston gave most of his employees a leave of absence, retaining only his executives and, covertly, the staff that maintained contact with the European arm of the Alston Image empire, which itself began producing and releasing content under the names of various front companies to create the impression that Alston Image was completely inactive.

Food became scarce as well, with production halted on all livestock farms and most other forms of agriculture. Officially, the only food products that could be legally produced were rice, water, and various wheat products. Meat was banned by vegetarians who found it offensive while vegetables were banned by various groups who found vegetarians offensive. Animal rights groups succeeded in banning the ownership of pets, forcing millions of Americans to release their family pets into the "wild." This resulted in many of the animals simply circling their former homes, begging to be let back in to their houses and their former owners watching in vain, unable to feed them.

Conservative activists succeeded in shutting down public schools, libraries, firehouses, police stations, welfare, social security and most forms of healthcare. In the days following the latter ban the protestors that now filled the streets wailed at the loss of their Medicare while demanding that the government stay the hell out of their healthcare.

Most of the country was out of work and millions were now taking to the streets, standing in thick, rancid clumps of humanity and screaming upwards at whatever buildings towered over them. The protests became an incoherent mania with little if any philosophy actually guiding the participants. Within a few days the streets in which they protested were bought by the private sector and privately funded police forces arrived to inform the protestors that they could either sign the Offense Prevention petitions being circulated by the private interests that owned the streets or be arrested for vagrancy.

With no police force to protect them, the more public figures within the Alston Image stable began living in the building itself to take advantage of the private police force that Alston hired. Made up largely of a portion of the SWAT personnel that had been put out of work when the government police force had been let go and they maintained watch over the inside and outside of the Alston Image offices with high powered assault rifles.

Despite the striking down of all other forms of government service, the military was unaffected. Due to the large number of private contractors doing business, the military industrial complex continued to thrive and continued to grow in size when vast amounts of the populace turned to military for employment. Because the military's first duty was, supposedly, to the government, it was with the understanding that they would regulate the private law enforcement groups that martial law was declared but with most of their money coming from private interests, the military police in their ominous tanks and battle fatigues did little to intervene when the private police officers got out of hand.

The sale of many products, including most forms of food, continued on the black market and many workers returned to jobs that were now conducted in secret. With their jobs made illegal, none of the workers were able to demand minimum wage or protest when they were forced to work seven days a week because no legal recourse was open to them. The militant throngs began to move en masse to the new sweatshops that were springing up across the country but were unable to afford most of the products they produced, with the lion's share being divided between the wealthy upper class and exports to the wealthy upper classes of foreign nations. Cheaper products were made available to the newly named "peasant class," who were forced to accept rations of inferior food and clothing from the organizations within the larger conglomerates that formed to create "communal conditions" for their workforces, all of which went under the public radar. Many workers became ill and mass outbreaks of food poisoning, tuberculosis, and diarrhea were untreated and unreported. Despite the lack of medical coverage and the frequent deaths of workers, there was always replacement labor: desperation coupled with mass hysteria drove the populace into the illegal factories.

The relatively meager profits that did pour in from Alston Image's overseas sales had to be heavily laundered before they could be received by the company. Nevertheless, Alston set about creating a reasonably hospitable atmosphere for his employees, converting conference rooms and offices into makeshift apartments with the dressing room toilets and showers providing for bathroom needs. Able to afford the expensive black market food, Alston made sure that those in his care were able to eat well despite having to also rely on the legal grain industries.

Contrary to his expectations, the confinement did not produce the kind of primal hostility common to cabin fever. Instead, a kind of closely knit community had sprung up, the sanity of the building's residents maintained by the unity of the philosophy that guided them. That philosophy, though none of them fully understood it, radiated from Alston's interactions with them which, by necessity, became more frequent. He allowed the performers to use the private gym in his penthouse and, amazingly, began eating in the cafeteria among his fellow residents.

The simple board and card games that were found on the various office computers became staples of the extended leisure time, with games of computer chess becoming popular activities. Alston began joining in on these games, taking up challenges from Dominic, Billie, and others as a small audience would watch, each contemplating the game quietly and applauding for whoever won. Alston found himself genuinely enjoying these moments, finding that the sacred, inner circle of friendship he'd shared with his most trusted associates could be easily extended to the rest of the people in his contained community. Still, he retained the reserved timidity that augmented his regal demeanor with an element of haunting uncertainty.

Sex was, predictably, another popular pastime, with the performers and other employees frequently taking care of each other's needs. Though she was as active with various men and women as ever, Hank couldn't help but notice a certain detachment in Billie's eyes, as though her mind reached out desperately to find the escape that sex was providing for her body while still remaining tethered to dark, sinister contemplations. She had gone out of town as she'd planned and returned a few days later, just in time to take up residency alongside Hank in the Alston Image offices. Though her inner distance was of constant concern to Hank, he broached the subject infrequently, finding that she would brush it off as quickly as he brought it up, usually murmuring "I'm just nervous about the concert I have coming up" as a canned statement of dismissal. This only served to concern Hank further—Billie was never worried about performances of any kind and the majestic aura of her sexuality seemed to have waned in the face of this new contemplation.

"Thanks for going to all this trouble to keep us fed, chief," said Rod Wielding one night as he and Slamdingo were hauling in crates of black market food from the loading dock under Alston's supervision.

"I hope you don't mind paying for our food and housing," added Slam.

Alston chuckled dryly "you're my employees—I always have."

If there was a silver lining to the underground industries it was that the streets were made relatively clear, with only a few hundred protestors lining the sidewalks at any given time. Although it was hardly safe to move back into their homes, the employees of Alston Image were able to come and go when escorted by Alston's private police force. There was little to do in the outside world, with most forms of entertainment being banned, but many of them found that they enjoyed riding off into the hills to just sit and observe the natural world. It was the kind of natural Zen that prisoners adopted to retain sanity.

In a surprise move, Alston joined Hank, Billie, Dominic and Diana Arland on a day trip to Big Sur, even giving them the use of his private jet to expedite the journey. Once there they rented a car and drove out to one of the rocky peninsulas that shaped the local coastline and sat on the outcroppings for hours, just taking in the mellow, meditative ambience of the foamy waters breaking against the rough shoreline and listened to the waves as they created a infinitely nuanced music over which long crimson bands of sunset eventually stretched, as though the sun, in its fading moments, had decided to reach out over the ocean and conduct the random symphony that had lulled the onlookers into solemn detachment.

After a couple of hours of watching the waters, Alston looked over at the others. Dominic and Diana sat on adjacent rocks near the center of the peninsula while Hank and Billie were huddled together on a single stone nearer to Alston. Though he was some twenty feet away, Alston could still see the curious stirring in Hank's eyes—it was the cold, steely eyed gaze of a veteran warrior who could never stare on a serene vista without imagining how a battle would play out on that calm expanse. Furthermore, it was a gaze that, on some involuntarily and deeply ingrained level, yearned to be in the throes of combat. Seeing that energy, Alston felt compelled to utilize it in some way. The restrictions of his country kept him from capitalizing on it as he would have in the past. Instead, he looked upon those dark, subtly arched eyebrows and the piercing eyes beneath them and began to think in terms of using the warrior instinct in Hank directly, in a way more visceral and heart wrenchingly committed to the cause of Alston Image than any of the paid guards that stood nearby ever could.

In the last rays of daylight they returned the car and boarded Alston's jet for the return home. The pilot had fallen asleep in the cockpit and, when roused, was surprised that the time had passed so quickly.

Duke Cunningham's success as a corporate attorney had come from a fundamental understanding that the courtroom was simply the site of a business deal in which the terms were not money and property but truth and perception. He understood that both the prosecution and the defense were presenting competing proposals to a board of directors that consisted of a primary decision maker and twelve advisers. The truth of reality being discussed was objective and unquestionable. The wise presenter of either side would not attempt to obfuscate the truth—this was a precarious path which demanded that lies be presented with the conviction and factual certainty of truth and whoever chose to walk such a path did so at extreme peril. There was no question of the reality of the accusations—Darcy's company had delivered the pornography in question and the cold federal laws concerning the transmission of obscene material were rock solid. The only hope for Darcy's case was for Duke to successfully argue that what had been transmitted was not obscene by any identifiable standard. If truth was the default then the bargaining token was perception and Darcy's freedom rested on Duke's understanding of the nature of the bargaining at hand.

The courtroom was at once a vast expanse of sharply hewed wooden grandeur, its utilitarian nature offset by the occasional Victorian flourishes in the minutia of the jury box, the judge's bench, and the church style pews that sat in long lines behind the balustrade that separated the theater of law from its audience, but alternately constrained and compacted by the fluorescent lights that echoed in the eyes of the police officers that stood by each of the chamber's exists.

Duke and Darcy sat at audience left before one of the two plain tables in place for the prosecution and defense and both were dressed with an intentionally conservative heir, Duke sporting the most bland of grey suits and none of Darcy's clothes suggesting any degree of sexuality. Even so, neither was so void of color and flamboyance as the prosecution's lawyer, Tad Felmer. In his formative years Tad Felmer had been raised in a staunchly conservative home in Shreveport, Louisiana where his army general father and housewife mother had made sure that he attended services every Sunday at the local Baptist church, participated in football and basketball in high school, never touched alcohol and sternly counseled him that sexual abstinence in one's teenage years was a cornerstone in the development of a good American. Maintaining such bolt-upright pride in his square jawed patriotism, Felmer had attended the University of Mississippi in the early 1960's and had been one of the loudest haranguers of James Meredith during the forced integration in 1962. He'd worked as legal counsel for the President's Commission on Obscenity and Pornography under Richard Nixon and had swung gingerly from there to involvement in the Messe Commission some years later. Now in his late sixties, Felmer was officially retired from the practice of law but served as legal council to Families for Families when asked. Today he stood at the opposite table, shifting through the papers in his briefcase and distributing them to the surface before him as though they were litigious tarot cards.

The jury was led into their box and seated then all in the room rose to recognize the arrival of Judge Vincent Cartwright who sat patiently as the bailiff swore in both sides then began with the calm weariness of a legal veteran: "Thank you all for being here today. The court shall hear the case of Darcy Collins v. the United States. The charge is the creation and transmission of obscene materials by mail. The jury is charged with determining whether or not Ms. Collins and her company, Darcy's Mainframe, have committed this act. The jury shall keep in mind that the charges against Ms. Collins are to be evaluated on the basis of the law as it existed prior to the establishment of the Department of Offense Protection and Enforcement and all new legislation that has been handed down since its founding. We shall now hear the opening statements of both sides."

Felmer approached the center of the chamber with a withered gait that was supported only by the lethargic haughtiness of his aristocratic air. "It is the goal of the prosecution to demonstrate that Ms. Collins has committed these heinous acts and we are confident that the materials collected as evidence will demonstrate that reality in no uncertain terms. As you hear the arguments made by both sides and the testimonies rendered you must ask yourself: 'what about the children? What about child pornography? What about Communism? What about National Socialism? Do I want to live in a world where human sacrifice on satanic ritual altars is the norm?' These are the questions at the forefront of the culture war that we are waging and which we cannot win if dangerous smut peddlers like Ms. Collins are allowed to roam free, looking with lascivious eyes at the patriotic children of America and dreaming of sinking their fangs into that pure, angelic white skin. Thank you."

Fighting the urge not to role his eyes, Duke rose and approached the jury, taking the time to make eye contact with each one of them as he approached. They were a diverse mix of people: a young college age woman with fair skin and red hair, a middle aged and obese man with an olive complexion, a sharply dressed black man in his middle thirties, an elderly Asian woman, and various other indicators of diversity. Duke knew that this could be played to his advantage: that a lack of cultural hegemony among the jurors would make it difficult for them to come to a common consensus on what was and was not obscene. "It is the goal of the defense to demonstrate that this trial is unfounded and unjustifiable—that the nature of the charges against my client are unconstitutionally vague and serve as nothing more than a smoke screen to advance the political agenda of various nanny state pressure groups. The question before you is not one of decent verses indecent but of liberty verses tyranny and of free thought verses the tightening clamp of the nanny state. I call on each and every one of you to weigh not only the merits of obscenity that will be presented but also the cognitive capacity that allows you to decide what is obscene and what is not. You will find that this cognition—no matter what its outcome—is based on your rationally identified personal values and that as such a legal and all encompassing definition of the standards of 'decency' in your community is not possible. Thank you."

The crushingly soporific ennui of legal proceedings sat in with each of the DVDs in question being presented and entered as evidence. A nervous tittering transpired through the audience as the titles *Darcy's Anal Orgasms Five, Mainframe Girls Mega Orgy Three, Sapphic Surrender Seven, Mother/Daughter Lapdance Fantasies,* and *World's Biggest Female Ejaculation Bukkake Nine* were labeled Examples A through F. From there the prosecution was allowed to call its first witness which turned out to be none other than Andrea Danvers, who entered the courtroom and rippled to the witness stand where she took the oath.

"Do you swear to tell the truth the whole truth and nothing but the truth so help you..." muttered the bailiff, fishing in his pocket and withdrawing a crumpled piece of paper from which he read "the great and holy mother goddess of vaginal supremacy?"

"I do," she replied and sat down, the rested position bearing little difference to her standing posture.

"Would you please state your name and qualifications for the court?" began Felmer wizened analysis.

"Doctor Andrea Danvers, professor of women's studies at Whitland College."

"Dr. Danvers, would you please enlighten the jury on the harmful effects of obscene materials on society and on individuals?"

"Well, the first thing that you have to understand is that what we're talking about here is not just nudity and it's not just sex. What we're dealing with here is *gonzo* pornography, which is where we see the real hardcore, body punishing sex where women are made to vomit, cry, and suck on penises that have just been in their anuses all while being called dirty and degrading names like whore, bitch, slut, cum dumpster, sperm receptacle, cunt, skank, flesh mattress, hoe, bucket fanny, minge, slag, hoe, abortion factories, slut bunnies, fuck holes, hose beasts, pecker puffers, fuck toys and many other awful things . Gonzo porn is by definition porn that feeds into men's deeply engrained sense of entitlement to women's bodies and what is rape if not giving men a sense of entitlement to women's bodies? And that is what the modern porn industry does—it delivers visual ownership of women's bodies through the penis which is a very potent means of delivery and it leaves women feeling helpless in the face of a massive social experiment in which pornified men are made into addicts to serve the needs of multinational corporations where-"

"Objection, your honor," said Duke, rising to his feet. "What exactly does this have to do with the effects of obscenity?"

"Sustained. Dr. Danvers, you will confine your answers to the topic at hand."

Danvers sighed pretentiously and began again. "To understand the effects of obscenity, we have to ask ourselves: is it normal to become aroused to images of sexual torture? Obscenity by its very nature is designed to portray the human body in a disgusting, degrading way and when that becomes the cultural standard then it becomes much easier in the minds of men to commit acts of sexual violence because they've become trained to think of it as gratifying."

"Would you like to demonstrate how each of the films entered as evidence meets the criteria of obscenity?" droned Felmer monotonously.

"Certainly. *Darcy's Anal Orgasms Five* consists entirely of scenes of women inducing orgasms in themselves by inserting vibrators into their anuses while simultaneously stimulating their genitals. In *Mainframe Girls Mega Orgy Five* we see a mass of women who have converged to have a sex that is devoid of intimacy and features scenes in which they lick one another's anuses. Now, the joke here is that the woman is having to eat shit and is done entirely for a male audience's enjoyment. *Sapphic Surrender Seven* shows women that are convinced to give in to their lesbian desires and this confers the message that female sexuality is for the men after all with its focus on women's breasts, buttocks and vaginas. *Mother/Daughter Lapdance Fantasies* perverts the relationship between mother and daughter and tells men that it's acceptable to expect mothers and daughters to have sexual relations. And the last one shows women spraying their ejaculate onto each other, which I think we can all agree is just gross."

"No further questions, your honor."

Duke stood, accepting the judge's offer to cross examine. "Dr. Danvers," he began, taking the podium, "would you like to explain to this court how the descriptions you've provided with regards to the evidence adheres to an objective definition of obscenity and not just your own personal revulsions?"

"No I would not."

"That was not the actual question, Dr. Danvers."

"Doesn't matter. 5th amendment."

"Dr. Danvers," interjected the judge "the 5th amendment protects you from having to testify against yourself. You are here as an expert witness. Answer the question."

"Very well—as a woman, I am able to give birth and that means that I know better than men what is and is not good for the human race. As a feminist, I know better than other women what's best for them. As a college professor I have an authority over non-academic feminists and as a bestselling feminist writer I have popular authority over less well known academic feminists, therefore my opinion of what is and is not obscene is, by virtue of my stature, the most accurate projection of the definition of obscenity."

"And can you put that definition into exact words?"

"It is words, images and other media that offend the sensibilities of someone such as myself."

"That sounds less like an objective definition and more like you've just sanctified your own opinion."

"I don't think of it that way. Rather, it is a recognition of my profoundly superior judgment as an inherently valid paradigm for society at large."

"How is that different from saying that you've sanctified your own opinion?"

"It's different because it recognizes the inherent complexity of my insightful prolixity."

"So in other words you're automatically right because you can state things in an excessively complicated manner?"

"No, I wouldn't say that. I would say that my heightened capacity for verbal complexity is-"

"You will stop evading Mr. Cunningham's questions or I will find you in contempt of court," interjected the Judge.

"Thank you, your honor," replied Duke. "But seeing as that is a fruitless line of discussion I would like to ask Dr. Danvers this: was it not you who asked my client to send you those DVDs in the mail?"

"Yes," said Danvers, visibly reluctant to offer such a definite answer.

"Then are you not also guilty of the crime for which my client is now charged just as a drug dealer and a drug buyer are both breaking the law?"

"No, because I was doing that as a representative of Families for Families, who were helping the FBI with its investigation. It's not illegal to break the law if you work for law enforcement."

"No further questions, your honor."

"You may call your next witness, Mr. Felmer," said the judge as Andrea Danvers slid down from the stand and left the room with a great, rolling indignation.

"The prosecution calls Ms. Darcy Collins," said Felmer, exchange places at the podium with Duke as Darcy took the stand and the oath. "You are the owner of Darcy's Mainframe, is that correct?"

"Yes," replied Darcy directly and succinctly, her shimmering blue eyes tinged with the solemn indifference the situation demanded.

"And what was your involvement in the creation of the films in question?"

"I own the company that produced them and was the executive producer on all of them. I acted in *Mother/Daughter Lapdance Fantasies, Mainframe Girls Mega Orgy Three* and *World's Biggest Female Ejaculation Bukkake Nine.*"

"And the same company of which you are the owner shipped these titles across the country, is that correct?"

"Yes."

"Would you care to tell me how the films in question are not obscene?"

"Define obscene."

"I think that much should be fairly obvious, Ms. Collins."

"You cannot be required to prove a negative. If you provide a definition of what obscenity is I will do my best to demonstrate how my films do not fit that definition."

"Well, your films strongly offend the prevalent moral authority of our times."

"Which is?"

"Well, look at the current political and cultural climate in the wake of Families for Families."

"They are not prevalent. They're a large minority that the U.S. government has unconstitutionally chosen to favor."

"But I think we can agree that pretty much the whole country now agrees with them."

"Only because they've established that they find public disagreement with their views to be offensive. If you go by that standard you're essentially allowing Families for Families to dictate the moral views of the entire country."

"Well then there's your definition of obscenity."

"But the judge has already declared that because of the time of my arraignment the law in this case must be reflected as it stood before Families for Families took over."

"I wouldn't say that they 'took over' Ms. Collins. The government simply chose to recognize the inherently superior rights of an oppressed minority."

"In what way were they oppressed? Were they being denied their constitutional rights?"

"They were being oppressed because the government refused to turn their ideology into law."

"If that's what it takes for people to have rights in your mind then freedom for you does not exist."

"Objection, your honor," said Duke. "Where is all of this going?"

"Sustained. Barring any cross examination, the defendant is relieved of further testimony."

"I have one question, your honor."

"Approach the podium."

Duke stood and came to the center of the room as Felmer seated himself. "Ms. Collins, would you please explain the artistic merit of the films in question?"

"Certainly. In all manner of artistic endeavor, any circumstance can be used as the symbolic presentation of a system of values. Look at the war films, for example, that extol a wide range of potentially contradictory values: patriotism, might makes right, violence is wrong, human life is of value, sacrifice is a virtue, brotherhood and camaraderie are deeply engrained bonds, civilians suffer most in war, battle leaves soldiers forever scarred and traumatized, and so on. The same medium, a motion picture about armed conflict, can be used by any filmmaker to communicate any moral values and the moral values presented by one can contradict the values presented by another, just as the concepts of value I just named are contradictory.

"But the thing that unites all war films is the acceptance that feelings associated with armed combat are a valid form of artistry regardless of the system of morality that underlies the plot. The same is fundamentally true of all genres: a romantic movie acknowledges that the concept of romance is artistically valid whether it is a movie about two young gay lovers in San Francisco or a husband and wife pair who are married in the Christian church. A horror film acknowledges that it is fundamentally valid to have an experience solely for the sake of experiencing the sensation of terror. In other words, any genre of artistic expression acknowledges that it is artistically valid to experience the feelings being presented regardless of the morality associate with it.

"The same distinction is over looked, however, in relation to sexuality. In western society it is only considered artistically valid to portray sex as being in the realm of moral decay, insanity, abuse, betrayal, manipulation, and a whole host of other negative experiences. To present human sexuality as being valid and proper to experience in and of itself is seen as frivolous, base, crude and unimaginative. What my films acknowledge is that the sexual experience is artistically complete in and of itself and requires no higher moral justification; that to observe a piece of art and find it sexually arousing is just as artistically valid as listening to the *Moonlight Sonata* and being moved to tears or just pleasant relaxation. From that point forward you can examine each of my films for the nature of their artistic message, but their validity as art is fundamental and absolute."

"Thank you Ms. Collins, no further questions. Your honor, I would like to call an expert witness of my own, Mr. Dominic Daniels."

"Bring him in."

Darcy returned to her chair at the defense table and watched as Dominic Daniels entered placidly and took the oath. As he sat she noticed how out of place Dominic seemed in the grey suit and tasteful yellow tie that he'd worn to the trial. Despite the uncomfortable contradiction between his suit and the ruffled gauntness of his actual body, he seemed graceful and smooth as he sat down in the witness box.

"Mr. Daniels," began Duke, "please explain your professional credentials."

"I am a director and screenwriter for Alston Image. I have received numerous accolades and am well regarded within my industry."

"I brought you here, Mr. Daniels, because you would serve as a third party qualified to address any incorrectly defined terms in the course of the trial. The term 'gonzo porn' was used earlier by Dr. Danvers. Was it used correctly?"

"No, it was not."

"Please explain the correct usage of the term."

"Gonzo as a genre comes from the concept of gonzo journalism made popular by Hunter S. Thompson. A gonzo journalist is someone who actively participates in the events that are unfolding, rather than passively documenting them. A gonzo film, therefore, is one in which there is no third wall and in which the director and the camera are acknowledged by the performers and the director and cameraman may interact directly with the performers, even being one of the sexual participants."

"The common objection to gonzo films is that they're inherently violent and cruel and thrive on putting women into dehumanizing situations. What is your expert opinion on that?"

"There are certainly films of that nature out there on the market. Whether or not those films depict actual dehumanization or simply performed, consensual acting has to be judged on a case by case basis but the reason that gonzo tends to feature a great many activities that might be seen as focused entirely on grotesque sexuality or bizarre, aberrant behavior is simply that gonzo porn is largely devoid of plot. There may be some sort of premise presented to justify why the people involved have come together to have sex, but very often the sexual intercourse itself is all that's presented and as such it is the sex, not the circumstances surrounding it, that demand the director's creativity. One of the avenues for such creativity is to go the route of disgust and compromise the viewer's sexual arousal with ideas and actions they may find unpleasant. Because modern society views sexual indulgence in and of itself as an act of rebellion, it is therefore frequent to see this creativity come out in ways that are outside the societal norms of sexual interaction."

"Thank you, Mr. Daniels. No further questions, your honor."

"Would you like to cross-examine the witness?" asked the judge to Tad Felmer.

"No," grunted Felmer irritably, as he pretended to occupy himself with various papers on the table. Dominic left the stand and the judge announced that the court would hear the closing arguments. Tad Felmer again approached the jury, this time with a slightly more militant tension in his eyes and mouth. "Ladies and Gentleman of the jury," said Felmer with the kind of aged tone of proclamation that seemed more appropriate to a campaign rally than a court of law. "You are gathered here on behalf of your community to make a decision that will have long lasting effects on the moral fiber of the country. This is an opportunity to be part of a landmark decision and I commend and thank you for taking your time to be here today.

"You must understand that there is no question about what has occurred here: the accused has shipped obscene materials in the mail and this is a crime in no uncertain terms. What I ask for each of you to consider the consequences of obscene materials being made available to the public. What does it say about the moral fiber of our community when we allow child pornography into our homes? After all, you wouldn't want to see your grandmother being raped by your children in a dark alley so why would you want to allow people to take pictures of it and sell them at playgrounds? That is the culture war that we are fighting.

"In the 1957 case of Roth v. the United States, it was determined by the Supreme Court that obscenity was in no way protected by the first amendment. Now, you have to understand which court rulings are inflexible and which ones aren't. Roe v. Wade can be overturned but Roth v. the United States cannot. The reason for this is that it's the job of the government to protect its citizens and that means that only laws which remove the necessity of choice—thereby *protecting* the citizens from consequences—can be upheld. Roe v. Wade *forces* people to make choices and that kind of force is exactly what the founding fathers wanted to protect us against. Think of those brave soldiers that fought and died in the American Revolution and ask yourself if you're willing to desecrate their memory so that you can open up your community to the leftist interests of a bunch of Hollywood smut peddlers. Only by having the community enforce the common interests of communal living can we ever hope to beat back the Communist threat posed by sexual promiscuity.

"The ruling made in 1957 is final and no other consideration of subsequent cases need ever be examined. The law is clear and all that remains is for you to vigorously prosecute Ms. Collins for attempting to profit off of illegal adult pornography that can only serve as the catalyst for child pornography and human trafficking. The defense rests."

"Thank you," said the judge. "The court will now hear the closing arguments of the defense."

Duke rose to his feet and walked to the center of the chamber, his solemn stride seeming to absorb every toxic fume of the withering fog that Tad Felmer had left seething in the eyes of those who now focused on the man who proposed to defend the indefensible.

"I hope that the inflammatory rhetoric of my opponent has not clouded your judgment," Duke began. "But in the event that it has, it is my duty and my pleasure to correct certain profound errors in his perspective.

"Rather than try to refute the concretes of what my opponent has said in his closing statements, I will acknowledge all of them: my client sent those DVDs in the mail and they were pornography. There is no refuting that. What I will refute is my opponent's premise. Ms. Collins lives in California, the products were shipped to Boston, she's being tried here in Washington D.C. and you were all selected from jury pools around the country. What community standards do you hope to apply and what community do you represent? You cannot speak on behalf of the entire country—we live in a country with a representative government and unless you have been elected by popular vote you have no right to determine policy. This is also true of the more localized level of society that we call a 'community.' At no point are the persons who decide policy in our country above electoral process.

"But assuming that there is a concise enough group of people among you that you could adequately judge 'community standards,' you are still tasked with determining honestly the standards of your community. You may not invoke the recent cavalcade of D.O.P.E legislation as the justification for your decision—my client was arraigned prior to their establishment. Think of your community as it was a few months ago. Can any one of you honestly say that you lived in a community that didn't tolerate the sale of these products? And if you didn't, can you honestly say that you didn't live in a community that tolerated the sale and purchase of the Christian bible—a book that is filled to the brim with incest, masturbation, whoring, sexual slavery, gang rape, sodomy, and plenty of other sexual taboos along with genocide, mass murder, human sacrifice, human trafficking, flying corpses, drug abuse, drunkenness, fratricide and worse? Do not say that your religious convictions give such a book the right to exist while damning others. Religion and state are separate entities in this country and for good reason.

"Would you then say that the literary and artistic qualities of the bible permit its publication but not the work of my client? The text consists exclusively of one-dimensional characters that follow an internally contradictory logic over the course of an inconsistent narrative that was trumped in literary merit by Sophocles 429 years before the Common Era. It fails as art and is rife with obscene activities. Its social value is seen only by a specific demographic who by constitutional finality cannot force their beliefs on others—in other words it's entirely subjective. And that is the ultimate justification for the bible's existence: that its value is open to determination by all people in a free society. But what allows you to see that value? If it were the only book in existence you would not be able to recognize its value by default. You have to determine its value by your own personal judgment and apply that value by contrasting it with other works in which you find no value whatsoever. That is the social value of all things that the law would determine to be obscene—that they demand the active rejection of your conscious mind. Thus, even the most revolting of entertainment is necessary for the functioning of a free society.

"But reflexive to this reality is the freedom for some persons to find value where others find none. If the social value of something is to be the determining factor as to whether or not it is legal to create, distribute or posses then you cannot make the decision to ban it without denying the preferences of some—even many—individuals in a society. My opponent invoked the word 'communism' to win the argument because he knows that you all know a deeply engrained fear of communism but not an understanding of what it is. Communism demands that individual rights be voided in favor of communal regulations. Ladies and gentlemen what this man is asking you to do in the name of patriotic service is the most un-American sham possible!

"Why do you think he cited an obscenity ruling from the 1950's? Because he actually expects you to ignore the ongoing legal debates over obscenity that have gone on since then. Miller v. California in 1973 decided that obscenity was a matter for local, not national, standards. In a society of privately owned property we respect the rights of private citizens to establish and maintain environments that cater to their own sense of moral conduct so long as that conduct does not do direct and unwanted physical harm to other citizens and therefore the question of local standards is settled by the right to private property.

"Consider the case of FCC v. Pacifica which established that only the repeat use of seven specific words during certain hours could be considered punishable or the case State v. Henry which struck down obscenity laws in the state of Oregon or Reno V. the ACLU which struck down indecency laws applying to the internet. Each of these cases represent a gradual acceptance of the first amendment as absolute in all matters of communication. The goal of my opponent is to incur fifty years of prison time for my client—effectively the rest of her life—take jobs away from the many people who work for her company, and criminalize her products on the basis of what? Some ill-defined concept known as 'obscenity' that they have demanded that you be protected from whether you want to be protected from it or not?

"Obscenity has never been properly defined by the federal government and the enforcement of law in a free society demands that its edicts be based on concrete reality, not some paradoxical hypothesis that is in a constant state of flux. When you go to deliberate on the fate of my client, ask yourself if you can truly find anything to enforce. If you are certain that she is guilty in your heart but not your mind then you have allowed yourself to fall into the sick but well guarded trap that my opponent has laid and the life of an innocent woman will be forever altered as a result."

The jury took ten minutes to reach its verdict and returned to the courtroom with the same reverent solemnity that they had afforded it during the proceedings. The juror nearest the judge, a middle aged black woman with a stern but compassionate face rose, opened the manila envelope in her hands and read from the page contained therein. "For the crime of creating obscene materials we the jury find Darcy Collins not guilty. For the crime of shipping obscene materials through the mail, we the jury find Darcy Collins not guilty."

The judge's face turned silently from the jury box to the twin tables before him at one of which sat Darcy Collins and Duke Cunningham with looks of quiet pleading on their faces and the other at which Tad Felmer and his lackeys sat forward and attentive, as if watching the winning shot of a bowling game teetering between a full strike and the gutter.

"Ms. Collins," said the judge with the indifferent magnitude of justice, "I hereby pronounce you not guilty. You are free to go." The gavel was struck and is sharp crack rang across the courtroom as Duke and Darcy rose to their feet and embraced in victory, not noticing as Tad Felmer took a single piece of paper from his briefcase, crossed the courtroom and presented it to the judge. There was a vague sigh into the Judge's microphone after he finished reading the page. "I'm sorry Ms. Collins," said the judge with visible resignation, "but Mr. Felmer has just presented me with a voucher stating that Families for Families has gotten the required signatures for a petition categorizing your freedom as an affront to their right to not be offended. You'll have to be incarcerated for the full term of your sentence."

The sound of the gavel, which should have still been echoing in the hearts and minds of each person in the courtroom, now seemed distant and castrated.

Chapter 19

BILLIE'S CONCERT loomed on the horizon. Her haunting detachment was broken periodically by the angelic affection she gave to those around her which was, now more than ever, bestowed with an odd sense of finality—as if she had only so much love to give and knew that the well was about to run dry. She spent a considerable amount of time with Hank—more than ever before—but he still felt that her quiet distance was her way of weaning him off of her affections—that so long as her body lay pressed against his every night, the warm shell of her body ever present, she could gradually release him from the powerful narcotic that was her spirit.

"Are you okay, honey?" he asked one night in the dressing room that had become their bedroom. She was sitting on the edge of their bed, miming the motions of playing a piano with her hands.

"Of course I am babe," she replied and then, sensing a heaviness to his words, "I'm just focused on the concert is all."

Hank knew what words he wanted to say and knew that their sounding would be like dragging a razor against the luscious membrane of comfort that was their relationship. He didn't want to say what needed to be said for he knew that it would mean showing fear and uncertainty on his part which could only be seen as a pathetic plea for a lethal dose of her drug. He asked anyway: "Are *we* okay?"

Billie released the invisible piano and leaned over to Hank, wrapping her arms around his waist and placing her head on his abdomen. "We're doing amazing, babe. And I mean it. I know I seem a little off right now and I know it makes me seem distant, but I'm still here honey. My mind can encompass the heavens, travel the stars in its contemplations, but you are forever the mooring ring of my heart." She kissed his naked stomach and they made love in a way that was more fearful and groping than Hank had ever known.

The following morning was the day of the show. They ate breakfast in the cafeteria and Alston joined them. "Are you still doing the concert tonight, Billie?" he asked.

Billie nodded. "Of course. Why wouldn't I be?"

"The protests. What with the things they say, I wanted to make sure that you feel safe."

"It doesn't matter. They can't scare me into hiding. That's how terrorism works."

Alston rose with eloquent, but practiced formality. "You have my support then; I just wanted to make sure you were okay with it all."

"I am."

"Good. I'll have my limousine take you there."

The performance was to be held at the Black Chapel, though promoters were only able to proceed by promising no sex would be had on the premises during the performance. The Black Chapel had been official shut down as a swinger's club, but could still operate as a restaurant provided that military police were on sight to maintain chastity and that the menu only consisted of the brown rice and the few vegetables that had been approved of by the D.O.P.E's new Department of Dietary Concerns branch.

Despite the clenching intestine that was the US government, the Black Chapel looked vibrant and alive the night of the performance, with tickets selling well among the upper class and the few working classes persons that were able to come by them. With most forms of entertainment being banned, the populace had been itching for some form of stimulus and solo piano was a welcome relief. Though various groups had tried to have the concert shut down, none could adequately explain how the performance was offensive to their particular minorities. A few measly protestors littered the streets near the venue, but other than that there was no significant blockage.

For once, Ralphie Barrel was cherishing his natural ability to go unnoticed as he navigated down the sidewalk along the side of the Black Chapel. The air was sharp and warm in his lungs and for the first time in a long time his senses felt equally charged, as though new synapses were connecting, reeling with the virginal rush that was their first exchange of serotonin. He was excited and alive and felt that it was some mythic force that rose from the briefcase in his hand. He was going to do something *real*. Something that people paid money to see people do in *real* movies. This was going to make him a legend.

Ralphie walked past the Black Chapel's back alley and glanced sharply toward it, making sure that there were no guards around. Satisfied that the venue's security was entirely occupied with the large influx of patrons through the front door, Ralphie walked on for another block until he was all alone, stopped and turned around to return in the direction he'd come. Still barren of persons, the slim alley welcomed Ralphie with veils of shadow that enveloped his black clad form completely, leaving only the ghostly paleness of his face and hands exposed to the light. What the alley subtracted in visibility it replenished in sound. Ralphie realized immediately that he'd stepped off the flat, muted pavement and onto a gravel path that echoed up to the tops of the surrounding buildings when his foot fell into it. Startled by the sudden rush of a sound that reminded him of crinkling wrapping paper, Ralphie paused and glanced around nervously. For the first time that evening, his environment had conspired against him.

Reestablishing his determination after seeing that he hadn't drawn any attention to himself, Ralphie stepped further into the darkness, his feet carefully finding arrangements of gravel that could bear his weight without creating significant noise. There was a garbage dumpster against the back wall of the club and a fire escape nearby. The fire escape was the traditional interlocking "Z" shape created by steel stairs and corresponding landings but the arrangement terminated some ten feet above the ground, with a ladder to cover the remaining distance. The ladder was pulled up to the first landing and Ralphie realized he would have to find some way to pull it down.

After setting the briefcase down against the side of the dumpster, Ralphie carefully closed one of the lids and scrambled up on top. Balancing precariously, he jumped and managed to catch the ladder by the bottom rung of the ladder, which came sliding down above him with a screeching clash of rust and steel. Ralphie landed on his side in the gravel, clenching his teeth to keep from swearing aloud. The ladder now hung lower to the ground and if he mounted the dumpster again, he'd be able to climb it.

Just as Ralphie was about to return to his feet when he heard another set of feet enter the alley and he rolled against the wall of the Black Chapel, pressing deeper into the protective shadows. The wide beam of a flashlight cast down the alley for a moment, revealing the dank textures of rock and brick but stopping short of the dumpster. Ralphie breathed an inward sigh of relief when the flashlight clicked off and the feet were heard stepping off of the gravel and back onto the sidewalk, the sharp click of their heels vaporizing into the crowd of bodies out front.

An instant later and Ralphie was back on top of the dumpster, the handle of the briefcase clutched in his teeth. It was not easy climbing the ladder this way as the contents of the briefcase made it fairly heavy but in short order he was on the first landing, the case back in his right hand, and was scampering up the fire escape. He wanted to ascend the steps more carefully, but the rush of adrenaline that had burst forth when he'd nearly been caught propelled him upwards with a new found vigor. He stopped just before the top of the stairs, smelling cigarette smoke. Peering over the side of the rooftop, he saw a younger man standing on the roof, taking a smoke break. Fighting the urge to ask where the kid had come by the cigarettes in the current market, Ralphie checked the boy's shirt, seeing the logo and slogan that identified him as a Black Chapel employee.

With a forced return to stealthy maneuvering, Ralphie snuck up behind the smoking employee and brought the side of the briefcase down hard on the boy's head. The kid, caught too of guard to express any degree of surprise, went instantly limp and fell to the ground. Ralphie leaned in and saw blood draining from the boy's ears. Satisfied that he was at least unconscious, Ralphie moved to the steel box structure on the roof that housed the door back down into the club.

The stairs went down one story before depositing Ralphie at a plain grey door identical to the one that opened onto the roof. Stepping through, Ralphie found himself in the maintenance corridor that he'd hoped to find. The panel next to the steel doors of a nearby elevator told him that the management offices were one floor below and the private theater boxes were a further floor down. Hearing the sudden and enthusiastic applause below, Ralphie realized that the concert had started and hastened his pace down the hall to a room marked "sound and lights."

The door into the room was slightly ajar and Ralphie leaned around the edge of the doorframe where he could see two people. One was sitting down at a board of dials and switches and the other stood behind him with a clipboard. "Bring the house lights down, Collin," said the standing man as the sound of piano music began on the concert stage down below.

"Collin, could you come here a moment," said Ralphie in a heavily affected tone.

"You stay here, I'll see what it is," said the other man, and Ralphie heard him walking towards the door. Pressing himself against the wall on the opening side of the door, Ralphie waited until the man with the clipboard, a wiry bald man with glasses, stepped out into the hall. Ralphie closed the door with his body as he brought the briefcase up again and knocked the man unconscious.

Able to hear Collin rising from a swivel chair and approach the door, Ralphie turned and, when the door opened, bolted forward and grabbed Collin by the throat. Collin was also a weak, nerdy sort and it didn't take much for Ralphie to strangle him. Once the wheezing, gurgling half breaths stopped and Collin went limp, Ralphie returned to the hallway and dragged the other man's body inside along with the briefcase. After locking the door,

Ralphie sank back against it, wiping sweat from his brow and suddenly out of breath. The rush of the moment was gone and the practical side of his mind urged him to focus on matters of escape but he forced them aside and slid across the narrow chamber of the sound and lighting booth to the little window that looked down on the stage.

Billie was sitting at the piano, playing. Ralphie felt the distant rumblings of the emotions that the music was meant to stir, but wouldn't allow himself to be swayed by their beauty; he was here for a singular purpose and its goal brought him back into the headspace of doing something *real*. He tried to find a good angle, but realized that from where he looked down, the open lid of the piano blocked Billie from direct view. He would have to wait until she got up. He tried to see if he could find Hank Steele and Issac Alston somewhere in the crowd and figured they were in the Alston box, but could only see them if he leaned out the window slightly, an angle that he wanted to avoid.

Withdrawing from the thin, rectangular window, Ralphie opened the briefcase, which was now stained with blood on both sides, and began assembling the contents it held. The dark clicks of the mechanical parts as they slid together were cold and satisfying. The most fulfilling of these clicks was that of the scope and Ralphie saved it for last.

The limo that met Hank and Billie at the front door of Alston Image seemed like a grand indulgence from some distant kingdom of Art-Deco castles and swing-jazz knights on fine porcelain steeds. It was a merciful caress of the royalty that Isaac Alston commanded when he was allowed to flourish and his most magnificent. The interior was covered in a cozy, puffy sort of leather that ensconced and enraptured the passengers.

Alston was inside the limousine when Hank and Billie stepped in, Hank nodding with an almost aristocratic heir at the chauffeur who opened the door. Inside, Alston sat at the far end of the chamber on a black leather couch near the driver. The entirety of the interior, its regal upholstery, mini-bar, and arrays of neon diodes that bounced and flashed in time with the radio's luxurious tones, seemed to pour forth from Alston, as though the finery existed simply as the understood accompaniment to Isaac Alston. Hank was reminded of his feelings at first stepping onto Alston's private jet. This casual pageantry was the mythical utopia that Families for Families held at bay, declaring that it was only those who spoke on behalf of the god of sickness and poverty that deserved to live in such a province.

"Dominic is riding separately," explained Alston as Hank and Billie settled into nearby seats and Billie hung a garment bag from one of the overhead handles. "He knew that I wanted to speak to the two of you alone," said Alston.

"Oh really?" said Hank, suddenly concerned.

"Don't be worried Hank," replied Alston with the kind of effortless calm that he commanded with the same deft grace as his opulent surroundings. "I simply wanted to take the opportunity to congratulate the two of you."

"On what?" asked Billie.

"On the success of your relationship. These last few weeks have put me in greater touch with many of my employees and your coupling has been a rather pleasing sight to behold."

Hank sensed that the kind of articulate, distantly stern demeanor that Alston used to virtuosic effect in his business dealings was awkward at best in these more intimate matters, but he felt honored to be one of two that were privileged with the patient task of watching Alston express himself this way. Alston's cold, precise demeanor was resolute in its contrast to the emotions that bubbled just behind his eyes, as though there were a quiver of innocent loving there that struggled to adapt to the chiseled surface. "I've been in this business for over two decades," said Alston, "and in that time many of my stars have had romantic flings with their co-workers. Some of those flings have been for a recreational reenactment of the scene they'd just filmed and some have resulted in marriage. But when I look at the two of you, I don't feel the kind of disinterested puzzlement that I'd experience watching my other employees together. The critics all talk about the chemistry between you two and, for once, that's not merely something I take into consideration in casting future projects. I really feel the chemistry—everyone does. Where do you think it comes from?"

"It comes from that moment when I first laid my eyes into his," said Billie with a soft certainty. "His eyes were commanding and vulnerable at the same time. There are very few men who can show that. Most men are simmering with testosterone and look into a woman's eyes as if she were the opposing team in an elementary school softball game. That can be fun for shooting a scene or a one night stand, but I look for a real man. Hank is one."

"I notice the Mrs. isn't with you," commented Hank as Alston contemplated Billie's answer. Hank then realized that he'd never seen Alston's wife at all.

"Patricia decided to take the kids and live elsewhere after the bomb went off. I can't say that I blame her."

"Does your wife support your business?"

"No," replied Alston, his demeanor relaxing. "She started out working in porn but quit after we were married. It was a shame—her career was just starting to take off, but she wanted to do the housewife thing. I went along with it because she was great with the kids. It was odd, though—as soon as our first child was born, she started getting really defensive about things. She didn't want people from the industry in our house; she didn't want the kids visiting the offices, and so on and so forth."

"Why did you stay married to her?"

"Because she's fantastic with the kids. She plays with them, spends time with them—if she weren't there I'd have to hire a nanny, so it's easier to just keep her around. And if she left me, there'd be no way in hell I'd ever see the kids again."

"What got you together in the first place?" asked Billie.

Alston thought about this for some time, appearing to contemplate not the nature of his response, but only its wording. "I'm not the sort of person that has much regard for the conventions of society," he replied slowly. "People have this kind of need to have this certain string of 'traditional' experiences in life: they want to get their learner's permit, get their driver's license, go to the prom, pledge to a fraternity, get married, have 2.5 kids, work a job and retire. There's nothing inherently wrong with any of those things, I just find them kind of bland because it's like people are born on this earth and they're given this playbill of those traditional experiences and then… that's it. They live for all of those specific moments and the rest of their lives are spent remembering or anticipating those moments. That makes those moments worthless to me. I want to create my own moments and I want them to be mine and mine alone. And I want them to happen whenever I wish to create them. So that's what I've always done. Even so, it seems like the rest of society expects you to want those moments as much as they want them. It's as if they just can't let it go. As a businessman I've always been in the place to delegate responsibility where needed, and so when I met Patricia, she seemed like a good sort to delegate the responsibility of family to. She was cheerful, alive, passionate, and focused in her work and she seemed to be unthreatened by the power that I held within the company, so I found her tolerable to be around. Over time, the ennui of married life kind of wore on her and that tenacity I'd seen in her before became a sort of withering aggravation. But she was my wife and she was able to handle the delegation of all of those 'traditional' moments that I was expected to have. It just made everything easier on a grand scale."

"That's always puzzled me about you," said Hank. "You seem to be so sure of yourself, so confident in everything that you do and how you respond to people, yet you keep them at bay as well."

"It's good to be puzzled," replied Alston. "But what I wanted to talk to you about was Billie. She's a great force in the company. Her vibrant smile, her charm, her wit; she's a very important person—the life blood of the company—if you will. She's an inspiration. A shimmering creature on a golden pedestal, though that pedestal is made of different things for each person that places her on it. For example, I see in Billie many qualities that I would like to instill in my own children—warmth, kindness, patience, intelligence and many others. Because of that, I feel a very paternal protection for Billie."

"And you're telling me to treat her right?" Asked Hank, confused.

"No," replied Alston. "I'm telling you that you're doing a wonderful job of that already and if she were actually my daughter, I'd have given you my approval long ago."

Billie smiled at both of them, and Alston showed Hank a polite smile and a nod. With these small motions Alston's posture returned to its royal perch and seemed to elevate Hank's status in its wake. When they arrived at the venue Billie stepped out onto the empty street, surrounded instantly by building security. She reached back for her garment bag then disappeared up the steps and into the club. Alston and Hank stepped out of the limousine and were also escorted inside but were taken to Alston's private box instead.

"I never asked how you enjoyed yourselves, you and Billie," said Alston as he and Hank took their seats at the edge of the balcony. "Despite the unfortunate business with Ralphie Barrel."

"It was great. I love sucking on titties and there were ten of 'em in my face. Did you by chance arrange all that?"

"I might have dropped a hint or two among your coworkers," chuckled Alston slyly.

"What makes you do what you do?" asked Hank.

"How do you mean?"

"What made you pick porn? You're a marketing genius and I can tell you love what you do. Why?"

"Because the sex industry is exactly where we need marketing gurus. Sex is the hardest thing in the world to sell because people are already sold on it but can't bring themselves to buy it. Add to that the fact that sex has been opposed and fought against since the dark ages. No other industry has such a history."

"But sex work has been around since the dawn of time. It's the 'oldest profession.'"

"It is, but it's also the most reviled. Anti-sex work loonies like to argue that it's a form of oppression of women handed down from patriarchal societies of the past—ignoring of course the reality of male prostitutes—but think about it: women have been able to take the money of men simply by virtue of their existence. Men in a patriarchal society don't have such an innate ability. In such a society, women are reviled as being temptresses because the men aren't comfortable with their own sexual identity and try to hide the creatures that make them aware of it. A woman, therefore, who uses her sexuality for personal gain—not the altruistic love that is demanded of their worthlessness—is thus reviled in the altruistic, collectivist societies of old. Hyper-masculine pride demands that men be able to attract women by virtue of their masculinity, not their wallets. In a society in which men actually think that they're entitled to women's bodies they resent the notion that they have to pay for them. To market a successful sex product, I have to convince my customers to see past the thousands of years of societal programming that teaches them that buying sex is a strike against their personal character and a vile, contemptible thing."

"So that's why it benefits from your expertise, but what draws you to it."

"I wanted to take a stand against oppression."

Hank chuckled and looked over at Alston, expecting to see the other man returning his jovial cynicism, but he saw that Alston was still looking at the stage distantly, as though unaware of Hank's misinterpretation. "Sorry," said Hank, his posture stiffening.

Alston raised a hand dismissively "It's okay," said Alston. "You, Billie, and everyone else that works for me were all born free in a world of slaves. That's my job—I protect the free from the enslaved."

The audience was filing in, their shapes merging into one vast expanse of patronage as they took their seats on the floor below. Smaller numbers converged on the private boxes and as those wealthier patrons filed in, there was a knock at the door to Alston's box. "Come in," called Alston and Dominic entered, his usual random assortment of fashions mediated by a dark blue blazer and tan slacks. With pleasant introductions and handshakes Dominic joined the pair as the lights rose and fell to indicate the start of the concert.

As the lights dropped into their theatrical repose, Billy took the stage. She was radiant—her dress hung limply against her frame even though the satin fabrics gripped her tightly in all the right places. She stood before the audience with the kind of classical beauty that radiated from movie stars of the early twentieth century. Her eyes sparkled as though they were captured by shimmering lunar light that rippled down the folds and sleek expanses of her sheer clothing. She was statuesque in the most sacred, transcendent sense of the word.

Billie turned with elegant poise and placed herself down on the piano bench. As if cutting through the majesty of the moment, she began to blaze through a series of songs from the Families for Families songbook, playing the melodies with basic chord accompaniment, covering six pieces in the space of a minute. Applause and whistles poured forth from the crowd as she smiled devilishly and laid into her actual performance.

The sound of the gentle, nocturnal performance recovered elegantly from the abrasive banality of the hymnal selections and navigated the dark, deftly trembling waters of Chopin, Brahms, Mozart and Beethoven before diving deeper into the works of Liszt and Grieg. The hypnotic tones cycled up and around the chamber with a calming stir that resonated throughout the souls of the audience.

It was an evening filled with the soaring, utopian tones that surrounded Hank in his fiancée's house. He felt a haunting chill at the thought of letting such beauty out into the world, unadulterated, but contented himself with the knowledge that it was being communicated by nimble and graceful hands of Billy Solar, who exuded in the music the same tender gratification in her playing that she did in her sex. The time seemed to melt away quickly, and ninety minutes concluded as fast as it began.

At the end of the show, Billie rose from her bench and walked to the front and center of the stage, bowing to the audience and smiling jubilantly as they gave her a long standing ovation. Then, just as she turned and waved to Hank in the private box, there was a whistling burst, muted by a silencer, from the sound booth high above. It was imperceptible to the audience but instantly following its report a single flash of crimson erupted across Billie's throat. Caught in the hot gel beams of the stage lights, the blood erupted in a jagged slice and Billie collapsed to the floor of the stage.

Hank was on his feet and tearing down the hall, the shock of the moment propelling him down a flight of stairs and into the melee of the crowd that was rushing for the emergency exits. The onslaught of panicked bodies hit him with the impact of highway traffic but his adrenalized rush towards the stage found him plowing into the frenzy, knocking aside one human barricade after another until he was able to vault onto the performance floor.

When Hank finally arrived at the stage, he found Billie laying in a widening pool of blood, the wound across her throat having ripped open her jugular vein. Her hands shook and the distant look in her eyes now seemed weak and disconnected. Hank wanted to do something—anything to help her, but as he looked around frantically, screaming the word "medic," he realized that this was all he could do and so, instead, looked down into Billie's eyes for support, finding, in her calm, collected countenance a peace that he could neither know nor understand as she died wordlessly in his arms. Fifteen minutes later, the EMTs arrived on the scene and began to pray for Billie, the only treatment they could legally perform.

Chapter 20

THE FUNERAL HOME stood at the top of a gradual and well manicured slope. The road from the main gates took a meandering course up and around the hill, terminating in a parking lot behind a bare, white building with massive double doors in front and back. The drive was surrounded on all sides by a diverse array of headstones and as the procession rose to the top of the incline it became apparent that the aisles of graves opened into a vast expanse behind the home, nearly vanishing on the horizon. In that distance, somewhere, was a tent over a recently dug grave. Tomorrow, Billie would be buried there under the stone of someone named Margaret Kovacs.

Hank watched the stones pass from inside Alston's limo, while Alston sat across the vehicle, watching Hank. Hank was vaguely aware of this, and some part of his mind—the part that contemplated with compulsive curiosity the ways in which Isaac Alston studied those around him—noted that this look was not the kind of professional consideration he'd given Hank at his job interview nor the probing inquisitiveness when he'd suspected him of being a rat but a quiet, neutral, though no less penetrating variety. Dominic was next to his boss, his gaze quieter and more contemplative.

"You ever do one of these before?" asked Dominic. Hank looked away from the window for a moment and shook his head before returning to his observations. "It's going to hit you the hardest after the funeral is over."

There was a pause and then Alston added: "I want you to know that when that happens, we're here for you." Hank nodded, but didn't break his distant gaze. Hank's deeply engrained worldview, which he had learned before he was old enough to read, the one that told him men don't burst out with strong displays of sorrow, wouldn't allow him to respond as he'd wanted to. He wanted to pull Alston close and cry on his shoulder. He wanted to cry for Billie and he wanted to cry for the kindness and friendship and support he'd found in Alston and Dominic. And he wanted to cry because he felt a strong urge to kneel down and kiss Alston's feet, but knew that this emperor would never allow that to happen. Instead, he folded that offer away and put it in the inside coat pocket of his mind, knowing that there would be a time, not too long from now, when he would not only open up the gates of his grief, but allow Alston to do the same. He longed for that moment, the bitter desert of this morbid meal, but instead breathed deeply in long, measured, intervals that did nothing to stop his sorrow from sinking further into the depths of his heart but at least kept it somewhat at bay.

Tim and Patricia sat together against the back wall of the limousine, perpendicular to the seats occupied by the others. Tim's eyes were swollen red from tears but his face was pale and dry, showing that he had shed his grief and become numb to what was about to happen long before he arrived at the cemetery. Hank wished he could somehow do the same, but outward grief was still a distant and unreal prospect for him.

Patricia wore a flamboyant black hat with a black veil and sunglasses, but there was still a coldness about her—she seemed to exist on the plane of reality that was about to attend Billie's funeral but that existence was only a token place holder in the reality that the limousine's other passenger's embraced fully. Indeed, Patricia's mind seemed to be on another wavelength altogether and beneath the veil of her placid exterior, she seemed to be contemplating something that ran in blatant contrast to the interests of those around her.

The vehicle arrived in the parking lot and pulled into an empty space. Alston was the first one out when the chauffeur opened the door, followed by Dominic, then Hank, then Tim and Patricia. Hank took one glance at Alston before they began their walk to the doors of the home. Alston's face had assumed its classic visage as the stoic visionary and he seemed to be staring down the funeral home and looking beyond it at the same time.

They crossed the parking lot to a pair of wooden oak doors that parted in gatefold fashion on their approach. The open doors revealed a deep maroon carpet that extended across the building to the front doors, which mirrored those in the back. In the center of this main aisle was a circular table which sported a large, solid white bouquet of flowers and a set of framed pictures of Billie through her younger years, terminating with a prom photo. There were no pictures indicating that she'd ever been a porn star.

When the quintet entered, they could all feel the pronounced change in the atmosphere, the air feeling especially sterile and flowery as if anticipating a visit from people of a "dirty" profession. Alston seemed to serve as a shield for the others, the automatic prominence and recognition he garnered drawing the attention of the more conservative attendees away from his four companions. With quiet, flawless poise he introduced himself to Billie's parents and motioned for Hank to come forward, placing a placed a hand on the younger man's back when he arrived.

"You must be Hank," said Billie's father in meek, forcibly polite tones. He was a tall, somewhat frail man who seemed to genuinely want to acknowledge Hank's importance in his daughter's life despite the electrified, razor wire fence that stretched between them.

Billie's mother, though older and slightly more squat as a result, still retained an echo of the slender curves that had made her daughter such a beauty. She too seemed to want to appear sympathetic to Hank but was similarly blocked. "Margaret told us so much about you," she added. Hank nodded and looked to the floor, then away altogether, his eyes scanning about for familiar faces. Rod Wielding was standing in a corner with a couple of the girls from the company, but most of the people were in the viewing room. Hank tensed at the thought of going in there.

Alston led the pilgrimage into the viewing room. Hank felt the moist, willowing familiarity of the pull in his throat and eyes as he drifted softly toward the coffin. As if sensing the dignified aura inherit to the arrival of royalty, the onlookers stepped aside as Alston and company moved towards the open casket. Hank saw his first wisp of Billie over Alston's shoulder and moved to his left when they came to a stop.

Hank's first thought on seeing the body was the dissonance in her visage. She laid still, arms folded over her stomach with a bouquet of white roses clutched in her hands. Hank's mind flashed for a moment on the frozen image before him and it was in this radiant instant the dissonance was strongest. She didn't seem *dead*, he realized. She seemed as though the flowers were a bridal arrangement that she held as though she were walking down the aisle during a wedding ceremony. Her calm, languidly determined features bore an expression that he'd seen before when she prepared for a shoot. It signified a moment of preparation before she stepped into the world of her work, leaving the external world far behind. Hank had secretly hoped that he'd see that focusing stillness in her just before she made the procession down the aisle to join him in marriage.

As he swallowed hard, Hank realized that *this* was what her detractors had accused her of being: an object. In life, when Billie's warm, delicate features had been animated by the vivacious spirit that surged through her body, she had been a sex symbol; a symbol of a human ideal realized by sexual expression. Her nakedness had been a joyous celebration of freedom and her sexual performances had been passionate dances designed to share that freedom with those who deserved it. And that freedom had made her the standard bearer of an ultimate ideal to be found in the hearts of each person who had known her. She had been a goddess to Tim, a friend to Dominic, a daughter to Alston, and a lover to him but now she was stripped of all of those connections and laid limp as an empty hunk of meat. She had been, truly and finally, objectified.

Hank saw a tear hit the side of the casket and realized that it was his own. Ashamed for reasons he could not fully understand, he turned to find that the entire room had fallen silent and now stood looking at him and his four companions. For the first time in his career as a porn star, Hank felt as though he were being ogled—that his visage was being preyed upon by the lecherous eyes of a depraved multitude. They seemed to be waiting for him to sprout horns, black leathery wings and a tail then defecate fire. They weren't looking at him as a regal thing of majestic beauty but as a disease ridden piece of gutter filth. He was a dirty needle stained with blood. He was schizophrenic whore that lived in a cardboard box. He was everything that Middle America stared at luridly through the cathode windows of their television sets but now he was standing among them; a real live *specimen* from that dark, murky underworld of pestilence and plague.

The various members of Billie's extended family were huddled together in various groups—older adults that had been quietly lamenting the young lady's demise, children too young and too distant in the family to have known Billie who waited silently for the event to be over, and various people from around Billie's age who had led the charge of hateful stares from the time that Hank and his party had entered the building. It was in these faces that Hank saw the most curious mixture of intents. Outwardly, there was an anger in their eyes that simmered at a white hot point.

"Who *are* you?" asked an old crone, her sharp, bony features drawing the edges of her voice taught around the barbed syllables.

"I'm Hank," he replied after a tense moment. "I am... Well, I was Billie's fiancée."

"Her name was Margaret!" boomed her father with a sudden snarl. The tension in the room seemed to vibrate out to the walls of the room, turn back on itself and reach critical mass. "It was the name we chose for her!"

"Her name was Billie," said Hank, meaning to whisper but instead emitting a wheezing shout. "It was the name she chose for herself."

Unable to withstand the withering glares any longer, Hank stormed from the room, his would-be in-laws parting hurriedly as he went. When he stepped out into the afternoon sun he wasn't able to restrain himself any longer and choked out a wet gasp as he laid his forearms against the hood of the limousine, sobbing in a way that was not like the orgasmic release he'd expected would come when tears finally found him but was rather a frantic, searching whimper. He felt as if the years of his life were stripped away like rings of a tree and the frightened, shivering child at his core was exposed. In this moment of deepest release he saw that child for what it was: a creature of simple purity. It was the part of his soul that had loved Billie with the tender, wispy affection of absolute freedom but that freedom demanded to be embraced only by the most confident, careful, and respectful of arms. Those arms had been Billie's, and she had enveloped that child with loving, effortless precision as no other had before. Now she was gone and that child fell endlessly through space, screaming in terror for a perpetually imminent crash that never seemed to come.

A gentle buffer against that terrifying crash came in the form of a comforting hand on his back. The soldier's instinct that would have told Hank to grab that hand and snap it at the wrist was dutifully dormant as he turned to see Isaac Alston's steady, comforting presence looking into his own. Though the eternally confident tone of Alston's demeanor was unwavering, his eyes were moist and sorrowful in their battle-hardened frame. He placed both arms around Hank and drew him close, the latter finding a new depth to the profound comfort and calm of his confident presence. On Alston's shoulder Hank wept as though he were daring the bitter, hollow void in his soul to continue expanding and eventually envelope him completely.

After a time Hank became aware that Dominic had joined them. He parted with Isaac and turned to meet Dominic's eyes. Instead of a redundant embrace, Dominic spoke with soft assurance, the composure cutting an odd angle on his normally fiery presence. "I know how you feel, Hank. Believe me I do. When my wife died I was the same way. Don't fight it right now—give in to the hopelessness. Let it fill you up and devour you. These feelings need to run their course and it's a hell of a course, but they'll get through you eventually. Right now you're just a conduit for those feelings. Just let them pass through you. I know that sounds impossible, but you've got one thing in your favor that I didn't have. The thing that has ruined your life isn't some microscopic infection that chewed up your beloved like it did mine. The thing that ruined your life is out there. Walking the streets. Eating, sleeping, shitting, living. You have my word—we'll find whoever did this. That's your ace in the hole, kid. Revenge."

Hank nodded and looked at the ground for a long moment before raising his head and focusing on the wide expanse of the cemetery. In the distance, just before the horizon, was a tent with metal polls that had been erected around a freshly dug grave. Tomorrow Billie would be placed into the ground out there, her body swallowed up by the flesh of the earth.

In notably stark contrast to the vicious glaring of the previous day, the morning of the graveside service was quietly ceremonial with neither Billie's family nor Alston's small group speaking to one another and only in quiet, short whispers to each other.

The pastor who spoke was withered save for a pronounced beer gut and spoke in a folksy, far-off tone about the wonderful little girl named Margaret who had always been the center of attention at church picnics, had loved to play hide and seek in the church playground, and several other whimsically nostalgic observations that made Billie sound as if she'd died at age seven.

Though there was no contact between the funeral's two reticent camps, both noticed that Isaac Alston was absorbed in a kind of sharpened contemplation, staring at the coffin as though he were decoding a secret message. When the service concluded and the casket was lowered, Alston was the first to stand and leave, making only a polite comment and hand shake to Billie's parents before trekking back to the limousine. When he arrived, the rest of his companions close at hand, a small pudgy man who introduced himself as Arvo Skarrat, was leaning against the side of the vehicle.

"I'm the executor of Ms. Kovacs' estate, Mr. Alston," he explained. "There's going to be a showing of her video will tomorrow and I want to make sure you get to hear it beforehand. She left something to you and your company."

"What?"

"I'll let her tell you, Mr. Alston."

When the others arrived at the limousine, Skarrat boarded with them and gave the driver directions to his office, a small one room affair in the upper floor of a town-square boutique. There were chairs arranged in front of a television that sat on Skarrat's desk. There was a VCR unit in the TV console and when all five viewers had been seated, Skarrat put a VHS tape into the slot. There was a moment of static, then a time code, and then a shot of Billie sitting in office they were presently assembled in. The lawyer's voice was heard saying "okay, whenever you're ready." Hank winced as he saw Billie make the same calming face he'd seen on her corpse.

"I, Margaret Jane Kovacs," she began, "being of sound mind am making this my last will and testament. Because of recent threats against my life, I have decided to make this statement concerning the distribution of my earthly possessions. First and foremost I wish to donate my human remains, my body, to Isaac Alston for use by his company Alston Image in any way they may see fit. Furthermore I authorize and give consent for my body to be filmed and presented in any product released by Alston Image.

"Working for you was amazing, Isaac. You defied and transcended every negative stereotype about the industry and for that I thank you and commend you from the bottom of my heart. When I was working for you I felt like my career was in the hands not only of a decent, hard working, and professional businessman but also a truly kind and generous person. You are the noblest, most praiseworthy person in your industry and while I can't begin to explain your personal views I know that they are what has driven your company from the very beginning. I only hope that one day the world will hear, understand, and appreciate your philosophy.

"Dominic—few people are worthy of having a friend like you and I'm eternally grateful that you thought I was. Carry with you the memories of our many good times watching classic movies, partying till we passed out, and laughing in joyous celebration. You are a master of your craft and it was an honor to appear in so many of your films. Never stop your work. Film until the day you die. This world may not deserve the beauty of your art, but it doesn't deserve to be deprived of it either.

"Timothy—I cherished knowing that I was the first woman you saw naked and it made me feel more beautiful than you could ever imagine. Know that I am only the first of many women in your life and if I do survive on some angelic level I will make it my duty to guide you to the right ones and help them appreciate you as much as you deserve.

"Because I know that my family's religious beliefs will cause them to disagree with the choice I have made regarding ownership of my remains, I wish to make this clear: all of my possessions are to be sold and pooled with the cash in my bank account, the total of which should equal nearly 2.2 million dollars. If my family does not contest this will then that entire sum is to be donated to the Christian organizations of their choice. If, however, they do contest this will then that sum is to be divided evenly between all the abortion doctors in the Van Nuys area. Either way, my body is the property of Alston Image.

"My last words are for Hank. I love you darling. Not lov*ed*. Not the past tense. My love for you lives and breathes and cannot die so long as you pump blood in your heart. I love you with all my heart and soul. When I first met you I saw that I had brought out the adorable, innocent child in a strong and handsome man and I knew that it was something to be cherished. My work for Alston Image was my purpose, but knowing that you found strength and happiness in my love gave that purpose validation. You were the deepest, gentlest, most passionate lover I've ever had and when you first entered me I felt our hearts reach out for each other. When I think about your sly smile, your penetrating eyes, your battle-hardened body and the witty charm behind it all, I know that whether or not there is an afterlife, my heaven was right here on this earth, cradled in your arms and I know you found yours in mine. I want you to promise me that no matter what you'll love again. As hard as it sounds now, I know that you'll find another woman and when you do, I want you to go to her with my blessing. I want you to drink every drop from the overflowing chalice that is your time on this earth, not waste it crawling in some vast, grey desert of sorrow and sentimentality. Let your happiness and celebration be your life's tribute to my memory. You were my soul mate, my therapist, my best friend, and my lover. We are held together by deeper bonds than any marriage could have ever bestowed and any death could ever break. I wish that there were a more profound word for what I feel but 'love' will have to do. I love you, Hank."

As the tape ended, Billie's eyes were filled with tears that were now mirrored in Hank's. Unlike the previous day, Hank made no attempt to hide this seeping expression. The tears rolled down his stoic face like battle scars that he was proud to wear. In the long silence that followed the tape, Hank reflected on how no ancient artifact on this planet could equal one one-billionth of the treasure he now carried in his soul.

"Can you really do that?" asked Dominic after a moment. "Donate your body to the porn industry?"

"I had to go through every loop hole and grey area in the law I could think of," replied Skarrat. "But technically there's no law against it. There's no legal precedent but if you can donate your body to science or to a museum, you can donate it to a company that makes porn."

"What will happen to the body now?" asked Alston.

"It won't be buried. The family will be shown this video in about an hour and while that's happening the body will be taken out of the casket, treated with stronger preservatives, and placed in cold storage until you're ready to use it."

Alston nodded and rose to his feet, shaking Skarrat's hand as the others left the room.

The flight home was uneventfully silent, with Hank and Dominic resuming their ambient, contemplative stares towards distant objects. When the Alston jet landed in Colorado to pick up Jesse from Patricia's parents, Alston and his wife descended the stairs to the concrete where Jesse waited with her grandparents. Tim ran down the stairs to hug his elder relatives and Alston knelt when his daughter came running to him, taking her up in his arms. When he finally parted he realized that Patricia was standing next to her parents with Timothy flanking them. "I'm leaving you, Isaac," she said dryly. "I just can't take this anymore. My lawyer will contact yours."

Alston rose to his feet, nodded expressionlessly to Tim, and returned to the plane.

After Alston returned to his house he remained there for three days despite the wreckage. He took no calls and held no meetings, though Dominic visited him and found him to be staying in one of the guest houses near the pool out back. On the fourth day, a Saturday, his employees were surprised to see him step out of one of the armored transport vehicles and enter the lobby of his company as though he were returning to a regular day on the job. Everyone who had been sitting around the lobby stood when Alston entered, though he walked towards the executive elevator as without acknowledging them.

"Mr. Alston," said Carol from behind the front desk. Alston stopped when she spoke. "The Adult Video News Awards committee called while you were out. They said that this year's AVN awards ceremony is being held in Billie's memory and they were wondering if you would give the keynote address. I told them that-"

But she was cut off when Isaac Alston quietly spoke five words that would echo across the entire country:

"Tell them I'll do it."

Chapter 21

"SO TELL ME how this thing is going to work," began Alston as Duke Cunningham sat down in his office.

"They want you to speak on the current state of the industry and, if you'd like, pay tribute to Billie. You can speak as long as you want about whatever you like within those parameters. Since there hasn't been much in the way of output this past year, they don't have many awards to give and there won't be a floor show. Dominic is going to get a lifetime achievement award and Billie is nominated posthumously for best actress for *Awake to the Skin* as is Diana Arland though Billie is favored to win. The other feature studios have a few titles between them as do the gonzo producers but for the most part-"

"I'm not worried about the awards. If we get something then I have another plaque for my wall. If not, whatever. I'm wondering about how this is going down. Isn't there going to be some kind of mass uprising from Families for Families?"

"There already is. They can't explain how the ceremony infringes on their rights so as long as there's no nudity or sex on display, we can assemble peacefully. As a precautionary measure the AVN committee has publicized the event as being held at the Black Chapel but it's actually being held at Caesar's Palace. Since the D.O.P.E crackdown, the facility has been used for nothing but evangelist religious gatherings and so there's been a lot of hush-hush finagling with regards to booking the event. Nevertheless, they're thrilled to be hosting it no matter how clandestine and are planning to broadcast it all over the internet. Technically video of the broadcast will become illegal the minute Families for Families is able to obtain a copy since they've already gotten the necessary signatures to establish it as offensive, they just need to get a copy so that they can list specifics. Melvin Crankshadow is notably quiet in all of this but Bob Match has been raising cane."

"That's fine—they can make all the noise they want. What day and time for all of this?"

"Friday after next at ten in the evening."

"That's when the ceremony starts?"

"That's correct. You're expected to speak at eleven."

"Very well. So talk to me about our European numbers."

"The DVD special edition of *A Wet Dream Within a Wet Dream* is doing well among horror buffs in Britain as expected and *Cum Hog Billionaire* is selling great as a direct download on alstonunderground.com"

"Where's that site being hosted?"

"On the books it's being hosted partially in Portugal and partially in Russia but really it's in Belgrade. Not the most secure place to do business but not then this isn't the most secure time to do business either. Don't worry—we've done it up to look like a pirate website—no obvious connection to you at all."

"Good enough. What kind of laundering are we doing on that line?"

"Plenty—we've got each transaction passing through about fifty hands before it gets to us. Loan sharking mostly but there's twenty different channels running the money so that's hundreds of people total. So far, we're good."

"Alright. What about politics. Nationally—any vocal opposition to this D.O.P.E. crap?"

"Not really. There are pockets of intellectuals that communicate on the internet, but it's just glorified cocktail banter romanticized with the lurid zeal of oppression. Basically kids that want to rail against the man, whoever that might be."

"That's what's public?"

"That's right."

"That can't be the totality of it. There's really no debate among pundits and the like?"

"The only people that get any air time are endorsed by Families or Families. If there's an uprising among intellectuals, it hasn't been televised."

"Have our PR department start probing the web more in depth. Even if just for my own sake. And start taking stock of editorials in the international press. There's got to be some way to gauge the opposition to this."

"You're hoping to gain some insight into their thinking?"

"No, I want to see if they're ready for mine."

The only way in which Melvin Crankshadow's office did not resemble the Oval Office was in its superior grandeur. Where the Oval office seemed to imply that the nature of the position was superior to the person who occupied it, Crankshadow's office conveyed that it was the conduit between himself and the ethereal powers of Heaven. A massive crucifix hung on either wall of the curving chamber and both of them banked outwards away from Crankshadow's desk towards the main door that led into the room, as if to imply that the towering crosses stood guard not only of the pastor but of the aura that surrounded him like the shimmering, almost blinding sunlight that poured in through the window behind him. The rest of the office was adorned with decorative shelves of books, though these were merely leather bound furniture of whose contents Crankshadow had never made himself aware. The walls were a pristine white that caught the invading sunlight with an immaculate reflection that surpassed the implied sterility of the color white in medical facilities.

There was a knock at Crankshadow's door and he responded with a chipper "come in." The figure that entered the chamber was concealed in a dignity sheath but Crankshadow was expecting her. "Is that you, sister Patricia?" he asked fondly.

The person in the dignity sheath nodded and sat in one of the chairs in front of Crankshadow's desk. "You wanted to see me, sir?" she asked.

"That's correct, sister Patricia. I want to commend you."

"For what sir?"

"For the sacrifices you've made in the name of the church. You're one of our longest standing members and you've shown that you have a vast willingness to serve the Lord. Have you ever stopped to think of the sacrifices you've made for the Almighty?"

"Well, some of them, I suppose, sir."

"Don't be modest. Your dedication is amazing. Few people could do the things you've done, or keep up a good face for as long as you have. As you know, in the name of spreading the word of God, we are often called upon to do things that we wouldn't normally consider ourselves capable of. When I found you all those years ago you were a tramp and a slut and I told you that you could use those skills for the good of the Lord. Don't you think you have achieved that in the last fifteen years?"

"If you mean my work in the industry and then with my husband, then yes."

"Then you know exactly what I mean. Few people would be so selfless as to prostrate themselves nude before the world, performing acts on camera that would be considered shameful to the citizens of Sodom and Gomorrah, become internationally known as a raging harlot, and seduce into marriage one of the most powerful porn kingpins in the world, but you did it, Patricia Alston."

"Don't call me by that name."

"But it's your name, isn't it?"

"Only for the sake of my mission. I don't wish to be known by it otherwise."

"You have my apologies. Nevertheless, I commend your sacrifices. You have learned that the only way to live a responsible, sane, moral life is to selflessly give yourself to others. To the Lord you've given your soul and after that, who cares what happens to the frail shell that is your body or the empty material gains to which it is attached. You are on the verge of becoming spiritually complete: you will have divorced your soul from all ties to this earth. You'll be ready to die—doesn't that excite you?"

"Yes... yes sir."

"Of course it does. Once you've renounced all ties to this world you'll be ready to finish out your years on this earth in quiet servitude, before finally being whisked away to the world of the Lord. But there remains yet one more tie to which you hold fast."

"What is that, sir?"

"The thing that you, in the course of your life of sacrifice, created with Isaac Alston."

"I planted the bomb that blew up our house. What else is there?"

"Your children."

"How do you want me to sacrifice them?" she asked, a sharpness entering her tone on the edge of her sudden breath.

"By giving them over to the church to be treated for porn addiction."

"That's all?"

"No—one final step will be required of you. Then the Lord shall forgive your sins completely. You must go to Isaac Alston and tell him that I've taken your children. Tell him that I sent my private soldiers into your home and stole them from you."

"He'll come after you with all of the legal weight in the world."

"That was the old world. Now he's in my world. You've already announced your divorce with him, yes?"

"Yes."

"And in this modern world, there's no judge that would dare to allow Alston custody of his children. My flock will petition the government on behalf of the children at my request. No matter what kind of stink Alston tries to raise, he'll only make himself look like a fool. I want you to tell him so that he'll think that no matter what your objections to his career, you're still on his side with regards to the kids. "

"I... I can't do that. Not to my children..."

"Mrs. Alston, there is no point in trying to argue this. I have legislation before congress that, when passed, will allow me to seize any child I want and put them into the program. You can either do this for me voluntarily or I can send my men to your house to abduct the children directly. Either way you'll be running to your husband with tears in your eyes."

There was no expression visible through the thick mesh net on the front of the dignity sheath, but the moment of silence that followed Crankshadow's words was ominous enough in its revere to convey a boundless world of fear and terror mixed with confusion and shame.

"Do you remember the friend that was at the church party where I met you when we were kids?"

"Yes."

"Have I ever told you what she said to me after you and that little boy with the toy airplane left?"

"No."

"She looked at me and said 'he is a fucking sociopath.' I didn't think much of it at the time and I thought less of it as you started witnessing to me at school, but now it comes back to me."

Crankshadow beamed with warm condescension. "Patricia, darling, I am not a sociopath. I simply know that human emotions are useless. There is no point in trying to empathize with our fellow man. Human kind is sinful, shameful, and deserving of death and damnation. I cannot love such vile creatures as that nor can it be good for my soul to try to connect my feelings and desires with theirs. The only way to love—the only true way—is to love the Lord and let his light guide us in all things. I have no regard for the feelings of my fellow man only because of my infinite love for the Lord. It his love that guides me in all of the wonderful things that I do for my fellow man and it is what must guide you to turn over your children to me and, by extension, to the Lord. Don't you want that too? To be free of all of these petty secular emotions that pull you down and tie you to this earth and its master Satan?"

"I... well, yes I do."

"Excellent. Now go forth and do the Lord's work."

That night, three men dressed in all black knocked on the door of the home Patricia shared with her parents. The casual observer the scene would have known only that they were welcomed into the home and left with the children shortly thereafter. Whether it had been at Patricia's consent or not, the children had left the house kicking and screaming with sacks over their heads. The casual observer might not have noticed the tightness in Patricia's jaw as she watched out the front door as the children were loaded into an unmarked car. Her face did not otherwise waver as the kids shouted "Mom" and "Mommy" at the tops of their lungs.

One by one, they found their way to Hank's room. Diana Arland had been the first one. In the days following the funeral she had come to the dressing room where Hank slept and made sure that he got up, showered, and ate breakfast, though she often found herself guiding him through these tasks with gentle encouragement. He ate when she told him to and dressed in the clothes that she gave him, but other than that he sat quietly in his room most of the day. After a time Diana found it easier to bathe Hank by entering the shower stall with him and, in those moments of mutual nakedness, began to lean into his muscled body in a deeper, more compassionately erogenous way. At first Hank flinched at the intimacy, as though giving in to physical pleasure would profane the reverence he had for his grief. She sensed in his body the wallowing despair of lost love's emptiness and the weary tension of accepting intimacy with another person, and held herself close to his sleek, muscled frame until the those tiny, infinitely minute feelings seemed to rise out of Hank and into Diana who transubstantiated them into closeness and compassion. Over time, Hank found tears in his eyes that fell from his face and ran down Diana's naked back, guided by her shoulder blades to join the bathwater than ran down the crevice between her buttocks.

When Diana sensed the hesitation to her presence leaving Hank's form, she began to kiss his body as she lowered herself to her knees. Lifting his penis with her hand, she took it into her mouth, her lips embracing it tenderly and with a kind of loving articulation that Hank had not felt all those lifetimes ago when she had shared a bed of carnal fulfillment with him and Billie during the filming of *Awake to the Skin*. Her sex then had been the wild, unrestrained ravenousness of festive sexuality. Now she felt more like a therapist. Moved by the empathy of her actions—which seemed to be devoid of any irrationally selfish desire, Hank allowed her to suck on his manhood, leaning back against the wall of the shower and letting the warm waves of pleasure mix with the deep report of her breath against his abdomen. He didn't feel in this attention a compulsion to chase his own orgasm—did not even feel his member stiffen enough to give him the longing ache that would have signaled his need to come—but instead gave himself over to Diana's administrations.

After a time she took him to the bed and made him lay there on his back while she mounted him. After sitting down on Hank and letting him enter her, she lay down against him, resuming the embrace they had shared in the shower, and began a long, tender series of motions that seemed to come more from the clenching and releasing of her vagina than the larger motions of her hips. She held Hank this way in suspended, wordless ecstasy knowing that any exchange of speech would give him an opportunity to seize up—to put words to the vast array of feelings that were inside him and, in their expression, give him cause to push her away. Though his thoughts were disconnected from the moment's pleasure, they were softened and comforted by Diana's presence and when he finally came, it seemed less like the sudden series of clenching that accompanied an ejaculating penis and more like the blossoming opening of an iris that swirled outwards to probe for more sunlight.

Over time, Diana brought a friend with her—one of Alston Image's transsexual performers named Saundra Bullcock. Now devoted to the silent attentions of Diana, Hank didn't object to Saundra's presence, knowing on a primal level that the trans-woman had been brought for some intended purpose. The three of them adjourned to the shower, and while Diana resumed the administrations she'd been giving Hank all this time, Saundra undressed and joined them. She and Hank had worked together in *Gender Bender Splendor Volume V* in which Hank had played both the giving and receiving roles in the course of their scene together and as such her form was not alien to him despite its anatomical contradictions. She had a long, beautiful penis that seemed to be the only remaining hint of her natural origins. Her breasts had been achieved with hormonal injections, not implants, and her naturally wispy voice and soft skin gave the remaining form a wholly feminine appearance.

As they bathed, Saundra asked Hank questions about how he felt— questions that penetrated him sharply but were guided by a notable level of compassion and skill. In the course of these dialogues, Hank understood why she had been brought into the equation: she had entered womanhood in contrary to the body she'd been born with and as such had spent her life learning the many different roles women had played in society. She knew how to be the diva bitch, the housewife, the tough as nails career woman, the mother, the school teacher, and a vast array of molds that she drifted in and out of with an elegance that defied the natural grace of most born women. Her feminine identity had come from establishing her individual identity above and beyond the synthesis of stereotypes that was mandated by her transformation. Here, in their quiet moments in the shower, she played the tribal mother—the wise sage that drank in the pains and fears of the community and breathed them back transmuted into words of strength and life. Hank realized that she'd been brought along as the academic clinician that would administer the structured therapy of female interaction while Diana gave herself over to the wordless dance of sexual performance.

After a time, Saundra began to join them in their sexual behaviors as well, and Hank found himself lost dreamily among a vast array of sensations that molded together to become a cloudy expanse of soft fulfillment metered at all times with the stiffness of anticipation and the rush of acceptance. The acts he committed with these two partners did not alleviate the feelings of loss and sadness that he felt for Billie but gave his body a gentle, pleasurable environment to drift through as his heart and mind, guided now by Saundra's kind words and patient understanding, could sort through the plummeting emptiness in his soul.

After hours of attention from the two women they lay in bed with Hank and cuddled against him, sharing a joint. In that contemplative state, the burning cotton candy smell of pot filling the room, he asked them a question: "Why are you all doing this for me? I know you want to help and in the name of all that is true I love it, but I don't understand why you feel so compelled to help or how you've known how to reach me in this way."

After taking a drag on the joint, Diana laid her head against Hank's chest and answered: "I'm a sex worker, Hank. It's what I do. People think that if you do sex work it's because you can't do anything else, but that only shows that they don't understand sex work. A prostitute can't simply be a docile, breathing corpse, even if that's what the client asks for. The thing is that nobody comes to a prostitute for sex—the sex is only a vehicle for the therapy that the prostitute provides.

"When I take a man into my body, his body confers to me the secret needs that even he can't put into words. I can feel the tension and the pain in his body and drink it into mine, transmuting it from his deepest longing into a sense of contentment and inner peace, even if just for a few moments. Sure, there are prostitutes out there that just stroll up and down the block giving out cheap blowjobs to whoever asks, but the difference between them and what I provide is the difference between fast food and a five star dinner. Yes, there are people that will just help you get your rocks off but that's okay.

"Can you imagine what life would be like if sex workers were revered rather than reviled? What if we were exalted on the level of doctors and teachers? I think most people are scared to ask themselves that question not because they think we'd devolve into some kind of blind hedonism but because they know that they wouldn't be as in control of the world as they'd like to be. Since the dark ages Western society has struggled to escape the grip of moralists who think that letting people have too much personal pleasure will lead to the downfall of civilization. And the people that those moralists reign over actually buy the idea that this hatred for professional sex is rooted in compassion and charity and a respect for human rights."

Two days later, Alston entered Hank's room, which was now populated as well by Dominic Daniels and Rod Wielding. The two additional men were clothed in contrast to the sprawling nakedness of Hank, Diana and Saundra, but all five were passing a joint around, each taking a couple of lazy puffs before handing it off to the next person. The last two members of the quintet had joined once Hank had pushed through the tears of the last few days and settled into the desert wasteland of ennui that, in its own bleak way, medicated his heart and soul. They joined not for discussion but to provide Hank with additional companionship in the silent wasteland he now navigated.

When Alston stepped into this grouping, his presence was noted in the sudden seriousness in the facial posturing all around him. Hank's room had become a delicate membrane for his soul's convalescence and Alston's presence was suddenly disruptive to that fragile ectoplasm. The company's owner moved with a commanding presence when he entered but now it was contrasted with a mania that strained in the corners of his eye sockets.

"Patricia was just in my office," he said with a new found tension in his normally resonant voice. "She says that Crankshadow has Tim and Jesse. That he came and stole them right out of her parents' house."

Hank sat up on the cot, suddenly focused in a way he hadn't been in a long time. "Really?" he said, though the word was a statement of interest, not disbelief. "To where?"

"They've been taken to the Families for Families center in Santa Rosa. He plans to treat them for 'porn addiction.'"

"That's insane," whispered Dominic from the folding chair where he sat.

"There's no way I can get them back through the courts—not right now. I'm going to have to go in and get them myself."

"You know it's probably a trap, right?" said Rod from where he sat on the floor. "You should take that security army you've paid for."

"They're for security—not warfare. They'd be nothing against the militia that Crankshadow probably has. I need to do this myself. With your help, Hank. You've got the military mind."

"Of course, Mr. Alston."

"Count me in too," said Rod. "I bet I could get Slamdingo to come along as well."

"I'm on board," said Dominic. Alston looked at him quizzically. "Don't give me that look, Isaac. Your family is my family. I know you've never said it, but don't think for a minute that's not how it is. I don't care how old I am or how inexperienced I am as a fighter—I want to do this. I'm your soldier and you know that."

Alston nodded, his face returning to its contemplative default for a moment before moving his attention back to Hank. "Mr. Steel," he said with a droll politeness, "would you care to teach Rod, Slam, Dominic and myself how to use firearms?"

Chapter 22

THE COLD METAL CHAMBER was a withered, water logged lime green that suggested the residue of nausea and dysentery. Pale, abrasive fluorescent lights beamed down from uncovered casings along the ceiling, giving the room a quivering countenance that was reinforced when the rumble of plumbing echoed hoarsely overhead. The floor was cold stone, with a flimsy fold-out bench along the same wall from which a short flight of metal stairs protruded. The stairs led up to a metal door, which was locked. The chamber was an inverted desert—where such a vast limitless expanse would cripple the unwitting traveler with its enormity, this tiny room threatened to crush the inmate's mind with its confinement.

Tim Alston had awoken to the stale miasma of the tiny chamber, unsure of where he was or how long he'd been there. After sitting in the room, pacing, banging on the door, and returning to the bench, he found himself slumped on the flimsy furniture. Hours and minutes bled into one another, and his heartbeat, at first racing and panicky, had quelled to a dull drone that throbbed in his neck and temples. There was a distant impetus in him to yell out for help, but the odd ambience of the room quelled his more feral inclinations. He simply wondered in a moist cognizance, feeling a mixture of tears, mucus and sweat in varying mixtures throughout his body.

Tim tried counting his heartbeats, assuming that they were around sixty per minute, to try and gauge the passage of time. Two excruciating minutes later he abandoned the practice and slumped back against the wall. He had some desire to kick back and forth to make the bench rock, as though it were a porch swing, but it the stiff metal legs, crossed to form X's on either end, were unresponsive. It occurred to Tim that the room seemed to be designed to be unyielding, as though its dilapidation belied a resolute indifference to his every action. Beyond terror, beyond fear of the unknown, he was simply *bored*. Over time he laid down on the bench, staring up at the ceiling and, unable to look up without being slapped by the anemic punch of the flickering light tubes, closed his eyes and put one arm over them to block out the glare. A few minutes of sleep came as a default of the posture but it did little to improve his state.

When his eyes opened, a man was standing over him. In the glare from above, it was difficult to make out the man's features, but after a time certain lines began to focus and sharpen until they produced the bare outline of his characteristics. The figure was wiry and thin, a gangly spindle of trim flesh that culminated in a poorly arranged puff of dyed black hair. The odd hair, along with his slightly swayed posture, told Tim that this was a man who had made a conscious attempt to appeal to young people in his appearance and had achieved a hackneyed impersonation of what such a youth might look like. Nevertheless, the man's full features began to reveal the details of their age as he came into focus and Tim could see that he was actually much older than he appeared, though still somewhere around middle-age.

Tim strained his brain to think of where he'd seen this person before, and it finally dawned on him: "You're Melvin Crankshadow," he whispered.

"That's right, young man," replied Crankshadow, his features forming an excessively poised smile. "Congratulations."

"For what?"

"For taking your first step."

"What first step? Where am I?"

"You're at the Institute for Pornographic Addiction, here at the First Grand Pantheon of Jesus Christ the Imperial Redeemer of American Liberty. This room is the Room of Acceptance, and I want to help get you out of here."

"Then let me out," Tim sat up on the bench, the belligerence of survival overtaking his fear for a moment. Crankshadow gave a practiced paternal chuckle and sat down next to Tim.

"I'm afraid it's not that simple," said Crankshadow as Tim struggled to acclimate to the pastor's after shave. "You see, you're here because of the choices you made. You're here because you need to admit that you have a porn addiction."

"I don't."

"I know it's very difficult to grasp right now," continued Crankshadow in a detached, condescending monotone, "but the first step in your treatment is admitting you have a problem."

"How do you know I have a problem?"

"I'm not going to argue this with you, Timothy."

"It's Tim."

"I'm going to give you some time to think about this. I'm going to come back in three hours and ask again if you want to admit to your problem. Then we'll see about getting you some food and a nice bath."

Crankshadow tussled Tim's hair and left the room through its only exit. Tim heard the door lock and, as that dry tone reverberated through the tiny room, became aware of his hunger. He wished that Crankshadow hadn't mentioned food because now he became aware of just how hungry he was. His stomach felt hollow as it gnawed at itself and his mouth felt numb and watery. He felt as though there were strings pulling down on his eye sockets. It was in the this state that he noticed a vent in the floor switch open and a thin trail of steam rise from it. Soon the room was filled with the smell of freshly baked pizza. The smell wafted through the room, its delicate spices making Tim's stomach cry out in need.

After a perceived eternity, the door opened again and Crankshadow descended the metal stairs, eating a piece of pizza. This time Tim sat up immediately on the pastor's arrival and Crankshadow smiled somewhat darkly at this recognition.

"Ready for dinner?" Asked Crankshadow as he lifted the piece from the plate and took another bite. Several strands of cheese hung in a limp hammock between the slice and his mouth. He took the strands in his free hand, turned his head back, and dropped them into his mouth, grinning as he brought his face back down to smile at Tim.

"Yes!" gasped Tim as though his stomach had seized control of his mouth.

"Then you admit to being a porn addict?"

The words crawled down dark staircases in Tim's brain and, whether it was out of an atavistic inheritance of his father's resolve or simply a learned emulation of the same, he shook his head.

Crankshadow nodded indifferently as he finished the last of the crust and licked sauce off his fingers. "Well, don't think about it too long," he replied. "I wouldn't want you to miss desert." Crankshadow left again and after a few minutes another scent now joined the smell of pizza—freshly baked cookies, hot chocolate and cinnamon buns.

Tim lay back on the bench again and this time his eyes closed from the dizzying blackout that was engulfing him. He found lucidity in his dreams and it was there that he contemplated the raw defiance with which he had found himself confronting Crankshadow. He thought of Billie as he'd seen her—not only naked but free and confident in that nakedness, her every curve sloping into the next with warm tones of vibrant flesh. When he'd seen her in that state, he'd known that he was seeing the most beautiful thing he would ever—or could ever—see. It hadn't been wrong—it had been right. It had made sense in his mind. He wasn't confused about his feelings in the slightest because there was absolutely nothing confusing about Billie. She'd been beautiful and that beauty was made radiant by the rippling fire in her soul.

Tim thought of what it meant to be an addict: the term culled forth images of shit-scented bums that sipped slovenly from paper bags in alleys or shot dirty needles in poorly maintained public bathrooms. It was a word for people who drank until they wrecked cars or gambled until they lost their homes. It was a word for people who couldn't stop destroying themselves. That was it, he realized: that was why these loonies kept trying to ban everything and sing the praises of some hysterical ghost creature that drove them on. They were the addicts. They were addicted to the flailing, feral masochism of forced mysticism. Their addiction had controlled them and they feared Alston Image not because it represented the antithesis of their god's desires but because it was that last ray of reality that beamed into the chemical fog in which they'd immersed themselves.

In that black, limitless dreamscape Tim came to understand why he was resisting and why if they did in fact allow him to starve to death he would not mind. He had known a thing of great beauty and where there was a single island of great beauty there was a surrounding sea of malignant contempt. He awoke knowing that he would give his own life before surrendering the beautiful to the ugly.

Tim woke again, slightly restored when Crankshadow enter the room, licking chocolate frosting from his fingers.

"Dessert was good," he said. "Ready to confess?"

Tim looked straight into Crankshadow's eyes with solemn determination. "No."

There was a wisp of change in the solidarity of Crankshadow's features, as though he were suddenly, though carefully, aware of the tractor beams that glared back at him from Tim's eyes. "That is most unfortunate, Timothy. Most unfortunate." He let the hand with the chocolate icing fall to his side.

"I don't care if you let me starve in here, asshole."

"We would hate for that to happen but it won't."

"Oh no?"

"No—you'll break like the rest. Everyone does eventually. Once you become dehydrated you'll be too delirious to hold on to this petty stubbornness. You'll admit to being a porn addict whether you mean to or not."

"How can I admit to being a porn addict if I don't know what I'm admitting to? How is that me taking personal responsibility for my actions?"

"You don't get it do you?" Crankshadow said, suddenly venomous. "You're not supposed to take personal responsibility. That's the last thing we want out of you. We—I mean the good Lord—wants you to give up being personally responsible. That's what's ruining you and the rest of humanity. You run around thinking that you can control your lives and take care of yourselves when really this world is dead in its sins and the only way for you to live a happy, fulfilling life is to give your life over to Jesus. He wants to be in your life. He wants to help you if you'll only let him."

"I've never tried to stop him."

"Don't mouth off to me."

"There's nothing wrong with porn! Nothing!"

"Oh no? Look at what happened to that strumpet Billie Solar!"

"Shut up!" Tim threw himself at Crankshadow who, despite his wiry frame, over powered Tim by grabbing both of the boy's wrists and throwing him to the floor.

Crankshadow was directly above him in an instant and glared down into Tim's quivering eyes as he squatted before the boy. "That fucking vile whore cunt deserved everything she got. She was an abomination before Christ Jesus and Ralphie Barrel did God's work when he put a bullet in that bitch. That's what porn does to you—in puts you in line for divine retribution. The Lord will weep for you on the day that he hands you over to the devil but that day will come and for whores like that bitch, it comes sooner than others. You don't think there's anything wrong with porn, do you? Well how would you like it if your mom did porn, huh? How would you feel about that?"

"My… my mom did do porn. I never thought there was anything wrong with it. It was just what she did. She was still my mom."

"So you *do* admit to being addicted?"

"No."

"Okay, you little panty waste faggot piece of shit—I'm going to let your shit your pants in this room for two days and when I come back I'm going to give you a choice—you can either give up and admit to your sins or you can see just what it feels like to watch your loved ones do porn."

Melvin Crankshadow was born to Bill and Julia Crankshadow in Birmingham, Alabama. At birth he was noticeably smaller than most babies, though the doctors were able to find no actual health problems. It was here that his parents, deciding to spare him the yoke of a proud, masculine name their son would never live up to, settled on Melvin. It was not long into his youth before his peers noticed the novelty of his name and began to chant it feverishly whenever he was around. As the larger boys gave in to the youthful onset of masculinity they began to actively bully him and Crankshadow would come home from Elementary school battered and bruised to a mother who, seeing the damage, would make him kneel down on the spot and pray for souls of the boys who had attacked him.

Melvin's father was distant and disinterested in his son, preferring to focus on his work as a used car salesman. Generally when Melvin sought help in matters of homework, his father would guide him through the course with a tone that was tinged with overt exasperation, acting as though the tutoring were a chore compacted by his son's inability to understand it.

The distance between Melvin and his father fueled a nearly clinical, academic interest in his father's behavior. Where his father was virtually mute around the home, he beamed with energy and a vibrant charisma when selling cars. He was one of the best dealers on the lot, moving three to four times the merchandise of his co-workers each month and it was in only a few short years, around the time of Melvin's tenth birthday, that his father was named owner of the lot that he had, for so long, dominated in spirit. It was this charisma and passion that Melvin sought to understand. His father didn't seem to have friends but at work he drew people in with a magnetic charm that left them feeling happy and cared for. This taught Melvin that friendship was built around sacrifice: when his father sold a customer a cheap piece of junk yard trash for six times its actual value, having convinced his buyer that it was the best deal available, the customer was then able to leave happier and a bit lighter because he'd sacrificed his judgment in exchange for camaraderie. This, Melvin learned, was at the altruistic core of friendship: getting people to feel better about the problems they'd never had before they met you.

The adults seemed to see in Bill Crankshadow the same vile malevolence they saw in his son. They regarded the whole family with suspicion, all of them unable to trust the man completely, as though he had secretly and quietly wronged each of them in a manner that mandated a reserved, solemn regard. There was one place where this dark appraisal was somewhat suspended and that was at the local church. At the local Baptist church which Melvin attended with his parents there was a suspension of judgment for in the lofty surroundings of religious imagery; the congregation adopted a more conciliatory tone with Melvin and his parents, the former always noticing how people seemed to stoop over a little bit at church—especially in the main chapel. This change in the Sunday air taught Melvin another lesson about friendship: that it required a constant overseer to keep both parties in line because, without such a figure, either party might be tempted to act on judgment, the suspension of which was central to friendship.

Melvin found that there was more to church than simply going each Sunday, absorbing the sermons, and leaving. Indeed, he found that the Wednesday night prayer meetings, Sunday school classes, and youth group excursions afforded him the opportunity to be on more even terms with his peers, finding them to be under the same spell. Desperate to improve their standing in the community, Julia encouraged her son's new found commitment to the church.

Melvin poured over the scripture, memorizing the King James backwards and forwards and soon began witnessing to other kids at his school. In a seemingly random fashion, Melvin would approach his various school mates and ask them increasingly penetrative questions about the Christian philosophy. Given that the vast majority of his fellow students were already Christian, they found the inquisitions tedious but otherwise inoffensive. Still, these interactions gave Melvin a chance to develop the instantly intoxicating tone that brought about his father's sales.

Melvin found that the sanctified atmosphere of the church seemed to carry into his own aura and that the bullies at school became more neutral with him, their behavior more indicative of the forced politeness he saw at the church, as though his association with the innermost workings of Christianity were endowing him with the same security monitor quality he felt beaming down from the images of Jesus all over the chapel. It was this aura that drove Melvin to look at the church as something more than a protective shield—he began to delve deeper and deeper into the psychology of the parishioners, often asking them highly inquisitive questions about the origins of their faith and how they came to believe in god. This, in turn, endeared Melvin to many members of the congregation who mistook his analysis for genuine interest.

The result of Melvin's study was a divergence in his mind. One part of him gloated at the simple fools who were so easily controlled by scripture while another part of him was craving something he'd never had before in his life: approval and acceptance. The more committed he was to the church, the more he gained the respect of its regulars and where previously respect had seemed like a tool of control, it now also seemed like something warm and generous. It wore on Melvin's mind not as guilt but as a sense of necessity: he had to choose either or—the logical dictates of his mind would not allow otherwise. Over time, Melvin realized that the answer had stared him in the face all along. There was one figure in the entire group that could have the warm comfort of acceptance and the glorious sense of power without contradiction: the preacher. The realization planted a seed in Melvin's mind and over time he came to realize that he was on route to becoming a preacher of the highest caliber.

Around the time of his twelfth birthday Melvin began to find his attentions drifting to the girls around him. Where previously his existence had been asexual and free of lustful considerations—which he'd long since written off as being the vices of lesser believers—he was shocked to learn of his burgeoning desires for the opposite sex. He'd already learned that men and women were meant to come together for one purpose: marriage and the producing of a child. Beyond that, the sexes were meant to remain strictly segregated with women devoting themselves to domestic pursuits and men chasing each other around in the woods. Any deviation from this mold—any attempts of men and women to cross collaborate in their social interests or come to communicate unnecessarily—was indicative of homosexuality.

Concerned that his newfound interest in the appearance of women was a sure sign that he was giving in to inclinations of faggotry, Melvin consulted the pastor at his local church and told the father figure that he was worried he might be gay. The pastor knew immediately that the solution for this was for more of Melvin's time to be spent in masculine pursuits among other men and recommended that he join the Boy Scouts. Here, Melvin found a fraternal atmosphere where he was encouraged to do the things that would make him a man, surrounded all the while by other young men. The raging desire to escape the constant thoughts of women propelled Melvin into the inner workings of Scouts with a new found vigor and he soon overcame his physical weakness with a near masochistic commitment to the physical activities of the troop.

One night, in the course of a three day hike, Melvin awoke to find his tent mate breathing hard and doing something with his hands beneath his sleeping bag.

"What're you doing?" asked Melvin, trying to look into the other boy's sleeping bag.

"Nothing," said the older boy. "Go back to sleep."

"Are you masturbating?" asked Melvin clinically, the term drifting into his mind from the dark annals of his limited sexual vocabulary.

"Yeah. Shut up—I don't want anybody to hear."

"Why would you do something like that?"

"Cause it feels good."

The words struck Melvin as a blur of confused thoughts. He was doing it for his own pleasure? Doing things for one's own pleasure was what aroused the attentions of others, who would naturally correct the behavior to return things to their proper state. Pleasure could only be taken solely for one's self if it was the satisfaction of either commanding based on an external morality or adhering to the morality of a commander. This was what established the order of things.

In desperation to gain his coveted status as the one in control, Melvin asked "isn't that fag stuff?"

"Nah, man. Putting on women's clothes, acting like a sissy, wishing you were a woman. That's fag stuff."

"So its faggy to be a woman."

"Yeah—that's why they act like fags."

"I'm not a fag."

"Never said you were."

"Then show me what you're doing."

Grunting in mild annoyance, the older boy unzipped his sleeping bag to expose his naked form. His largely hairless body rose and fell with the up and down administrations his hand made on his young organ.

"What do you think about when you're doing that?"

"Bitches."

"You mean girls?"

"Same thing."

"Then you're a fag."

"No I'm not."

"Yes you are—you're thinking about girls."

"I'm thinking about wanting to fuck girls. Fags want to fuck boys."

"That doesn't make sense."

"Shut up and go back to sleep."

Confused and frustrated, Melvin turned the other way and closed his eyes, sleep coming only after the other boy had breathed harder than before, exhaled slowly, and gone to sleep himself. On their return from the hike, Melvin had informed the boy's parents that their son was showing signs of homosexuality and had masturbated in front of him. Horrified, the parents slapped their son around until he admitted that it was true. The boy was shipped off to military school some days later.

Melvin began to study the teachings of Christian scripture in greater detail with respect to the nature of sexuality. From the Garden of Eden going forward, they depicted women as being manipulative seductresses and Melvin came to realize that sexuality was an inherently feminine concept, one that was used to corrupt men and he now understood why it was wrong to "lie with man as one lies with woman." It was a vile and evil thing, to treat a man as though he were on the level of a temptress.

Still, Melvin found himself bound by a desire for all of the young temptresses around him. It was a desire he could not escape and one he dared not admit, as it would tarnish his now crystal clean reputation with the churchgoers.

There was a crucial night in Melvin's development, however, when he'd attended a church dinner party with his parents. The dinner was held in the home of a man and woman who were prominent within the church—the man was a deacon and the woman was a Sunday school teacher. They were respected in the local community and Melvin knew that this meant he had to seize on their auras—to gain whatever countenance allowed them to move in such respected circles. His spiritual development depended on it.

It was to Melvin's surprise and frustration then when he found himself hurried off to the "kid's room," which was the bedroom of one of the two daughters that the family had. Upon his exile to the frilly, light blue chamber, Melvin found himself welcomed reluctantly by the two girls, though not with the hormonal vigor that they approached other boys.

"I'm not into fag stuff," said Melvin before either of them could say more than introductory pleasantries. The girls were taken aback but continued in their amateurish efforts at the formalities of hosting, asking Melvin if he wanted to play a board game with them. Melvin searched among their games, passing on Candy Land and Are You my Mommy in favor of Scrabble, which seemed to be gender neutral. The game progressed with an uncommon solemnity as Melvin found that the girls didn't seem compelled to act as temptresses. Still, his odd desires returned and he found himself looking at the bits of flesh—legs, knees, face, arms—that were exposed on each of them with an unavoidable fixation. When the other two girls were focused on the board, he would turn his attentions to their skin, marveling at its softness and the way they seemed to be blissfully unencumbered by the gruff melee of angry self-torture that passed back and forth among the boys that Melvin followed about.

The girls were pleasant and enjoyable—and Melvin found himself carried along by their spell. The word 'spell' occurred to him suddenly and he became worried that the spell was Satan trying to tempt him. This was compacted by the arrival of a fourth child, this one a boy of about seven years. As soon as the little boy entered the room, the focus of the two girls shifted and Melvin felt their coquettish charm turn into a pseudo-maternal interest in the young boy. Wailing inwardly at the realization that he had in fact been under their spell all along, he was enraged. The rage was not, however, at the girls. Something inside him told him that the girls were wonderful creatures that had been led astray by the arrival of the little boy and that their wonderful charm of femininity they had exhibited as young women could be molded into something proper and good—something that could only be achieved by returning their attention to him. He knew that they were only going for the boy because Melvin's own masculinity paled in comparison and, as such, there would have to be a display of power to determine who the true alpha male was.

The little boy had a red toy airplane that was attached by a long white cord to a handle so that the plane could be flown by turning in place or running ahead of it. When asked about the plane by one of the girls, the boy explained that he had brought it to fly in the family's big front yard. Melvin glared at the plane from behind the two girls as his mind endowed it with the properties of adorable charm that made the little boy's disposition so adorable. To win the battle, the object would have to be brought down like a flag burned in war, thereby demoralizing the other side.

In a burst of fury, Melvin lurched forward and snatched the airplane's handle from the little boy's hands. Running down the hall with the toy flying machine trailing him in the air, Melvin rounded one corner after another, the girls and the boy shortly behind him. The girls were yelling for him to give the plane back but he ran on harder and harder, charging through the dining room. Steering clear of the living room where the adults were gathered, Melvin ran outside and ducked around the side of the house. When the boy and girls found him, he'd stomped the toy plane to bits and ripped the cord off of the plastic fuselage. Melvin apologized with sarcastic bravado and left the remnants of the plane for the boy to pick up.

Reentering the house through the glass patio door in the back, Melvin found himself in a study with a computer, rows of books, and an ornamental whip mounted on one of the shelves. The girls and the boy followed in through the patio entrance as Melvin closed the interior door. The girls were about to confront Melvin and demand to know why he'd done such a thing, but he spoke first:

"It's time to play school," he whispered. "And I'm the principle. You all need to be punished." He jerked one of the girls down to a couch and began spanking her. After a few repetitions he pulled the other one down as well, spanking her clothed bottom. The girls seemed to respond to this rough behavior. They started giggling as though they'd forgotten the act of bullying Melvin had just committed. After a moment he looked over to the little boy, who stood rooted to the spot. "Your turn," he beckoned, though the little boy did not move. "I said your turn!" barked Melvin, jumping up from the couch and grabbing the little boy by the arm. Looking into the little boy's watering eyes, Melvin administered an Indian rug burn to the boy's forearm as he yanked him across the room to the couch. The girls moved aside as Melvin threw the boy down on the couch and began to spank him over and over again. The boy began to sob wildly, his face red and contorted, as Melvin slapped his open palm against the boy's buttocks. Enraged by the showing of weakness from the younger boy, Melvin pointed at the ornamental whip. "Do you know what that is?" Melvin hissed. "It's a cat-'o-nine tails. It has nine whips and if you get hit with it enough times you'll die. If you ever tell anyone about this, I will whip you with that until you're dead, do you hear me?"

The boy jerked away from Melvin, stood up, and stepped back slowly, raising his hands as though he were ready to box. Melvin was taken aback, not by the sudden willingness of the boy to fight, but by the unbelievably pathetic nature of the defensive posture. The boy's fists were raised but his shoulders still cowered, as though the preparation for battle were only a formality in anticipation of certain defeat. Melvin understood now why all of the other boys had picked on him—he had been this wretchedly pitiful creature that now stood before him. He realized in that instant the laws of the world—that his self worth was dependant on how many people he kept subservient to himself.

"Get him!" shouted one of the two girls and they lunged into Melvin, knocking him down to the couch and hitting him wherever they could. The little boy suddenly joined in as well, pulling at Melvin's hair. Melvin launched out a hand and slapped the boy just as the door to the study opened. The little boy's mother, who months ago had bought her son the toy airplane for his birthday and spent countless evenings in the parking lot of the neighborhood pool teaching him how to fly it, was now standing in the doorway, looking at the frozen melee.

"Are you okay?" Asked the boy's mother.

Melvin looked up at the boy, who was again on the verge of tears. The boy's features suggested that he was grappling with whether or not to tell on Melvin and it was with tremendous satisfaction that Melvin heard the boy say "I'm okay."

"Are you sure?" His mother asked.

"I... I'm sure..." said the boy. The mother closed the door carefully, looking down at Melvin all the while. There was a moment's awkwardness as the pile of fighting children disentangled followed by silence as all three tried not to look at Melvin, who was starting with laser beam precision at the little boy. A few moments later Bill Crankshadow opened the door and, with grim formality, told Melvin it was time to go home.

The next day the little boy would sit staring at a bowl of oatmeal on the breakfast table as his father asked him over and over again if he was sure everything was alright and was there anything he wanted to say about what had happened last night. Each time the boy had shaken his head and responded that nothing had happened. The red airplane was thrown out with the trash.

Melvin wasn't punished for what happened because, as far as anyone of authority knew, nothing had. He'd known that the boy would never tell but was surprised to learn that the girls remained silent as well. He never saw the boy again, but when the girls would pass him in the halls at school they would be noticeably cold and silent towards him. This, in Melvin's mind, was a victory: he had crushed from them the vile temptress behavior. More so than that, he told himself that this was an act of love: the girls had been beautiful and pure when they'd played with him, but when they'd played with his adversary, the little boy, they'd turned into temptresses and the punishment for such a defilement of their virtues had been to have their capacity for warmth of any kind amputated.

One of the girls happened to show up at his church some weeks later. Her name was Patricia and though she was reticent toward Melvin at first, she later confided that she had gotten pregnant and had an abortion without her parent's knowledge. Melvin began to administer the kind of compassion he'd learned from watching his father and the pastor at the church. He would help her find the way to salvation through Jesus Christ, he told her. He would help her find her place in something much bigger than herself.

Later on in the school year, Melvin had been out on the playground during recess. The sixth grade at his school was still a part of the Elementary, which was vexing to Melvin who'd wanted to impress and integrate with the older boys. In the course of recess, Melvin noticed a teacher, Ms. Lillian, had brought her class out for their turn on the playground. Ms. Lillian was a beautiful creature of twenty-eight on whose finger an engagement ring shimmered proudly. Her shinning smile and eternal patience brought forth thoughts of honeysuckles on a bright summer day. She was perfect and when Melvin waved involuntarily at her as she passed, she waved back and he knew that perfection was for him and him alone. As the students went off to play, she'd sat down on a bench and Melvin had watched her for a time, until another boy this one of some five or six years, had brought his teacher a picture of a heart with his name and "Ms. Lillian" written on it. The teacher had given the student a hug and a kiss on the forehead, thanking him for the drawing and shooing him off to play. This corrupted her in Melvin's eyes, but he knew that he didn't have the authority to confront her directly.

A few minutes later, the boy separated again from his friends and went to a nearby water fountain on the edge of the playground. Making sure that the teacher had immersed herself in a book, Melvin walked up to the little boy, leaned in to his ear, and whispered "if you don't take your pants off and show the rest of the kids you pee pee, I'm going to make you go to Hell." The little boy looked horrified at the thought and Melvin took out the imitation gold cross on a chain that he wore around his neck, holding to the crucifix to the boy's face. "You see this? I can use this to make you go to hell. And it will also tell me if you ever tell anybody on me, and then I'll make it give you AIDS. Do you know what that is? That's what god gives fags to make them suffer in Hell while they're still alive." The boy turned around to face the jungle gym where most of his classmates were playing and began to unbutton his pants. Melvin ducked away around the corner of the school building. Watching from a distance he saw the boy's pants fall to the ground and as the boy's classmates began to notice they reached over and tapped the shoulders of those around them, bringing the oddity to their attention as well. There was a pause among the crowd of some thirty students and then they exploded with laughter, the sharpened barbs of their tinny voices resonating in the little boy's soul like the reports of a thousand machine guns.

When Ms. Lillian noticed what had just happened, she shouted the boys name and came running over to the scene, where she pulled up the boy's pants and grabbed him roughly by the arm, dragging him off to the principal's office. She no longer wore the bright, charming face that she'd had only minutes ago. Now she seemed aggravated and sickened. Melvin's heart was warmed by the knowledge that he'd saved this beautiful woman from certain damnation and put an adversary in his place.

Melvin began to favor this new method over any physical form of bullying. Beating up another kid by hand left only physical wounds that would heal over time and leave the opponent stronger and better able to withstand pain. But wounds to the brain and soul ran far deeper and those that bore them would feel them flare up, their stitches breaking open, anytime they were in Melvin's presence. These were the truest lashings Melvin could provide and he was able to administer them with magical psychology.

A few years later, Melvin discovered a pornographic magazine in his father's nightstand. Enraged that his father was contributing to the corruption of these women into temptresses, he thumbed through the pages of the glossy magazine, seeing one woman after another unclothed and penetrated by muscular men. He knew that each of these women had been corrupted. He stared on in horror at the acts of sodomy and vaginal adultery that the ladies performed, telling himself all the while that he could save these poor women. The magazine was called *Big Tits Wet Slits* and Melvin looked up and down the front and back covers until he found the words *A Publication of Alston Image.*

When he graduated high school, Melvin entered seminary with the intention of becoming a youth pastor. The radiant charisma of the limelight proved too strong, however, and he found that he was frequently preaching before large crowds at various mega-churches. The grinning swagger that had made his father such a successful car salesman had made Melvin a star on the stage, where he bathed in the glory cast upwards to him.

Tim Alston began a focused meditation, laying on his back and staring at the ceiling while he began setting things aside. The thought of what was happening to his mother, father, and sister right now entered his mid and he set it aside. The thought of what was going on elsewhere in the building entered his mind and he set it aside. He felt as though each thought that entered into his mind carried a weight that would consume some small amount of his vital energy and setting these thoughts aside—not allowing his mind to dwell on any of them, seemed to alleviate the tension in his head and the aching in his stomach.

After some time, Tim realized that he needed to relieve himself and did so by pissing down the vent in the floor through which the smells of food were wafting. The vent snapped shut as he did this and he felt a small victory at knowing he'd stopped at least one of the tortures.

Time was one of the first things that Tim set aside, but it was also one of the most persistent—he longed for some way to keep track of time but soon realized that knowing this would only hasten the return of all of the thoughts he'd already put aside. The feeling of being alive became one of polarized ennui, as though he were suffering the effects of heatstroke while freezing. Eventually, something in his mind disconnected and he entered a hovering ambience where he felt no conscious thought at all, only the transparent lilt of thoughts and feelings being crumpled up and tossed into his subconscious.

It was in this state of hovering detachment that Tim heard the sound of the door's cold steel locking mechanism slide in and out of itself, the door opening once more. He heard Crankshadow enter, the waifish footsteps once more filling the tiny chamber, but they were now accompanied by the sounds of at least two others. One of them stopped as soon as Crankshadow entered the room and the other seemed to buck and kick frantically.

"Now what?" asked Tim when Crankshadow approached the bench. As the pastor neared, Tim could hear a change in the footsteps: the sharp click of shoes was gone and replaced by the thick sound of bare flesh on steel. He opened his eyes and looked down to see that Crankshadow wore no shoes. Following up the figure's legs he saw that the man was clad only in a bathrobe.

"Do you admit that you have a porn addiction? That you're powerless over your addiction and that only God—the one true god—can save you?"

"No."

"Bring her in!" Said Crankshadow and Tim sat up to see Matthew Simmons, clad in military fatigues, enter the room with a video camera in one hand and a captive in the other. It was a girl of about five years old who had been stripped nude with her face painted garishly in slutty makeup. Her cheeks were emblazoned with rouge and the wide caverns of starvation around her eyes bore several layers of multi-shaded blue and white eye shadow. Her hair hand been done up in pigtails with droopy pink bows. It was Tim's sister Jessie.

Tim jumped to his feet but was shaky and uncertain once he got there. He looked around frantically as Matthew locked the door and turned on the video camera, staring into its monitor screen. Tim heard the record button beep and the red light in the front of the camera ignited. Almost silently, Crankshadow removed his bathrobe—his eyes not leaving Tim's as his hands danced fluidly and calmly through the pulls that undid the knot in the robe's belt—and dropped the garment to the floor. He stood naked before Tim, his frail, rodent countenance towering above the boy despite only being a foot taller, and began to stroke his penis until it was erect. Like a withered carrot stuck into a sickly mushroom, the poorly hewn tool stuck straight up, its length engorged with blood.

"Do you now see what your demon sister has done to my manhood?" whispered Crankshadow, bending down until his eyes were inches above the boy's own. "Your demon sister is a temptress. She was born a temptress, like all women, and unless we save her soul she will die a temptress as well and then she'll burn in Hell for all eternity. Do you want her to go to Hell?"

"Will you be there?"

"No."

"Then yes."

Crankshadow slapped Tim across the right cheek and turned away in annoyance, kneeling down next to Jessie, who stared at the floor, her eyes moist and reddened. "This demon consumes all of us," Crankshadow hissed as he began to grope the cowering girl. "I'm not above it and neither are you. We are all demons at heart and without the love of Christ Jesus, we are nothing but sinners. And with the salvation of Christ Jesus we are still sinners but we are sinners who have been forgiven. Don't you want to be forgiven for these sins you're committing? I've been forgiven. I know the truth of Jesus Christ and I know that he will forgive me of my sins for no other reason than that I acknowledge the significance of his death on the cross. No sin is greater or lesser in the Lord's eyes and because of that all sins can be forgiven. Don't you want that peace of mind?"

"No."

Crankshadow pushed the girl to the ground and brought her up on her hands and knees, kneeling behind the quivering child and pushing his withered manhood into her. Her voice meant to produce a scream but instead brought forth an amplified cry of distorted shame as her tears splattered on the floor. Tim ran forward, not knowing how he would intervene but doing so nonetheless and was thrown backwards by a sideways slap to his throat from Matthew, who was steadying the camera with his other hand. Wheezing and chocking, Tim panted hoarsely on the ground and, as his vision became clear again, realized that blood was now dropping to the floor between his sister's knees.

Tim had seen his sister nude before—even in recent memory—when she received baths from their parents and her visage had always seemed to be fundamentally removed from the women that modeled for his father's company. Those women had developed not only the curves of sexual adulthood but the matured confidence required to use them. His sister had none of those things—no breasts, no pubic hair, nothing but a narrow, razor thin opening to distinguish her from the boys that were her age. That opening was being forced apart now with a force that reached past her tiny body and into the invisible realms of what her body lacked, as though demanding that she take on as fact the delusion of having a type of body—a sexual body—that was not there. It was in this transgression that Tim saw the reality of Crankshadow's evil: that he demanded the unreal from the unable. It was not sex that was evil but Crankshadow's deluded insistence. Jessie Alston screamed as though her voice had reached beyond itself, into a howling abyss where it flailed with primal abandon for the traction of mercy.

The look on Crankshadow's face as he climaxed was one of bitter triumph. His contorted lips bent around clinching teeth as he closed his eyes and threw his head back. The camera turned to focus on the expression, drinking hungrily from the contortions as the little girl vomited. The pastor's face seemed to shamefully but flamboyantly demand adulation for the triumph of disgust over pleasure.

"Now do you see what smut like what your father puts out does to people?" Hissed Crankshadow, pivoting on his knees to face Tim, who was sitting in the corner with his knees drawn close and his face covered by his arms. He raised his head, forcing himself to look directly into the pastor's eyes and not at his crying sister who was still in the receiving position she'd been forced to take.

Tim was careful in his words, as though endowing each of them with the certainty of his convictions and the clarity of intransigent bravado: "My dad and his 'smut' didn't do that to my sister. You did. It's all your fault."

"You are worthless scum," menaced Crankshadow, rising to his feet and putting on the robe. "You're saying that people should be allowed to go down the road that led me to do that to your sister."

"No. I'm saying the road you went down was yours and yours alone."

"You're exactly like your father."

"Thank you."

"I had hoped that this little exercise would make you see how it feels when the people you care about fall victim to pornography, but I can see that there's no changing your mind. You aren't possessed by a demon, you are a demon."

"Thank you."

"I hope you repent of your sins young man. If it comes to it, I'll find the longest, thickest penis in my entire ministry and force it into your rectum. If watching the horrors of porn won't make you repent then maybe becoming a part of them will." He turned to Matthew: "Let them rot in here together. No food, no water." And with that he stormed out with Matthew close behind.

After the door closed Tim rose to his feet and went to hug his sister but she screamed and told him to stay away.

Chapter 23

THERE ARE NO WINTERS in California, only intervals in which the sun's eternal presence is somewhat benign. The sprawling expanse of the state, which is larger than some countries, is given at any time to a range of temperatures but through them all there is a dry, arid quality that pierces the skin and leaves it baked and brown. It could well be argued that this eternal summer has made the brains of the state's populace somewhat gelatinous and whimsically vacant while others would argue that it has made them more mellow and thoughtful but between the two is the simmering anger of perpetual heat stroke. It is the anger that fuels thuggish cops and common thugs to duel with clenching teeth and straining eyes in an ongoing struggle to seize the whipping hand, one from the other in constant cycle. For the more mellow residents of California, namely Los Angeles, there is an ongoing inward struggle to push one's self into one of the two non-threatening categories and away from the scorching crimson ravishment of the lethal third. Still, the undertow of such mania is strong and visceral, forever stroking the soft membrane of complacency with a sharpened claw. In recent times that membrane had been ripped open completely, unleashing the swarms of baby cockroaches that had been the plethora of anti-porn protestors into this world stepped Isaac Alston, Hank Steel, Dominic Daniels, Luther "Slamdingo" Stevens and Rod Wielding.

They left on the night after Patricia's visit in a used Mazda that Rod had been able to find cheap and purchased with cash he'd been given by his employer. The car was primitive and cramped compared to the luxury that Alston normally enjoyed, but he seemed indifferent to the setback as he guided the vehicle out of the Alston Image lot with Dominic in the passenger's seat and the remaining three pressed together in the back. They rode in silence but in each of them the same adrenaline mounted: vision was becoming sharper, sounds were becoming more detailed; the mind was waking its body more completely and preparing for battle. The metronomic pulse of their hearts was reaching out its plasma soaked fingers to tap out its meter on the backs of their eyes, in the inside of their throats, and the inner curves of their arms. All five knew that it was pointless to try and suppress this feeling that rose within them and each knew, with a wisdom that only comes when the rational mind is working in mature harmony with its savage, primitive counterpart that the killing self had awoken its secret holds on the tendons, muscles and nerves of the body the only course of action was to guide it and control it. And the only way to control it was to gently assure it that if it held fast and waited patiently, it would receive a satisfaction greater than its desire for wild flailing would allow. Somewhere, in the near future and at an ever shorter distance, was their enemy and the rational mind was putting aside the defensive mechanisms that would cause them to look for protection and instead look only for offensive pathways. It was a feeling that was harrowing in its calm.

Hank and Slam had been able to track down a number of weapons which were now hidden under a blanket in the trunk of the car: two AR-15s, two Glocks, a Bretta 9mm, and an AK-47 along with five hunting knives, all of which had been for sale on the black market at several times their actual value. Ammunition had been expensive as well but Alston had been more than willing to put up the paper.

The city around them was a decimated morass of apocalyptic dimensions. Where the protestors had gathered—some of them still meandering around in anemic clumps—there were wide swaths of graffiti proclaiming the end of times and the Hell that awaited fornicators, all decreed in bumper sticker levels of literacy. As the car navigated the brittle streets its occupants did nothing to conceal their identities—they rode through town with the solemn grandiosity of old west gunslingers, their faceless reservation in the midst of the firestorm that mounted before them serving as a single, eloquently understated challenge to the rivals that stood in their way.

They drove away from town to a wide expanse of California desert where guns could be fired in relative seclusion. By the time they arrived the dawn was breaking and they were able to see well enough to walk away from the road and out into the wilderness. The jagged, irregular cut of the rocks and disheveled lilts in the sand presented them with a biological shooting gallery to hone their skills. Dominic went first with the AK-47. "You want to keep it pointed down," explained Hank as he looked over Dominic's shoulder. "The way it fires will send it upwards, so if you're inexperienced you'll want to let the gun raise itself to the level of your target." Dominic nodded and carefully lined up the base of a cactus some ten feet away. The caffeine rush of the weapon's report cracked in a rapid column of bullets that went up the length of the cactus, splitting it in half in a series of pulpy bursts. For the first time all day there was smiles and applause among the group and Dominic and Hank high fived. Similar tutorials followed with Hank taking the other four through a dry run on using the different weapons, then showed them how to hold an edge weapon with the blade coming out of the hand in the direction opposite the thumb, keeping the inside of the arm protected during lateral thrusts.

When they returned to the car it was mid day and the simmering anticipation of violent release was mediated by the bonding force of camaraderie. Still, when they returned to the car their solemn demeanor resumed, the energy and intensity again brought to a fever pitch through the clenching Zen of silence.

By the time they arrived in San Bernardino it was early evening and the sun was just starting to retreat. They ate food from packed lunch sacks and though none of them were particularly hungry they knew better than to waste the expensive food and all of them ate their meals in their entirety.

San Bernardino was nearly a ghost town—trash filled the roads and the few pedestrians that were seen out on the street looked like the zombie descendants of third world slave labor. They moved without even the kind of implicit authority in their steps that would justify the direction they wandered. There was an atmosphere of sorrow that loomed ever present in the hollow hearts of each dry human husk. Their eyes probed the world before them in sharp, uncertain flicks that cowered wide-eyed in their sockets, afraid to take in the world around them but still looking for a destination that they dared not find or stop looking for. It was the eternal struggle of imposed poverty—to never appear too idle or too busy and it was a limbo that was difficult to watch.

There weren't many other cars on the roads and that few that were drove with an overly performed sense of formality—as though the rigor of intense structure in all behavior were an end in itself. Realizing how odd they seemed in their out-of-town vehicle, Alston navigated the car through the outer edge of town, doing his best to remain out of sight of the various roving gangs of private street cops.

The First Grand Pantheon of Jesus Christ the Imperial Redeemer of American Liberty was located just off the Rim of the World highway amidst the shallow hills so endemic to California. They drove past the placid set of onyx slabs that made up the building and Hank took note of the barricades that stood between them and the main structure. "There's two guards on either side of the main gate and I saw at least three golf carts with guards patrolling the parking lot, but given its size there would have to be more. The hills are going to be our best bet for an approach, but I would imagine that there's gunmen up there as well."

"Did anyone else notice," interjected Dominic "that the barbed wire on the fence surrounding the complex was on the inside, not the outside?"

"It's probably not new arrivals they're worried about," said Alston. "They're in the retention business."

The hills that surrounded the First Grand Pantheon encased the structure in a wide bowl that opened on one side to face the highway. The hills were festooned with a dense network of pine trees and after driving for a mile they quietly drove the car into the woods, leaving it burrowed deeply into the shadows of the night and brush.

"Move like I do," said Hank as they exited the vehicle. They distributed the guns and knives, with Dominic taking the AK-47, Rod and Slam taking the AR-15s, Alston taking the Beretta and Hank taking the two Glocks. The knives were distributed among the five and the quintet made their way into the woods. They followed Hank's delicate motions, doing their best to impersonate the manner in which he hunched over and stepped gently. The inches of their careful paces stretched the short distance to the compound out to a withering eternity, but the party was far to drawn into each movement's tiny mediations to be wearied by the distance.

Just as the hollowed out luster of illumination that shone from the crater of the compound broke the horizon, the five men could see a guard walking perpendicular to them through the woods. Slam readied his weapon but Hank placed a light hand on his shoulder to stop him. Holstering the guns, Hank brought out one of the blades and began to move away from the group, the rest of them knowing instinctively to let him step out alone.

The guard was dead before the other four could register it. Hank moved as though he'd stepped sideways into the cool evening breeze and been whisked along its currents towards the guard, who became rigid when Hank's arms encircled him then went suddenly limp in a cloud of blood that erupted from his throat. Hank stepped back and guided the freshly rendered corpse to the ground so that it sprawled silently. Hank returned to his squad mates, a blackened swath of the guard's blood soaking his chest in a glorious Rorschach spray that stood out only slightly against his black shirt. "No guns till we're inside," he whispered and motioned for them to continue forward. They moved on until they reached the lifeless corpse of the guard and Hank bent down to remove his helmet and bullet proof vest. "We'll put these on the kids when we're heading out," he said, handing the helmet to Dominic and the bullet proof vest to Alston, both putting on the articles. "If this was a patrol they'd be in groups. Solo means that there's one every twenty yards or so."

"Do we take them all out?" asked Rod.

"No—it would take us three hours to walk around the perimeter at least. This is going to have to be as covert as possible," replied Hank, dragging the corpse into some dense bushes.

They navigated through the underbrush, keeping to the shadows as they came to the circular fence that contained the compound. The lights in the parking lot were only sporadically activated, and as the other four looked over Hank's shoulders, he pointed out a pathway among the dark spots in the parking lot that led up to the side of the building. The others took in the path and looked back to Hank for further instruction. Before them was a chain link fence with a thick spool of razor wire running along the top. An iron fence post was directly in front of them and it was here that Hank and the other two stronger men pried up the fence, bending it just enough for each man in the group to slither through.

Once inside, the expanse of the parking lot lay before them in a shadowy sprawl. They now stood at the top of a six foot white brick wall that surrounded the perimeter of the parking lot and served to hold border off the surrounding hills where they'd been truncated to clear space for the parking lot. Hank led the path to the asphalt by turning and dropping down so that he landed silently. The rest of the group followed as best they could, light claps seeming to resound infinitely across the delicate evening when they reached the ground.

They moved through a dense network of shadows and the poor covering of the few cars. Hank navigated them in a wild, zigzag fashion that kept them out of the line of video cameras atop the lamp posts. At each covering, whether shadow or car, Hank stopped the troop and evaluated their position. These moments reeled about them as though taken over by the ambient gaze that poured in from the hills.

When they finally reached the rear of the building they were confronted with a double door that was locked with chains and a large padlock. "No getting in here," muttered Hank.

"Can we shoot the lock off?" asked Slam. "Like in the movies?"

"Not really. Unless..." Hank looked over at the vest and helmet. "I might be able to pull it off with the AR-15, but if I do... our cover is blown. I really don't think that—"

"Put down your weapons and turn around slowly," came a commanding voice from behind. All five men turned reflexively and opened fire, leaving six dead guards in golf carts in the wake of their volley.

"Shit from movies never works," said Hank. "Kind of like when a dipshit preacher tries to bait a trap for the good guys." And Hank moved over to one of the bodies, found a key ring with just a few keys on it, and returned to the group. "Outside guards," explained Hank. "Not enough security clearance to do more than secure the external doors, but it should be enough to get us inside." He tried the keys one after another until one turned in the lock and the chains fell to the floor.

"No more time for subtlety," said Slam, "Full force from here on in."

Hank nodded in agreement and bolted through the door, the others fast in his wake. They were in an industrial sized kitchen facility and quickly rounded the expansive cooking island to burst through the opposite doors into a long white maintenance corridor. Hank went first and stepped in backwards, throwing himself against the opposite wall with guns extended in both directions. The others followed, looking in both directions quickly as they followed Hank down the corridor, moving in the direction of two more double doors, these with a sign reading *TO STAGE* above them.

Through the doors they were met with the enormity of the main chamber, its arena seating extending up to the roof on all sides. Hank looked around and, seeing the gold lined doors in the back of the stage, motioned for the others to follow. Bursting through the doors and into the main concourse, they saw a further set of doors, these emblazoned with the words *Office of Melvin Crankshadow.*

Two guards came around the right adjoining corridor and fired, one of the bullets slicing across the top of Hank's shoulder and casting a sleek spurt of blood in its wake before embedding itself in the wall. Hank returned fire along with Slam and Rod, the high powered weaponry knocking the guards down and giving Hank time to rush them and fire point blank.

"Slam—you watch the left corridor, Rod you take the right, Dominic you give them back up. Mr. Alston and I will handle this." And with that he kicked open the doors to Crankshadow's office.

"Where the fuck are my kids?" bellowed Alston as he stormed through the double doors into the wide oval shaped room. The preacher's head snapped forwards, his wizened eyes held open wide.

"Your children are safe in my care," Crankshadow spat back, his condescension shaken but not decimated.

"Don't give me that shit!" screamed Alston, firing his gun. The shot landed in the center of Crankshadow's desk and splintered through the varnished wood, making the scrawny preacher jump backwards in his chair.

"Put down that gun if you ever want to see your children on visiting days at San Quentin," hissed Crankshadow. "My guards will be here any minute-"

"And they'll die like the rest," said Hank, the sharp gruffness of his military tone serving to counterbalance Alston's fury. As Hank rounded the corner of the desk Crankshadow could see that Dominic, Rod and Slam were standing guard in the hallway, assault rifles at the ready.

Hank leaned in to look at Crankshadow's computer, swiveling the mouse to bring up the desktop. Scanning over the files and folders, he saw one that bore the title ALSTON KIDS and clicked on it. Inside the folder was a single high definition video file, which he opened. The video appeared in a media player and began. Soon Alston could hear the sounds of voices crying, one in disgust and one in agony. "What is that?" he hissed. "What are you watching?"

Hank steadied his weapon on Crankshadow. "Give me the keys to the room in this video," he barked. "NOW!"

By now Crankshadow seemed to be sinking into himself, his pale complexion draining further into the pure nakedness of fear. He reached into his pocket and extracted a small key ring. "It's one of those," he whispered, glancing hurriedly at Isaac Alston as he did so. Hank pocketed the keys and stopped the video from playing.

"What was that?" demanded Alston.

"Just a minute," said Hank, typing at the computer. "Open your email and send this video to that address," said Hank.

"That's the FBI," whispered Crankshadow, almost pleading.

"You're god damn right it's the FBI. Now do it!" Hank steadied the barrel of his gun on Crankshadow's temple as the preacher shakily did as he was told. A ping went off to say that the email had been sent and Crankshadow sank back in his chair, eyes stuck on Alston like a condemned man to the switch throwing hand of an executioner.

"Now—show it to me," said Alston. Holding Alston's eye contact the whole time, Hank set the video playing again and turned the monitor to face his boss. Alston's jaw clenched as he saw what was happening. His mouth opened but his teeth continued to bear down with such wrenching ferocity that they seemed ready to crumble as he watched his daughter being raped. A single gunshot reported across the room and the monitor split in half, a burst of sparks erupting as the bullet tore through it. Alston turned the weapon on Crankshadow and fought with all his muscle to make steady his aim. "Okay holy man," he growled. "Make Jesus stop the bullets!" he screamed, firing two more shots. One of them landed in the middle of Crankshadow's chair, the other penetrating his kneecap. Crankshadow howled in agony as Alston took aim again "Make Jesus stop the bullets!" he cried, his voice transcending the distortion of screaming and into a monstrous realm of feral hysteria that surged up into his infernal eyes as he fired another shot, this one hitting Crankshadow in the groin. The preacher's pants began to fill with blood that ran out the cuffs like piss from an incontinent child. His face was contorted as though screaming but all he could produce was a barely audible whimper as Alston advanced on him. "Make Jesus stop the bullets!" and with this Alston began firing again and again, the shots landing in the preacher's chest in rapid succession then erupting out the back of his chair and shattering the plaster on the wall behind him as the slide crashed back and forth on the gun, whipping visceral snaps of ravenous flame into each bullet's shimmering wake.

Crankshadow's hands were frigid in shock, one gripped white knuckle around the arm of the chair, the other frozen in mid air. The quivering in the preacher's jaw was the only sign of motion until his increasingly pale lips began to grope for words. "At least…" gasped Crankshadow, the words making him cough up blood. "I'll go… to heaven…"

"Thank God," said Alston with dark satisfaction and fired the rest of the clip into Crankshadow's face. The cringing terror of resignation in Crankshadow's expression was split down the center, the three bullets separating the skull in a plasmatic eruption. The preacher's head hung in two pulpy sections, the top of his spine visible through the eviscerated grey matter that had spewed across the back window.

Alston lowered the gun, the tension leaving his body for a moment as he examined the lead laden corpse in the chair before him. Hank stared into Alston's face with a dark, solemn appreciation. He had seen Alston in his purest form for a moment—the form that hid at the heart of every human being and only sprang forth in the moments when one realizes their own ability to take life. It was a beautiful, strangely serene moment.

"You done here, Isaac?" called Dominic from the hallway. "I think I found the holding cells!"

Alston gave one last look at the plasma splattered corpse of Melvin Crankshadow then turned and followed Dominic out of the office and down the hall.

Tim hadn't moved much since his sister had been raped. He'd stayed in the corner where he'd cowered and tried to sleep. Occasionally he would urinate into the corner but he hadn't defecated since he'd been in the room. His sister had sat silently in another corner of the room after her crying had subsided. He'd tried to hug her again at one point but she'd thrown her fists at him chaotically and screamed. He didn't know what to do next—his mind was empty of all thoughts or feelings. He felt as though his only tie to the existence around him was the dull aching in his bowels and stomach.

He was roused from his state when he heard gunfire somewhere in the building. At first he thought that the guards had taken down an intruder, but then the gunfire seemed to be relocating. After a time he heard Melvin Crankshadow screaming. Then other voices: Dominic. Hank. His father. There was the sound of many sets of feet charging down the halls and he heard his father banging on doors and shouting "Tim? Jesse?"

"We're in here, Dad!" he shouted hoarsely as he ran to the door and beat on it. "We're in here!" He heard the lock being manipulated and different keys being tried until, in a sudden click of salvation, one of them threw the dead bolt and the door opened.

"Tim!" Said his father, bursting through the door and pulling his son into his arms. Tim realized that his father was sobbing in their embrace. "Where's your sister?" he asked, pulling away. Tim stepped back and pointed to the corner where Jesse was still cowering. Naked and still stained with blood, urine and vomit , she looked out from between the closely crumpled knot of her knees and arms as though she was afraid to even look at her father.

Alston's companions watched at a cautious distance, knowing that they were seeing Alston in a state more human than any of them had ever imagined. He lowered himself to one knee and laid his gun down on the floor. He didn't open his arms wide but simply let one rest on his knee and the other hang by his side. She was looking deep into his face now—probing in her own childlike way for the points of tension and solemnity that told her this was not only her father but a beacon of that calm, guiding force that the title demanded. She eventually began to unravel, standing shakily to her feet and running to him, where he held her in the midst of the sorrow, agony and relief that swirled through the room.

Dominic realized that his shirt was the least torn and stained and so he took it off and brought it over to Jesse, draping it over her. The adult size shirt fit her like a long dress and Dominic took off his helmet and placed it on her head. After putting Tim in the bullet proof vest, Alston picked up his daughter and headed for the exit.

"Dad?" asked Tim as they stepped into the dank, windowless corridor outside. "What about the other kids here?"

"He's got a point," said Hank. Alston tossed him the keys and turned his attention back to his kids. There was some rustling of locks for a few minutes and then Hank returned. "No kids on this level, but look who I found." Darcy Collins leaned her head into the room and saluted. "If there's anyone else, the FBI will be here soon. Let's get out of here." Alston lifted his daughter and carried her in his arms as they made their way for the door.

They sprinted down the hall to the flight of stairs that were its only access and ascended them quickly, arriving back at the main concourse which circled the chapel in one direction and led to Crankshadow's office in the other. Alston put a hand on Tim's back to hurry him along as they stepped over the dead bodies on their way back to the main chapel.

Hank led the way back through the building, looking around carefully then seeing sets of guards coming through two of the far doors. "Go!" shouted Hank and the group broke into a run, Hank firing into the approaching melee but only slowing them down. In the next instant they were running back down the maintenance corridor and into the kitchen, bursting out the back door and hitting the asphalt with full force as shots began to sound. "Don't stop!" shouted Hank "just keep going."

They reached the brick wall unscathed and Dominic helped volley Tim up to the fence where he wriggled through the opening followed by his little sister and then his father who turned around to help pull Darcy through. Slam and Dominic sprayed bullets at the tiny cache of guards that had amassed at the door, but neither side was able to make any hits and the defensive nature of the opponents told Alston's party that the mercenary guards had learned of their boss's death.

The car was where they'd left it, but Alston gave the keys to Dominic. "You drive," he ordered and climbed into the back with Tim and Jesse. Hank got the passenger's side while Slam and Rod piled into the back and Darcy sat in Hank's lap. The car sped off through the woods and hit the open road with a screech. Alston exhaled audibly.

"Let's get you guys home," said Dominic, though more to himself.

"Hank..." said Tim urgently. Hank looked back at the boy with concern. "It was Ralphie Barrel that killed Billie. The preacher told me he got him to do it."

Hank nodded and looked over to Alston. "We have an errand to run in Vegas," he said darkly.

"We'll be in town for the AVN awards anyway," said Alston.

They drove in general silence the rest of the way home, with Jesse crying occasionally and Alston whispering soft words of comfort. Dawn was breaking as they arrived at the Alston Image offices where Carol met them at the door. Alston explained the recent events to her as best he could and she agreed to take care of the kids while they went took care of business. He then escorted the children up to his office and had them take turns using the office's bathroom to clean up. After dressing Jesse in a different T-shirt and telling Carol to go find some clothes in his kids' sizes, he sat on the couch in his office and held them both close as they cried on his shoulders.

"When will we see mommy again?" asked Jesse.

"I don't know," Alston replied. "She disappeared after she came and told me about you guys. I don't know where to."

"Dad," said Tim sitting up. "When they came and took us from Grandma and Grandpa's house, mom unbolted the door and talked to them for a couple of minutes before they rushed in and grabbed us. I couldn't tell what about, but I heard Melvin Crankshadow's name a few times."

Alston looked his son in the eyes for a long time and then said "Tim, I want you to tell me the truth about something: when the bomb went off in our house, was your mother out in the back yard with you?"

Tim thought about this for a long time. "No," he said finally. "She told us both to go play outside—way in the back of the yard—and then she came out right as the bomb went off."

Alston looked up and saw that Dominic and Hank had stepped off the elevator as this revelation had been made. "Patricia," said Dominic, "Is the feminine form of 'Patrick.' What's the feminine form of 'Judas?'"

"We set up one of the dressing rooms as a hideout for Darcy," said Hank. In the awkward silence that followed, he said "Mr. Alston—you told me awhile back that Judas was the noblest character in the Bible. Why?"

"The point of that story is sacrifice, Hank," replied Alston with a choked return to his normally contemplative tone. "Judas made the greater sacrifice—he had to betray his mentor and be damned to Hell for all eternity. That's far more profound than a god that dies and goes to his own heaven."

"And what do you think of sacrifice, Isaac," asked Dominic.

"Sacrifice," said Alston, "is the consolation prize for failed virtue."

"Was Billie a sacrifice?" asked Hank with a sudden but respectful sharpness.

"Only if we let them win," replied Alston gravely.

They left later in the day, in the mid afternoon. Clean, showered, and wearing new clothes they sat out for Las Vegas, forever on lookout for the police but more consciously focused in their thoughts on the subject of the vice president of Intersect Productions.

Ralphie Barrel took a drag off his cigarette and cleaned his sniper rifle with a proud smirk. He could not believe his luck—that Isaac Alston, history's most dickless loser, was finally stepping out of hiding and into his crosshairs. For once he felt like somebody. When he wore fancy dress clothes he no longer felt like they belonged to someone else. He had ripped open the shell of the Alston Image empire and now he was going to fire another set of shots into the heart and brain of its heart and brain.

The rifle lay on its side on the coffee table, the stainless steel briefcase it traveled in sitting open on the couch next to Ralphie. He unscrewed the silencer, looked it up and down then blew into it. Satisfied that the extended barrel was unobstructed, Ralphie reinserted the silencer into its slot in the briefcase's padded interior and began examining the scope. It was dark in the house but he performed the ritual more for the sake of seeing the individual instruments of the weapon gleam in the moonlight. It made them look slick and flawless.

His departure from the Black Chapel the night of Billie's murder had been quick and painless—in the rush of panic that followed the blast he'd been able to collapse the weapon into its case and join the chaotic throngs that moved out the front door. The melee had been enough cover to side step into an alley and back track to his car. When he'd reached the highway back to Nevada, the briefcase carefully stored in his trunk, he began to feel the adrenaline ebb and his sense returning. It was the same sense of satisfaction he'd gotten from shoplifting as a child: the feeling of scampering out of the reach of the law and melding back into the flow of the populace until his past actions had been ironed out by the ignorant tide of public dismissal. There was no better feeling in the world—not even fucking a hot bitch.

The doorbell rang and Ralphie looked up, startled. He quickly boxed up the remaining pieces and slid the briefcase under the couch before going to answer the door. Not looking through the eyehole when he opened the door, Ralphie looked out to see an empty front step. Confused, he leaned out slightly and saw nothing unusual except an unrecognized car parked just up the street. He started to step back inside when Hank Steele emerged from the bushes like an unseen tiger in jungle underbrush.

Ralphie realized what was happening as the wind rushed from his lungs. He tried desperately to breathe but was barricaded by the wall at his back and the arms that braced him. There was no faltering in Hank's eyes that would allow Ralphie to slip in with his usual sly retort. There was nothing there but an unadulterated killer's eye. A loaded gun in his mouth would have been merciful compared to the burning in Hank's glare.

"You killed her." He hissed. "You did it. You killed her." Hank's voice quivered as though he were about to cry but the wavering expanded into a malicious, cavernous snarl. Ralphie felt his cockiness melt along with his bladder control.

"The fuck is that smell?" said Dominic as the other four stormed in through the front door.

"Little bitch pissed and shit himself," said Hank with righteous scorn. He flung Ralphie to the floor where the vice president of Intersect Productions crumpled to the ground and tried to rise to his feet before the heel of Hank's jackboot came down on his back. The air rushed out of Ralphie's lungs again followed by a burst a blood and teeth when he hit the ground. Alston kicked Ralphie in the stomach and pistol whipped him before stepping out of the way and letting Hank retake the reigns. Hank stomped down on Ralphie's back, this time smashing a kidney as Ralphie vomited blood.

"People are going to hear," said Rod. "Kill him and let's get out of here."

Ralphie wanted to protest but his mouth could only grope vacantly for words that had already bled out of his frantic mind in unbridled desperation. Hank kicked Ralphie under one arm and Ralphie was spun onto his back where he lay as Hank jumped down on top of him. Broken and quivering, Ralphie gave himself over to the raping of his mortality.

"Which eye did you look down the scope with," growled Hank with a raving mania. Ralphie sobbed through the blankets of blood that covered his face, trying to shake his head pitifully. "Which eye did you look down the scope with?"

"Right," whispered Ralphie as though he was a humiliated child. "Right..." and his eyes filled with a horror they dared not know. Hank had produced a knife from his belt. It was a hunting knife—slightly curved and serrated on the inside like the kind used to skin a doe after a hunt. Hank guided the knife down with withering precision towards Ralphie's right eye. He tried to scream and jerk his head but the elbow in his throat made it come out as a gurgling noise. The triangular tip of the blade came down closer and closer and he tried to close his eye but another hand belonging to a third person was holding his eyelids back. The new fingers were dug in deep, a thumb and forefinger stuck beneath his eyelids, making his vision blur in and out. The blade came closer and closer and then it penetrated—Ralphie screamed as the agony of his eviscerated eyeball scourged through his nerves, his vision suddenly ripped in half.

Then—as suddenly as the burst of burning blue-white pain had shot through his broken body—Ralphie felt himself detach from all of the pain and float downwards into himself. He felt as though he fell through the wall of pain and into some kind of soft world where the pain existed only at a distance, like the winds of a hurricane that were only a cool breeze when felt a few hundred miles away. He was safe for a moment as a membrane coated itself around his fragile nerves. He no longer cared what happened next. He no longer cared that a hand gun was being pressed into his voided eye socket. He didn't care about all those things that happened distantly.

Hank pulled the trigger and Ralphie's head exploded, its right hemisphere shattered across the living room floor. Slam rose to his feet as did Hank. "Here," said Dominic coming out of Ralphie's bedroom. "I found this under his bed." He tossed a bag of cocaine to Hank who caught it and emptied the contents on Ralphie's body then rubbed the bag clean of finger prints.

"Looks like Ralphie just got in bad coke deal," said Hank shakily as they made for the front door, dashed across the lawn, and piled in to the car. Alston slammed the gas pedal and the vehicle screeched off towards the mouth of the neighborhood.

"We need to get lost, man," said Rod. "We need to get out of town and split up—lay low or something."

"Not yet," said Alston firmly. "I still have a speech to give."

The casino was dark and subdued and if it weren't for the cars and limousines in the parking lot, it might have been assumed to be completely barren. The waterfalls out front and the streams of lights were dormant, replaced instead by work lights over the various doors, their garish illumination perverting the seductive nature of the building. There was only a trickle of protestors outside the building, having apparently been tipped off about

282 | Jordan Owen

the AVN Awards Show's actual location. Their signs bore phrases like PORN KILLED BILLIE SOLAR.

"I recognize that guy," said Hank as they drove past the small crowd and into the main lot of the casino, pointing to one of the sign bearers. "He was one of the protestors outside our house. Back then he was railing about how Billie would burn in hell for what she had done."

"That's their M.O.," replied Dominic from the passenger's side front seat. "Damn them then pity them."

They pulled up into the casino's main lot where they were met by several representatives from the AVN awards and a parking valet. The valet took the car and the quintet was led inside by a young woman with a clipboard and walkie-talkie who was accompanied by two body guards. "I've got Alston, Dominic Daniels, Hank Steel, Rod Wielding and Luther Stevens," she said into the walkie-talkie, "I'm bringing them back now." She led them through the golden front doors of the casino and into a Hades of darkened gambling machines. Row after row of slot machines sat empty and dark under the dim house lights and what little color and shine was visible seemed like a vain groping into the anemic light for some trace of their former glory.

The party took an abrupt turn down a maintenance corridor and then through two double doors into another hallway, this one lined with a row of dressing rooms. There were other technicians and back stage people there, all of them dressed in black and carrying the same theater tech gear that the young woman leading the five had carried. Two older women with slightly graying hair emerged from one of the dressing rooms and led Alston inside.

As the door closed behind them they began undressing Alston and taking his measurements. They said nothing about the blood on his T-shirt and jeans or the bruises on his chest and put his clothes into a trash bag. After taking his measurements they instructed him to bathe and he entered the shower stall in the corner of the room and bathed in what felt like warm liquid salvation. He could feel the water massaging his weary muscles and taking the shuddering edge off of his fatigue. As he stepped out of the shower he was rejuvenated enough to forget that he hadn't slept in almost two days. The two women in the dressing room brought him a tuxedo hemmed to his measurements and he dressed quickly and mechanically, not wanting to give himself time to contemplate the meaning of the new clothes, what occasion they were being donned for and what was expected of him. Before he was able to fully realize what was happening, he was fully dressed and the same woman that had led him back stage was escorting him through the double doors that led to the wings of the stage. Dominic, Hank, Luther and Rod had been similarly dressed and were being led down the hall to a side corridor that would take them to the audience. They each made a token gesture to Alston as they passed, with Dominic putting an hand on Alston's shoulder and beaming into his eyes for an instant, then Luther and Rod shaking his hand. Hank was last and he simply nodded with quick but sincere salute. The sharp, steady look in his eyes passed into Alston in that moment, carrying with it the certainty that would allow Alston to bridge the gap in his mind between the cold hard reality he intended to impart and the delicate sculpture of the words themselves.

He stood in the wings, the first row of the audience just visible over the side of the black silk wing nearest the front of the stage. There were voices all around him, saying to one another that the internet and satellite hook ups were online, that the broadcast was good to go. All else dropped away around him when the M.C.'s voice boomed over the PA system "Ladies and Gentlemen, here to deliver this year's Key Note Address, the founder and Chief Executive Officer of Alston Image, Mr. Isaac Alston."

Chapter 24

THE SUDDEN SUSPENSION of all time, all space, and all thought gave Alston the silent canvas on which to lay the precise cracks of his dress shoes against the hard wood of the stage and he felt himself rising into the broad shouldered presence that had brought him his empire. When he reached the single microphone at the center front of the stage he became aware of the audience for the first time. They were all dressed in black and devoid of the drunken, barely clothed frivolity inherit to the ceremony. Instead, each of the thousands of faces was solemn and sober and immersed in the darkness that shrouded them.

His voice sounded alien to him when its rich tones were carried over the PA system but he felt himself regain its command quickly as he began to speak:

"Ladies and gentlemen, I stand before you bearing the final ember of fire from the gods—that last dying spark of what had been our humanity. The very essence of who we are has come under attack in a manner crasser, baser, and more primitive than the natural act that it attempts to oppose. Our industry, an industry that springs forth from all that is good, proper, and fulfilling to the human race is on the defensive end of a war against those who are determined to make contagious their own desire for self-immolation. While I may be literally addressing the people in this room tonight, I am in truth speaking to two groups. The first are the diluted fools who seek to destroy us for reasons which they themselves do not understand. I do not harbor any hope of reaching their intellect because none is to be found. I only intend to demonstrate that our lifestyle is not rooted in the blind absence of concrete values or the denigration of humanity, but the opposite. If, by some miracle, they are able to understand and integrate my ideas then they will evolve into beings whose existence transcends the frail prison camps of their outdated morality. If they fail to understand then they may carry to their grave the burning itch of knowing that the truth was extended to them on no uncertain terms. The second group—more precious and filled with potential than they will ever know—are those who have, on some secret level, known the truth and to them I am only about to put words to a reality that they have known only as a feeling of wrongness and injustice that stands in grating contrast to what they know to be the natural state of the human race.

"It is a profound and unforgivable error that history's oldest profession has never had a philosophy that accurately and adequately defended it. Since the dawn of human existence there has been no shortage of philosophies which have sought to contain and restrain sexual indulgence and there have been a small smattering that have championed it in various ways but no system of thought has been established, codified, and advocated that has properly justified the existence of professional sexuality. I am here to do just that.

"When the arguments against pornography are distilled to their most basic essence, they fall into two camps and, ultimately, you have heard only these two arguments against the existence of pornography and professional sex : the spiritual argument, which holds that it is offensive to some ethereal entity when human beings indulge their senses and the secular argument, which maintains that sex is an inherently victimizing act which cannot being indulged without one or both of the practitioners being taken advantage of. The lives of those embracing either or both of these philosophies may differ along with their justifications and tactics, but their enemy is the same: sex. The desired end result of the crusade is always the same: a puritanical world of infantile robots that are controlled on the basis of a deeply engrained fear of their most natural instincts.

"Consider this example: Joe Average walks up to a newsstand and purchases a pornographic magazine. As he turns to leave, he is confronted by two people. The first is a Bible waving minister who cries 'how dare you corrupt your soul with that filth. You are a sinner of the worst order and deserve to burn for all eternity! Throw away that garbage and turn your life over to god!' Then the second person is a shrill, androgynous 'progressive' who screams 'how dare you denigrate women in that manner! That sort of swill can only serve to turn you into a rapist or a child molester. This proves that you hate women and children!' And what neither side realizes is that all Joe Average hears is 'don't look at that magazine. Don't indulge your sexuality. Renounce your sexuality but for *our* reason instead of the other guy's reason. The other guy's reason is obviously ridiculous—you should *not* read that magazine for *our* reason.' Both sides think that they are offering Joe Average some new moral standard that will enhance his being but neither realizes (or wants to admit) that their motives are the same: to stop a person from enjoying their sexuality. Debate in this country has been reduced to both sides taking the same position for different reasons and believing that they are offering a choice. This is the stagnation of our modern society that our industry is in a position to transcend. While the left and the right join forces as an over arching 'anti' society, we can become a beacon for true progress and societal development but to do so will require the establishment of a complete philosophical system for our industry and the lifestyle that springs from it.

"I do not create pornography to appeal to humanity's most basic instinct. I create pornography to appeal to humanity's most basic *essence*. Out of all the species on this planet it is we who have reached the highest plateau of existence and if we have a purpose in this existence it is to let the joy of our celebration echo endlessly across the feral valley of those creatures beneath us. As their existences are mandated by a series of instincts we rise above them by applying volitional consciousness to our base desires. From this awareness springs all of our hopes, dreams, innovations, successes, and moments of happiness. The purpose of life is determined for each individual by the realization of their personal identity. Personal identity is established when the needs and desires that affect all human beings are given a form and context which is unique to each individual. No personal identity is possible without personal preference and to remove the capacity for personal preference—to demand that one single preference must be adopted by all persons—is to demand that human beings reduce themselves to the level of lower animals.

"It is our ability to customize the nature in which our base instincts are carried out that separates us from the lower creatures. Where they seek food with no concept of fulfillment save that of staying alive and indulging in the tastes of whatever happens to be around them, we create the vast landscape of culinary wonders that allow us to draw personal pleasure and identity from the act of eating. Where lower creatures dig out burrows or make nests, we raise to the sky the most majestic of skyscrapers and sprawl out in all directions the comforts of modern living. Where they use their eyes as a tool to help determine threat and non-threat, comfort and non-comfort, we use the stunning capacity of our perception to reshape and recreate our view of the world with art and films. And where they use their hearing to identify oncoming predators, we use it to create that most remarkable of art forms, music. In all of these matters, it is one's ability to choose based on their own personal preferences that will allow them to find happiness and enjoyment in whatever they choose to indulge. This is the basis for the construction of one's own identity: the concepts, both concrete and abstract, that one chooses to reflect their own nature. In all matters except sexuality, these choices are largely neutral in the eyes of the modern world. The decision to prefer Italian food over Chinese, for example, does not carry with it any sort of moral distinction, but merely communicates an aspect of the decider that has been arrived at based on their personal preferences. In a free society, all matters of personal expression and choice should be so morally neutral and—in most cases—they are. There is one aspect of human existence, however, where few societies have been able to allow true moral neutrality and that is the realm of sex.

"Where preferences in clothing, the arts, living spaces, and all else are left up to the individual, the moralists that dominate philosophical discourse with a bridge troll countenance will tell you that sexuality must not be open to personal preference—that to indulge in your own desires in this regard will lead you down a path of destruction and that only a rigid moral code—theirs—can save you from yourself. The first lesson that you learn in such a philosophy is that the purpose of sex is the creation of life but that the purpose of life is not sex but the overcoming of sex.

"The spiritualists will tell you that the purpose of life is to appease the feral whims of a deity who shows all the patience, awareness, compassion, and foresight of a petulant toddler and that to appease his divine prudishness we must be reborn in mind and spirit as children ourselves. The secular puritans will tell you that sexual expression has a deleterious effect on 'the children.' This emphasis on childhood on the part of both camps cannot be understated for it is at the root of their schemes, lies, and false convictions. A child is not capable of navigating the world and as such must rely without question on a set of irrefutable truths provided by its caregivers. As it grows it gradually gains the ability to asses these truths and discovers their flaws. As an adult it then must endeavor to correct these flaws in the set of truths that it passes to its offspring. This is the process by which societal evolution is able to take shape, and to require an adult to surrender its decision making capacity and return to a child-like state, with governments, religions, and slogans in place of parents, is to cripple both the person and the society yet this is the goal of the puritans who propose to deprive us of our stock in trade.

"Critical to the puritan's neutering of our adulthood is their view on women. The spiritualists, aware as we all are that the even the most brutish of men can be toppled at the hands a seductive woman, condemn women as being the paladins of all that is evil and in so doing damn them to a base level slavery where the wonder of their existence must be hidden under veils and paternalistic property rights.

"In a primitive society in which a man's identity is determined only by the extent to which he is a physical being capable of hunting at protecting, it is women who are left to the work of the mind, even as society ignores their capacity for it. Because patriarchal society is predicated on the tribal notion that the ability to hunt and protect the status quo represents the totality of existence, it holds in suspicion all that is new, innovative and exceptional. In a patriarchy men are expected to exist for the sake of a few, primitive functions and women for a single primitive function—that of motherhood. Patriarchy holds that the function of a society is predicated on a strict set of basic limitations for the sake of the greater good of society but simply predicates them on gender rather than ethnicity, age, religion, or any of the other means by which the collective is identified and it is for this reason why patriarchy is just as oppressive to men as it is to women.

"Yes, men have made a great many of the intellectual innovations through the ages, but at every turn they were opposed and beaten down for one reason: that the work of the mind and the process of educated inquiry upset the definite, primitive understanding of the universe and forced human kind to either embrace a new, more expansive idea or fall by the way side. For this reason the men who made these observations and innovations were held in a level of contempt nearly as damning as their female counter parts. To fail as a man, men argued, was to become consumed and over taken by the aspects of human existence that had been relegated to womanhood: sexual identity, the nature of existence, preoccupation with matters of empathy and compassion, and the arts and literature. The brutal oppression of the patriarchy weighed fatally not just on women but on all people who wished to live a life of the mind and it is the life of the mind that has brought us to the wonderful modern world we have today.

"Patriarchy is not just rule by men but rule by a certain type of man—a man who demands that orders be passed down from a single source and obeyed simply by virtue of the provider's existence, hence the parental nature of the position. The direct alternative is the matriarchy which demands simply that the same type of person—only now a woman—be put into the position of that male figure. Notice in both genders that the authoritarian personality type is quick to declare that their identity is indicative of what they see as the best quality of that gender: an unflinching parent-knows-best attitude. It is not the gender, but their self declared role as society's parent, that is the failing of both systems.

"In recent times, the devotees of the various new age movements have convinced themselves that as women they have some special magical powers that go back to ancient pagan times. What they fail to realize is that these so called 'powers' are all just metaphors created by ancient peoples to explain the natural presence of womanhood. A woman's ability to induce feelings of arousal in men was deemed witchcraft. Her own awareness of her sexual desires was considered demonic possession. The solution to this—the cop out that has thrived for thousands of years—was to declare that sex had the sole purpose of producing children. People who say that the essence of womanhood is motherhood are bigoted fools and no more correct than saying that the essence of manhood is fatherhood. To say that parenting is the essence and purpose of one's existence is to say that human beings are viral by nature—that our only purpose is to propagate and advance a resource consuming, planet killing species.

"The essence of womanhood, as established unintentionally by the patriarchal societies of the past, was to be vessels of sexuality. In such a society, men's sexuality only existed to the extent of their involvement with women. Men who sought to develop a sexual identity of their own—to recognize themselves as sexual beings in their own right—were castigated as weak and inferior. This was not without purpose—in a primitive culture in which might was the only thing that made right, a thriving society would require that its men be capable fighters able to fearlessly and ruthlessly triumph over any aggressor while the women, most directly capable of taking care of the children, were tasked with domestic activities. While this arrangement may have been a valid means of maintaining existence, it did nothing to develop the standards and the quality of life. It was first through the arts and then the sciences that humanity began to develop to the point that it is now. In the arts, human kind learned to reconstruct and reflect the nature of the world around them in a manner that was endowed with meaning and symbolism in contrast to the absurdity of reality. From there the sciences allowed for a process of critical thinking, experimentation, and evaluation that allowed the human race to find a path towards the ideals romanticized in art. The role of women in *this* arrangement, the arrangement of the mind allowed to achieve innovation, is one of metaphorical creativity, no matter the gender of the inspired innovator. Their ability to create life endows them not with the slavery of unquestioned motherhood but symbolic beacons from which that which is new and triumphant can be created.

"By changing the accepted purpose of our sexual capacity from being entirely reproductive to being an act solely of personal gratification, we are able to transcend our primitive origins. All copulating beings can have sex to reproduce and while they may do so for the pure physical rush of the act and not the knowledge that they are creating offspring, it is the ability of a human being to recognize the act as having a volitional capacity—to produce children or to enjoy one's self—and the greater ability to incorporate the choices of that volition into one's own identity—that makes one a sexual human being. Those who have attempted to hold sex as a utilitarian function have sought to reduce our species to the level of animals.

"You would think, with the porn industry's resounding rejection of the sexual utilitarianism that has kept women oppressed that the radical feminists, a group whose name proposes to embrace a woman's very essence, would embrace us and indeed the 'sex-positive' feminists have. But they are the exception, not the rule. A cancer erodes modern feminism. Your self-appointed scholars are all too quick to erupt into a shrill firestorm of rabid finger wagging at the mere suggestion that a woman is capable of choosing when and with whom she will have sex. To circumvent the individual's right to choice they attempt to distort the definition of rape into something that can be invoked by any moralist to override the consent of whomever they decide is a victim. Last year my company released a film in which a young woman comes home to find her roommate's boyfriend passed out on the couch, decides to extract his penis, and then proceeds to have sex with him. Did this man—in his unconscious and vulnerable state—rape this woman? Of course not. Did the actor playing that character rape his co-star? Never. What about one of the bondage film we released in which one of our starlets walks up to a man restrained by hand and foot cuffs and pours hot candle wax on his penis until he comes—did he rape her? Not in the slightest. But according to the newly expanded definition of rape, the women in my pictures were deprived of better opportunities in life and a decent education and because they didn't receive those opportunities in their formative years their capacity for choice has been forever scarred and they must surrender their foolish perception of free will because no matter what they think the sex they choose to have is automatically rape, so sayeth the matriarchy. What is of greater oppression to a woman: the person who tells her that she can make her own decisions or the person that tells her that she is unable to choose anything?

"Rape is: the act of forcing a person to have sexual relations with another person either by brute force, coercion or deception. Various moralists and pseudo philosophers of the modern era have determined that rape is some sort of metaphysical abstraction whose definition can be stretched and expanded to include any sex act not sanctioned by an uninvolved third party. When a puritan accuses me of condoning rape by producing pornographic films, magazines, and websites, I reply that all of the models depicted, male and female, came to my company of their own free will and signed papers confirming that they, in their rational and adult minds, have consented to perform for my company. This is the first, last, and only response such an accusation deserves because it encompasses the entire definition of actual rape. When the puritan in question attempts to move the goal posts and declare that what I am doing constitutes an act of rape even after the participants have been shown to consent, then the only response they deserve is a statement of fact: that *they* are the ones who do not respect the rights of each person in a free society or understand what it means to consent to sexual intercourse. The reality of the situation is that they do not have to respect the choice that a person makes with regards to their sexuality, only the right of that person to make the choice. A moralist who declares that the definition

292 | Jordan Owen

of 'rape' extends beyond the bounds of its literal definition is simply using the firestorm associated with the word to get their way and is—in essence—saying 'because I said so.'

"The radical feminists have proposed, nobly, to remove rape from society but they have failed to understand that the nature of the requisite freedom is not to be free *from* rape but to be free *to live without rape*. Being free from something is a logically flawed notion. Being free 'from' means a person must only be removed from the possible threat to be considered free. By this logic a prisoner in solitary confinement is free *from* the outdoor elements, physical harm, emotional betrayal, communicable illness and nearly any other potential threat. This is the implication to live free *from* rape and it is only a backdoor into the enslavement of women that the sex-negative in our species have always sought. To be free from rape simply requires that sex, the circumstance of rape, be made impossible.

"Notice the inability of the sex-negative schools of thought to precisely articulate what it is that they consider to be acceptable sexual practice. They are experts at portraying any sexual activity as repulsive and brutal but are embarrassingly hesitant to articulate what they consider acceptable. Because they are authoritarian in nature they are cautious when it comes to declaring any form of sex as being universally acceptable because this creates an area in the minds of their followers where approval is not required. Even the more radical feminist groups that declare lesbianism to be the only acceptable sexual practice for women declare that it should be practiced not out of personal choice but out of a woman's presumed desire to distance herself from men and because this overrides individual choice and determines a mode of sexuality that is meant to be practiced for the greater good, it is just as oppressive as telling a woman she ought to do nothing with sex but get pregnant again and again until her period is a long forgotten anomaly.

"The alternative, freedom to live without rape, is incorrectly defined. A thing must be identified by what it is, not what it is not. A tree cannot be identified as 'not a rock.' So, to be free to live without rape means to be free to live a life based on your own choice; a state which contains the freedom to have only consensual sex because rape, by its definition, is sex that is not chosen. Because of this definition it is a logical contradiction to say that two lovers engaged in a rape-fantasy role play are somehow contributing to the potential for actual rape—their psychological premise of mutual consent will not allow this to happen and it is an act of authoritarianism for an outside party to override the consent of those involved.

"In a system of 'freedom to,' the blame is placed on the perpetrator. In such a system human beings are able to pursue their personal freedom to its natural limit because personal freedom ends where the freedom of another begins.

In a system of 'freedom to,' the restriction of law is placed on the perpetrator to ensure that the logical limit of personal freedom is not overstepped. In a system of 'freedom from,' personal liberties are restrained and removed until the victim cannot place themselves in the position of victimization. The notion that the removal of pornography from a society will, by extension, create an atmosphere where human beings are not compelled to commit rape is like saying that a world without contact sports will create an atmosphere where human beings are not compelled to commit assault and battery.

"Make no mistake about the nature of my remarks. There are and have always been the brutish, primitive men who beat down women; those who stand in the way of women and attempt to guide them into lives of quiet servitude or worse into lives of savage torment. They are the pig-headed fools who the noble leaders of the women's movement fought so hard to destroy and they must remain destroyed. Any man who prevails on a woman physically, mentally, or emotionally to hinder her progress in life or gain a degree of intimacy to which he is not entitled by her consent is a worthless and despicable human being devoid of any merit of honor, dignity, empathy, love, compassion, or self worth and excuses himself from the realm of human endeavor. But to accuse all men of carrying the despicable traits of these monsters is bigotry of the highest order. To say that the desire and inclination to rape is a latent instinct in all men and that all they need is a certain stimulus to push them over the edge is a statement that undercuts the nature of a free society: that all are innocent until proven guilty.

"The modern concept of equality is to declare all people as being equally worthless. Just as the mystics will tell you that we are all equally damned to hellfire in the eyes of their God so the secular moralists will tell you that we are all rapists, murderers, and thieves at heart. When all people are guilty by default then the origin of their guilt is absolved of its status as a crime; it is only in the face of a proper course of action that an improper course of action can be identified as incorrect. It is this capacity to differentiate between right and wrong that defines the difference between responsible and irresponsible. Responsibility demands the capacity to identify the proper course of action and a moralist who refuses to recognize this capacity is an authoritarian.

"But in contrast to the civil rights that the women's movement has fought so hard to gain, the radical feminist movement that has corrupted the mainstream is simply another form of female enslavement. They propose to empower a woman with control over her body by teaching her that she is incapable of choosing what is proper to her own body: a contradiction. They seek to have her celebrate her womanhood by embracing asexual sterility: a contradiction. Their philosophy may be worded differently but they accomplish the same ends as their mystical and conservative counterparts: the enslavement of the woman. This is at the root of why the puritans of both camps have attacked our industry so viciously and why they have been so eager to join forces. Ours is an industry where women are in change in all manners, from performance to business and everything in between. Both sides refuse to acknowledge the reality that this is an industry where a woman can flaunt her sexuality *and* demonstrate her ability to create and maintain a successful business. This truth strikes hard at the case of the sex-negative among us who declare that a woman can be either successful or sexual but never both and certainly never the two combined.

"You who have long declared that pornography leads to the objectification of women as being purely sexual and therefore inferior have never had the courage to look at the true implications of your position. I am now going to have you stare full-on into the cold mirror of reality: why is it impossible for women to be viewed in a purely sexual context without devaluing them as human beings? Why must the successful, educated, career oriented woman submerge her sexuality to the point that it barely exists if at all? Your educators will tell you that this is an outgrowth of women trying to compete in male dominated career fields that had previously been regarded as boy's clubs. It was necessary, therefore, that women should take on a harsher, colder, and more ruthlessly business oriented tone to override the negative attitudes around them. The temporal necessity of this solution has given rise to a malignancy in modern feminism which declares that the only two positions proper to womanhood are either that of a cold, asexual business person or a professional rape victim. Into this dark and seething dichotomy my industry has offered a third option: that a woman can be fully recognized as a sexually positive entity and still command the same level of professional respect as her male counterparts. Do you now want to say that there have been legendary instances of sexual harassment and abuse in our industry? Yes—there certainly have been. But we have made the progress that the rest of society would not and that forward thinking attitude has been at the forefront of our business practices.

"Our society, a society of capitalism, has become as bankrupt of ethics as it is of revenue. Do not blame the economic downturn on government intervention. When a government intervenes correctly in business affairs it is acting only to preserve the rights of its citizens by returning to them the money or property that was stolen by way of fraud. And you wonder why we, the porn industry, will be immune to the tide of much deserved government regulation that will soon drown the market? Do not blame some secret conspiracy—government and pornography are impotent bedfellows to be sure—but consider instead the simple fact that we have succeeded where all the other markets failed. When the toy manufacturers pushed for relaxed health

standards in order to fill their toys with lead and dairy farmers sold knowingly contaminated milk to impoverished communities, we were embracing
the latest innovations in PCR DNA testing to better self-regulate the health of
our performers. Our industry is a shimmering bastion of the self-regulatory
ethics demanded of responsible, free market capitalism and our attackers
know it. That is in part why they gnash their teeth in petty jealousy.

"They say that indulging the existence of our industry promotes tolerance and acceptance of human trafficking, white slavery, and child molestation. To say that I have something in common with a white slaver because we
both deal in sex is to say that a bank owner and a bank robber are somehow
comparable because they both deal in money. Just as a banker's gains are not
served by submitting to robbers, my business cannot thrive by tolerating the
presence of slave drivers and as such human trafficking is as antithetical to
my business purposes as it is repugnant to my heart and soul. I seek to exploit
and trade on the basis of the *product* of human labor. For a slave driver, the
human being *is* the product. The idea of selling one's body is euphemistic at
best and clouds the true nature of the exchange. When one sells one's services
as a sex provider what is being purchased is consent. The actual body cannot
be separated from its owner, so an actual exchange of property for money
does not occur. In human trafficking, the will of the body's owner is overruled and a state of slavery is the result.

"What the opposition to pornography refuses to acknowledge is that
legal pornography is created when all parties involved—the models, the producers, and the consumers—come to the table out of volitional choice. Contemporary feminist theory—which is a denigration of the word 'theory'—
will say that women are incapable of making that choice. They declare that
all pornography is rape on no uncertain terms and that the women involved
are too naïve, too uneducated, too abused and too poor to make a better
choice for themselves and as such must have society intercede on their behalf
to save them from making a choice. Is this not the same attitude as the male
chauvinist pigs who declare that all women require a man who is a father
figure that looks out for their best interests and pats them on the head when
they say silly things about freedom and empowerment? The anti-porn, sex-
negative feminists have done nothing more than change this societal father
figure to a mother figure and announced that you are no longer oppressed
because the gender of your oppressor has been changed.

"So long as we hear the argument that the modern porn industry is an
outgrowth of patriarchy, it must be observed that modern pornography runs
contrary to the history of patriarchy. Throughout history it has been the patriarchal societies that have shrouded their women in opaque clothing that
hides their form. It is patriarchy that burns women at the stake as witches and

adulteresses and it is patriarchy that opened the Magdalene houses where a woman could be incarcerated for even appearing to have sexual capacity. And it was patriarchy that established the rigid moral codes of chivalry that demanded that respect for women be predicated not on the genuine respect of one person to another but rather out of detached and hypocritical interest in preserving one's honor in accordance with the standards of society.

"Look at the Islamic fundamentalists that run certain parts of the Middle East. They have embraced completely the view on women that is now being advocated by anti-porn feminists. They hold that men cannot control themselves in the face of a woman's sexuality and that such sexuality must be hidden from view and punished. While modern feminists toil for so called 'equal rights'—which to them is not a campaign for a level playing field but a campaign for universal worthlessness—they have forgotten the lessons of history and thrown in their lot with the vilest forms of Puritanism.

"Human trafficking should be considered distinct, however, from consensual prostitution. A man or woman who seeks to sell their body sells the service of gratifying others and is no more despicable than a masseuse, a chiropractor, a surgeon or any other person who uses the motions and actions of their body to positively stimulate another. A person who acts in a managerial fashion for such a person, but makes no claim of property on the person, is not a slave driver and neither of these professions should be considered illegal. You cannot own something which you cannot sell, and ownership of one's own body is central to a free society, second only to the ownership of one's own mind.

"And that is the root of this sleazy scam our opponents are running: when they teach you to be ashamed and afraid of your body, they succeed in taking control of your source of sensory input for the world around you and in so doing control your perception of the world. When you accept their interpretation of reality over the functionality of your own mind, they control you completely.

"In an objective reality—which is what we live in and no amount of Platonian masturbation can render it otherwise—there must be a standard of value which transcends all personal subjectivity. That standard of value must symbolize and objectify the exchange of consent in its purest form: the consent of the seller to the buyer. That objective symbol—which the critics of the sex industry decry in fear of its true and unyielding nature—is money. To the buyer, the exchange of money for product is the ultimate demonstration of respect: it means that they wish to take the thing which you sell in exchange for the value you have ascribed to it and acknowledge the totality of your ownership. In other words, they respect your capacity to determine the value of the material concretes which validate your freedom. To the seller, the exchange of money represents completeness of ownership provided that the thing which is being sold is something that the seller has a right of ownership to in the first place, meaning that it is their property and not stolen. The human body is unquestionably the property of the human being that lives inside it and no amount of linguistic obfuscation on the part of the anti-porn lobby can render it otherwise. No matter what they may claim about wanting to save sex workers from their career paths out of an altruistic concern for their well being, the cold hard reality of the matter—as cold and intransigent as the money that they fear—is that they are the ones who are attempting to gain a dictatorial hold on the consent of another human being, not the client who uses their money to purchase the services or products of another person.

"To remove from the table of exchange the objective value of money is to invalidate all other means of exchange. If you barter your services for the services or goods of another then you are simply replacing a symbol of objective value with the specifics of what that symbol would be worth. If you withhold sex from a partner on the grounds that they have not provided you with certain luxuries or demonstrated in themselves the personal character which you find requisite in your choice of lovers then you are simply broadening the scope of what will constitute the bartered deal and are hypocritically considering yourself superior because you trade your consent on the basis of something other than money.

"Because the sex industry is one in which the primary workers own the means of production by default it is thus above the standards of bottom-up business reform inherit to other forms of labor relations. The owner of the business interest is forced to deal with each employee not as members of a union but as individuals, each with full control over their means of production: their bodies. When the critics of capitalism turn their attentions to the porn industry, there is nothing there for them to nationalize and nothing that can be seized and because opposing an industry requires that you oppose the product and its means of production they are faced with a reality that they are terrified to acknowledge as it would reveal their 'argument' to be what it is: the simple reality that they are anti-sex. To say that you oppose an individual's right to ownership, sale, production, and exploitation of a thing is to indicate that the thing itself is fundamentally unsafe and must be removed from availability and if this is your attitude then you cannot say that you are pro-sex.

"The anti-porn lobby will cry that they are not opposed to sex, only to the industry. Their favorite analogy is to say that if they were opposed to the fast food industry, nobody would accuse them of being anti-food. But in the light of their opposition to our industry, carry this argument to its fullest extent: imagine that they were to say that they were opposed not only to fast food, but all restaurants and to the exchange of money for food and declared that only certain types of food were acceptable for human consumption and that those foods must be prepared in your private gardens and eaten out of sight in the privacy of your own home and that the food must be completely bland and devoid of taste so that you nourish your body without the enjoyment of taste, then a rational mind would have to come to the conclusion that the people advocating this masochistic lifestyle have some problem with food and eating. It is only rational, then, to conclude that persons who believe that sexuality must be uniformly banished from public sight, kept locked up in a hidden room where it is only used for utilitarian, pseudo-altruistic purposes, and never ever sold under any circumstances are in fact people who, on a basic level, are opposed to human sexuality no matter how much they themselves may proclaim to enjoy sex in their own lives. If they actually do enjoy sex it is only as an act of hypocrisy.

"The ability to capitalize on sex does not create uniformity in sexual identity. Just as any other capitalist industry has a wide diversity of products to appeal to a wide variety of interests, so the capitalistic nature of pornography observes all manner of sexual interest in a society and provides product accordingly. Those who have taught you to think that capitalism dictates the nature of our culture are the ones who want you to feel out of control of your own life. Capitalism reflects the full range of tastes available to consumers and it only supports conformity to the extent that the society in which it operates is conformist. There is no absence of diversity in the world of modern pornography and if a consumer is unable to find a market that caters to their interest then they are most likely unable or unwilling to operate the internet.

"In a capitalistic society, personal identity becomes the basis for trade: the necessities of your purchases are derived from the base instincts which make you an animal, but the specifics of those purchases are derived from your individual identity as a human being. The result of those who have taught you to despise capitalism is to declare that the capacity by which you may attain the material concretes of your abstract identity is fundamentally wrong. Without the ability to attain your material concretes how are you to make concrete the abstract sense that you call your 'self?' We are beings that interact with a material world and the extents to which we may manifest our personal identities in that world determine the extent to which we exist as individuals. A slave with no rights whatsoever can think of themselves as having individual value and recognize their existence as unique from all others but such a recognition is meaningless if they cannot manifest their identity in material reality. Thus, to formulate an identity one must either purchase or create the specific factors that define the abstracts of their person.

"Identity is not formulated in a vacuum. The creation of one's own sense of self demands that one always evaluate the nature of their responses to the world around them. When one learns of the capitalistic nature of the world they can internalize it as a negative, thinking that those who wish to profit on their abilities and the abilities of others are evil, or they can internalize it as a positive and see that the exchange of value for value is a mark of respect. When the developing individual learns that that sex has the capitalistic elements of pornography and prostitution they can only view it as a negative if they have been taught so by external forces. This wrongness is rooted in the notion that it is wrong to trade for goods and services. The full and complete embrace of this idea would lead to the downfall of society because the only alternatives to trade are force, theft, coercion, and begging.

"Some would declare that love is the alternative to trade, but love is only the recognition of specific values as they relate to you, the individual. You do not charge your children for the food you give them because of what they represent to you, and that meaning is payment in full. The same is true of your spouse and all other loved ones: you love them because of the values they represent. Communism, socialism and all other forms of shared wealth have proposed to make this sort of connection a basis for national policy: that at the point of the government's guns we can somehow genuinely adopt the kind of love for all of humanity that would make us want to overlook the realities of trade but such a concept is simply an obfuscation: in all relationships with loved ones, the trade that occurs which gains them your love and vice-versa, you exchange based on values that are unique to those persons. To seek to find those values in all persons is to declare that all persons are interchangable and thus devoid of value.

"Because sexual fulfillment is an outgrowth of the fulfillment of one's own ego and philosophical values, it is impossible to say that they will need 'harder stuff' when their usual porn interests get old and tiresome. To indulge in that which you find fulfilling is not something that needs to be expanded upon because it is complete in and of itself. Anti-porn crusaders are fond of claiming that there are men (always men, never women) who find themselves bored with depictions of vaginal sex and look for images of anal sex, then images of bondage, then torture, then snuff films and then child pornography, all in the interest of finding 'harder and harder stuff' to which to gratify themselves. If this is true and porn for these men is nothing more than a need to debase and harm others then it is *they* who need to check on their own values and their own identity because that path of ever increasing degrees of victimization is only a path to their true identity.

"There is no such thing as 'harder' material, only material which caters to a greater degree of expression in certain interests. A person who is comfortable with their own sexuality will learn what circumstances are required for their satisfaction and seek those just as they seek their favorite foods, books and movies. Satisfaction cannot be improved upon or dulled if it is grounded in a true sense of self. A man who is comfortable with the fact that he is turned on by women dressed in school girl uniforms realizes that it is the implications of the uniform, not the age of the person who wears it, that provides his thrill. As such he does not require an 'enhancement' of his satisfaction by seeking out actual school girls either in porn or in life. The same truth applies to the indulgence of all acts of sexualized symbolism, whether they are male or female, straight or gay in nature.

"Observe the ever popular fable of the devil that appears to people and attempts to purchase their souls. For each of his victims, the exchange is always the same: whatever it is that the victim desires above all else. There are many ways to interpret this myth but it is foremost in our culture a fable with a chilling moral: do not admit to yourself the truth of your identity or the truth of your desires and that to do so can only lead to your downfall. From such a perspective can it be any wonder that men and women are terrified of admitting their true nature?

"What is the essence of nearly all romance novels? A protagonist who has grown weary of their spouse and embarks on a journey of unchained eroticism with a new partner who transcends the ennui of married life. The psychological crux of these stories is to abandon the pure for the profane, the social for the personal, and the life of performed delusions for the life of effortless honesty. Only in a society of such honesty can freedom exist, contrary to the cries of the puritans who have long declared that society must function to constrain the individual.

"It is in the name of a free society that all persons must champion the responsibility of the individual. But an individual can only have the mind of an adult. One of the longest running and most revolting stereotypes in our industry is the slimy hack porn director who lures half-witted teenage girls to his apartment under the guise of auditioning for a starring role on the silver screen, only to have her end up sobbing on a bed as she's penetrated over and over again. Why does this happen? Why does she not see him for what he is and tell him to go to Hell? Because she has been stunted with the mind of a child. She lacks the mature capacity to make a rational judgment. An adult can recognize a charlatan when they see one. An adult stunted with the mind of a child cannot—yet this is the desirable state of being as declared by today's moralists!

"What purpose does crippling an adult's mind to the level of a child's accomplish? Jealousy at the personal liberty of another is the root of the problem, but what is the nature of the philosophical abstraction that they seek to concretize in their puritanical utopia? To know this one need only observe the folklore that drives them. They attempt to teach us that humankind is the result of a creator who placed a man and woman into a utopian environment in the Garden of Eden and told them not to eat of a piece of fruit which would give them the knowledge of good and evil, then damned them when they ate it. To not point out the blatant hypocrisy of this statement is to do an injustice to thought and reason: their god expected them to know that obeying him was good and disobeying him was evil when they had *no knowledge of good and evil!* And with that they are banished from paradise for wanting to think for themselves—the essence of an adult. Their philosophy teaches a person to regard all that is new, nonconforming, gratifying and expansive as fearful and uncertain.

"Since the dawning of human history there have been those human beings who retain a residual exaggeration of the cowering, hiding instinct of our savage ancestors—the ones who would run and hide at the first sign of danger whether it came in the form of a thunderstorm or a ferocious beast. As their minds developed through the generations they retained their abstract, fundamental sense of fear and began to create elaborate mythologies to explain the merciless nature of the universe. As they attempted to integrate these mythological explanations with their survival instinct they came to believe that happiness and the indulgence of pleasure led to a dropping of one's guard that would lead to misfortune. When this perspective was fully integrated with their mythologies they came to believe that the gods they worshipped were offended by human happiness and that to find happiness in anything besides spiritual supplication would lead the gods to reign down upon them. It is this savage, primitive fear that is at the root of puritanical morality: do not indulge because the gods will strike you down. Because of this savagery that they have scorned and castigated those who considered themselves above such fear and it is out of this mindset that modern day puritans seek to enslave those who are free in mind and body, neither of which can be independent of the other in their freedom.

"That is the basic driving force of their abstract jealousy: fear. They fear intelligence as if anything proper to the human condition ever came from stupidity. They fear change as if change is the result of some abstract mania and not a natural desire to transcend the stagnant. They fear freedom, as if oppression were what brought them the modern society in which they now live and the right to express their point of view. They fear education because the process of education is one of inquiry, which reveals their moral code as the baseless pleading that it is.

"Central to the premise of all movements of moral authoritarianism is the necessity of an overseer to decide on the behalf of the populace what is proper to the existence of each individual. Even if this were a matter which could be decided universally, with each person needing the same forms of intellectual, emotional, and physical stimulation to fulfill their needs, it would still undercut the purpose of the personal decision when the nanny state makes it for them. Pride is the aspect of the mind which nourishes the ego and, by metaphorical extension, the spirit. Pride is not found in the autocratic dictates of an external authority, but in one's own ability to see the positive results of their values manifested on the basis of their actions. When the decision not only to choose one stimulus over the other but which one is inherently correct is made for the individual by a moral authority then the individual can derive no pride from adhering to it. Authoritarians, those who demand slavish loyalty to their socio-political construct, declare that pride is the feeling of satisfaction that one feels by committing with patriotic blindness to the dictates of authority but there is no pride to be found in mindless servitude. Slavish devotion does not create pride but the *suspension* of pride. Just as a chronic drunkard does not feel happiness in intoxication but a temporary freedom from the need to be happy, so blind patriotism cannot produce pride but rather an artificial, potentially addictive, uniformly bland sense of dull sustenance in the place of pride.

"Your, moralists have taught you to obsess over values but never to understand what it means to value something. To value, they say, is to restrain one's self. They teach you that you achieve values to the degree that you are able to deny what you desire in favor of that which you do not. If a spouse is faithful to their partner not out of love but out of a sense of duty to family values then they deny themselves the validation that would come from choosing fidelity of their own volition and, alternately, the possibility of finding a more preferable partner. The same is true for the other partner—if they are unable to retain their spouse based on their own character and must resort to a guilt laden diatribe on the importance of maintaining the nuclear family, then they fail to develop the personal values which might have allowed them to retain their partner on genuine merit.

"To attain value is to apply the act of thinking in two central capacities: one must identify what values are to be gained and what actions must be undertaken to gain them. The latter hinges on one's ability to leave behind that which is useless and embrace that which is beneficial and it is this axiom that brings about the failure of conservative morality as applied to the right. The former requires that you recognize value as a function of personal again and this axiom brings about the failure of conservatism as applied to the left. If you retain the past at the cost of the future, you doom the present to failure. It is a genuinely progressive mindset, whether it leans right or left of center, that can gain in value and the stubborn unwillingness of the puritans in the face of progress is not a noble stand against impossible odds but the necrotic tissue that slowly overtakes an infected wound.

"Because they fear the process by which values are gained—the process of inquiry and causal experience—the authoritarian moralists castigate those who are willing to commit to the process and instead demand that personal values be surrendered to blind following. They declare that a man of honor must renounce himself for the good of society but not the actual people of that society, only the principles by which they are governed. To surrender the concrete to the immaterial is the foundation of mysticism and no honor can be found in that trade just as no honor can be found in the surrender of personal values for those of the collective which is itself an immaterial abstraction.

"We see here the cycle of desperation employed by those who conspire to enslave women under the guise of championing them. They do not champion individual women—indeed their only use for the actual women that surround them is to turn them into professional victims that will, through impassioned testimony, indoctrinate the next generation of tithing supporters. Any truly great societal movement must be able to demonstrate how it is benefiting each individual which supports it and must have clearly defined goals. When the goals of the movement are achieved, and the lives of the individuals improved to their targeted degree, the movement is no longer needed. In the absence of benefits to the individuals involved, the movement, no matter how noble its premise becomes a self-perpetuating, eternally unattainable goal. And when the unattainable goal becomes the life's work of generation after generation of supplicated supporters, the actual goal of enslavement is realized.

"If a woman is to achieve happiness in life, it must be done for her own benefit and on her own terms. If your goal in life is not to achieve your own happiness but to put yourself in a position that will further the agenda of your cause, then you have given your life over to a moral authority and renounced your capacity for happiness. If you campaign for higher pay then it must entail higher pay for *you*. If you campaign for a workplace free of sexual harassment then it must include the workplace of your job of choice. And if you campaign for sexual freedom then you must be free to indulge your own as you alone wish, with no pompous gasbag shaking a finger at you and squawking 'the personal is political.' These circumstances proceed from your sense of individualism, which is the basis of rational pride.

"This is what the phony logic of the anti-porn lobby fails to grasp: that your desires for sex stem from the abstract principles of your system of values and if you accept that the nature of your character—not some external force that modifies your values without your control—is the basis for your rational capacity then you understand that you cannot pursue rationality to the point of irrationality. In an objective reality no amount of rational pursuit can give way to the irrational. Just as you cannot drink water to the point of dehydration or add two and two until they make five, so you cannot indulge in rationality to the point that you are irrational. A sexual identity rooted in rationality has no capacity for rape, child molestation, or other acts of sexual abuse and no amount of rational sexual stimulus can create a need for the irrational. If you want this in simpler language then understand it thusly: if you seek out greater and greater degrees of real abuse in your sexual interests to the point that you are committing acts of sexual crime then you are not being corrupted by external forces but gradually giving into the self that you were all along and tragically taking your victims with you.

"The irrational is that which works against the precepts of your capacity to function in a free society which are the capacities of ego, intelligence, empathy, individuality and honor. To compromise any of these capacities is to embrace the irrational as your motive factor. When the irrational is your premise there is no amount of rationality that can proceed from it. The wrench that has been thrown into the gears of modern man's rationality is the assertion that one's own judgment bears no hold on their ability to choose the rational and as such must behave irrationally in the guidance of a larger force that will guide their irrational actions into the semblance of rationality. Some seek out this guiding force in the churches while others find it in the secular substitutes of various governments or other ruling bodies. When you accept their puppetry guidance in the place of your rational capacities then any performance of those values is only theatrical at best and cannot be derived from your actual character or speak to its quality. If you accept as truth that you are a sinner then virtue becomes hypocritical. If you accept that you are capable of virtue simply by the reality of your character then you have opened your mind to rationality and to its precepts.

"Ego is the part of your mind that identifies yours as a self unique to all others and that the separation of your mind from those around you demands that your exposure to the output of other minds be done consciously. If you stumble blindly though the world allowing every advertisement, slogan, political speech, television show, religious leader or any other media entity deprive you of your capacity for rational judgment then you have chosen to surrender your rational capacity. When you surrender your ego you surrender your capacity to recognize that the responsibility of your actions is yours alone. The motor powered by the ego is your pride, which can only be recognized and engaged in the singular. If you take pride in anything that does not involve your own achievements then you are taking pride in the irrational and have embraced the mindset that allows human beings to take pride in the false accolades of race, gender and nationality.

"Intelligence is the capacity with which you grasp the objective concepts present in the world around you. It demands that you choose to use your mind actively in your perception of the world and consciously choose to evaluate the world as a conscious human being, not an instinct driven animal. Intelligence is expanded in its function by the accumulation of knowledge and requires knowledge to thrive. To cut off from the active mind a potential piece of knowledge, no matter how subversive and disturbing that knowledge may be, is to deny the intellect another meal. Modern moralists have deprived the intellect to the point of starvation on the low protein diet of their abstinent philosophy and declared that the absence of intellectual stimulation is intellectually fulfilling.

"Empathy is your ability to recognize sentience, emotion and intellect in other people and, by virtue of that recognition, gain an impression of their feelings, needs and desires. The trick pulled by the anti-porn lobby is to take a back door route into undercutting your sense of empathy by declaring that certain universalities exist in human experience: that all people will find an experience to be good or bad, uplifting or demeaning. By this standard you are removed from the need to have actual empathy and can instead champion certain causes or ideas without the actual emotional connection that validates them and you are then able to be inhumanly cruel in the name of humanity and heartlessly ruthless in the name of compassion. This is the reality of the religious leader that humiliates and tortures his flock in the name of salvation as it is the reality of the college professor that makes their students feel ashamed of their sexual identities in the name of sexual freedom.

"Honor is the safeguard of one's pride which declares that the terms of one's values are not open to negotiation. Moralists of all stripes are frequent to declare that honor is found in accepting the values of a concept greater than one's self, but this can only serve to invalidate the honor of the individual. When your honor is predicated on the dictates of authority then the only thing you can hope to gain is the approval of the members of a society that endorse that authority, who are, themselves, devoid of the personal honor and pride that would make their praise something worth achieving.

"Herein lies the root of all mysticism and the source of the fundamental breach between reason and faith. An argument predicated on reason demands that the mind continue to function to remain convinced of its validity. An argument predicated on faith is not an argument at all but a gradual convincing of the target audience to turn off its mind and let its decisions be made by a higher authority. A decision to not think is a contradiction in terms and cannot be arrived at rationally, yet the moralists of today attempt to subvert reason by convincing their audiences to select between multiple reasons to stop thinking. Whether you surrender your sexuality to an authority because of religious, social, or political motives, the end result is always the same. Your moralists have taught you to feel no pride in your sexuality and no sexual honor save for achieving the state of a panting, sniveling Spaniel that results from accepting their idiotic notions and because you have surrendered your honor, your pride, your values, your sexuality, your body, and your mind, no happiness can be achieved.

"The volition of your own mind is the only source from which genuine values may proceed. If you select as your moral code a set of guidelines based on your observations of the world then you achieve the value of the strength of your convictions. If your moral code brings you happiness in the course of your life without harming others then you gain the value of self-esteem. When your moral code is modified by your own rational thought process then you gain the value of wisdom. In each case it is only the morality of the individual which can validate a decision. If a nanny state makes that decision for you then the decision loses the validation that you would have gained for your effort.

"When you surrender your capacity for choice to the dictates of another, you also surrender your capacity to make judgments about the character of your new leader. When this happens you become incapable of asking the question 'who is this new ruler and why are their ideas superior to my own? What truth makes it so?' The dark day in which you lose this ability is the day in which you have helped give birth to a dictator. This is the paradox of a free society: that freedom exists only to the extent that the individual is capable of making choices but that respect for the right to make choices also means respect for the right of others to choose to surrender their right of choice. It is against this paradox that the intelligent of society must struggle. From the time of the ancient cultures which delivered to us the towering innovations of government, mathematics, philosophy, literature and art, the great thinkers of the ages have also stood as the vanguard against the cowering hordes that have never understood the concept of choice. We, the sex industry, stand as the vanguard of human sexuality against those same hordes that have gone unopposed for far too long.

"Those same cowering hordes have torn down each great society in succession and erected the quivering monuments of one Dark Age after another. Though their actions are contemptible and undeserving of sympathy, one must realize that it is only their parasitic nature which drives them and that responsibility falls to the intellectuals not to defend the great innovations of the mind, but to end the battle altogether. Think of the cattle runs designed to gently and quietly guide cattle to the slaughter. The process of educating the unthinking, cowering hordes of humanity has been likened to the process of developing such a run. But human beings are not cattle! The job of thinking persons is not to gently guide the unthinking, but to throw down an ultimatum: a demand that they either choose to use their minds or wither away on the outskirts of societal progress, never burdening those who can think and choose and who choose to live! The United States was one attempt to throw down such an ultimatum. Its founders declared that the requirements of a free society were not wishes to be granted but the recognition of the basic requirements for human existence. They declared that no human being may surrender that truth or distort it for dictatorial purposes. The goal of the cowering hordes in such a society has always been one of micro-analyzing such declarations to find minute ambiguities that could allow them to overthrow free society in the guise of championing it. If free society is to continue to exist, then the thinking must confront the cowering hordes not with a gentle civics lesson on the nature of government but with an unflinching, cast iron declaration that no ambiguities exist: that freedom is predicated on choice and that the choice to take the rights of others is only the choice to give up one's own freedom.

"The fundamental divide in all schools of philosophy has been between the authoritarian and the libertarian. The libertarian asserts that human beings will, given freedom, generally choose the good and choose to accomplish their goals in ways that do not harm others. The authoritarian asserts that human beings are inherently evil and as such must be controlled by the rigid standards of uniformity. The libertarian is fit to govern because he understands that force is used to control those who fail to practice the good by infringing on the rights of others. The authoritarian is eternally unfit to govern—he believes that the use of force is a wide reaching blanket to cover all people at all times so that they are never faced with any choices. The paradox of freedom requires that freedom be extended evenly to both the libertarian and the authoritarian or, in other words, freedom demands that it be extended to those who will actively work against it. The best that a libertarian can do, then, is establish a society in which the authoritarians are surrounded by constitutional padding that will allow them to rail at the top of their lungs and thrash about to their heart's content without unseating the liberty of those who can think. The United States made a profound and legendary attempt to create such an environment with the Amendments, but even this has not been water tight enough to keep the authoritarians in check. It has failed because the populace of this country refuses to educate themselves on the nature of freedom and the freedom that exists for them in this country. The most pitiful act of shallow indifference any populace can suffer is that of accepting the freedom they enjoy as a default and never coming to understand its nature. It is this that allows modern moralists to deprive you of freedom in the guise of championing it.

"Politics are believed, wrongly, to be two dimensional. The assumption is that there is a left wing and a right wing and that to go too far in either direction is to reach a dictatorship, whether it is Communism on the left or Fascism on the right. This is inherently incorrect because it posits a slippery slope fallacy in which the authoritarian bent of one side must balance the authoritarian bent of the other side and thus holds that people are only free to the extent that they are able to shift their country's political landscape back and forth between two dictatorships at regular intervals before they are shifted too far in one direction; it holds that freedom is a state of constant flux that is eternally under attack from itself and if freedom cannot not be attained, only pursued, then it has become the basis of a dictatorship no matter how noble its origins. The reality of the situation is that both the left and the right contain authoritarian and libertarian branches. The means by which politicians maintain their careers and accomplish their agendas is to pit the libertarian branch of one side against the authoritarian branch of the other. It is for this reason that persons on the left and the right appear to join forces. No matter what the political origins various anti-porn groups may proclaim as their virtues in contrast to the failings of the other side, they are nothing more than authoritarians joining the ranks of their fellow authoritarians. If you choose to renounce your sexuality for liberal reasons or conservative reasons, you have simply come to the same conclusion for a different reason. The divide is, therefore, not between those on the left and the right who favor freedom, but between those who understand and respect freedom and those who do not. Between the left and right leaning libertarians on one side and the left and right leaning authoritarians on the other. The recognition of this divide allows for those on the left and those on the right who understand and respect freedom to dialogue about the nature of the actual differences in their opinions, without worrying that coming to a central conclusion that falls down the middle of their ideologies will leave them open to the dictates of authoritarians.

"This is the nature of political advancement by means of authoritarianism: no matter what the window dressing of their movement, be it right wingers advocating for a return to traditional family values or leftists decrying pro-letarian injustice, their goal is to control. Stripped of their supposed causes, authoritarians on the left and the right are laid bare as what they are: the cretinous parasites who crave authority for its own sake and lead the masses in an unedning, blind uprising against imagined foes and purpetually imi- nent apocalypses. If you go around their circle you will arrive at oppression whether you choose the left or the right as your starting point. When you realize that all their roads of political action lead to the same point you will realize why the authoritarians of the left and right have been able to join forces in the anti-porn debate: because their moral code has brought them to the only possible conclusion despite setting off in different directions. For far too long they have walked this eternal circle and it is time that the curtain be pulled back to reveal the crude machinery of pulleys and gears that keepsthem running in an eternally raving loop. The conception, labor pains, and birth of this realization are the process of education.

"Education is the process by which the mind rises from childhood to adulthood. As such it is critical that whoever is guiding the process allow the student to think, in ever increasing degrees, for themselves. An educator who refuses to allow this to happen, who eschews the sense of wonderment and desire inherit to the happiness found in gaining knowledge, and imposes instead an ever expanding sense of fear and reliance on groupthink, is not a teacher but a cult leader. They do not nourish the brain, they wash it.

"The moralists of our age have declared themselves to be your educators, and you have accepted the faulty notion that you require their education because you have not sought out actively the identity and pursuit of your own values. And it is in this naïve state they have told you that you are morally depraved for following your sexual desires, spiritually deviant for failing to adhere to their code of religiosity, and intellectually dishonest for refusing to shut off your mind.

"One of the most important linguistic modifications made by the anti-porn lobby is that of the word 'force.' Force in the proper context refers to the use of either physical or psychological coercion to commit certain acts against one's will. Because the vast majority of porn professionals did not arrive at their careers by means of this type of force, the puritans on the other side have been forced to modify the definition. They bring into play the notion that ideas and images carry the force of their implications, which is true, and stubbornly state that this kind of 'force,' which refers to the ability of a presentation to alter your opinion based on a strong argument, is analogous to the kind of force that maliciously controls a person into doing the undesired. They contend that our modern mass-media culture bombards the populace with images that the citizenry will be unable to expunge from their brains and that after a certain point the human mind will somehow shut down and blindly follow whatever media trend it has been most harshly bombarded with. Theirs is the attitude that the mind will eventually receive so much information that it will cease to function and that when it ceases to function it must be deposited, by the unthinking robot body to which it once belonged, in the hands of those few people that somehow know *better* what's best for all people. They see the mind as the plastic spinner in a board game that gradually loses its momentum before coming to a halt on some random outcome. They propose to hedge their bets, then, by weighting the spinner in their favor by removing all other possible outcomes. Theirs is an ongoing gamble for your mind to grind to a halt on a position that best suits their goals.

"The authoritarians of society, whether they consider themselves to be on the left or the right, have made it their duty to protect you from decisions by removing those decisions. They use these methods to remove all stimulants to the body because stimulants, by their logic, can only hasten a person to the inevitable result that their mind will embrace a deviant philosophy when it breaks down. We the sex industry propose that the human capacity for choice is the basis for the capacity for human happiness.

"If one is to deconstruct the arguments of the anti-porn lobby, one must begin with the immaterial arguments based on emotional reaction and empty speculation. The first thing to address is the manner in which they view human sexuality. They seem to think that sex is a straight line that inevitably leads to criminal behavior. The first step, in their eyes, is masturbating which if left unchecked will lead to masturbating to pornography, which will lead to a stunted view of the opposite sex, which will lead to misogyny or misandry, which will lead to outward expressions of sexual violence, which will lead to rape, which will lead to pedophilia, which will lead to murder. This is an argument that is insulting not just to the porn industry but to all of humanity—the idea that indulging our sexuality will inevitably lead down a path of self destruction and antisocial behavior—and it is about as reasonable as saying that driving a car will inevitably lead to a crash or that eating at restaurants will inevitably lead to food poisoning.

"When pressed for a concrete argument that is not predicated on religious dogma or blind emotional firestorms, those opposed to pornography will offer a small number of very specific arguments. The first is that pornography spreads disease. This is a gross misrepresentation—SEX spreads disease. The porn industry spreads print and digital media. When this topic comes up the puritans will jump immediately to the relatively few STDs that are incurably fatal, rather than the multitude that can be cured or controlled with medicine. The fact that there are chronic and fatal STDs is not a call for less sexual freedom—it is a call for further advances in the field of medicine that the suffering obsessed dogmatists have sought to oppose! If the spread of STDs were their true focus than they would be working proactively to help find cures rather than scorning the adults that are capable of thinking in the guise of pretending to care about them. Legalizing an industry mandates that it be made safe for all workers involved and as such legalizing the business of direct to client sex providers demands that their health be closely monitored, but in pornogrpahy there is no potential for the spread of STDs to the consumer and, as a result, only the performers themselves should be concerned with their own working conditions. On-site safety regulations are meant to protect workers from that which they choose not to be exposed to, not that which they wish to encounter. On a construction site hard hats are required because the persons on the site do not wish to minimize the potential for harm to their heads. On a porn set in which performers ejaculate onto one another, there is no violation of worker rights because the workers have made the informed decision to be exposed to the bodily fluids in question. For regulatory bodies to disregard the choice of the workers themselves in the guise of pretending to care about their needs is the ultimate sham of the authoritarians.

"The second argument is again rooted in people filled with blind rage sticking their nose where it doesn't belong. It is the argument that performing in a pornographic film is psychologically traumatic to the performer. Again, the simple questions: *why? How?* They hold up teary eyed former starlets who testify that the experience was horrifying and unpleasant but never stop to consider that maybe it was only so difficult for *them*. Just as not every person alive is physically, mentally, or emotionally capable of playing Major League Baseball or serving in the armed forces, so not every person is equipped in the same areas to perform in the porn industry. It is up to each individual to search inward and decide for themselves if they are capable of performing in our field. In the modern age there are more than enough non-biased resources for men and women to learn about the nature of what will be expected of them and there are certainly enough documented examples of the sorts of acts they'll be performing. Again, it takes a mature, intelligent, and informed adult to decide if they are capable of doing this and it is not the responsibility of those who are happy with their decision to bear the brunt of the aftermath of those who aren't.

"These arguments are characterized as having the same penalty: an incurable disease will follow the contractor for the rest of the lives, as will the stigma of appearing in pornography. The first is only the result of inadequate medical options but the latter is immaterial and transparent: the only reason that the stigma of having appeared in a porn film will haunt a person is because the prejudiced society that surrounds them will forever hang it over their heads! Thus, the argument to the latter amounts to saying 'you should not do this because we will persecute you for it and we would hate to do that.' The sort of people who champion this flavor of idiocy have been known throughout history to force Scarlet Letters on those who violate their code of sacred suffering and the time has come to either wear such letters with pride or overthrow those who bestow them.

"The next accusation that we face is that we use degrading themes, stories, and titles in our work. To this end, yes—we very frequently do. Our opponents throw this up as if vulgar titles alone are somehow enough to win an argument, but they staunchly refuse to understand why we do it. Though I cannot speak for all of my colleagues, I will make this statement and let them decide if they agree: to give a pornographic film a name, theme, or story line that is outside the norms of so called "decent" society is a way to purge the psychological restraints imposed by that society. A woman who is told from birth that she is a shameful, wretched, disgusting temptress simply for the anatomy she was born with or that she must protect her sacred, creamy white purity from the evils of the flesh may find it liberating and empowering to give herself over to the aesthetics and vocabulary of whoredom and may wish to be in a position to have others call her vulgar names as an act of championing the shedding of her psychological restraints. A man who has been told from birth that his every sexual desire is the end result of a deep-seated desire to oppress and abuse women may find a similar liberation in watching bukkake or even participating in it. By acting in a manner by which these people can overcome their hang-ups with the use of performance art and psychodrama in a controlled and safe environment with partners who knowingly consent to the act, pornographic performers are not degrading themselves and their audience, but providing a therapeutic service that no priest, rabbi, or caliphate has ever accomplished.

"Radicals for Puritanism have long railed that pornography—and indeed sex in general—is a violent thing. Is there a violent aspect to sexuality? Yes! Sex is an act of controlled violence the same way walking is an act of controlled falling. Pain and pleasure are only a hair's width away from one another and one can easily influence the other. As such, the infliction of pain is an element of sexuality as are all acts meant to stimulate the body. One must then ask where the line is drawn: how harshly may a lover gnash at a partner's genitals with their teeth? How hard may one partner thrust into another? How deeply may they dig in their fingernails? The simple answer is that just as there are those who wish to be long distance runners and those who wish to simply walk, so there those who desire the extremes of pain in their sexuality and those who wish only the most directly pleasurable sensations and all must be free to decide for themselves where they fall on the spectrum of sexual interaction and be free to find consenting partners. Our opponents may not understand our justifications for acting out in this manner, but their ignorance does not form the basis of a right to take away our rights.

"They say that we stereotype women as being consistently willing to have sex with anyone. This is as preposterous as saying that professional sports programs stereotype athletes as being consistently willing to play ball with anyone. Would you rather we show women who are *unwilling*? They say that we stereotype women as having no value outside of their ability to perform sexually. Do they ever stop to think that sports programs stereotype athletes as having no value outside their ability to perform on the field? Do you value a plumber for anything more than his ability to fix pipes? Do you value a computer engineer for anything more than her ability to design and build computer technology? A person who cannot perform sexually may be useless to the porn industry but that does not mean that they do not have value elsewhere or no inherent value as human beings. Intelligent, thinking adults understand this. Petulant children do not.

"They say that pornography promotes rigid standards of beauty which few people are capable of attaining. Setting aside the fact that just about any body type can be found in pornography with a simple internet search, ask yourself: if you watch a sporting event, do you want to see athletes that are scrawny, weak, and physically inept simply so that you do not feel put down by comparison? Or do you want to see an athlete whose body is at the peak of its physical perfection so that they can play the game with the greatest skill possible? How much more absurd would it be to demand that expert players intentionally perform poorly so that their less talented spectators are not intimidated by their abilities? This is the level of absurdity that comes to the fore when the beautiful, sexually capable people of a society are hidden away for the benefit of those who are plain and incompetent at best.

"Imagine the absurdity of a man who wants to play catch in the backyard with his son but can't because he feels ashamed that he cannot live up to the skill and ability of the players of professional sports. Why is this absurd? Because the purpose of playing catch with one's child is different than that of playing professional sports. The game of catch is a means to spend quality time with the child, bond with them, and help them with basic coordination. The professional baseball game is meant to be an exhibition of the absolute best in physical ability and to entertain the audience. In both examples, the game of baseball is the only constant but the purposes for which it is played in both situations are different. By the same token, no man or woman should feel unable to perform sexually with their partner because of what is seen in porn. When a couple comes together to have sex it is generally with the intention of celebrating the connection between the two people but in porn the purpose of sex is to provide entertainment by showcasing the interactions of the physically exceptional. In this case, just as in sports, the purposes of the professional and amateur involvements are not the same and for this reason no couple can rationally consider their relationship to have been intimidated by pornography.

"Because our opponents cannot provide a proper counter argument, they resort to a deeper level of emotional bullying and attempt to guilt us by asking 'would you be ashamed if your daughter were appearing in porn?' In their minds, if you answer yes then you are a hypocrite for enjoying porn and if you answer no then you are a degenerate. But what they fail to understand is that my daughter is an individual person who is free to live as she wishes. How is it moral for me to demand that another person pay compensation for my emotional shortcomings? They argue that porn should be outlawed because it has the potential to produce addiction for some people but how is it moral for one person to demand that the rest of society bend to accommodate his personal flaws and addictive nature?

"Those who ask this question always use the hypothetical daughter, never the son and never other members of my family. Now the parental implication is obvious—in a modern society if my mother or sister told me that she was going into porn, I would have no recourse to stop her and the decision would not reflect poorly on my guidance. But why am I never challenged with how I would feel if my son were doing porn? Let us consider the history of societies that could actually be considered patriarchal: if you were a man in the Old Testament times, one of your most important goals in life would be to pass your worldly possessions, title, and property down to your first born son. Because there was no such thing as genetic testing at the time, the only surefire way to make sure that your son was in fact yours was to marry a virgin and keep her under strict observation. Thus, a woman's highest role in society was to be married off as a virgin so that she could produce only the offspring of her husband. We see this reflected symbolically in traditional bridal attire, which is white to reflect virginal purity. Thus, the shame that fathers are meant to feel at having a promiscuous daughter is rooted in a deeply ingrained cultural tradition that has never been properly expunged by progressive philosophy. It is tragically ironic that the so called "progressive" moralists—those who claim to be championing the anti-porn lobby for the sake of advancing society—would resort to a tactic of emotional blackmail that is rooted in the most deeply primitive of misogynistic traditions.

Now consider the inverse—in the same relatively primitive patriarchies men who were able to impregnate many women and produce strong, healthy offspring were prized and held in high esteem. Consider the many wives and sons of a fictitious historical figure like Jacob, who in Judeo-Christian mythology sired the children of Israel. It was necessary for the survival of the species for one man to have many wives since one man could impregnate many women. Additionally, the mortality rate was high among both children and the mothers who gave birth to them so a man was expected to be virile and sexually capable. From this primitive origin we can see the beginnings of the societal construct that prized sexual prowess in men and virginity in women.

In the recognition of such a double standard it is the responsibility of a progressive society to remove it through the equalization of societal recognition. This can be accomplished one of two ways—either the men can renounce their sexuality until they are on the same controlled, guilt ridden level as their female counterparts or women can be taught to overcome their chaste social programming and embrace sexuality and sexual abundance on the same level as men. The sex negative feminists and their ilk want the former and I want the latter because it is in this light that we understand why women doing sexually promiscuous work is indeed liberating and empowering.

"Now that the petty objections of our opponents have been laid naked and vivisected on the chopping block, let there be no illusions about the nature of those who pose them: the root cause of their hysteria—the reason for which they have spilled blood and burned witches and cast adulterous persons to the wolves is their *envy*. They envy us for embracing our sexuality when they are still struggling to admit they have any just as they fear all freedom and castigate those who live in its celebration. That is the root of their objections. Let us cast them aside, that they may rot in the fiery pits on all sides of the shimmering path which we alone are able to walk.

"Why then is the expression of sexuality so critical to a free society? Let us consider the fact that we transcend our animal natures by concretizing our abstract emotions. Love and happiness are the highest emotions—the reward of the achievement of one's values—therefore the manner in which they are expressed is crucial to the degree to which they are experienced because it is the abstract made concrete that allows for the experience of emotions on a human level. A free person, who freely pursues their own happiness, must be allowed to express that happiness in a manner that is proper to their individual existence. If sex is the ultimate physical expression of affection—whatever the manner and degree of that affection—then to restrain its expression among consenting adults is to restrain their capacity for the expression of happiness and by extension their ability to feel happiness.

"The Christians have a popular theme which runs through their bible and it is encapsulated in song: 'this little light of mine. I'm gonna let it shine.' Like many simple truths to be found in religious texts, this statement is, ironically, made more insightful when it is removed from any connection to a god or magical thinking. A statement like Matthew 5:14 which reads 'Ye are the light of the world. A city that is set on a hill cannot be hid. Neither do men light a candle and put it under a bushel, but on a candlestick; and it giveth light unto all that are in the house.' Or in Luke 11:33: "No man, when he hath lighted a candle, putteth it in a secret place, neither under a bushel, but on a candlestick, that they which come in may see the light." Removed from deific trappings, these ideas carry a profound truth: when one has a thing of happiness in their lives, they do not hide it away, stifling it for the sake of coddling the miserable. Instead, one is compelled to display their glorious happiness proudly and without shame, the natural by-product of this being that their happiness, on display for the entire world to see, will compel others to pursue their own happiness. And this is the essence of a truly free society—one in which the right of the individual to pursue their own happiness forms the basis for our mutual compassion, respect, and empathy.

"But such beneficial ideas lose their relevance and insight when they are mutilated to reverence for a tyrannical deity, as in Matthew 5:16, 'Let your light shine before men, that they may see your fine works and give glory to your Father who is in the heaven.' With such a statement, a beautiful idea becomes corrupted by the vilest and most despicable thing ever conceived of by the human race: the god of abstinence and necrotic altruism. This god demands that you derive all of your happiness from the awe and humility you feel in his presence then demands that you honor this forced, spoon fed happiness by masochistically performing acts of expression devoid of that which makes them acts of expression. He demands that you sing music that has no syncopation or harmony. He demands that you shut off your rational mind when you attempt to educate yourself. He demands that you to have a sex that is devoid of passion, rhythm, stimulation, enjoyment or fulfillment, instead demanding that you find all happiness resulting from sex in the conception and eventual birth of a child, as if there were something joyous in passing on the 'original sin' that has plagued humankind for the centuries.

"Don't misunderstand sex as having the sole and primary function of producing a child. Just as the common good of a society is served when individuals achieve their own personal happiness, so the natural results of all pleasurable acts are byproducts of the selfish indulgence of pleasure. One does not satiate their hunger for the moral satisfaction of having fueled their body—instead we eat to enjoy the taste and the warm rush of stimulation the nutrients give our bodies. By the same token, boys and girls do not sit up nights fantasizing about the children they might one day produce. Some may tell you that they do—and may even claim that they come by this naturally—but I assure you: they are only parroting the values that have been forced on them by years of conditioning. Remove the rigorous conditioning from an individual and their first concern will be the act of sex, not the long term result. This is validated by homosexuality, which cannot be performed for the sake of producing a child yet is seen as a completely comparable alternative to heterosexual sex by those whose natures and desires mandate its indulgence.

"If a person tells you that your life's purpose is to raise up the next generation and that all your actions, including sex, should be predicated on that purpose, then they are only confessing their desire to be reduced to the level of a virus. A viral entity has no goal save that of replication and each cell of its subsequent generation is similarly geared towards this purpose. A virus is lower than a parasite: a parasite requires its host to continue living in order to further its own goal of continued living. A virus seeks only to consume and replicate blindly until it dies, either as a result of its hosts immunities or by default when all of its host's resources are used up. In society, a parasitic person may feed off of the lives of others and the resources of the earth but may still aspire to create some temporal enjoyment for themselves. A viral human being, however, is devoid even of this hollow aspiration. A viral person seeks only to exist in the ultimate state of altruistic abandon: a life that exists for no purpose save that of creating further life.

"The attempt to relegate a woman's sexuality to the realm of child bearing has been the hallmark of the viral strain of human beings. They insist that a woman surrender all of the things that would elevate her sexuality above the level of an animal: pleasure, passion, lust, personal gratification, personal volition, sexual fetishism, and identity. A woman whose sole purpose in sexuality is to produce children is a woman who has become what the anti-porn lobby claims to rail against: a semen receptacle. A man who believes that his sexuality has the sole purpose of creating offspring is the one who truly confesses that he is base, crass and a primitive and that he sees a woman as nothing more than a functionary—a tool to accomplish nobler means. He sees her as a sacrificial animal that exists for the purpose of viral replication.

"To say that sex is performed primarily to produce children is to say that it is an act of altruism at its core. But your orgasm guards against that. Your orgasm is your reward not for producing children or living up what the mystics declare to be your purpose in society. It is the reward your body gives itself for having been properly stimulated and nothing more. Once sexual gratification is recognized as egoistic—meaning that its nature is geared towards the self, not society as a whole, we learn that the profit motive is the greatest protection and celebration of sexual freedom possible to human kind. The profit motive requires that you establish a value for that which you posses and a precedent of reciprocal value in those you wish to share it with. If you put a price on your sexuality—meaning that you set the terms of exchange between you and another person on a set of identifiable factors—then you establish that your sexuality is a thing of value that serves your personal gain. If you choose money as the basis for your consent then you have used the purest symbol of value—the dollar—as the determining factor and because you cannot receive money without gaining its value then you have done a thing which is purely egoistic and therefore purely in the service of your sexual identity.

"The anti-porn lobby is quick to harp on the subgenres of pornography that cater to violent interactions such as bondage and sadism. 'What positives could ever be found in such things?' they scream as though I were advocating mass genocide. They try to assert that the reason a person would be interested in such activities is because they are either a woman who has been brainwashed by the patriarchy into thinking that they deserve to be brutalized or a man that has been brainwashed by the same into thinking that he has some right to bully and demean women. The reality of the situation is far more intimate than they would like to imagine: in the submissive participant, the qualities of strength and endurance are brought out and used as the basis for orgasmic pleasure. It is culturally acceptable in fiction for men to be shown enduring torture because they are able to display their extraordinary capacity for endurance. Why is the same not acceptable for women? Alternately, the psychology of the dominant person in BDSM scenarios is intensely emotional and requires that they be able to read their partner perfectly and eternally balance the administration of pain so that their partner is fulfilled but never actually harmed. Both positions require a perfect, unbroken amount of trust. Have you even done a trust fall, the exercise where one partner falls backwards certain that their partner will catch them? Then you have performed the essence of BDSM.

"Why would adults delight in fantasies that would involve the aesthetics of childhood such as being surrounded by toys and stuffed animals? The anti-porn moralists are quick to scream that such scenarios are meant to cater to latent pedophilia and provide the viewer with a form of simulated child pornography. The insult of their position is that it is so often argued with a question: *what could this mean if not a means to create legal child pornography?* They ask this question with a sort of open ended finality, as if no other possible answer exists. But what are the redeeming qualities found in childhood? Wonderment. Discovery. Innocence. These qualities and others may be indulged in by adults who construct youthful scenarios for their mutual amusement and this psychology is reflected in the adults who delight in wearing adult sized versions of baby and young childhood clothes in their lovemaking but are strictly appalled by actual child sexual abuse.

"Only a fool would dare to say that pornography caters exclusively to fantasies of men dominating women. Are there forms of pornography that show men dominating women? Yes. But is that the entirety of the medium? No. The field is full of genres that cater to such interests as women controlling men in BDSM scenarios, penetrating them with strap-on dildos, humiliating them in 'clothed female/nude male' experiences, reverse gangbangs, female ejaculation bukake, and a whole range of other fetishes, all of which are as acceptable as they are liberating.

"The puritans, with their philosophy that all people's desires are uniformly wrong, fail to understand that finding a consensual partner is central to sexual fulfillment, even if the act performed between those partners depicts violent or anti-social tendencies. We are creatures which seek—to varying degrees—the companionship of those persons who best reflect our values, interests, and desires. So long as one's sexual desires require more partners than masturbation provides, they must find consenting partners. To find a consenting partner is to receive the validation of one's own desires in the actions and perspectives of another. This validation of the self is crucial to the fulfillment of one's sexual needs with others and is arrived at rationally via their capacity for empathy. Because an unwilling partner cannot reflect the values and desires of the attacker, it is impossible to say that a rapist is motivated by a desire for sexual satisfaction. If a rapist claims to be motivated by their sexual desires then they are in, reality, motivated by the desire to overpower the social constructs by which human beings interact. If a man drugs his date and has his way with the unconscious body then he is satisfying not his sexual desire but his desire to escape from the knowledge of his own inadequacy, namely his inability to seduce her by consensual means. Because the effects of rape are beyond the realm of consent, no consensual act may be considered indicative of them, including acts which portray consensually and fictitiously the control, terrorizing, and dehumanizing of a victim.

"Often scenarios are constructed in porn which involve the depiction of a victimizing act—one in which an actual relationship of trust and respect is compromised, such as adult to child, teacher to student, boss to employee, and so on. In all of these situations, there is both a dominant and a submissive and a scenario that reflects the psychology of the dominant/submissive relationship in sexuality that is like a dance in which one partner leads and the other follows but neither are considered greater or lesser as human beings. These fantasies are designed for the adults who can understand and respect this relationship. If you desire to genuinely have sex with a child or rape and brutalize another person then your desire is not for sexual fulfillment but for the victimization of others. Thus, the psychology of such a person cannot be considered a strike against those who can appreciate the meaning and purpose of sexual symbolism.

"It is in the expression of selfish joy that I am a merchant. My products are stimulants as much for the mind as the genitals and as such the offer a plethora of ideas and methods by which the happiness of sexual fulfillment may be expressed, experienced or studied vicariously. In a society of rational individuals, each bringing their own mental constructs and life experiences to the table, some of the practices my products depict will seem abhorrent and others will seem beautiful. It is up to the work of their rational minds to determine which is which as this is crucial to their individual awareness.

"In any society one can find the prostitute, a position which has always existed since the dawn of human history. The sex professional is not inherent to any one particular era or to the nature of patriarchy. Because of the egoistic nature of the orgasm and its pursuit, the prostitute is a social inevitability. Yes, the same men who proclaim the virtues of chastity, abstinence and virginity in women are often found in the bedrooms of brothels but this is only because they have chosen to take a stance that is contrary to their existence as rationally sexual beings. The contempt for the prostitute is that he or she is not only engaging in sex for enjoyment but furthermore that they are doing it for the sake of their own profit, not the profit of society which would have been in the form of a child.

"Look at the puritanical ideal of womanhood—the Virgin Mary. Their female ideal is a woman that is able to produce a child without having sex and therefore without the potential for an orgasm. Such is the blind, viral nature of their idealism—you have mastered your body not when you know how best to stimulate it but when you know how best to disconnect from it. When they relegated matters of sex to the woman, they did so with the intention of making her the scapegoat of all sexual desire. They tasked her not with sexual identity but with the transcending of sexual identity.

"They declare that their god has given them instructions for a single, pure, perfect form of sexual intercourse that has a sole purpose. In a society of primitives, it is understandable why such masochistic superstitions had to be imposed. A tribal group that has no means of refrigeration is well served to regard certain kinds of meat as 'unclean' and would naturally consider them demonically possessed. A society of primitives that has no knowledge of bacterial infection is wise to believe god wants their food and their dung kept separate. Such a society is equally well served, for practical purposes, to restrict its sexual habits to a specific set of actions confined to a specific institution; namely missionary sex to produce children within the context of marriage. With no concept of contraception, disease transmission, reproduction, or even basic hygiene, it is advantageous to restrict sexual reproduction as a whole.

"The problem is not the temporal validity of these solutions but the manner in which they are maintained today. In the sophisticated modern world, where medical innovations and technology have, for all practical purposes, replaced the masochistic regulations on human sexuality it is only as an outlet for social control that such regulations are still enforced. In this way, they are the true plague: the lies, superstitions, phobias, and more deeply ingrained socio-religious memes that are passed from one generation to the next in the guise of perfect knowledge. If you seek your absolute truths in flimsy beliefs that are in all ways flawed then can your really be surprised when the world around you appears to function on the premise of confusion and hatred? Can you be surprised that your god appears to be some classroom bully that hovers over you with a magnifying glass as you run a maze with no exit?

"Backed into a corner and facing no other avenue of retort, the puritans of all camps will ask why, if sexual freedom should be universally accepted, should people not be allowed to have sex with children or view child pornography? The answer is that a child has not attained the physical, philosophical, and psychological development necessary to make informed decisions about the nature of their sexuality and as such an adult convincing a child to embrace sexuality on terms the child cannot rationally comprehend commits an act of rape.

"Do you still dare to cry that pornography causes or encourages pedophilia? Look at the Catholic Church! You will find no group of religious leaders more committed to the practice of sexual denial and lifelong abstinence yet they have become known the world over as a den of child molesters. The world wide revulsion that is Catholicism has gone to extraordinary lengths to hide and protect its vast throngs of pedophile priests yet they have the nerve to lecture at the sexually liberated about perversion! You have all heard the joke about the Rabbi who, arriving in Vatican City for the first time, remarks 'if this is poverty, I can't wait to see chastity!' Such a humorous aside is far darker in its truth than its author could have ever known yet it is the reality of this world wide bastion of abstinent insanity.

"As our society collapses under the overwhelming guilt that is sex negativism, I stand before you with this simple truth: your sexuality is not sacred. It is not some wafer thin, pale white shimmering fawn to be kept hidden and coddled lest the horrors of the big bad world should foul its childish perfection and render it totally unlovable. The cognition of sexual morality is this: accept that sexuality is a natural and healthy part of who you are. Decide what is proper to your existence by exploring the documented practice of a wide range of sexual acts or invent new, as yet undocumented activities. Find consenting adult partners with whom to engage in these acts and take precautions to ensure that disease will not be spread and unwanted children will not be conceived. Within these morality there is no sexual abuse, no act that is fundamentally wrong, and no detriment to society at large.

"The establishment of one's sexual identity is the result of two factors which are reconciled by the sex act itself and these are the natural and nurtured selves. The natural self, one's body, mind and genetic makeup, are determined by the DNA and physical health of one's own genetic line as well as the birthing process. These factors are the default in each person and no two sets of factors are exactly alike and these are the factors that determine, on a fundamental level, how the person in question perceives and interacts with the world around them. The nurtured self, however, is contingent on the social factors surrounding a person during their developing years. The factors that determine a nurtured self are: the geographic environment, the social climate, and the culture in which a person develops. All geographical environments are more accepting of certain body types and not others just as all cultures advocate certain principles and values and not others. The degree to which a person's natural self succeeds or fails in adapting to these factors determines their nurtured self. Because the psyche consists, at its core, of these two elements, then the mind must establish a persona based on the common ground between the two. This is where sexuality becomes the psychodramatic stage on which the combat between nature and nurture plays out. A healthy sexual identity is created when one is able to enter the theater of sexual intercourse knowing what part they play and how to play it. To deny someone this right is to deny them the certainty of their fundamental identity and thus keep them in a perpetual state of angst and confusion. When you express your abstract sense of yourself using the physical concrete of your body to acheive sexual satisfaction, then and on that day have you acheived sexual identity.

"Do you now see why professional sex is crucial to a free society? If you have understood my words then you have understood that value is the gaining of the concretes of one's abstract morality and that sexual value demands one's ability to capitalize on one's sexuality. You have understood that the nature of capitalism is not to control and shape society but to reflect it. You have learned that no consensual sex is performed in the absence of trade and that trade demands the capacity for choice. And if you have understood all of this then you now know that no middle ground remains between those who champion sexual freedom and those who oppose it and that pornography and prostitution are the cornerstones of sexual freedom, not the antithesis.

"You have the decision laid bare before you: will you be an adult with full responsibility for your life or an eternally dependent child whose every decision is sterilized and removed by the authoritarians? No authoritarian will tell you that they seek to take your rights away and drive you into oppression. They will tell you that they do the things they do for your own good or for the good of society or country or whatever abstraction they use to obfuscate their true intentions. Their pursuit of power is not the drunken malevolence of gaining power for its own sake as is the assumption of those looking for an obvious villain. They seek power out of the fear they have of the freedom of others because at their most basic level they are still those tribal primitives who superstitiously believe tragedy will befall all those whose faces show even the tiniest spark of happiness. You can be your own person or you can be more meat for their insatiable power hunger. You cannot be both.

"I was asked to appear here today to talk about the state of the porn industry. This can only be stated accurately by looking at the state of the human spirit. In this day and age the human spirit is under attack from all sides and it is caving in. As you look out at the vast, sterile wilderness in which the sunken-cheeked drones now stumble, looking aimlessly through blood shot eyes for the next reassurance that their dry, empty existence will be transformed beyond the grave into an infinitely more wonderful eternal version of the same state, ask yourself what it is that has brought them to this level.

"The fundamental battle is one that has been waged since the beginning of time between the successful and the unsuccessful. Between the fulfilled and the unfulfilled. Between the beloved and the bitter. Between the beautiful and the grotesque. Those who are loved for their physical, mental, and emotional beauty have been attacked mercilessly by the ugly, idiotic, worthless and hateful since our species gained the capacity to differentiate such attributes. We are told that the beautiful ought to cover and hide their beauty, for fear of shaming the ugly. We are told that the intelligent should remain silent and dormant in their brilliance lest their innovative insight break the safety net of communal ignorance erected to coddle the frailties of the stupid. And those who know and understand the nature of true, mutual and requited love are told first to keep their love and happiness a deep, dark secret so as not to sadden the already emotionally repugnant. They are then told that they, the lovable, are only of noble character if they commit themselves to 'romantic' relationships with the abusive, revolting, and boring of the world. They are told that they ought to love someone in spite of their shortcomings, but never that there must be virtues that outweigh those shortcomings. You, the worthless, whine that we should love you despite your lack of success, beauty, intellect, personal integrity, self confidence, and aesthetic awareness; that we should love you for who you really are. Well what are you? What are the redeeming qualities by which we should love you? Love to you is something to be handed over by a beautiful person to a grotesque person in exchange for nothing! You whine that you would be perfect lovers if only you got the chance, never stopping to think that perhaps your thinking that is why nobody ever gives you the chance!

"We the beautiful have given you the opportunity to observe us and learn from us. Throughout history we have made our achievements known—the great secrets of the universe, of science, of mathematics, of literature, of music have been published throughout the ages by the most intellectually beautiful and you have decried them as heresy and witchcraft. The most aesthetically beautiful have shared their designs, artworks, and talents and you have called them pretentious and arrogant. And the most physically beautiful have shared their bodies and, through merchants such as myself, given you a glimpse into their bedrooms, that you may know the innermost secrets of their sexual enjoyment. And this last group has been regarded with the most suspicion, the most hatred, and the most venom by the herded masses that are nothing more than a sniveling underworld of bland, sensory deprived proles.

"Do you still cry that the current state of the world is not the result of the results of the sex-negative and their crusade to deprive us of our ability to live by choice and thought? Look at the very thing that has been the catalyst for the current state of the country. Do any of you actually know what it is about *The Lotus Wave* that has made it so controversial and shunned? You don't even know and yet you've torn the entire fabric of society to shreds out of the fear that this movie might make you confront something new that you aren't prepared for. I am among the privileged few that know what is contained in that forbidden script and I am still determined to unleash it on the world. Do you think I do this without purpose to manifest some gleeful state of anarchy? Hell no! I intend to create this movie with the full knowledge of the effect that it will have on society and I demand that society confront those effects and nail shut the casket of sexual oppression once and for all.

"In the name of every person who has found in themselves a thing of beauty, whether that be in mind, body, or spirit, I now stand before you to declare that we will not surrender to the jealous, the ugly, and the worthless. If you wish to call us elitist, you may since that is a term that only acknowledges the echelon above you on which we reside. You who have called me and those of my industry vile and subhuman for creating pornography know this: we are the guardians, the innovators, and the standard bearers of beauty. Your moralists are the standard bearers of sterility and stagnation. They tell you that we represent the seamy side of life, but never stop to consider that it is the seamy side of a garment that holds it together. Your freedom from tyranny, from blind dogmatism, and from every irrational pain you have ever endured is directly proportionate to the freedom with which we are able to operate.

"I have broken my public silence tonight not so that I could enlighten you with some new revelation but so that I could bring to the surface the truth which you have drowned. If you wish to revive it, breathing new life into its long neglected lungs, then do so with these words: I am proud of my sexuality. I will live in its celebration. I will accept no alternatives because no *living* alternatives exist."

Chapter 25

THE LAST WORDS of Alston's speech hung in the air, not as an echo but as the harrowing stillness one feels when made aware that words are at an end and violence is imminent. But even that tension was benevolent and when the thousands of attendees rose to their feet it was to applaud in brazenly enthusiastic unison. It was an applause that Alston, the lifelong look of solemn defiance still on his sharpened face, drank in with a naked certainty that had always eluded him. Now, it was laid bare before him. Their cheering, their applause, their whistles, all of it came together in a joyous thunder that returned to him a thousand fold the investment of his heart and soul. He had spoken directly to the dormant truth in each of them. Their applause ripped a passionate wound in Alston's soul that drained the infection of his lifelong withdrawal from others. They had heard his words and welcomed them with an embrace that restored his appreciation for humanity. Though his face was still locked in its fixed precision, he found himself thinking a silent *thank you* to the multitude.

In some distant world, one that reached impudently into the ether of the moment's grandeur, Alston was vaguely aware of his wrists being pressed together behind his back, of handcuffs ratcheting shut, of Miranda rights being read, but through it all his gaze remained fixed on the soaring choir that applauded his convictions. In the afterglow of such a report, Alston realized that the cheers were becoming boos as the military police officers escorted him off the stage.

As Alston was led towards the wings, Diana Arland stormed up the steps to the stage, shouting "what's the charge? What has he done?"

"Breaking and entering, murder in the first, aiding in the escape of a convicted felon," said one of the cops with clinical graveness.

Alston found himself being escorted through the main arteries of the casino, drawing curious stares from the technicians as he went. Within minutes he was being loaded into a paddy wagon with Hank, Rod, Slam, and Dominic, all of whom were similarly bound. They sat on two steel benches that ran the length of the vehicle's interior and Alston joined Slam on the bench opposite Rod, Dominic and Hank. They were consumed by darkness when the doors closed and after they felt the vehicle begin to move they could hear the hellacious cries of the protestors and the blunt, metallic thud of fists banging on the sides of the wagon.

Some thirty minutes later they arrived at the local police station and were escorted inside where each of them was thumb printed, photographed and led into the holding cell. A few drunks and similarly petty offenders littered the large, dimly lit room where a single bench and a toilet adorned the back wall.

"Well," said Dominic distantly as he rubbed his wrists where the handcuffs had been, "here we are." None of the others responded to him. An hour later Alston was offered a phone call and contacted Duke Cunningham. When he was led back to holding, Alston addressed the other four members of his crew:

"Duke's on the case. He's going to see what he can do. I don't know how we'll get out of this one, boys. I'm sorry."

"Don't be sorry," said Slam. "It was worth it."

Alston nodded and looked down at the ground for a moment. "It was damn worth it," said Dominic, and Alston looked up to see him smiling wistfully and beaming up from where he sat. "I can't tell you what an honor it's been, sir."

"Oh captain, my captain," said Hank with gentle salute. Alston smiled for the first time in a long time and found himself carefully basking in the moment's soft exposure. It was a nice feeling—admiration—and for the first time he was able to enjoy a moment's sentimentality. A distant flood gate was opening within him, and soon he would feel the full brunt of the admiration that all those touched by his work had felt for him. He found the smile broadening, miring itself in the dulcet tide of satisfaction apparent in his companions. He moved towards the bench and Dominic and Rod moved aside to allow him a seat.

"We should be reeling in horror right now," said Alston ponderously. "Why aren't we?"

"You're coming around to something we've known all along, Isaac," replied Dominic. "You finally said it in that speech and it couldn't have happened any other way. If there's one good reason you've never spoken to the public all these years it's that you were a pearl among swine. They didn't deserve you and didn't want to hear you. They only sought to castigate you as their latest in a long line of scapegoats. But you wouldn't let them, and it turned you into god. Their hellish condemnations were the act of worship that elevated you above all the rest, and all you did tonight was acknowledge that you were finally ready for the mantle they'd bestowed."

"Thanks, Dominic."

There was a pause before the conversation was resumed and in that moment Alston found himself reflecting on the recent events. The murderous anger that had surged through him when he'd killed Crankshadow and the vindictive glee with which he'd watched Ralphie getting tortured seemed distant and other-worldly, as though he were remembering the most satisfying moments of an otherwise dismissible film. Instead, he found himself basking in the admiration granted to him by his four companions. It was not an admiration that he had actively sought, but was instead an appreciation of these men's wisdom at admiring him. What he realized was that he was finally ready to accept their admiration.

"I knew you understood," said Hank. "I knew you understood what I meant that day I told you what it meant to work for you. Part of me wanted to think that you really were as cold and dead as your exterior let on, but I kept telling myself that you understood the full grandeur of what it meant to be in your Empire. I tell you this—the more I think about it, the more I realize I wasn't worried about losing my job so much as if you understood what it meant to me to be working for you."

Alston smiled again and nodded. "When you walked in, Hank, it wasn't your dick, your muscles, or your voice that told me that we had a winner in you. It was your eyes. When I looked into your eyes I saw a complete human being: a passion for living that could be channeled for love or violence and when you spoke to me I could tell that your passion had been used for violence most of your life. It was time for someone to throw the switch and use that passion for things constructive, not destructive."

"You're a good man and a good friend, Mr. Alston."

"Thanks, Hank. And it's Isaac."

In the hours that proceeded they spoke fondly of memorable times at Alston Image through the years, Dominic discussing the shoe-string budget with which they shot the first few films and Rod and Slam relating their favorite shoots and the beautiful women they'd known throughout. This led to the inevitable discussion of Billie, a topic which Hank was able to look back on with a bittersweet smile, realizing that Billie's memory was becoming the angelic backbone of Alston Image as it already was in his heart.

Just before dawn, Duke Cunningham arrived at the holding cell and, though slightly disarmed by the jovial tone of Alston and his companions, was beaming from ear to ear. Alston stood and crossed the barred chamber, Dominic, Hank, Rod and Slam at his sides.

"You're going to be charged with capital murder, Isaac. They're going to try you first and try the other guys if you're guilty."

"Has the D.A. seen the footage?"

"He has. He already told me he'll never get a conviction."

"Then why are they going to try me?"

"Families for Families has all the pull now. It's going to be a big spectacle to satiate their followers. If they have the signatures they'll be able to convict you anyway. It will be Darcy Collins all over again."

"What about Darcy?"

"She's back in federal custody. Just holding for the time being."

"How much is bail for us?"

"They'll take a five hundred thousand for each of you."

"I'll pay it."

"Are you sure, Isaac?" asked Dominic.

Alston snorted "my car cost more than that."

"What defense can we possibly work up?" ask Hank. "We have no alibi."

"I don't know," replied Duke. "With the laws like they are now, it's a wonder they're even having a trial."

When Alston was arranged on capital murder charges, Bob Match had a field day declaring that the vilest traitor since Ulysses S. Grant was finally being prosecuted. "That Mr. Alston would dare to enter a plea of 'not guilty' is a mockery of our legal system," he boomed across the airwaves to a diminishing viewership. "Surely the Department of Offense Prevention has the necessary signatures to render this trial irrelevant. Come on America—trial by jury is *not* what the founding fathers would have wanted!"

But not even Shouting Match with Bob Match could drown out the president's State of the Union address, which was the shortest in history: "My fellow Americans," he began. "It is my distinct regret to report that our experiment in accommodating the needs of the extreme-conservative fringe of the Republican Party has failed. I have no progress to report because none has been made. My administration will no longer bow to the demands of the minority party and will instead pass the full brunt of our agenda. The Unlimited Sanctity Act will be repealed along with all faith-based government programs. Religious organizations will now be required to pay taxes because forcing Americans to pay higher taxes simply because we refuse to tax religion is just absurd. The Department of Offense Prevention and enforcement is henceforth dissolved and all regulations made under its control are hereby repealed.

"The Constitution shall be amended to guarantee that congress shall pass no law infringing on the rights of the people to copulate consensually, or of the people to profit thereof. Furthermore, another amendment shall be passed declaring that each person's body will be their own property to do with as they please in all matters.

"These measures will help to ensure that the authoritarian menace that has plagued our nation is kept under control. We have seen a rise in corporatized religiosity and pseudo-academic posturing that has threatened to destroy our nation and the values that make it the greatest nation on earth. This injustice was recently highlighted by a great man and a great American. Also everyone has healthcare. Thank you."

"They're going to have a hell of a time giving an American hero the death penalty," said Duke Cunningham as he and Alston rode to the courthouse in Alston's limousine.

"Let's just get this over with," replied Alston. His suit and tie were uniformly non-descript and it was odd to see him in such utilitarian attire.

When they arrived at the courthouse, Duke and Alston were immediately surrounded by federal agents, one of whom placed a bullet proof vest over Alston as he emerged from the vehicle. The surrounding huddle made it difficult for Alston to see the crowds that had gathered on either side of the frigid steps leading up to the pantheon of litigation that towered above him. The massive assembly was a burnt casserole of reporters and protestors but through it all there was a hopeful new strain in the crowd's otherwise necrotic DNA: the ones who were there cheering for Isaac Alston. Diana Arland and Felicity Hatchback had organized the Alston Image contract players into a robust throng that was joined by an infusion of players from other studios. The stunning beauty of the women and the regal handsomeness of the men stood in harsh and withering contrast to their opponents who were either pitifully emaciated or morbidly obese with only a frail smattering of homely miscreants in between. As he reached the steps, Alston caught a glimpse of Diana Arland, her face stoic and determined. There was a shine in her eyes as though they intended to stand in defiant contrast to the overcast day around them. The other women that stood around her seemed more naked than they ever had on film. Their beauty, like the shimmer in Diana's eyes, was unshaken by the harsh malignancy of the herd of protestors on the other side of the concrete steps. Their faces were the canvases of their conviction and each was painted with the majesty of a conscience unencumbered by the guilt of humanity and, in that harrowing release of long imposed tension, were the most beautiful creatures imaginable.

"Whore!" screamed a boney teenage girl on the other side of the pavement as she threw a rock at Alston's supporters, hitting Janet Drillride. The police were on her in an instant, cuffing her and leading her away. Her sign, which read *PORN PROMOTES VIOLENCE AGAINST WOMEN,* was left to gather rain water in the mud.

"Thanks for the irony," shouted Janet, her cheek now freshly bruised and her lower lip bleeding down her chin. Despite her injuries she did not move from her position as Alston was lead inside.

As the rage of the crowd noise was muted by the towering wooden doors of the courthouse, Alston became uniquely aware that the dome of static that had surrounded him for most of his life was now lifted—the screams were at once individual and intelligible, his psyche no longer feeling the inherit need to blend them together in reflexive defense. He felt as though he could have taken on each of the hundreds of naysayers out there one-on-one and took satisfaction in the knowledge that every single one of them was too chicken to fight that way. The guard by the metal detector eyed the proud smirk on Alston's face with an arched brow.

The courtroom was the same one that had been used for Darcy's trial but when Alston and Duke entered they found the benches to be lined with spectators, Dominic, Slam, Rod and Hank among them. After the pair was seated at the defense table Diana, Janet and Saundra Bullcock entered along with several other Alston Image contract girls who sat down alongside their male counterparts. Alston looked around once at the dense audience, making eye contact with Dominic who nodded solemnly.

The room was called to rise for the judge who entered with uniform efficiency and took his position. It was Judge Cartwright again. Duke's heart sank a little even thought he'd known this all along. There was a morbid tension to the trial's introductory proceedings as though the judge were inflicting a certain deliberate strain on the moment. "The case of Isaac Alston verses the United States of America will come to order," he said in an excessively dry, frustrated monotone. It wasn't clear what his intent was in this but Duke wondered if it had something to do with the Collins trial.

Just as he'd given one look for acknowledgement to Dominic and the others, so Alston took a single expressionless look at the prosecution. Tad Felmer had returned and brought with him the instantly recognizable Andrea Danvers. Next to Andrea was a scrawny wastrel that Alston identified as her husband but was unable to remember his name.

"Ladies and gentlemen of the jury," began Tad Felmer as though he were presenting the Ten Commandments in some biblical film from the 1950's, "what you have before you is a clear-cut case of right and wrong. This man, Isaac Alston, led a small militia into the First Grand Pantheon of Jesus Christ the Imperial Redeemer of American Liberty and brutally murdered the pastor Melvin Crankshadow along with several of his guards and freed a federal prisoner."

The judge cracked the gavel "Ms. Collins was found innocent, Mr. Felmer, and was released into Families for Families' custody. In light of recent action by the administration her innocence and freedom are now being upheld. Please continue."

"Of course your honor. As I was saying, there are numerous witnesses and plenty of video camera footage showing the defendant to have entered the facility with his co-conspirators. The case is irrefutable: this man, Isaac Alston, murdered a holy man. And what is a holy man if not the bedrock of the great nation that is—"

"That's enough, Mr. Felmer. The jury will now hear the opening remarks of the defense."

Tad Felmer shuffled back to his table, noticeably quelled as Duke took the floor. "Contrary to what Mr. Felmer would like you to think," began Duke earnestly, "this issue is not so cut and dry. The nature of your decision will be based on what your values are. Do you believe in blindly following a person simply because they represent a set of ideals or do you support a person consciously because their values are a mirror of your own? My client's children were taken from his custody by the woman that bombed his house and handed over to a religious fundamentalist for brainwashing. My client entered that facility with the intention of rescuing his children but was then brought face to face with something that no parent wants to even contemplate: he saw one of his children being raped by the man that had kidnapped them. Put yourself in the shoes of my client. Remove from your minds the protective escapes of a pornographer and a preacher and evaluate each of these men for who they are and what they've done. But more importantly, think about your own values and ask yourself what you would have done in that situation. Thank you."

There was a hovering tension in the air as a DVD containing the footage sent to the FBI as well as DNA tests matching the semen found in Jesse Alston's vagina to that of Melvin Crankshadow. The prosecution entered security camera footage as evidence and called Alston to the stand. Alston crossed the room with the same steadied grandeur he'd exuded on the stage at the AVN's. The eyes of the jurors and the television cameras bringing the trial to the attention of the whole world were upon him. Now, in his completed form, he welcomed them. Once sworn in he took his seat next to the judge and sat evenly, with both hands on the short arms of the chair and his feet side-by-side at shoulder's width. It was as though he were sitting in the electric chair already but prepared to dialogue at length with the executioner.

"That was quite a speech you gave, Mr. Alston," said Tad Felmer with a serpentine countenance. Alston was silent. "Well?" he said irritably.

"Is there some protocol for pleasantries in the course of my trial?"

"I thought you'd like to let the jury see your human side."

"They already have."

"When?"

"In my speech."

"Oh really? I would have said that it was when you shot Mr. Crankshadow."

"They saw it there too."

"So you don't deny it?"

"No. Not at all."

"Then why are we even here? Why didn't you plead guilty?"

"Because the jury is not only assembled to determine whether or not I committed the acts in question, but whether or not they constitute a crime."

"Murder is a crime."

"But in the defense of my child?"

"Your children were in better circumstances than you were able to provide for them."

"Better? By what standard?"

"They were in a safe, moral, Christian environment rather than in the decadent sleaze that you traffic in."

"They were never raped or molested in my custody."

"Mr. Alston, surely a smart man such as yourself should realize that was only done in the interest of showing them the dangers of the porn industry."

"A man with less awareness of the human condition than myself would be awestruck to hear you defending a child rapist."

"Mr. Alston, I certainly don't condone the actions taken by Mr. Crankshadow, just his purpose in taking them."

"So do you condone my purpose for shooting the preacher?"

"No."

"And why not?"

"Because those actions were being taken by a pornographer and therefore are morally indefensible."

"So you've created a point of view where its acceptable for a man to rape a child but not for that child's father to commit lethal retaliation?"

"You make it sound so simple, Mr. Alston, but in fact it's a far more complex matter."

"In what way?"

"We've been over this, Mr. Alston: he was a man of god and therefore good. You are a man of the flesh and therefore evil."

"So it is within the rights of a holy man to rape children at his will?"

"No—you see, Mr. Crankshadow was serving the will of the almighty, not his own. Don't you respect the will of the almighty?"

"I will never respect a rapist or those who champion him. Not in this world or the next."

"Do you believe in god, Mr. Alston?"

"I do not."

"So you deny his existence?"

"No—'denial' implies that there's something there to deny."

"So you doubt the existence of god?"

"No, there's no doubt about it in my mind."

"So you claim to know everything then, do you?"

"I haven't said that."

"Well you claim to know that god doesn't exist."

"I have no belief that he exists. I don't claim to know for certain whether he does or not."

"You don't call that a contradiction?"

"I do not."

"You're a very proud man, Mr. Alston."

"I am."

"You don't see that as a problem?"

"I see it as a virtue."

"Well, Mr. Alston, I think our preliminaries are done. I've arranged to have you examined by a couple of experts."

"If you say so."

Trembling piteously, Mercer Thompson rose and, like a vibrating dildo, drifted to the center of the room. "Mr. Alston... I... uh... was wonder... uh... how you feel about... well, things as they appear, as such as... they might appear..."

"Sit down, Mercer," said Alston evenly.

"Yes sir."

After smacking her husband upside the head, Andrea Danvers rose and took the floor. She appeared to be floating back and forth within herself as she tried to stand on the strength of her convictions and the stubby protrusions of her legs. Despite the utter silence in the room, nobody could hear Dominic whisper "step into the ring, bitch."

"Nobody can deny that your daughter was raped, Mr. Alston," began Andrea Danvers. "But do you now realize how the parents of women you rape must feel?"

"I've never raped anybody."

"But you *have,* Mr. Alston. What they experience on the sets of your films is rape."

"No, it is not. We have them sign contracts to prove it."

"I don't care if you sign a million contracts—that's rape."

"Then you don't respect a woman's right to choose."

"I would respect their choice, Mr. Alston, if they made the right one."

"The right choice isn't for you to determine."

"Mr. Alston, if you have any respect for women at all and if you love your daughter, then you'll understand why I'm fighting for the women that you keep locked up in the Alston Image building."

"I don't keep them locked up."

"I understand that they all live at the building now and seldom leave."

"They live there now because it's not safe on the streets for them."

"Exactly. And that's why I'm fighting for them."

"No, Andrea, you're fighting for them because it allows you to cast yourself as superior to women whose physical beauty towers above your unsightly visage."

"That's objectification."

"No, Andrea, it's the truth. And this sadistic charade of political correctness that you masquerade as a 'cause' is extraordinarily transparent: you get to insult the pretty girls as being stupid, uneducated, traumatized and whorish in the guise of pretending to care about them. You get to humiliate the pretty girls by making them feel guilty for enjoying the benefits of being beautiful. It lets you get attention from the boys by shaming them into coming to you for support. I can say with utter certainty that none of the women in my employment feel victimized or have any sympathy for your viewpoint."

"He's right," said Felicity Hatchback, whose words were met with nods and murmurs from the rest of the women there to support Alston and with a sharp glance from the police officers in the room.

"You see, Mr. Alston? You've got these poor women so brainwashed that they actually think that they agree with you!"

"The only brainwashed person in this discussion is you, Andrea," said Alston, an authoritative firmness entering his otherwise darkly serene voice. "You've actually succeeded in brainwashing yourself into believing your own propaganda and while I don't know what vast succession of gullible rubes has allowed you to perpetuate it this long, I can tell that you've never had any brush with reality. The failure of those who have argued with you in the past is that they cannot bring themselves to believe that you actually mean the full implication of what you imply. It speaks to their character that they give you the benefit of the doubt and assume that you'll see the logical failings of your arguments if they're brought to your attention. But you've trained yourself not to see reality. The world to you is not a place of cause and effect but a place of knee-jerk reaction: you've identified the words in our language that will create a firestorm of unfocused, unhinged dismay and then, in that moment of insanity, project an idea that, were it seen through the lens of sanity would be shown to be illogical and irrelevant but seems acceptable and workable in the midst of rampant controversy. Did you not hear what I said in my speech about how you and your ilk need to keep the world on the level of a child? I can look into your eyes and see that on some deep, long suppressed level, you realize that the reason you need you need to maintain this infantile charade in the minds of those around you is that you have never grown past the childhood technique of getting your way by 'crying wolf.' So please, Andrea, continue with your accusations. Continue to try to put me on the defensive with words like 'rapist' and 'misogynist' and 'child abuser.' You will find that I am immune to such things not, as you assume, because I've made myself intentionally ignorant of the truth but because I have embraced it and learned, as all persons of rational capacity have, that reality exists independently of your perception and that no matter what your convictions, it will not surrender to your demands."

"Mr. Alston," said Andrea through a jaw clenched so tightly that the bursting of her molars would have generated no surprise whatsoever.

"Do you really think that stressing the formality of my last name will make me see the validity of your argument, Andrea? Do you really think that I'm the one here who is out of touch with the official nature of the situation? It is only in recognition of the moment's seriousness that you and I are even having this discussion, Andrea."

"So you do take what I'm saying seriously?"

"No, just the fact that it's being said before the bar of law, whatever mockery of the judicial process this may be."

"You are an unreasonable man, Mr. Alston."

"Thank you."

"How can I ever get you to see that what you do is rape?"

"You can't because it's not. No outlandish display of your falsely found convictions can ever make it so. You can convince a person to reject reality but it will not change the fact of reality."

Andrea bit down harder and breathed thickly through clenched teeth. "It is rape, Mr. Alston." Alston remained silent. "It is rape! It is rape!"

"Click your heels together and see if that helps," said Dominic with a grinning sneer of pure, guiltless levity.

"Order," said the judge, banging his gavel in response to the chuckles that filled the chamber.

"Mr. Alston, do you just have no compassion for humanity?" growled Andrea.

"If I agree with you then I will help you turn thousands of women into rape victims. If I stand against you, I am aiding in their emancipation. How can I or any moral creature side with you in the interest of compassion for humanity when those are the choices?"

"I can see that you're... you're a... a..."

"Scour your vocabulary, Andrea. You won't find a word there that will put me on the defensive."

"You've raped women! Your company rapes women!" Here jowls were quivering.

"The women gave their consent."

"Their consent is not good enough!" she barked, suddenly screaming.

"And what is, Andrea? What is necessary for these women to be able to think for themselves?"

"They can't! That's the point! That's why I'm here for them!"

"Of course, Andrea. All those mean things the cheerleaders said in the locker room lose their sting when you get to pretend they need your guidance."

"Shut up! Shut up you rapist!"

"Go ahead Andrea—suck that word dry."

"I'm just trying to help the porn stars!"

"They don't want your help."

"You don't get to decide that for them."

"I don't want your help," said Diana Arland, rising to her feet.

"I don't want your help either," said Janet Drillride, standing next to Diana.

"I like what I do and you can't change my mind for me," said Felicity Hatchback.

"This is who I am and if you don't like it you can fuck off and die," said Saundra Bullcock.

"None of you know what's good for you!" bellowed Andrea, spinning around on the line of performers. "And that fucking tranny is just an abomination!" There were gasps all around the room.

"Not a big fan on transsexuals, are you Andrea?" Said Alston, his steady voice suddenly soaring to fill the chamber.

"Transsexuals are just men that reinforce the patriarchy by embodying gender stereotypes. They are unacceptable! If you want to cut your dick off that's fine but that doesn't make you a fucking woman. I know what makes you a fucking woman!"

Dominic Daniels was on his feet. "So everyone in the whole world has to just bend over and accept you because you're a fat ass pig cunt with a cob up your ass but you can't show a little tolerance for someone you don't like? Fuck you in the eye you sick twisted bitch!"

"I'm not intolerant! I just know what gender paradigms require a temporary suspension of cultural acceptance for the transcendental needs of the matriarchy! I'm not intolerant—I have a husband!"

"Your husband," barked Hank, now being physically restrained by Rod Wielding, "is a spineless, limp wristed little runt that was born for the world to push around and if you think he's a man cause he has a dick then you don't know what it means to be a human being. Everyone says you're a man-hating feminist but that isn't it. You hate women too. You hate women more than men—you go on and on about empowering women but all you do is crush them! That's all you are is a goddamn bully that gets to treat people however the fuck she wants because nobody wants to have those names attached to them. If the people you call 'rapist' or 'racist' or 'sexist' actually were any of those things, you wouldn't be able to use those words against them and you know it. You feed on people's better natures. You see people with a heart and a soul and you rip them apart and you're so goddamn fucking pompous that you actually think you're doing the world some good!"

"Shut up male oppressor!"

"Don't you fucking call me a male oppressor—I love women. I love women more than you can possibly imagine because you don't even know what love is! I just lost my fiancée and it's been killing me! It's eaten my soul to the pulp and it's because I loved that woman more than I loved myself or anything else on this blessed hell hole of a planet and you're going to look me in the eyes and tell me that I'm the oppressor? What would you have done with Billie if she'd gone to you for 'help?' All you'd ever do is make her feel like shit for who she was and have her go around like your little lap dog confessing her sins to rooms full of your adoring fans. You think porn objectifies women? You're the one that collects women's scalped dignity and holds it up as a badge of honor. You're the one that reduces them to the subhuman! And you don't even have the self-awareness to realize what a parasitic cretin you really are!"

"Your honor, why aren't you stopping this?" pleaded Tad Felmer.

"Because I want to hear it," said the judge.

"You're all rapists. Every single one of you!" shrieked Andrea. But then her eyes fell on Slam, who had now joined Rod in restraining Hank. "And you," she said, a note of dramatic pity entering her hoarse voice, "you're just a poor black man that's been taken advantage of. You poor, poor, thing. Surely you know on some primitive, tribal level that this isn't right. Surely you realize that this is just the modern day form of slavery and that you're being kept in bondage for-"

"Shut it, lady," bellowed Slam. "I'm not some ignorant fool you condescending, racist piece of shit. I make damn good money doing what I love and if you know what's good for you then you won't invoke the suffering of my ancestors to try to get in my good graces. Its pigs like you that keep minorities down. You don't want to admit that you're racist so you act like you pity me. Fuck you bitch!"

"What did I tell you, Andrea?" said Alston from the witness box. "Not one of them wants you, Andrea. But the wall is still there if you want to beat your head against it."

Andrea whirled around at Alston with raging venom in her blood shot eyes but the spin took her off balance and she caught herself by bringing her right arm down on the prosecution's table, cracking the edge that she fell against. "It's rape!" she screamed, her bulbous lips quivering as she advanced on Alston, now massaging her left arm. "It's rape!" she screamed in a burst of phlegm and saliva as she began to shake her left arm wildly, as though trying to cast off an octopus. "It's rape!" She stumbled back a couple of paces and then started advancing again. "It's rape!" She was heaving in and out for breath and squeezing the fat glob of her left breast furiously. "It's rape! Rape! Rape!" she screamed the word over and over as she collapsed to the floor and rolled over on her back.

A police officer radioed for an ambulance as Andrea began flailing her arms and legs, beating the ground like some grotesque giant child throwing an apocalyptic temper tantrum. "Rape!" she screamed as a pulpy froth began to seep from the corners of her mouth. "Rape!" she screamed until the word was lost in the gargling distortion of her bug-eyed hysteria. The word became nothing more than an incoherent sound; a squawk of reeling, voracious hellfire choking up the craw of a mass of flesh determined to strip itself of all human countenance. Then the sound was no longer a projection but a wheezing plea for oxygen from a brain that knew on its most primal level that the flow it received from its heart was finally overdrawn. In the last moments of Andrea Danvers' existence, the word "rape" was heard a final time as dull, vomited thud from her throat that seeped out the cavernous, tongue flailing chamber of her mouth and vanished in the soiled air of the courtroom as her bowels kidneys released.

Chapter 26

"**IF WE CAN AVOID** inducing cardiac arrest in the prosecution, the trial shall continue," droned the judge, the weariness of judicial professionalism weighing heavily in the tone of irritability that colored his voice. There had been a two hour recess so that Andrea's body could be removed and the audience had been instructed that further disruptions would be held in contempt of court.

Security camera footage was presented showing Alston and company entering the building and shooting down the guards, none of which was denied by the defense. Murmurs were raised among the audience when the prosecution was forced to admit that none of the surviving guards from Grand Pantheon staff were available to testify because the entire security force had been hired from mercenary circles as opposed to the private police forces and had thus fled the country after learning their employer was dead.

When at last the prosecution rested, Duke Cunningham called for the video from Crankshadow's computer to be shown. As if making a hollow stab at a cinematic atmosphere, the lights in the room were dimmed and a screen was lowered as the bailiff pushed a digital projection unit on a rolling table to the center of the chamber. With a sharp, almost sarcastic click, the projector came to life. When the video began, Duke Cunningham turned his gaze down to the desk, not wanting to see what was being shown. He looked over at Alston and saw that the man was not looking at the screen but fixedly at the judge. It was a colder and more focused stare than Duke had ever seen on the Eros Emperor but it was dangerously feral. Like an expertly muscled attack dog that growled quietly as it sighted an intruder, Alston's eyes were a challenge to the judge. As the foul events of the video proceeded like the accelerated metastasizing of an uncontrolled cancer, Alston's eyes challenged the judge to look into the screams and cries of the two children on the screen and extrapolate their father's guilt from the soul wrenching sounds. The jury watched in agony: one woman wept openly while another sat with her hand over her mouths. A man in the back row of the jury box clenched his jaw and held the arms of his chair tightly in his hands to stop from shaking. No amount of advanced knowledge of the nature of the trial had prepared them for what was before them. On the projection screen Crankshadow loomed larger than life and his teeth, gritted in withered pleasure, underscored the ravenous malevolence in his straining eyes.

When the film ended Duke Cunningham rose to his feet as the lights came back on. "The defense rests, your honor," he said flatly.

Tad Felmer spoke briefly and haltingly in his closing remarks. "Nobody can deny that what Melvin Crankshadow did was reprehensible. But Mr. Alston killed a man. That's what you're here to determine. We've verified on no uncertain terms that it was Mr. Alston who committed the acts in question. His guilt is obvious and unquestionable. The law is laid before you and now you have only to enforce it."

Duke rose and took the floor in exchange with Tad Felmer. There was a quivering stillness in the air as Duke made eye contact with each juror then closed his eyes and took a deep breath. "Imagine it was your child," he said finally and returned to his seat.

The jury was given its instructions and left to deliberate. Alston and Duke retired to the hallway where they were soon joined by Diana, Dominic and the rest of the entourage. "Well..." said Dominic, hands in pockets, as he groped for the right words to punctuate the situation.

Alston raised a hand with polite dismissal. "We'll search for platitudes after the verdict."

"We gave 'em a hell of show, nonetheless."

"Nonetheless."

"Mr. Alston," said the Bailiff as he leaned out of the door to the courtroom. "The jury is ready."

Dominic arched his eyes as if to say "that was quick" and the group returned to the courtroom. When they had all returned to their places in the chamber the jury was led back into its box from the adjoining room and assembled in their respective seats. The straining calm of the moment was akin to watching a basketball sail through the air in the final seconds of a tightly scored game.

The juror nearest the bench stood to read the verdict. "On the charge of breaking and entering, we the jury find the defendant, Isaac Alston, to be not guilty. On the charge of vigilantism we the jury find the defendant, Isaac Alston, to be not guilty. On the charge of capital murder, we the jury find the defendant, Isaac Alston, to be not guilty."

"Mr. Alston," said the judge with polite warmth in his formal tone, "You have been found not guilty by a jury of your peers. You are free to go." And with a crack of the gavel Alston and his supporters were on their feet, Alston first embracing Duke, then Dominic, then Diana and Abe in turn. There was thunderous applause and cheers filled with the unrestrained joy of absolute triumph. Those who had come to support the prosecution seemed to be trying to shrink further into their non-existent shells.

"Judge!" bellowed Tad Felmer over the celebratory din, "I will remind you that Mr. Alston's guilt has already been determined by a D.O.P.E petition signed by the members of Families for Families."

"And I'll remind you that your theological views do not put you above the respect all U.S. citizens are expected to show for the court system. You can spend the night in jail for contempt." The mirth of Alston's side turned into a toxically piercing laughter as Tad Felmer was handcuffed and led away.

After returning to Van Nuys Alston arranged for counseling for his children and commissioned the rebuilding of his house. For a time the protestors returned to their usual patterns but with their charismatic leader gone they lacked the rabid voracity that had fueled them for so long. They meandered about listlessly and occasionally shouted at the cars that entered the gates but for the most part they were a benign herd and Alston Image employees were able to return to their homes and start going to work in their regular vehicles again.

A phone call came in from Hotei Shibasaki. "I've watched your speech Mr. Alston. Do you have a body for the film?"

"Yes."

"Then the project is yours. How soon can we begin?"

Several days later, Artie Barrel arrived at the Alston Image offices. Alston was quietly attending to some contractual papers when Carol buzzed his office saying "Artie Barrel here to see you, sir."

"Send him up," Alston replied, nonplused.

When Artie stepped through the door of the elevator, Alston could see a profound change in his demeanor. The arrogant, boastful swagger that he had projected so insolently a few months ago was drained from him and he walked into the room slowly, his eyes cast down at the ground, holding a faded cap in both hands. When he arrived at Alston's desk he glanced at the empty chair in front of him and back to Alston, but no invitation to sit was forthcoming.

"Well?"

"I… I'm sorry Mr. Alston."

"I agree."

Artie looked as if to say that he would have winced at the sentiment had there still been such energy in him. Instead he just nodded distantly.

"My boy's dead. They're saying it was a drug deal gone wrong."

"So I've heard."

"My business is dead too. I aint got nothing left."

"And?"

"Well, I was hoping to make a career out of the church, but that's gone now too. I can't get a job doing anything. Nobody will return my calls anywhere I look."

"So you're coming to me to inquire about employment."

"Yes sir."

"Certainly. I'll find a position for you."

There was a startled look on Artie's face. "Really? Just like that? Well thank you sir—you won't be sorry. I've got tons of experience directing and I could—"

"You'll be working as a janitor," interjected Alston with a calm, mediated tone. Artie's face dropped again.

"What?"

"Take it or leave it."

"But why? After all my experience-"

"Your experience is exactly what I'm taking into consideration, Artie. If there's one thing I know it's that there are certain people who *need* to live in total poverty. People who'll waste every extra dollar on shooting smack or betting on horse races. You give them one tiny iota more than they need to survive and they'll end up in a worse situation than if they had no money at all. You're one of those people, Artie, but your spending vice is pride. Not the kind of worthy pride gained from the satisfaction of one's own accomplishments, but the sneering, corrosive false pride that drives you to summon a multi-billionaire to your beer-can strewn hovel so that you can waste his time making idiotic threats rooted in a half-baked pseudo morality. I know what you're like to work with, Artie, which is why as soon as you come to work for me I'm going to put out a memo to everyone in my company telling them not to acknowledge your presence unless it is for matters strictly relating to trash cleanup. If you speak to any of my female employees I'll slash your pay for a week. If I get even one harassment complaint I'll fire you on the spot and I'll put my personal attorney on the case against you if your victim decides to press charges."

"That's not fair!"

"Then don't accept the position. But if you come to work for me, you will work in a disciplined manner. Since you could not learn that of your own free will, I shall have to impose it on you."

"Will I have any chance at promotion?"

"Never—you'll work entry level for minimum wage until the day you retire, if that ever happens."

"You're a cruel man, Mr. Alston."

"You're a man who deserves cruelty, Mr. Barrel. Now take the position or not."

"Can I think it over?"

"Think about whatever you want, just get out of here and stop wasting my time."

Artie turned and shuffled out of the office. Two weeks passed in which Alston neither heard from Artie or thought of him. Then, while enjoying lunch with Dominic and Hank at an outdoor bistro, Alston was informed by the latter that a news story had reported Artie as dead by a suicide. "A bullet in the brain, they said," explained Hank. Alston shrugged and continued eating a chicken salad.

In the wake of Crankshadow's death the protests became sporadic and anemic at best but intensified among pundits. Bob Match had constant interviews with Alice Grausam for two weeks in which they agreed at length on the patriotic importance of seeing Alston hang before finally diving at each other across the news desk and making out.

When large-scale corporations went belly up, their resources were quickly bought up by younger start-ups, ushering in a new generation of burgeoning corporate giants. The protestors that had chocked the streets around the Alston Image offices finally dissipated completely when they were able to return to work under conditions that were fair and ethical.

In the midst of new found economic stability, *The Lotus Wave* entered production. Hotei Shibasaki was flown in from Japan to direct and Altson met him at the airport. Seen in the unflinching fluorescent light of the airport terminal, the lines of wear in Shiabasaki's face were more readily apparent than ever. Nevertheless, there was a certain satisfied tranquility in his decrepit features.

"I honestly never thought I would get to do this, Mr. Alston. Thank you."

"The same in return, Mr. Shibasaki."

When they entered the lobby at Alston Image, those milling about the lobby paused and turned as though some long forgotten deity of an ancient faith had been returned, in body form, to its most sacred hall of worship. Carol was the first to notice, the distant boredom of her uneventful day being wiped away with the sudden realization of Shibasaki's presence. Dominic, who had been carrying on a conversation with a member of his lighting crew, stopped and turned open mouthed at the entrance. Even though all had known that the project was going forward and even that Alston had gone to the airport to meet Shibasaki, the arrival was still one of awe.

"Mr. Daniels," said Shibasaki, catching Dominic's eye, "I was most impressed with *Awake to the Skin*. Perhaps you'll work with me on my new project."

"Of course, sir," stammered Dominic, his cocky assuredness suddenly lost in a haze of unexpected humility. "And thank you very much."

In the days that followed, the script for *The Lotus Wave* was xeroxed and delivered to each of the cast members, with Hank Steel taking the male lead. The table reads for the script were a solemn and nearly worshipful affair, with each cast member finding their characters to billow up off the page itself, requiring little effort to become them. The reads also became a salon of sorts for Dominic and Shibasaki to discuss the nature of acting and dramatic performance. Dominic found in the old man the kind of kindred spirit he'd longed for since his days in film school and, in Shibasaki, these qualities were amplified by the warm countenance of accomplishment in the fragile yet resonant tones of his voice. Rather than be a mirror of the kind of starry eyed longing that Dominic had seen in so many of his peers during his university days, Shibasaki was the dream made flesh: the proof that such desires could be made manifest in the real world. Here was a man who had climbed the proverbial mountain and now greeted all new climbers not with the disdainful amusement of an expert to a pesky novice but with the respect due to one bold enough to undertake such a journey.

Alston noticed a change in Shibasaki as well—gone was the tough exterior that had been forged by years of yelling at factory drones to be replaced with the light gayety of a mind given over completely to its most creative impulses. Alston found the old man to be quiet and thoughtful but that meditative nature was no longer consumed by a bitter, jaded grimace.

Set construction began and Alston found himself visiting the sets more often than usual, though his usually commanding countenance was now reserved and replaced by a youthful sense of wonderment at the process. Shibasaki carried this aura on a vastly more personal level as he beamed at the building process with a satisfaction that showed the set was being constructed to the exact specifications he saw in his mind as though he controlled the process by some telepathic CAD program.

Hank felt a catch in his throat when Billie's corpse was wheeled in on a gurney and loaded into the casket. Placid and untroubled, the solemn face was still virtually unchanged from the last time he'd seen it. Though the rest of her form was already covered with the dress that the costume department had chosen, Hank was bleakly pleased to see that it retained its shape after all it had been through. Nobody questioned him when he spent most of his time sitting silently next to the casket on the set while Billie was in it. At one point Dominic, who was serving as an assistant to Shibasaki, overheard Hank whispering to the body, but carried on as if unaware.

When filming was at last ready to commence, Shibasaki commanded a sacred aura when he looked into the lens of one of the cameras then sat down in his director's chair. The clapboard fell and the first of the scenes filmed in the viewing room of the funeral home began. Hank entered the scene exuding the sharp sense of control he'd shown in his first scene for Alston Image but tempered with the delicate balance of dramatic performance. He delivered his lines not with the sense of ironic disinterest that so many porn stars recited dialogue, but with the stirring grace of a genuine actor. All but one of the scenes in the viewing room were performed in the first day. The last, Shibaskai insisted, would have to be the last scene that was filmed overall as the anticipation of the scene's performance needed to carry throughout the rest of the filming.

There could be no doubt the scene that Shibasaki wanted to save until the very end. The set for the viewing room remained erected while different parts of the soundstage were used for other rooms and private residences were rented out when necessary. Billie was loaded back into storage, her form showing a vague wisp of deterioration but nothing that couldn't be covered with makeup. During the remainder of the filming, Hank became wary and reticent in Shibasaki's presence and a cold, resentful mood began to build between them, though Shibasaki seemed to take it in stride. As if anticipating the potential build up of anger in Hank, Diana Adler was always nearby to attend to Hank when she felt the tension mounting. Though her moments of taking him away from the set—often for a drive or a visit to Billie's old house—caused a hold up in production, it was generally tolerated, especially by Shibasaki, who seemed to be consciously orchestrating the pain from a distant plateau. The resulting on-camera performance was not acting, Alston realized, but something that raged up from the depths of Hank's soul and ensnared the other actors that surrounded him. His sex scenes were filled with glorious bursts of the anger that had always tingled in his eyes and the heat and passion that resulted was a heat and passion of a man's soul laid barren by a plague and finally seeing the first tender blossoms of new life reaching for the surface. When he watched the resulting performance from Hank, Alston saw in Shibasaki's face the answers to the questions he'd always asked when looking quizzically at other people.

When at last it came time to film the final scene of the film, Diana made it a point to lead Hank away from the production crew as they brought in Billie's body and prepped it for the scene by dressing it in a break-away version of the dress she'd worn earlier. Billie's genitals has long since gone dry, and the technician who filled the corpse's orifices with artificial lubricant glanced around worriedly to make sure Hank was nowhere to be seen before performing the act.

When Hank returned to the set the rest of the cast and crew looked away as he stared at the body for a long moment. After that suspended instant, Hank looked over to Shibasaki and said "I'm only doing this once." With that he strode onto the set and Shibasaki frantically motioned for the cameras to begin rolling when he realized that Hank was about to perform the scene then and there. One of the cameras zoomed in slowly on Hank's snarling face as he began to deliver his lines while glaring down at the body: "So this is it, sis? Are we truly done? Are you truly done with me? I could fuck you for the rest of your life, but can you fuck me for the rest of your death? Well?" he bellowed, gripping the casket by its side and throwing it to the floor. He began stomping and kicking at the casket with a furious energy, screaming "Can you fuck me for the rest of your death?" Hank's hands plunged into the splintering casket, pulling out the corpse and lifting it to his lips, giving it a long kiss before throwing the limp mass to the floor like a ragdoll. Bille's form collapsed to the floor with a morbid supplication as Hank dove down upon it, his eyes becoming quivering, misshapen triangles as he ripped the clothes off the body. The form, now naked and framed by the ravaged tatters of fabric, lay empty and soulless before Hank as he unzipped his pants and took out his penis. He steadied himself with one hand above the body and began to masturbate harder and harder with the other, his face dark and blood curdling as he thrust himself into Billie's limp remains. His thrusting was wild and unfocused as tears streamed down his cheeks and he pummeled the body harder and harder. Dead and devoid of pain, the body did not react to his thrusts, instead remaining sickeningly docile. When the madcap rush of the necrotic moment consumed him and he felt ready to ejaculate, Hank withdrew his tool in time for it to spray wild ropes of semen all over the cadaver in random arcs. Unable to look down at the body any longer, Hank feel to his side next to Billie and cried openly and nakedly. Distantly, in another universe and in another place and time, one of the cameras was zooming in on his face, capturing the final frames of *The Lotus Wave*.

The next day, Alston drove to the house that had been Billie's and knocked on the front door. Hank answered, looking haggard and pale, his once sharp eyes dull and moist amidst the puffy redness of his cheeks. He held a bottle of vodka limply in one hand. Clad in an under shirt and boxer shorts, he simply looked at Alston for a minute before turning and walking back into the house, leaving the door ajar.

Alston followed Hank in to the house that was now actively disheveled, not commenting on the over turned dining room table or the fist shaped indentions in the walls. He turned a corner and entered the living room, finding Hank sitting on the bench in front of Billie's piano. Alston entered, crossing the untold miles of history in the modest room and leaned against the instrument, looking down at Hank. The moments of silence that followed, in which Alston observed Hank and Hank stared fixedly into the keys, were endowed with a groping longing. The air itself seemed to be swirling aimlessly, longing to wrap itself around the piano's now long forgotten reverberations.

"I have made a living," said Alston carefully, "filming people doing sexual acts that are beyond most people. Until now I've always known that my performers have the right mind to carry out the acts that I wanted them to perform without being traumatized. In all of the orgies, threesomes, bondage scenarios, and every other extreme fetish, I've always placed in my performers the trust that they would be able to handle the psychological effects of such work and that it was within the bounds of their own sexual identity to do what I was asking of them. I don't have that certainty here. I need to know how this is affecting you. I need to go through this with you."

Hank was lost in thought for several briefly infinite moments after that before answering. "Isaac, I knew that going onto that set and fucking my fiancée's corpse was going to wipe me out. I knew it was going to be like nothing else before or after. And it did wipe me out—it's been like a waking death ever since. But even so, I have this certainty in my mind that it was my choice to do that scene. My heart hasn't accepted it yet, but my mind is fixed on that fact: that it was my choice. I understand what you meant now in your speech, Isaac. My decision is validated by the fact that it was mine and mine alone. I don't feel like I got my just desserts or something, I feel like I have something to be proud of and that comforts me because I know that one day my heart will join my mind in that place."

"That's very good to hear."

"I feel like if those assholes at Families for Families had gotten a hold of me they would have wanted me to blame someone greater than myself— you probably. Then society. Then the government. Then capitalism. And I'd blame everyone but myself and it wouldn't be a real healing that I'd get in return. I'd constantly need them there to stroke my wounded pride and tell me that it wasn't my fault. They'd be my addiction. I might as well shoot heroin at that point."

"You're exactly right."

"Thanks Isaac."

"Don't mention it."

"No—I have to mention it. I have to talk about it. You deserve pure adulation and all you've ever gotten for your work is hatred and ridicule. People need to study that speech. Anyone who disagrees with you needs to get a transcript and read it again and again until they finally understand that you aren't some kind of savage monster—that you're more human that any of them."

"Thank you, Hank."

"And they need to understand that you're a good friend."

Alston nodded and straightened slightly. "I also wanted to tell you two things—that Billie is to be cremated and her ashes will be given to you. Also, the family has decided to let you keep the house if you want it."

"That's nice of them."

"Well, I've had Abe at their throats for the past few weeks. Nothing he can do to threaten them really, but I can keep the whole mess tied up in court for eternity if I want and since organized religions are being so heavily taxed now, the family doesn't really see any point in accepting the donation anyway."

"Things are getting better."

"They are. Do you want me to hang around?"

"Thanks, Isaac, but I'll be fine. I need to be alone with my thoughts for now. I'll call you if I need you."

"Certainly. I just don't want to find you hanging in a noose the next time I come over."

"No worries. If there is actually a Hell then I want to forestall seeing Ralphie Barrel for as long as possible."

Alston snorted and chuckled. "Good enough for me, Hank."

Three months later the premier of *The Lotus Wave* was held at the Black Chapel, its ceremonial proceedings serving as a better tribute to Billie's memory than either the funeral or the AVN Awards had ever been. With all prohibition lifted the event was a time of rebirth and revelry, with lavish catering and an array of wines enjoyed by a packed house that ranged from porn industry luminaries to mainstream celebrities. Press covered the event extensively and when Alston stepped from his limousine he was greeted by a barrage of camera flashes which he stood smiling broadly. As the purple residue of the bulbs cleared from his eyes he was able to make out the press that stood on either side of the red carpet leading up to the entrance.

"How has your business been since the D.O.P.E was closed?" asked one reporter.

"It's been great—look at all this!" said Alston, chuckling and gesturing broadly to the proceedings. "We're rereleasing our entire catalogue and we have some new titles in the works—I just green-lit *Go Swell it on the Mountain* and *A Handful of Bust.*"

"You seem to be newly comfortable in the public spotlight," said another reporter, pointing a microphone in Alston's direction.

"Actually the public spotlight is finally ready for me," replied Alston with a smirk, turning to leave then adding "for all of us," before ascending the front steps. As he crossed the threshold into the ante-room of the Black Chapel, he was greeted by a pleasantly grinning Dominic Daniels, who held a glass of red wine.

"You're like a new man tonight, Isaac," Said Dominic, embracing Alston.

"It's a new world," said Alston.

"Hopefully the night's proceedings will come off without a hitch."

"So long as nobody is murdered or raped, I'll be happy," replied Alston with a momentary dip into dire thoughts. They made their way to Alston's private box and his good humor returned when he saw Shibasaki. The elder man sat placidly in one of the chairs that had been moved up to the edge of the balcony. There was an unusual peace about him—he neither reveled in the newfound attention that his work received nor dismissed it. He seemed merely at ease, the hard-assed slaughter house boss persona of many years now a fading memory melting away from a frame that was weary of its burden.

Down on the main floor, Alston could see his contract players sliding into place, Hank moving proudly among them. He also noticed Darcy Collins, draped in a slight but lavish evening dress, the long fatigue of her wearisome legal battles a thing of the past. She was radiant under the white house lights that caught her skin and made her glow sharply like the first rays of sunlight on eyes awoken from a long and troubled slumber. Alston felt his heart strain at her sight and he was quietly surprised to feel such an idle, uncontrolled longing in himself.

The lights dimmed and Felicity Hatchback walked out on stage in front of the lowered curtain, stepping in front of a microphone. "Last year Alston Image founder and CEO Isaac Alston set out on a journey to locate a legendary filmmaker and the only man more reclusive than himself," she began. "His search was difficult and fraught with anti-sex activists but today his labors have come to fruition: we are proud to present to you the final installment of Hotei Shibasaki's Wave trilogy, a set of films that the director himself honestly believed would never be completed. The vision of Isaac Alston carried many of us, his loyal employees, through the fear and uncertainty of the recent national climate and it is time for the rest of you to share in that vision. But first and foremost, we must commend the work and philosophy of Hotei Shibasaki for it was this that inspired Isaac Alston in the first place. This is

Mr. Shibasaki's night above all else. I know that you all are really here to see *The Lotus Wave,* not sit and listen to me, so here it is!"

The lights darkened and the film commenced. The Alston Image logo shone proudly in the opening frames and Alston felt a swelling of pride like he'd never known before. He felt Shibasaki look over at him and returned the smile that he saw on the old man's face. The shimmering tones of the soundtrack enveloped the room and lifted the minds of all those present into the haunting limbo of the film's inner world.

As Alston watched the picture he heard a part of his mind predicting tomorrow's press with lines like "not since Deep Throat has a pornographic film so captured the nation's consciousness" and "*The Lotus Wave* marks a new era in filmmaking: one in which the sex on camera is real and undeniable but so is the legitimacy of the picture's artistry." Alston snapped out of this contemplation when it struck him that the press had no idea of the necrophilia that would close out the film. When the pivotal climax finally came, there was no great motion—nobody made for the doors, nobody shouted in disgust, they only watched, their expressions not changing. Then, in a rapture whose salvation was grander than any the highest of holy men could have conceived, the credits began to roll and the audience stood and applauded. A single spotlight burst on, shining down not at the stage but on Hotei Shibasaki. Alston and Dominic were on their feet in that instant and turning in to exchange handshakes with Shibasaki before joining in the applause. The old man smiled with a grin that seemed to be an outgrowth of transcendent pride, satisfied tears brimming in his weary eyes.

There was an after party held in one of the Chapel's conference rooms, with the cast and crew mingling with the Alston Image execs and their various guests. The catering was superb and as Dominic bit into a roasted chicken breast he looked around and realized that Alston was nowhere to be seen. He made eye contact with Darcy, whose eyes said that she was wondering where Alston was as well. Stepping into the hall, they asked a security guard where Alston had gone, to which the guard replied "he wanted to go up on the roof, so I let him." Concerned, Dominic and Darcy ascended the utility stairs and stepped out on the roof. Alston was standing at the edge, hands in his pockets and one foot on the low barrier wall, his weight mounted by his arm on that knee, looking out into the vast sprawl of metropolitan California. Dominic felt a voyeuristic twinge in seeing his leader in this transcendental state, one where the softly billowing palm trees carried the mild breeze of the costal night into gentle mind sculptures of the romanticized image of Hollywood: a glimmering dreamscape of unlimited possibility. The lights of the city seemed to kneel in acknowledgement of Isaac Alston's silent, thoughtful gaze.

"Come on out, Dominic," said Altson, his head turning slightly. He noticed Darcy. "You too, babe."

They walked out to the ledge, joining Alston in one of Western culture's fine pleasures: the look of city lights in the night. "You're missing some good catering," said Dominic.

"The FBI has mounted a nationwide manhunt for Patricia," said Alston as though not hearing Dominic.

"So that's what's on your mind?"

"Not really. I'm not even worried if they catch her. I was just thinking about how she's out there right now, on the lam, trying to lay low, trying to dodge the law. That's what she's been her whole life—on the run. Now the police are just a manifestation of the things in herself that she's always run from."

"You never stop with the philosophy, do you Isaac?"

Alston smiled thoughtfully and carried the look into Dominic's eyes when he turned to him. "When there's nothing left to contemplate there's nothing left to live for. The beauty of growing in life is that it's a journey without end—but you get to stay at nicer and nicer hotels along the way."

"Wow—that was concise."

"I aim to please."

"It's good to see the lights back on in the valley isn't it, Isaac?" Said Darcy, stepping in close and resting her head on his shoulder.

"It's the most beautiful thing I can imagine. The lights of utopia returning en masse."

"You know," pondered Darcy, "I was at a bookstore the other day and I was so happy to be back in one that I found myself opening the books and inhaling just to smell the fresh ink. I walked out of there with a small stack of books but while I was checking out, this mother was standing there with her young son—he couldn't have been more than about five—and he pointed to one of the nudie magazines behind the counter and said 'mommy, who don't those women have any clothes on?' and do you know what his mom said?"

"What's that?"

"She said 'when people grow up, they start liking the way other grownups look without any clothes on and so those magazines are for people who want to enjoy that.' The little boy seemed to accept that and they went on their way. I felt like I was living in reality again for the first time in months."

"You're welcome."

"Good evening, ladies and gentlemen," said a voice from behind them and they turned to see Hank Steel approaching with Diana Adler and Saundra Bullcock by his sides. In both hands he held Billie's urn. "I'm glad you could be here for this." The hardy enthusiasm of his voice had returned in the face its months of necrotic frigidity.

"We're going to lay Billie to rest," said Saundra, patting the top of the urn in Hank's hands.

"This seemed like an appropriate way to go about it," added Diana.

"You're sure you don't want to hang on to those ashes?" asked Dominic.

"No, I don't," said Hank, approaching the edge and unscrewing the top of the urn. "Holding on to Billie would hold me down. If she's taught us anything it's that you can keep a beautiful winged creature in a cage or you can enjoy watching it fly free. You can't have both."

"She taught us what beauty is," said Diana, looking down at the urn.

"She taught us what passion is," said Saundra.

"She was a true friend," added Dominic.

"She was our rock," said Alston, a single twist of a choke in his throat betraying the depth of his words.

"I love you, darling," said Hank, kissing two of his fingers and running them down the length of urn as though baptizing it. As if compelled by instinct the other five repeated the ritual, each giving the urn their own reverent blessing.

With nothing more to say, Hank held his shoulders back and his chin high as he opened the urn and, feeling a particularly strong breeze, turned the vessel over. The ashen contents poured forth and caught the breeze that carried them off into the newly rejuvenated lights of the San Fernando Valley where they would mix with the veins and arteries of the Eros Empire.

Acknowledgements

The journey to bring this novel to life began in the spring of 2009 with the idea to write a novel set the porn industry that would defend this often misunderstood and misrepresented world against the attacks that have been leveled against it and offer a philosophy to those who work in adult entertainment. More so than this wider goal, however, I wanted to tell an engrossing story about the lives, dreams and ambitions of these often maligned and overlooked people. Both of these endeavors were accomplished with the industry insight and moral support offered by countless persons in and out of adult entertainment. Outstanding among them were Dr. Chauntelle-Ann Tibbals for her thorough and insightful analytic coverage of modern pornography, director Michael Whiteacre and retired adult actress Lydia Lee Hawk (aka Julie Meadows) for their outspoken advocacy and work to raise awareness of the pro-porn side of the debate, Christina Doxstader for introducing me to Ben Ohmart at Bear Manor Fiction, and lastly to Brad Strickland, who was kind enough to have long conversations on the art of writing and book publishing with an eleven year old kid and awesome enough to pick up that discussion sixteen years later when I was writing this book. I owe each of you my eternal gratitude for your support, guidance and enthusiastic friendship. It has meant the world to me and more.

– Jordan Owen
Atlanta, 2011

www.ingramcontent.com/pod-product-compliance
Lightning Source LLC
Chambersburg PA
CBHW051131030726
47504CB00004B/818